IN THE
DARK

USA TODAY BESTSELLING AUTHOR
LILA ROSE

Editing: Hot Tree Editing
Formatting: Lee Ching with Under Cover Designs
ISBN: 978-0-6484960-5-2

Becky Johnson,
for being the amazing editor she is.

PROLOGUE

I didn't want to ask for help. Mum was already upset about something she'd heard down the street. But my fear was raw, palpable, leaving me breathless and shaky. I didn't know what was going on or why pain spread through my body.

With my arms wrapped around my middle, sweat covering my body and stabbing pains shooting through me, I staggered into the kitchen. The scent of bacon filled the room and my stomach growled in response when I inhaled the familiar greasy scent.

How was I hungry when I was hurting so much?

Am I dying?

Tears fell unbidden, dampening my cheeks. I quickly wiped them away.

"Mum." I coughed. She stood at the stove, her back to me.

She turned, tongs in her hand, and screamed.

I covered my ears; still, her scream drilled into my head, hurting me even more.

"Mum," I yelled. Even my own voice hit me like a sledge-hammer to the brain.

Her screaming stopped. Wide-eyed before me, she gaped. "Leila? Your body…"

"Help me. It hurts." I collapsed to the ground on my hands and knees. "Please."

"No. No… Look at you—you're wrong." She sobbed, her hand covering her mouth in horror.

Another fierce wave of pain rushed through me. Crumpling

to my stomach, I moaned. Slowly, I shifted my head sideways on the cool vinyl floor. I watched through watery eyes the skin on my arm and hand shimmer and shake, as it… changed.

What is happening to me?

Mum inhaled deeply, her voice low and calm, devoid of emotion. "You've always been different. I— You're not my daughter. No. I can't… You're bad. This… it proves it."

Icy terror rippled through me, cutting through my pain when I watched her own transformation—sad haunted eyes turned cold and hard.

From out the corner of my eyes, as I lay helpless on the floor, she stood above me with the hot pan in her hand.

Dad yelled from somewhere for my mum to stop, his footfalls fast approaching. But it was too late.

The pan collided with my head.

I woke with Dad sitting on my bed next to me, patting my head, and all I could think was, *Isn't that appropriate now?*

I knew what I'd become, even before I'd passed—no, before I was knocked out.

Should I be in shock?

Should I be scared?

I wasn't.

I'd always suspected something was missing, that I wasn't quite whole, because I wouldn't have had the "eye problem" without a good reason. Finally, I knew and it left me… feeling complete.

"I'm sure you can understand me while you're like this," Dad said as he bent to rub his face against my cheek. "I want you to know I love you with all my heart, no matter which way you are. You'll always be my daughter, and one day I will come back for you. I-I need to take your mum away for a while. She can't cope right now, but she does love you, Leila." He paused and sighed. He knew I wouldn't believe what he'd just said. My mum had never loved me. Dad cleared this throat and added, "Don't worry, okay? Your Uncle Jack will be here for you. I'm so sorry I have to leave this way. It's for the best though… For *your* safety."

Wait, he's leaving? I struggled to sit up only I had no control over my new form.

"No. Don't move, sweetheart. One day, all of this will make sense, I promise, but now isn't the time. Your uncle doesn't know about this." He gestured to my whole body with his hand. "I'm leaving it up to you to tell him, if you want. He won't be by until tomorrow. You'll need to hunt soon, so I've left the back door open for you. When you can, go into the woods. Your instincts will take over."

He scrubbed at his face with one hand. "God, I wish I didn't have to leave. I understand you'll be upset, but… I have to do this." He nodded to himself. "Uncle Jack will keep you safe. I know you're strong, in mind and body, especially for a thirteen-year-old, and that you think you can take care of yourself. Still, I hope you'll let Jack help you. I do love you, sweetheart."

He gave my nose a peck, stood and walked out of my room… out of my life.

Chapter One

FIVE YEARS LATER

I was naïve when I thought my first year at college would be different to what high school dealt me.

It seemed people weren't willing to grow up when it came to me. Every day, taunts were thrown my way. I supposed what didn't help was the college was a small one, the only one in our tiny country town, and right next door to our old high school. It even effing resembled our old school; the classrooms were nothing like I'd seen in movies or brochures. They were set out as if we were still fifteen. What also didn't help was that it had so many of the same students who pissed me off in high school, who, of course, continued to piss me off still.

I needed to get through the three years of my computer science course, with a minor in history, and then I'd be out of there. My plan was to work in data analysis, either online or in a small business where I wouldn't have to see many people.

For the time being, however, I had to endure it *and* more specifically, history. Foolishly, I'd picked the subject for an easy ride. It was actually a subject I liked, but not so much anymore. If it wasn't for the dipshit up the front teaching it, I may have looked forward to the lectures.

Jesus Christ.

I banged my head against the table and silently screamed. Dr Geffen, the history professor, had just said that World War II started back in the 1600s. I was convinced he'd downloaded a fake PhD from the internet just to use the title. No one corrected him, and I was sick of doing it. Plus, I was sure he was sick of sending me out of the classroom for disrupting it. Sometimes though, I thought he looked forward to yelling at me in some way. Therefore, I stayed quiet. I'd review what I actually needed to learn at home.

At the start, I'd been surprised no one failed history, until I discovered he gave the test answers away for "special favours." I preferred not to imagine what.

"Can this go any slower?" I mumbled into the desk.

When the lecturer raised his voice higher than normal, signalling the end of the session, I quickly opened my eyes and jumped in my seat, fright filling my body. My hand covered my fast beating heart. *Great, I fell asleep in class.* However, that part didn't bother me. It was the fact my head had been turned sideways and my eyes landed on Isaac Grey, who was a few tables over, and great, just my luck of course, I'd been drooling. I quickly wiped away the saliva and glanced to see that… hell, he'd been watching me.

Good God, had I snored?

Isaac was my most recent crush. Hell, my only crush. Though, I wasn't sure if they were honest feelings. It was more that he intrigued me. He'd actually caught a lot of attention from the opposite sex with his charcoal-coloured hair that hid his tantalizing green eyes. He wasn't a 'big jock' body type, more lean and tall with an always-tanned look to him.

He moved to our town about three weeks earlier. Arrived at the college and chose not to sit with or speak to anyone. Isaac liked to stalk around campus with his big, brooding attitude.

My type of guy.

Another reason he was my type of guy was… okay, as corny as it was, I felt a connection to him. As if, when he first walked into class, something inside of me reached out to him and grabbed hold.

Forget, it. You sound ridiculous. Leave it at the fact he's smokin' hot.

Many of our fellow students tried to talk to him; they all

wanted to be the one to gain his attention and receive a word in return. Still, he never disappointed me in his responses to their attempts, which consisted of head nods or shakes, and my favourite one was when he walked away from them.

Me? I hadn't bothered trying to get his attention. Even when my body seemed to crave it. *Stupid body.* I kept to my side of the room and he kept to his, while I tried to ignore his wonderful, intoxicating scent, an aroma I was yet to figure out. Still, it stood out above the rest, even more than the others my nose didn't recognise. There were a few.

"What?" I grumbled at Isaac and quickly averted my gaze.

Okay, as first words went with such a hot dude, I could have done a little better. Then again, maybe not, especially after the drool issue.

Out the corner of my eye, I saw Isaac shake his head, rise from his seat and walk out of the empty classroom.

Gathering up my things, I headed to the gym for the compulsory P.E. session. Normal colleges didn't subject their students to a physical education class. However, mine did, damn it. The dean thought it a brilliant idea to have us jump around like idiots to get our blood pumping so we'd stay awake for any afternoon sessions we may have. It was built into our enrolment contract. Apparently, I forgot to read the small print when I signed up and my uncle handed over the fees.

I loathed it with a passion.

College sucked just as much as high school did.

Three years, Leila. Three fucked-up years and I'll be able to leave these idiots behind me.

When I arrived, I went straight up to Coach Bacon. Not a student lived to see the next day if they even thought of ridiculing her for her last name. I didn't even know if she was a real coach, but she insisted we call her it.

"Coach B., I can't do gym today." I smiled while holding my stomach.

Her dark blue eyes met mine before I looked to the ground.

She was one of the people who didn't flinch away from my stare. As staff went, she wasn't too bad.

She placed her hand on her slim hip. "Let me guess. Is it because you have a headache? Or could it be you feel too sick? Or wait, my personal favourite, you hurt yourself on the way here? You do know that one day you're going to have to participate in physical education, Leila."

"And I look forward to that day. But I can't today, because I have cramps. Really, really bad cramps. You know, that time of the month cramps."

She quickly wiped at her smile with the back of her hand before she tucked her short blonde hair behind her ear. "I know it's no use arguing the importance of P.E. with you, Leila." She glanced down at her clipboard and muttered, "Go and sit down somewhere."

I began to walk off until I heard her speak, "Now what can I do for you, Isaac? No wait, let me guess. You have cramps as well."

Dear God, how long had he been behind me? Please, please, please tell me he didn't hear what I'd just said.

Isaac didn't respond; instead, Coach Bacon growled out her frustration and said, "Fine. Go and find a seat to the side." She turned her attention to the waiting students. "All right, everyone. Get into teams for dodge ball."

Humming my way over to the far right side of the gym, I sat down on the cold floor and crossed my legs. Hopefully, I was far enough away from all the flying dodge balls. Movement beside me let me know someone was there. I glanced to find Isaac had followed me and proceeded to sit down beside me.

My heart took off in flight. Why did the big hunky idiot have to go and sit there?

Leaning my head back against the brick wall, I closed my eyes and ignored his presence. Which was always bloody hard. Like every time in history, his scent soon filled my senses.

I think I preferred the days Isaac participated in P.E; at least then, I got to watch his amazing body move. Actually, I even liked the days he didn't participate and he'd sit by *himself* somewhere else in the gym… *Not right next to me.*

Why today? Why now?

For a while, I sat and listened to the ball being thrown around. Listened to the girls squeal, the guys laugh and the impact of the ball when it hit someone. Then a muffled conversation caught my attention. I opened my eyes in time to find Isaac's hand inches from my face. He'd caught the ball before it made impact with my head.

I stared at his outstretched smooth hand in front of me and watched as he threw it back to the one who'd tossed it my way. Mick Delaney, a jock and boyfriend to the gorgeous Hilary, one of Jenna's, my arch-nemesis, cronies. I sent daggers his way, only he ignored them and kept his gaze on Isaac, before he decided to walk over to us.

"Good catch, man. You should try out for the basketball team."

Snorting to myself, I said to the ground, "Idiot."

"Shut. Up. Freak," he snarled. His face heated as he glared at me. His hatred palpable. It was a reaction I was used to from the majority of students.

"Whatever, jackarse," I mumbled under my breath and glared at his back as he walked off.

He didn't even bother to wait for an answer from Isaac. Then again, he probably thought Isaac was also a freak, considering he sat next to me. I would hate to think I'd caused another to be deemed a freak by association.

It cemented my reasoning not to have friends, as well as explained why my early-childhood friends had left me. They didn't want to hang out with the weirdo of the town.

No one trusted the eyes.

My right eye was normal, a moss green colour like my dad's. The problem I had was my left eye. It was black. The iris was all black like my pupil.

It wasn't as if I could help it; it was the way I was born. People hated it or they didn't trust it... me. When I'd been born, my parents put me through every test known to mankind. They wanted some kind of explanation. But no one knew. Another pain-in-the-arse situation was I couldn't even wear contacts to hide my disfigurement. I was told they would have worked, if I weren't allergic to them.

Go figure.

No normal life for me.

Which was why I didn't understand Isaac's newfound attention. I glanced over at the guy, who stared back while sitting quietly beside me.

Glancing away, I muttered half-heartedly with a shrug, "Thanks."

"It's fine."

My head spun his way. I looked at him with wide eyes then away again.

He spoke.

I would've thought his voice would have been a deep, gruff one. Not the soft, light—yet *all* male—one he used. One that made my heart stumble.

As my shock subsided, I said, "Oh, Lord, he speaks. I don't think my beating heart can take it, please, no more."

Glancing his way, I received a sweet half smile. Only, it didn't reach his eyes and quickly disappeared after I witnessed it. "Are you mocking me?" he asked.

My heart pounded wildly. I held my head high, gave him a full-blown smile and pinched my thumb and forefinger together. "Maybe just a little."

He nodded and stared at me. His eyes flicked all over my face, as if he were taking it all in, studying me. I looked away first.

Great, have I just blown my chance of having a half-decent conversation, because of my stupid teasing?

Coach called time, announcing the end of the lesson and the end of the day. I looked to Isaac and back to the ground again.

Yep, I guess I blew it. Oh, well.

Shrugging, I got up from the floor and dusted my butt off; the floor was never the cleanest to sit on. I'd taken a couple of steps forward, but stopped when I heard an intake of breath behind me.

"Goodbye, Leila Morgin."

Looking over my shoulder, I met his gaze with my puzzled one. Why was he speaking to me of all people?

"Yeah, see you. Isaac Grey."

I made my way home by foot, because I hadn't bothered to apply for my licence, strange for an eighteen-year-old, but really, the world would stay that little bit safer if I didn't. Besides, I only lived a few blocks away in the house I grew up in. It was an old farmhouse with a wooden shed off to the side of it. The property was large enough to have no neighbours sticking their unwanted noses in. It was quiet and very peaceful. How I liked things.

My house was a four-bedroom weatherboard home. Not too small, but really too big for just me and my absent guardian. My uncle was rarely home. He never told me what he got up to, but some days I pictured him either doing something very illegal or he was involved with the government for some reason. However, the truth was probably that he was off hunting and drinking with his mates somewhere. As long as he showed when it was time to pay the bills and give me money for food, I preferred to have him absent. We didn't get along very well. Dad had always said it was because we were too much alike, both of us being stubborn. I couldn't see it.

I supposed, at least one member of the family had stuck around. Even if we didn't see eye-to-eye. I looked too much like my dad and uncle to second-guess it, but I often wondered if my mum was my real mother. From memory, it seemed she hated me forever.

Since my parents left, Dad would sometimes call; usually, I left those missed calls on the answering machine for my uncle to return. Though, they hadn't called for a while.

Dad had been my everything. My best friend, a confidant, a role model, a peacekeeper.

It still hurt…

Shaking my head, I unlocked and opened the creaky front door. I threw my backpack down and headed to the kitchen for an apple before walking through the dining and living room, and down the hall to the end bedroom, my bedroom. On the way, I passed the bathroom and the other three bedrooms with their doors closed, where dust had settled on the knobs.

I opened my door and fell to my bed, heaving a sigh.

I had no time for thinking. Though… *Isaac?*

No. Instead, I reached for my history books and searched through them to revise what I was supposed to be learning.

Sometime later, my stomach growled. I gave up the books for the night and went for my usual run. After that, I would then come home, eat, shower and fall into bed, the same as I did every night. I loved to run though. It did so many things for me; more importantly, it kept me sane—most days anyway.

CHAPTER TWO

Darkness surrounds me. Every way I turn, I see nothing but black. My heart beats hard in my chest. My hands tremble along with my legs. I want to run, to scream, but I don't.

Because I know I'm waiting.

It isn't until I see two small red dots in the distance that I relax somewhat.

"Yes," I whisper. "That's what I'm waiting for."

The dots drift closer and closer.

And in a blink of an eye, which always makes me jump, they're right in front of me, so close I can reach out and touch them... No, touch the face that belongs to those red eyes.

I want to.

I need to.

Even though a small amount of fright fills me, I still know I'm safe.

The red eyes study me.

"You're mine," the voice growls... Right before I woke up.

Every Goddamn morning since I turned eighteen, I'd had the same dream. The same darkness, the same red eyes and the same voice claiming me.

None of it made sense, and I hadn't spoken to anyone about it to see if they could understand it.

I didn't see the need to worry if it was set to be my future, if the red-eyed person would find me. I wasn't worried by the dream; confused yes, but not worried. There was also nothing I could do about it. It came no matter what and, each morning I woke, I pushed it aside to continue on with the day.

On the walk to college the next day, the same sense I'd had for a while filled me. That someone was watching me. I shrugged it off; it was probably just me. I did tend to get a little paranoid.

The paranoia lingered, though, as I walked down the hallways. I felt more eyes on me than usual.

I stopped in my tracks when super bitch Jenna Avery stepped in front of me. Her evil cronies Tina, Hilary, Montana, Sofia and Monica standing close behind.

Quickly, I flicked my eyes to the ground.

"Hi there... ah, what's your name again?" I caught her smile through my hooded eyes. She shifted her long, blonde hair over her left shoulder.

Rolling my eyes, I told her, "You know my name, Jenna." We'd only been attending the same school together since first grade. In addition, she'd been a pain in the neck since then too.

"Oh, yes, Leila. Such a pretty name for such a..."—she shook her head—"Anyway, I saw you yesterday in the gym, when Isaac talked to *you*. I want to know what he said."

Sighing, I raised my eyes and noticed there were more than Jenna and her tarts listening in.

It was then I spotted Isaac walking our way.

He stopped just behind the crowd and met my gaze with a curious one, his brows high.

Honestly, I didn't know why—maybe it had been because Isaac was there, giving me confidence—but for once, I stared straight at Jenna and watched her shudder from my gaze.

"So you want to know what Isaac said to me yesterday?" I slyly smiled.

"Yes," Jenna snapped.

Shrugging, I said in a bored voice, "He confessed his undying love for me." I covered my mouth and faked a cough to hide the laugh wanting to arise.

I saw Isaac roll his eyes and the twitch on his lips.

"Yeah, right." Jenna glared. "As if he would like something like you." She laughed, others joining in. "You might have more luck with another species."

Wincing, I realised I shouldn't have started it. Me and my big, stupid mouth. What could I have said to that?

My mind went blank.

I was stumped, because I felt it was true myself. Who would even think of falling for the freak show?

Looking to the ground, I hoped I seemed to be walking away with as much dignity as I could manage. Which was what I started to do. I pushed my way through the laughter, the jibes, until someone grabbed my wrist.

My body was spun around. My eyes landed on the hand that held me and I knew who it belonged to because it had been in my face just the previous day. I followed the hand up his arm, to his shoulder, and then to Isaac's sober face.

The hallway grew quiet. My ears rang from how silent it had become.

I waited for Isaac to say something—anything. He didn't. Instead, *oh, God,* he pulled me close, wrapped one arm around my waist, the other went to the back of my head, which helped me lean into him, and then… he kissed me.

My first kiss.

Shit, I don't know what to do.

Thankfully, my body took over. I wrapped my arms around his neck and dragged him closer still. *Yes.* His lips parted, and mine followed suit. His tongue ran lightly around the edges of the inside of my mouth.

That was when I woke up and the anger took over.

It was my first kiss, damn it.

It shouldn't have been like that. Like a pity kiss.

Breaking free of his grip, I stepped back and searched his face to find he *did* pity me. His chest heaved in heavy breaths, his eyes sad and wary.

He was only kissing me because he felt sorry for me.

Hell, that hurts. My… shit, I didn't even know what it was, but I wasn't happy being away from him. My *everything* wanted him to take me, surround me and let me stay that way forever.

Freaky thoughts, Leila.

Isaac must have read the pain upon my face. He took a step towards me, his hand reaching out. I turned and stalked quickly away.

When I made it into the girl's bathroom, I looked at my watch. First class had already started. I had study time anyway, and knew I should be using that time to do exactly that, especially because I refused to cry over it, not there around people anyway.

Still, I needed the breather.

Turning to look at myself in the mirror, I raised my hand and ran a finger along my lips.

Stupid, kissable, delicious prick. I wished it never happened. I wished I could take it back, get him to give me back my first kiss.

But I couldn't and it wasn't fair.

I fisted my hair as my mind kept repeating how his lips felt against mine, how his arms around me felt right, kept me warm. And then there was the foolish way I'd accepted him in.

Why did he do it in the first place?

Gripping the sink, I fought my emotions. I wanted to cry, to scream. However, all of it had to wait until later. When I was home… alone.

Waiting in the bathroom until break time, I made my way to my locker, yet another reminder our small country college was like high school by installing lockers.

It was hard to block out the students who whispered and giggled as I walked past.

Once I grabbed my lunch, I headed for my usual spot, the library.

Planting a smile on my face, I walked in and saw Jim, the

librarian, at the front counter. He was the only person here who treated me as if I were normal.

"Hey, Jim." I waved.

"Miss Morgin. Lovely to see you, like always. How has your day been?"

My smile faltered. "Ah, okay."

He looked at me sternly, sliding his glasses down his wrinkled face to do so. "You lie to me, Miss Morgin. But I will let that pass. If you need to talk, I'm always here."

My fake smile fell from my face. His kind words made me want to cry even more. "I know," I managed. "Thanks. I think I'll just eat my lunch and read some. See you later, Jim."

"Maybe you will, maybe you won't. Nevertheless, remember, don't let anyone see you eating in here, young lady. Then others will think they can do it."

"I know." I gave him a quick salute and grin then headed up the back to my secluded spot in among the tall stands full of books. No one entered that far up, so I knew I was safe there.

It always made me feel better if I was able to eat and read in peace. My break was over far too quickly and I had double history next. My stomach dropped, and my food threatened to come back up.

I ignored the feeling, and with dread intact, I made my way to history, which wasn't far from the library. I glided into class and straight up the back with my head held high. Isaac already sat in the opposite back corner to my table. I dismissed the way he seemed to want me to meet his gaze. The way his head and eyes followed my every move, watching and waiting for me to glance at him.

Sitting down, I opened my book and thankfully, for once, Dr Keffen didn't take forever to arrive. I was happy to see he was in one of his moods, ordering silence throughout the room while we watched a documentary on Adolf Hitler.

Jenna turned in her seat from up the front to smile and wave at me. She laughed with her friends and quickly turned back around before Dr Keffen had the chance to say anything.

I glanced out the corner of my eyes, to see if Isaac witnessed Jenna's little show, but his eyes were glued to the television, which was probably a good idea. The documentary could stop my brain from working, for a while at least.

I zoned out, barely registering the words or images on the screen. Dr Keffen turned off the television and walked out. I looked around bewildered. Apparently, it was the end of the session. He was probably eager to get more alcohol into him. I quickly gathered up my things to leave before all the other students left me alone with Isaac.

I was lucky enough to leave without him saying anything to me. Although, deep down, I rather hoped he would have said something. I had an urge to give him a piece of my mind.

There was just one more double class to suffer through before I was able to head home.

At the end of the day, I went outside to find it was raining. Head hunkered down, I walked the short distance home, grumbling the whole way. My clothes were drenched by the time I arrived.

Finally, inside my house, I stripped off my soaked clothes in the hallway and headed straight for the shower. I sighed under the welcoming spray. After warming my cold body, I reluctantly stepped out and dressed in leggings and a tee. Although the temperature had dropped outside, it was always warm inside. Even my own body temperature ran a little warmer than most.

Making my way to the front door to grab the wet clothes I'd left, I bent to pick them up, but I froze. Inhaling deeply, the air from the gap under the door brought a very familiar tantalizing scent.

What was he doing here? Did he knock? If he had, I didn't hear it, and usually I heard most things.

Drawing in another deep breath, to try to steady my racing heart. I opened the front door, expecting to find Isaac waiting.

When I saw he wasn't in sight, I stepped out and breathed in the air around me. He was close, but where?

Grabbing my big duffel jacket hanging on the rack beside the door, I slipped it on and yanked on my rain boots. Pulling the hood over my head, I walked outside, down the front steps and followed his enticing scent, which lead me down to the shed. I was about to open the door, when I heard a soft noise from behind me. I spun and came face-to-face with Isaac, wearing a long-sleeved black shirt and black jeans.

"Effing hell, Isaac, sneak up on girls much?" I glared, grabbing at my chest.

"My apology." He smiled derisively.

"Yeah, sure. What do you want? How did you find my house?" I asked, crossing my arms over my chest. *Do you want to stay for a coffee? A snack? An afternoon delight in my bedroom?* What was wrong with me?

"Can we speak in there?" He pointed to the shed. "I'm feeling like a drowned rat."

I heaved an annoyed sigh. He actually looked good standing in the rain, his black hair slicked down on his head. His clothes also clung to him so I could see the outline of his chest. Of course, I was a little reluctant to let him into the shed.

Still, I turned, opened the shed door and walked in.

"I came here to apologize for what happened today."

I spun back to face him.

He gave me a small smile. "For how I found out where you lived, well, when I moved here, I was warned to stay clear of you and this area, where you do your witchcraft or commune with the devil."

"Yeah." I snorted. "I do both. Look, I don't want your half-hearted apology and really, there isn't anything to apologize for. So you can take your pity kiss and stick it where the sun don't shine, because it will never happen again."

"It wasn't a *pity* kiss," he said in a whisper that held a hard edge to it.

Okay, I wasn't going to believe that for a second. I'd seen the look in his eyes.

Which reminded me that I was staring at Isaac. I turned my gaze to the wall.

"Yeah, right. Now, if you don't need anything else, I'm heading inside." I stepped around him, but he was soon in my way. "We could have been friends, Isaac. Then again,"—I shrugged—"I don't really need them."

I managed a couple of steps away from him before he called out, "Why can't we still?"

"What?" I asked, facing him, only with my eyes off to the side.

"Why can't we be friends now?"

"What kind of game are you playing at, Isaac? Why would you want to? If you're just trying to impress the other girls by taking pity on the freak, then you can forget it. They won't care."

"I don't concern myself with the others. They're childish."

"News flash: most people our age act like that."

He shook his head. "I don't believe that with you. I don't get along with many people, but I could with you. I don't pity you, Leila, and I'm not playing any games."

I moved my eyes to study him. He seemed to be serious. Then again, he always seemed to be serious.

Was it time I took a chance on someone?

Could I trust him? The new guy, the one guy that drove my senses wild and stole my first kiss.

Yes, yes, yes. Trust him, jump him, spank him. I seriously needed some private time; he was driving my hormones crazy.

Sighing loudly, I said, "One chance, buster, and if you stuff me around in any way, I will stomp on you."

He let out a breath, which could have been a laugh, I wasn't sure.

God, what was I getting myself into with this guy?

"Wanna come inside? My show's about to start and I'm not missing it."

"Ah, I don't think that would be a good idea. Most parents don't like me."

"Don't worry about it. My folks aren't home."

He gave me a dubious glance, looked over my shoulder and then back to me before he nodded. Without another word, I stalked off, not caring if he followed.

Yeah, right. I wanted to be that six-year-old girl again and jump for joy, yelling over and over, "I have a friend." *And a hot one I want to lick at that.*

After I removed my jacket and boots, I noticed Isaac standing just outside, peering in.

"Coming in or what?"

"Thank you." He gave me his half smile, which made my stomach do flip-flops. I quickly looked away.

Was having Isaac in my home really a good idea? I hardly knew the guy for God's sake. He could have been a serial killer or something, or he could knock me out and rob the place. Funny though, if it came down to it, I didn't care too much. It was nice to have someone in the house with me. My always busy, always drinking and hunting uncle didn't really count.

Sitting down on the couch, I switched on the TV and ignored the fact that Isaac Grey was in my house. His gaze ran over the pictures hanging on the walls. I flicked through the channels.

"*This* is your show?" Isaac asked, standing behind the couch.

"What's wrong with *Glee*?" I glared. No one should ever diss *Glee* in front of me; the show always brought a smile to my face.

"No, nothing, I suppose. If you like singing," he said with a fake cringe, while trying not to smile.

"I don't know if this friendship can continue," I said, shaking my head at him. "You can either sit down and shut it, or leave now."

He stood behind me quietly until the commercials came on.

"Isaac, what are you doing?" I asked without looking at him.

"I-I think I may be a little wet to sit on the couch, and I didn't want to interrupt your show. You seem scary when it comes to it."

A laugh escaped me as I jumped up from the couch and looked at him with wide eyes. He *was* still soaking. I averted my gaze to over his shoulder and cussed at myself for not being considerate enough to notice.

"True about the show, but still, you should have said something earlier. Hang on, I'll go grab a towel, and I'm sure I have something for you to wear that will fit. Wait one sec." I rushed off to the linen closet, grabbed a towel then dashed to my bedroom. I searched through my clothes for a hooded jumper and found some old tracksuit pants of my dad's. I ran back to the lounge, threw the towel at him and placed the clothes on the edge of the couch before sitting back down in time for *Glee* to start again.

Isaac cleared his throat behind me.

"Yeah?" I asked.

"A room to change in? Unless you would prefer me to undress here?" Humour laced his voice.

I pretended to think about it for a minute, tapping my chin with one finger. "Go down the hall to the end room. You can change in there."

It wasn't until the next commercials came on did I realise Isaac hadn't returned. Worried with what he was getting up to in my room, I went after him. The door was closed. I knocked before entering, in case he was that slow at getting dressed—or I hoped he was. I opened the door without a reply and found him over by my window, looking at the pictures that hung on the wall beside it.

Dear God, he's not wearing a shirt.

Thank you, Lord.

In my dazed state, I froze and took in the glorious view before me. He was beautiful. He hadn't turned around, so all I could see was his back; still, his back was something to write home about. In fact, I could recite a sonnet about how his tanned skin shone from the wet rain. How his shoulders cried out to me and made me want to sprint over, just so I could run my hands all over them.

He turned around, and I found the front view was just as good as the back. Nice strong arms and a six-pack that yelled, *Hello, take notice of me.* And good God, I was. That was until he placed my hoodie on.

I let out an annoyed breath at him for interrupting my ogling. A blush rose to my cheeks and I looked away, but not before I saw the smile on his face. He knew I was perving, and he enjoyed every minute of it.

Oh, hell, what did I get myself into?

"I wanted to see what was taking you so long," I said after clearing my throat a few times.

"I hope you don't mind my looking around. But I thought if we're to be friends, it would be best to see how *my friend* lives." He grinned. Smiling suited him. I didn't understand why he didn't do it more often, even at school.

"You can just ask me questions instead of snooping," I lightly suggested. It wasn't like I had anything to hide. Well, not there in the house anyway.

"True." He nodded. "Do you mind if I ask one now?"

Shaking my head, I leaned against the door frame and teased, "You don't have to ask to ask me a question, Isaac. You just do it."

He let out a deep, carefree laugh. It was beautiful and caused goose bumps to appear on my arms.

"All right then." He studied me for a moment. "Why is your eye black?"

Biting my bottom lip, I moved my gaze to the floor and then back up. I knew it wouldn't take him long, like all curious people. "I don't know." For the first time, the lie felt bitter. "I was born this way. Believe me when I say I've had test after test and no one has any answers."

"Does it bother you?"

Another sigh escaped me. I met his gaze for a second, then it met the floor again. "At the start, yes, of course it did. Especially when so many people question it and they make their own assumptions from it, saying I'm a witch, or a demon child, or the one that never goes away: freak. But you soon learn to ignore all of it and continue on with your life... As good as you can anyway. So, no. It doesn't bother me now."

"You must get lonely." It was a statement, but I chose to answer it anyway.

"Look, I can understand that you feel sorry for the freak, but seriously, if that's all this is then get lost." I straightened and looked to him with a glare. He quickly moved his gaze from my belongings and focused back on me with his own glare.

"Leila,"—Damn him and his sexy voice saying my name—"I don't feel sorry for you. I only wanted to say that I know what being lonely can feel like. I haven't allowed myself a friend in such a long time. To a point, I can no longer handle being without companionship."

"I don't get it, Isaac." I shook my head. "You say you haven't allowed yourself a friend, but all you have to do is speak up and you'd have dozens of willing people. I mean, sure the majority would be girls who only want you for your body. And you'd have a few guys who would only want you for your mad ball skills... Still, they'd be your friends."

He groaned and ran a hand through his inky hair. "It's not the same. I am... different. I think you are as well. And I found that since you had no one else around you that it would be easier to get to know *you*."

"So I'm the easy target friend," I joked. I didn't care that he wanted to be friends with me because he saw that I didn't have anyone else to hang with. While I knew it wasn't because he felt sorry for the lonely freak, it was because he didn't care for crowds. He was a person who liked solitude, but when that got to be too much, it was always good to have just one other person to go to. My belly warmed at the possibility. He'd chosen me to be that person.

"Are you always going to take offense to everything I say?" he growled.

"Okay, *buddy*. If we're friends, you have to learn to know when I am joking. Dammit, Isaac, you're making me miss *Glee*." I bolted back to the living room.

Isaac eventually came out and sat next to me quietly. He was smart enough to leave me in peace while my show finished.

The whole time I watched the cast of *Glee* break out into song, I wanted to punch myself. For some reason, I couldn't seem to wipe the silly, happy smile from my face. Though, my guess was because of who was sitting beside me.

CHAPTER THREE

"That was the most—" Isaac began.

I quickly placed my hand over his mouth. "No, you don't. You do not say one bad word about *Glee*," I said, meeting his eyes that held humour, with a scowl.

He gently pulled my hand away, only he didn't let go. Instead, I watched wide-eyed as he placed it with his own on his thigh. I moved my stare away, knowing I was blushing. My heart beat hard in my chest, and suddenly, vultures pecked away in my stomach. It wasn't the sweet butterflies fluttering around. No, my nerves had me so tied in a knot I felt like I was going to throw up.

No guy had held my hand.

Well, besides my dad, but he didn't count.

"Why do you always look away? I've noticed you hardly ever meet someone's gaze."

"Pff." I pulled my hand free and made it look like I needed to tuck my hair behind my ears.

Even though nausea was heavy in my stomach, I liked the way my hand felt in his; the warmth and tenderness gave me… emotions I wasn't used to feeling.

Emotions that scared me.

Just friends, just friends.

"I'm sorry if I've made you uncomfortable," he uttered. "It's only that I wish you wouldn't look away. I like your eyes, Leila. My father once told me that if you refused to meet someone's gaze, they would think they're superior to you, they would see you fear them. I don't believe that with you."

"Look. It's nothing." I clenched my hands into fists.

All of it was alien to me. I didn't know how to act or what to say. God, even how to look. I was used to averting my unwanted gaze because of the way it made people feel. And now... now I had someone telling me it was a sign of weakness.

I couldn't let it continue.

It wasn't in my nature.

After a deep breath, I looked up to meet Isaac's gaze.

His smile and the look of pride in his eyes gave me more confidence. And sent my heart into hyper-drive.

Stupid hormones.

He reached out and ran the back of his hand slowly down my cheek. "Perfect."

Biting my bottom lip to stop the moan wanting to escape from his touch, I shrugged, as if his compliment was something I heard every day. Acting like it was nothing, when it was the total opposite. His comment... I wished I could bottle it and take it with me everywhere I went just so I could listen to it over and over.

Oh, hell. I wanted to look away. I had to fight with myself to keep my eyes on his. To me, it was natural to avert my unwanted gaze.

A pain in my chest started.

Was I about to have a panic attack?

"Would you mind if I used your telephone to call my father to collect me?" Isaac asked, as if he had sensed my inner turmoil. I sent him a small smile of appreciation, a change of subject was just what I needed.

"Do you always talk so proper?" I teased.

"Do you not like it?" he said, laying it on thicker.

I rolled my eyes. "It doesn't matter whether I like it or not. Friends don't judge each other."

"Too right, or else I would have said something a long time ago about your slang."

Gently, I punched him in the arm.

Or did that class as flirting? I didn't want to flirt with my only friend and stuff things up. It could chase him away and I'd never… Bugger it all, I knew nothing about flirting, so I would act how I'd usually act and be myself. Isaac could either take it or leave it.

Therefore, I sat up straight with my hands folded in my lap, and in my best posh voice, I said, "Please, feel free to use the telephone, Isaac Grey." I smiled and asked, "Is that better?"

He raised his eyebrows. "No." He smiled and shook his head. "It's not you."

"I know, right?" I nodded.

"Pardon?" he smirked.

With a roll of my eyes, I ordered, "Just go and call your dad, wise guy."

He went to the kitchen and used the phone near the living room. It was times like these I was glad I was different.

Glad I had great hearing.

"Father."

"Isaac, where have you been, son?"

"At a friend's house. Would you be able to come and get me?"

"I'll have your brother do it. Sorry, my boy, but I'm a little busy at the moment."

Isaac has a brother? I never knew. He passed my address on and said goodbye. Before he could come and sit back down, I stood and walked into the kitchen.

"I should've asked if you wanted something to eat. I'm starved. I didn't realise it was so late. What can I get you? Do you have time for something? How far away do you live?"

Pausing my search in the freezer and fridge, I glanced over my shoulder at his amused expression.

It was strange how easily I was finding it to meet his gaze. I was in awe of Isaac because he made me feel so comfortable, I could be myself around him.

"It's fine. I'm not hungry, and we live on the other side of town. On a property like this actually, and feel free to eat something yourself. Shouldn't your parents be home soon?"

"Worried you might run into them?" I asked while getting out my usual dinner, a microwave meal. Tonight, chicken stir-fry. *Yum. Not.*

"Actually, yes."

"I never picked you to be one who was scared of parents." I laughed. "But you don't have to worry, they won't be home tonight."

"Oh, are they out of town?"

"No," I said flatly. Why was he so interested in where they were? "Anyway, enough questions about me. Tell me something about yourself."

He looked as though I'd asked him to kill someone for me. His nose screwed up, a dark look passed in his eyes and his whole body tensed.

"Come on, Isaac, it isn't that hard. Let's start with how many family members you have."

He stared down at the kitchen bench he'd sat at. "There are four in my family. My father, my brother, my sister and then myself."

"Yes, *and?*"

"And what?" He looked over my shoulder, out the kitchen window.

"Isaac, why are *you* being so difficult? Sorry, unless you don't want to tell me. I was being rude, wasn't I?"

I could have kicked myself. It was a perfect example of how all of it was alien to me. I wouldn't answer any question on where my parents were, and there I was, pushing for more information out of him.

He rolled his eyes. "It's fine. All right, my brother, Jeremiah, who you will meet in a moment, because I am sure he will not leave until he is introduced to the person who… until he meets you. He is, ah… nineteen, a year older than myself. My sister, Jezanna, she's sixteen. Our mother passed away a year before we moved here. My father is still pained by it."

"I'm sorry."

"Thank you."

Crap, I didn't want him to leave feeling low, especially when I was the one who annoyed him into talking. So I asked a few light questions, like about music. I told him my favourite was the Black Eyed Peas.

He pulled a disgusted face. "I listen to The Smashing Pumpkins."

"Who?" I asked.

He smiled. "I see that I am going to have to enlighten you with some taste."

We moved onto everything else we could think of while I ate my dinner until a bang on the front door made me jump. Usually, I would've heard a car pull into my drive, but I must have been too engrossed in our conversation to notice.

Which was not good enough. My uncle had always taught me to be cautious.

"I'll answer it, since it will be Jeremiah. Leila, I must apologize in advance for my brother. He is, uh… well, I'm sure you will soon find out."

Okay, that did not sound good. I admitted to myself he had me worried. I waited anxiously in the kitchen while Isaac left to answer the door.

"Brother," a deep voice barked.

"Jeremiah, please come in."

I listened to their footsteps approach. Isaac's quiet footfalls and Jeremiah's loud heavy ones. Isaac walked in first, followed by Jeremiah, and when he spotted me for the first time, he stopped abruptly. His eyes grew wide and he sucked in a breath.

It was the usual reaction upon seeing my eyes for the first time.

I was impressed with myself though. I didn't look away.

Isaac shook his head as he sat back on the bench. I glanced from one to the other. You could see the resemblance. Both had charcoal hair and deep green eyes. Only Isaac's were more alluring than his brother's. Really, the only difference between them was that Jeremiah had a soldier's build. He was taller, his hair shorter, except at the front where his fringe hung over his eyes.

Jeremiah had an ample amount of time to say something. To get over his shock and quit bloody staring, but he hadn't.

"Hi there." I waved. "I'm Leila Morgin. I'm sure you can see by now that I have one black eye. No, I don't know why that is. This is how I was born. Now can you quit staring?"

If they could have, I was sure his eyes would have grown wider. I glanced at Isaac, who was trying to repress his laughter.

I glanced back to Jeremiah to see if he'd made any progress, and thankfully, he had. He was now glaring at me.

Yay.

"I'm sorry, Leila. You took me by surprise. Still, it was very rude of me, so I will apologize again."

"Don't sweat it. Most people scream and run when they first meet me." I nodded.

For a second there, it seemed like he was going to laugh. Instead, he asked, "You have a nice home. Are you parents in?"

Groaning, I snapped, "No, not right now. Why?" Seriously, what was with asking about my parents?

"They're not, but I am," a gravelled voice answered behind Jeremiah. Jeremiah spun around quickly, while Isaac stood, a noise falling from their lips.

"Way to go, Jack." I glared at my uncle.

Admittedly, every time he returned, a little tension would leave me and I'd sigh with relief. Once more, I had no idea where he'd been. At least he'd come home. Sometimes he looked a little more worn than usual, as he did now.

Rolling my eyes, I controlled my laugh as I watched him

take on a pose of a tough man in front of the boys. His feet were spread apart in his tattered blue jeans and cowboy boots. His arms crossed over his large chest, which caused his flannel shirt to look too small for him. He held his short brown-haired head high and glared at the strangers with his piercing blue eyes.

Shaking my head, I said to Isaac and his brother, "Ignore him. He's just the hired help."

Uncle Jack snorted. He carefully walked around Jeremiah and Isaac without taking his eyes off them, and stopped at my side, only to ruffle my hair, which I hated and had told him over and over.

"What's up, kiddo? And who do we have here? If I had known we were having guests, I would have been home earlier."

"Whatever. Where did you go this time?"

"*Hunting.*"

A low noise, one that sounded like a growl, came from Jeremiah and Isaac's direction. I looked at them, screwed my nose up and raised a brow in question. They said nothing.

"However, it doesn't matter about me right now, kid. You're bein' rude. I think introductions are called for."

"Isaac, Jeremiah. This is my annoying, pain-in-the-butt Uncle Jack. Doofus, Isaac and I go to college together and Jeremiah is Isaac's brother, here to pick him up after we had wild monkey sex." All three of them nearly choked on their own saliva. They ended up spluttering and coughing to regain some oxygen back in their systems.

"Seriously, kid. You're gonna kill me one day."

Smiling, I nudged his ribs and offered, "I shall try my best."

"It's a pleasure to meet you, *Jack*." Jeremiah glared. "Isaac, are you ready to leave?"

"Yes." Isaac nodded. "I'll see you tomorrow, Leila," he said with his usual sober expression. Had something happened here without my knowledge?

"Yeah, see you then. Nice meeting *you*, Jeremiah. I'm sure we'll be seeing a lot of each other now."

He turned from the doorway to glance at me. "We'll see." He smirked then left, with Isaac following.

"Damn it, Jack, look at what you've just done."

He scoffed, walked over to the top cupboard and grabbed out his stash of bourbon. He checked the level to see I hadn't drank any then continued to pour himself a large glass, which he drank down in one go.

What was it that had him on edge? I hadn't seen him like this since my parents up and left, leaving him with the responsibility of me.

He turned around, concern written all over his face. "I don't like it, kiddo."

I sighed. "What?"

"Them."

"Don't do this, Jack," I yelled.

"I have a right to," he yelled back.

"No. No you don't. You don't get a choice of who I hang out with. Come on, Jack, when was the last time you saw me with someone—anyone? I need this. I need normal."

He snorted. "You won't get it from them two."

"What does that even mean? You always say cryptic shit and never finish it. Is this one of those times, Jack, or will you finish?"

He stared at me in silence, annoying the hell out of me. My hands fisted at my sides.

"You know I'm always gone for you, right? To keep you… to keep all this running." He gestured to the whole house.

"I call bullshit. I know for a fact Dad sends you money."

"Just leave it, Leila."

Ooh, he called me Leila. This always marked the time he'd shut down on me.

"All you need to know is I care about you. I'll have your back." He sounded weary.

Concern for him fluttered through my system, but I rolled my eyes and turned back to my cold dinner. It was always like this. He'd come home for a couple of days and say some things I didn't understand. We'd fight, we'd make up and we'd fight again. Then he would leave.

I couldn't listen to Jack on the Isaac situation because my uncle was someone who hardly cared enough to hang around. So I'd continue to be around who I wanted. Could I have said the same for Isaac? Had Jack scared him away? Or would Jeremiah have ordered Isaac to stay away from me? There was something about Jeremiah I didn't understand.

Still, it wasn't worth worrying about right then because it was time for my run. I walked to the back door and opened it.

"You running, kiddo." It was a statement, not a question. Jack knew I liked to run. It was something I did every night.

Only, he didn't know *everything* behind it.

Chapter Four

Darkness surrounds me. Every way I turn, I see nothing but black. My heart beats hard in my chest. My hands tremble along with my legs. I want to run, to scream, but I don't.

Because I know I'm waiting.

It isn't until I see two small red dots in the distance that I relax somewhat.

"Yes," I whisper. "That's what I'm waiting for."

The dots drift closer and closer.

And in a blink of an eye, which always makes me jump, they're right in front of me, so close I can reach out and touch them... No, touch the face that belongs to those red eyes.

I want to.

I need to.

Even though a small amount of fright fills me, I still know I'm safe.

The red eyes study me.

"You're mine," the voice growls...

The house was quiet when I was driven awake from my dream the next morning. On a day my uncle was home, I would usually hear him bustling around the house or his loud snoring coming from the front bedroom. So the quiet could only mean one thing. He'd left again. I hadn't expected him to leave so soon; usually he stayed for a couple of days. At least I was able to walk around my house without getting into another argument.

I shoved the disappointment down and got ready for the day. After I showered and dressed, I walked into the kitchen and was surprised to find there was a note on the bench waiting for me.

> *Morning, Kiddo,*
> *Sorry can't stay longer. Something came up. I'll be home soon though. Please be careful, and for once listen to me about your new friends.*
> *Jack*

I crumpled up the note and threw it in the bin.

When was the last time I'd listened to him?

He'd never liked me running at night. He actually never wanted me to be alone in the house while he was away. Even suggested once that one of his *girlfriends* should stay here with me. However, after I threatened to shave his eyebrows off and wash all his clothes in starch, he relented and left it alone.

I grabbed my umbrella and walked out the door. At the end of my long dirt driveway, a black Hummer waited there.

I opened the passenger door smiling to myself. "Hey. Nice ride," I said to Isaac.

"Thank you. I thought you would like a lift since it's raining," he explained as he pulled away from the curb.

"You thought right, and now that we *are* friends, you can think of yourself as my personal taxi service. Especially when you drive something this sweet. You never know, maybe if I showed up in this, people might start liking me. I might actually get asked out—"

"Why would you want that?" Isaac growled.

"Isaac, if you haven't noticed, I am a girl, and I do have needs." *Not that they'd ever be fulfilled.*

"I have noticed," he whispered.

"O-o-o-kay. So tell me, how much shit did your brother give you?"

He shook his head and smiled. "What about your uncle?"

"Pfft. No one needs to worry about him. We hardly see each

other. He's always out with his mates drinking, and whatever else he does."

His eyebrows furrowed. "He doesn't inform you where he's been or what he's been doing?"

"No, and really, I don't care." I shrugged.

It was easy to say I didn't care, but sometimes I wished Jack and I were closer. Then I could tell him the whole truth about myself. Still, my worry that if I did, he would leave, prevented me from opening up.

"Enough about him. I noticed you ignored my question about your brother. Out with it."

"He said nothing."

"You're lying." I pouted. Something I had never done in my whole life. "Let's get something straight here. We don't lie to each other. Well, unless it's a huge life-threatening secret. But if it's something little, you have to spill."

"I'm not sure how this friendship is going to work," he teased.

"Hey, too late to back out now." I grinned.

He chuckled. "Fair enough. Jeremiah said that it would be in my best interest to stay away from you."

I knew it. "Why? He's worried you'd get the rep as the freak's friend?"

His jaw clenched. "I wish you would stop calling yourself that. I don't like it."

I raised my eyebrows. "Yeah, okay. I suppose."

"He doesn't care what you look like, or what your rep may be." He sighed. "Jeremiah's just being protective."

"That's nice, I guess. That he would look out for you."

"Not only me, but you as well."

Say what now? "I don't understand," I said, and shifted in my seat to look at him, but his gaze remained on the road ahead. I knew he wasn't going to say anything more on the subject, which annoyed me. I had one person already being cryptic in my life; I didn't need another. However, I reminded myself I wasn't someone who liked to be pushed into a subject I'd prefer left alone, so who was I to do that to another.

"Who in the world is this playing? It's terrible," I asked. The music inside the car had been playing softly, but loud enough to comment on, as well as being a good conversation change.

He smiled and pulled the car into a spot in the car park both the high school and college students shared. "That would be The Smashing Pumpkins."

"And you pick on my taste in music. You have issues, Isaac Grey, and I don't think I'm going to be able to help you."

He let out a roar of laughter. "I was under the impression I was helping you."

I snorted. "You got that wrong. Are you ready?" I asked, my hand on the door handle.

"Ready for what?" He looked on with confusion.

"For the gossip, the whispers, the stares. You do know because we came together, people will think we're... *together*." It was times like these I wished I'd been able to head off to a college in a big city. A place where students could pass each other by with ease, remaining invisible if they so wished. I'd had no choice but to remain home, where it was safe and I knew the lay of the land. I just wished my town had been big enough to attract a different calibre of student. Instead, I had to put up with the ridiculous nonsense of feeling like I was still in damn high school.

He shrugged. "Let them think what they want. I don't care."

"I don't either. But don't say I didn't warn you." I got out of the car. Already, I felt multiple eyes on me. What made it worse was when Isaac came around and placed his arm around my shoulders.

I had to admit, it did fit there perfectly. Still, I had to ask, "What are you doing?"

"Giving them something more to speak about. Unless you would like me to stop? That is, if you don't want others to think that we *may* be together?"

The game could be fun, the best fun I'd had in a long time. But what could be dangerous from doing it was the way my heart already raced from just having his arm on my shoulders. The way I wanted to wrap my arms around him and tilt my head up to see if he would kiss me.

Yeah, playing the girlfriend could damage my brain and heart.

Though, I may as well enjoy it while I could. There was a chance that the game of pretend girlfriend was the only way I would ever receive the feeling and actions of anything remotely like actually having a boyfriend.

Isaac's arm slid away as we walked down the hall.

"What are you doing now?" I hissed.

"I thought you wanted me to stop?"

"No. It's all good. Let the game begin." I gave him my best smile and received one in return as he bent and kissed me on the nose, then replaced his arm to my shoulders.

Be still my beating heart. No wait, I think my heart just stopped as soon as Isaac's sexy lips touched my nose.

Jesus. I was a dead woman, melting into a puddle of mush because that was the cutest, sweetest move I had ever seen.

Oh, God. I was going to be sick.

Damn that vulture in my stomach.

He led me to my locker—again something I never saw in other campuses from their brochures—so I could grab the books I needed for my double computer science class. I opened my locker door. Isaac stepped up behind me and placed his hands at my waist. His body was so close to mine that I felt him along my own from top to bottom.

My heart sang with joy.

Then choked on rap music because I was nervous.

I quickly grabbed my books and closed my locker, hiding my hands because they were shaking so badly. I turned in his arms and looked up into his eyes. I was surprised to see that, for once, his eyes were smiling like he was. He looked happy. I only wished it were because of me, that he really wanted to be with me, instead of pretending.

I thumped my forehead against his chest and snorted.

"Are you all right?"

I let out a huff of laughter. "Yeah, all good."

"I better head to class."

And I really shouldn't have agreed to this.

With no classes with Isaac that day, I didn't get to see him. I wanted to, but chose not to, choosing to chicken out instead by hiding in the library at lunch, away from him and away from all the questions. Jenna and her flock asked me multiple times what was going on whenever they spotted me. By the end of the day, they gave up. Thank God, because I was about ready to kick them all on their shins, and then knee them on their noses. What was laughable was when Jenna even had some cute guy approach me to try and get any type of information. Still, I didn't budge.

After my last class, I made my way to Isaac's car where he was already inside waiting for me. The closer I got, the faster my heart beat. I opened the door to his smiling face and climbed in.

"Hey." I smiled.

"How was your day?" Isaac asked.

"Good." I shrugged as he started the car. "Lots of questions, as I'm sure you got. I didn't say anything to anyone though."

"I didn't see you at lunch."

"Sorry. I probably should have told you. I usually go to the library to see Jim. It's a nice and peaceful place."

"Are you okay, Leila?"

"For sure." I gave him my best reassuring smile. I only hoped he didn't notice it wasn't a real one. "So are you going to drive or what?"

"Actually, I was wondering if you would like to go somewhere with me? Unless your parents expect you home. Or your uncle?"

"Isaac." I sighed. "No one expects me home, so that sounds good." *A way to take my mind off things.* "Lead the way."

We pulled up out the front of an old, run-down pub. The sign was half hanging off the top of the building. I turned my head sideways to read it. Boozers.

"I don't have an ID," I said while getting out of the car.

"You'll be fine," he assured me. He took my hand and led me to the black steel door. As soon as he opened it, a number of scents hit me: men, women, alcohol, cigarettes and sweat.

We walked down the long dark corridor. At the end, it opened up to a large, rounded room. People were everywhere. Some played pool, others danced, most drank and smoked, and from the smell of it, it wasn't just cigarettes. Isaac led me towards a booth table to the left, near the bar. He gestured for me to climb in first, so I did, and then sat closely next to me.

"I'm thinking this place is nothing like you've been to before." He smirked at my worried expression.

"You could say that. How do you know about this place?"

"One of my father's friends owns it. It's a safe place for me to come and… relax."

I couldn't help but wonder what he meant by safe.

"Would you like a drink?" he offered.

"Sure, but, ah, non-alcoholic."

"Of course." He leaned toward me. Was he about to kiss me? Only, I didn't find out because from whatever look I had on my face—which I was sure was curiosity—it stopped him short, and the smile fell from his face. "My apologies. I was getting used to pretending." I nodded at him before he left the table.

I bit my bottom lip as confusion settled in. Why would he want to kiss me when no one from school was around?

Could… no, he couldn't have *wanted* to. *Does Isaac actually like me?* I snorted. That thought was just ridiculous. Wasn't even sane. No… but… No, just no. Then I'd go and get my hopes up and like him back, make an idiot of myself if he didn't like me.

Jesus Christ. I sound like a whiny cheerleader girl.

Nevertheless, it's Isaac and all his gorgeousness.

Shut up, you fool.

Confusion was definitely my middle name.

I wasn't alone long. A guy, not much older than me, walked up and stood in front of me. I looked up into his light blue eyes. His own eyes widened upon seeing mine.

In habit, I looked away, my eyes landing on Isaac waiting at the bar. Just seeing him gave me courage, so I stared back at his blue eyes.

"Evenin' there, love."

An English accent. Yum.

"Hi."

"Hope you don't mind my sayin' so, but you have beautiful eyes."

Glaring at him, I asked, "Are you for real, or just playing some stupid game?"

"I never play, unless in bed." He winked. "Name's Caelen." He held out his hand to me. I looked at it, then up to his smiling face and placed my hand in his.

"I'm Leila."

"Caelen, what are you doing here?" Isaac asked. He placed the drinks on the table and turned to face Caelen, who let go of my hand and stepped back.

"Ah, Isaac, so good to see you, chap. It's been too long. I was just introducing myself to Leila here."

"I didn't know you were back."

"Luckily for me I am, or I wouldn't have met Leila. Would you mind if I sit with the two of you?" he asked as he ran a hand through his shoulder-length blond hair.

Isaac looked down at me. I shrugged. He sighed and

nodded, then sat down next to me. Isaac nudged at me to move around.

Caelen smirked. "No matter, lad. I'll sit this side." He placed himself to my other side, a little too close for comfort.

"Lad? Isn't that what you would call a much younger guy?" I asked.

Caelen's eyes brightened and looked over at Isaac, who, I noticed out the corner of my eyes, shook his head slightly.

"Yes, it is. I just like to tease him. Now, tell me about yourself, Leila. How did you two meet?"

"College."

"How interesting. What made you go back, Isaac?"

"Caelen, don't," Isaac warned.

My brows drew down at the obvious warning Isaac issued. "How is it that you two know each other?" I asked after taking a sip of my drink.

"Isaac and I go way back, even before he moved here. Boy, I could tell you some stories about this guy." He thumbed toward Isaac.

"Caelen," Isaac growled low.

Interesting.

I thought I would have hated coming to a place like Boozers. But in the end, I had a really good time, thanks to Caelen that was. Isaac sat in the booth like a zombie, not saying much at all. Therefore, when Caelen asked me to dance, I jumped at the chance. Besides, I'd never been asked before. I pulled my hooded jumper off and walked out onto the dance floor in my jeans and red, sleeveless top. Caelen pulled me in close and I soon got the hang of things, swaying to the music. After a few songs, we went back to the table for a drink.

It was also in case Isaac wanted to ask me to dance, but he didn't. So I continued to dance with Caelen, who I found was funny because he liked to crack jokes every chance he got. Sweet, in a 'roll your eyes' way, and so charming, I lost count how many times he made me blush.

It was a brilliant night until Isaac came up to us on the dance floor, handed me my jumper, and told me we were leaving. His voice was sharp, annoyed. I mumbled my goodbye to Caelen, who gave me a light peck on the cheek. Then I followed Isaac out to the car.

The drive home was quiet and tense. We pulled into my driveway and up to my house. I presumed Isaac wasn't coming in because he kept the car running.

"Isaac, what have I done?"

"Nothing."

"You're lying to me."

He turned to glare at me. "Like you lied to me after school when I asked if you were okay?" he snapped. After taking a deep breath, he continued, "Look, it's nothing. I don't think we should play the couple game any longer." *Was that a good or bad thing?* "Besides, it would be hard if others saw Caelen and yourself down the street together."

"What's that supposed to mean? We only danced for God's sake. Besides, the game was your suggestion in the first place."

"Yes, and I shouldn't have."

I gaped at his harshness, and then sighed. "When will I see you next?"

"I'm not sure."

"Fine," I bit out and climbed out of the car. I stomped up the stairs to the front door. Before I opened it, I felt Isaac behind me. The strange thing was, I hadn't even heard his car door open or his approach.

"I'm sorry, Leila," he said. I turned to face him. "How about I come and collect you this weekend? You could come and meet my father and sister," he asked.

He was quick to change his attitude, why? Still, I wasn't

passing up the opportunity to know Isaac more. "That would be nice." I smiled.

He glanced over my shoulder to the house. "Are your parents or uncle home?"

"Isaac." I blushed. "They're never home. My parents are off travelling, and my uncle is always somewhere else. He left again this morning. I practically live here on my own."

He looked down at me with wide eyes. Had he been surprised by my confession? It seemed like he was going to say something; instead, he pulled me into a hug, his arms wrapping around my shoulders. I stood there for a second in shock, and then placed my arms around his waist. I inhaled his familiar scent and revelled in his comforting heat. All too soon, he dotted a kiss on my forehead and then walked away.

For the first time, I was too tired to go for a run and opted to go to bed.

Excitement drummed through me with what tomorrow would bring. I was going to see Isaac again and I'd get to meet his family.

Even if he frustrated me, he was worth keeping.

Chapter Five

I waited around the house for Isaac to show and, I hated to admit it, I did wait all day.

He never showed.

Then I considered maybe I had the day wrong; he could have meant Sunday. Only, I had no way of knowing. For one, I didn't have his phone number, and two, I didn't know where he lived, which boiled my blood in frustration.

Sunday came and went with no sign of Isaac.

Of course, that made me even crazier.

It left me wondering if something had happened. Still, I thought he could have called if something had come up and he wasn't able to make it.

I actually rang all the names in the telephone book ending in Grey. His family wasn't one of them. Then again, there weren't many. Ours wasn't a large town.

Of course, my warped brain then started thinking that Isaac had just been playing mind games with me, toying with my emotions. Until another part of my mind told me I was being silly. He wasn't that type of person. Still, another, yet more annoying, part snapped back and said I hardly knew the guy.

It was amazing the things my mind would come up with when emotions were flying high.

Monday morning, I gave Isaac enough time to pick me up from my house before classes started. He didn't show. So I walked to class. With the sun beating down on me, I was glad

I'd opted for my jeans and a long-sleeved cotton top. Not my usual hooded jumper.

After searching the whole school, I realised I'd searched in vain; he wasn't there.

Concern caused my stomach to churn. What if something had happened? If not to him, then maybe one of his family members and he was upset. He could've needed a friend and I hadn't been there for him. Instead, I was wallowing in my own stupid thoughts.

Even if I was unwelcome, I needed to find out where he lived to see if he was okay.

I drove myself insane while I suffered through a long, boring day. It was made worse as I had no luck sneaking into the office at lunch to look up Isaac's address. Frustrated at my inability to be stealthy or even rational, I decided to follow another idea.

Walking up to the shambles of the place called Boozers, I opened the door and entered. The music hit me as well as all the other God-awful smells. I stalked down the corridor and stepped out into the open area. Glancing around, I noted it was quieter than the other night.

Suddenly, the hairs on the back of my neck raised. I felt all eyes were on me. Instinct told me to run, but I couldn't.

Two girls around my age sidled up beside me. As soon as they saw my eyes, one gasped and the other squealed in disgust.

Jesus Christ. I sighed.

"O.M.G, Heather. Look at her eye," the short blonde one whispered to the taller redheaded one, Heather.

"I know. I'd be so embarrassed if I had that thing. What are you doing here?" Heather asked, only her annoyed tone made it sound as though I shouldn't even be stepping foot in the place.

However, I wouldn't let them get to me. Jutting my chin out, I said, "I need to find Isaac Grey. Have either of you seen him?"

They both giggled with glee. "He hasn't been in today." Heather sighed longingly before she glared at me and asked,

"Wait, why do you want to know? You know he won't like you. He's ours."

Blondie took a step towards me. "Yeah, bitch. Stay away. Don't think you can come in here and take over."

Holy crap, had I stepped into a parallel universe where we were in some primary school show? They acted like it and it made me want to twat-punch them.

"Come on, Chloe. It's not like he'd choose her over us anyway." Heather sneered.

"Yeah." Chloe laughed and slapped her small hip. "We are T.A.S.T.Y."

What in the hell was going on here? Isaac? Choose me over them? Was he with them?

"Hullo, love, fancy seeing you here again. I had hoped."

Turning, I smiled when I found Caelen standing right behind me. It was good to see his friendly face.

"Hi, Caelen."

"Rack off, girls." He shooed Heather and Chloe away with one hand. They didn't seem fazed by it. They pouted at him, winked and actually skipped off.

Caelen ignored my eye-roll and asked, "Have you come here on your own? Not a good idea, sweetheart."

"I know. Look, ah… Do you know if the manager is in?"

"'Fraid not, love. Why're you after him?"

"Damn. He knows Isaac's dad and I need to know where Isaac lives," I said. Frustrated, I ran a hand through my hair.

"Don't tell me that bugger has run off and left you broken-hearted already? Not to fret, pet, I can help you in that area." He winked.

Snorting, I said, "It's nothing like that. I, um, he told me where he lives, but I lost the piece of paper and I have to get some things to him tonight." I shifted from one foot to the other.

Stiffening, I felt movement behind me. I didn't have to turn to know others were walking towards us. I could sense them. For a fraction of a second, I saw panic sweep through Caelen's eyes and that told me whomever was advancing was bringing trouble with them.

"Righto, love, I can help you with that. Come, I'll take you to *Isaac's* house." He gestured with his arm towards the main entrance.

Glancing over my shoulder, I witnessed what that one word caused. When Isaac's name was spoken aloud, it stopped the menacing few advancing toward me.

Why?

Following Caelen out to his red Mustang, I did not hesitate getting in. I trusted Caelen and I knew the reason why was because he'd seen me with Isaac the other night.

We drove in silence, which kind of worried me. Caelen liked to talk, even if most of it was bull. After fifteen minutes and just out of town, we pulled up at the end of a driveway. I looked down it to see a huge, three-storey home. Turning back to Caelen, who was doing what I had been, staring at the house, only I saw worry rolling off him. His brows furrowed in the centre and he shook his head.

"Sorry, love, wrong house. Come to think of it, I really can't remember where he lives." He went to put the car back into gear, but I stopped him by placing my hand on his.

"You're lying. Why?"

"Look, it's just not the right time to visit your crush," he said harshly and continued to drive off. Panic set in, feeding my adrenalin. Something was wrong and I didn't want to leave. I opened the passenger door and jumped out, rolling along the road before snapping up to stand.

My eyes widened when I found Caelen standing in front of me. How had he moved so fast? "You cannot go in there." He tried to shove me back in the car.

What had him on edge?

"Caelen, what's going on? Tell me." I wiggled and fought his grip. I saw, from his wide eyes, he was shocked I was able to fight him. Hell, I was even surprised I had strength to push him as well. But, I wouldn't let anything stop me from going into Isaac's house. I stomped on his foot, kicked him in the balls and started running.

"Fine, you stupid wench, get yourself killed. No skin off my nose."

With those words, it confirmed I was running into danger. Still, I didn't stop. If Isaac was in trouble and there was no one else to help him, it was up to me.

Opening the door quietly, the smell of blood hit my nose. The hairs on the back of my neck raised and unease clenched at my heart.

I followed the stench, ignoring all the rooms I passed, while I walked softly, but quickly, down the hallway.

Fear and dread boiled up inside of me. I wanted to run, but the other part of me wouldn't have it. The urge to protect was more important than anything else.

My senses were on high alert. I didn't want anyone to sneak up on me. As I got closer to the end room, I heard muffled voices.

A scream ripped through the house. I ran and burst through the door.

My eyes landed on Isaac first. He lay on a table, arms and legs bound with silver. Blood covered his naked chest. Next to Isaac, on a different table, was Jeremiah. He was also half-naked and bound like his brother. At his side was yet another table and it held a young girl, who I presumed was Isaac's sister, Jezanna, in a flimsy nightgown.

They all looked alike. All weary, worried and bloodied.

My eyes reached Jezanna's and my heart went straight out to her. She looked petrified.

I calmed my own fear. I had to do something—anything.

"Leila, get out." Isaac's voice dripped with fury.

The next I knew, I was being held by my throat up against the wall.

Panic flared as my breath left my body. My wide eyes settled on the older man who'd grabbed me. He had short, red hair, freckles that consumed his face and light brown eyes.

"Who do we have here?" he asked with a deep gravel voice. He repositioned his hands, moving one forearm against my upper chest so I could breathe. I gasped in lungfuls of air while his other arm pushed my stomach to hold me firmly against the wall.

"Leave her alone," Isaac snarled and struggled against his restraints. A stronger scent of burning flesh filled the room.

Jezanna cried out for him to stop, which calmed him enough for me to hear, "You fool, you shouldn't have come." Jeremiah coughed and spat blood to the side.

"An interest of yours, Isaac?" Freckles asked. "I can see why. What strange eyes. What are you doing here?"

Settling my nerves, I calmly replied, "Just came for a visit."

"Well, sweetness, you came on the wrong day. Lenny," he bellowed.

"Yes, sir?" said the giant coming through the door, which joined onto another hallway. Lenny had to crouch to fit through or he would have hit his bald head. He was the biggest man I had ever seen.

"Finish what you started. I'm sure this pretty thing would love to watch." He took a small step to the left. Still, he had me pinned.

Lenny the giant, walked over to Jeremiah and pulled something from under the table, my eyes widened when I realised what it was.

A long carving knife.

"No," Freckles barked. "Do Isaac, this one feels more for him and I want to hear her scream."

Lenny stepped around Jeremiah to Isaac. He made a show of licking the blood off the knife while he watched me with his dark piercing eyes. I looked on. Shock and fear coiled in my stomach as he slowly placed the knife on the left side of Isaac's stomach—the closest side to me.

"I'm sorry, Leila," Isaac uttered. My eyes found his as Lenny's cut went deep and slow, straight across Isaac's stomach. Isaac's only sign of pain was when he tugged at his restraints. I wanted to cry, to scream, but didn't. I wouldn't let the monsters have satisfaction from it.

I kept my gaze on Isaac, as his own was on me. Lenny brought the knife up a little higher, near Isaac's chest, and started again. Isaac opened his mouth in a silent protest. It opened enough for me to witness Isaac's canine teeth slide down to a point at the end.

Vampire.

"You didn't know." Freckles laughed. "Oh, how dear. Yes, sweetness, I can see it in your eyes the shock. What I don't understand is why you aren't screaming."

Lenny stopped to watch the conversation. He was grinning a toothless grin. I wanted to wipe his smile right off his face.

Maybe I should have been shocked, scared or repulsed with finding out what Isaac was.

But I wasn't. It didn't matter what he was.

Really, I felt at peace with it. I wasn't the only one out there in the world who was different. And that alone brought a smile to my face.

Faking a yawn, I said, "This doesn't interest me." My eyes went to my captor. "Why aren't you doing anything, Freckles? I see Lenny has blood all over him, but you're all clean. Oh, wait, I get it. You don't like to get your hands dirty."

"What the hell are you doing?" Jeremiah yelled.

Freckles ignore Jeremiah and answered, "No, that's not it. I like other things. But what I don't like is to see a human speak to me as such." He pulled me towards him and then thrust me back against the wall, knocking the wind out of me.

That's going to leave a bruise.

"Seriously, that's all you got?" I rasped. *God, I hope this works.*

"Leila, say no more," Isaac warned.

"No," Freckles said through clenched teeth—fangs. "To answer your question, it's not all I've got. But I'm not going to show you, my dear. Lenny, come here."

Freckles got Lenny to place his hands on me where he'd had them.

I smiled wider. It was exactly what I wanted. I had a feeling Freckles was the strongest out of the two, so Lenny would be an easier target.

Jeremiah and Isaac could put up with being hurt a little longer while I was busy. What I didn't expect was Freckles to bypass both guys and walk to their sister. She started whimpering as he used his left hand to run his fingers from her foot all the way up to her hair.

"Now, I will show you what I've got… what I enjoy." He bent and kissed her on the forehead.

Fuck. What did I do?

"I will kill you myself for doing this, Leila," Jeremiah screamed. Isaac hissed at him. Jeremiah continued ranting, only his rage was addressed at Freckles. "Fucking leave Jezanna alone. She's done nothing but what we've asked."

"Hey, Freckles," I called. "Why don't you leave the girl alone? I'll do whatever you want."

"No," Isaac growled low. "You will leave them both alone. You only came here to end my life, so do it."

"So many decisions." He smiled. "I thank you, sweetness, for the offer, but I prefer them younger." Freckles chuckled while he patted Jezanna's hair.

"Sorry, Freckles." I sighed. "But I can't let that happen."

"Boss, I think she's doin' something." Lenny gasped.

All eyes turned to me.

Indeed, I was doing something. I dropped all of the barriers around my mind.

Now, they can sense what I am.

"Impossible. There are none left." Freckles choked.

Well, I guess that answered one question I'd had for many years. I was the last of my kind.

Without hesitation or thought of how much it was going to hurt, especially from doing it so fast, I changed.

Lenny was good enough to hold me upright, as my body spasmed and shook, then my hands and feet turned into paws.

Goddamn it.

Pain engulfed me as my head grew, my features changed, my teeth lengthened and fur popped out of nowhere.

That one still amazed me.

My clothes fell from my body, having been torn and stretched, unable to stay together as my body grew.

Lenny let out a strangled sound once he realised he no longer held a girl, but a large cat.

Before he reacted, I pounced.

My strong jaw reached around his neck and my teeth sank in with ease as I ripped half his neck away. He fell to the floor screaming—well, he would have if it weren't for the missing voice box I spat out next to me on the floor.

Looking up to Freckles, I pushed with all my might from Lenny's convulsing form and jumped onto Isaac's table.

CHAPTER
SIX

I was a little appalled at myself, at the calm easing through me, especially considering I'd taken a chunk out of someone's throat. However, with a mixture of adrenalin and survival instincts, not only for myself, but Isaac and his family, nothing else mattered. I knew if I didn't do anything, we'd all be killed, and I wanted to live. I cared for Isaac and there was no way anyone was taking him away from me. It was not happening.

Mine.

Standing on top of Isaac's table, I swished my tail from side to side while I watched Freckles's shocked face.

The feline part of me thought it was fun and wanted to play more with her prey.

Succumbing to instinct, I climbed across to Jeremiah, causing Freckles to back up away from Jezanna. I pounced again and landed on top of him, sending his body to the ground. I thought vampires were supposed to be strong?

Was he in shock?

My teeth sank into Freckles neck. He screamed. Turning with his flesh in my mouth towards the door, it crashed open to reveal Caelen. My heart lurched with relief. I had sensed something was coming, and knowing he was on our side calmed me a little.

"Caelen, help her," Isaac ordered.

"Help who, lad?" He looked around, confused.

"Leila."

"Bloody hell, mate, don't tell me that huge cat is tiny Leila?"

Dropping the vampire's neck, I stumbled to the side a little. *Shit.* His blood seemed toxic to me, enough to disorientate me.

"Caelen," Isaac yelled.

Something was happening. I knew I didn't have much strength left, and what I was about to do would drain me even more. Still, I had to. I reached my mind out to Caelen's and with a small battle, I squeezed my way in to his to make the connection I needed. *Caelen don't. I'm fine. Untie them.*

"Righto, woman." He stalked over to Isaac first and started on his chains by covering his hands with the clothes that had fallen from my body to prevent the silver from burning and weakening him, as they had the others.

"What the hell are you doing? Help her," Isaac snarled.

"Sorry, mate, she told me to untie you lot first."

Stumbling back to Freckles, I felt him move. Too disorientated to stop him, he raised a knife and plunged it into my ribs. A howl escaped me.

I swiped at his face with my paw. I was growing too weak from his blood and the power I expended to connect with Caelen. I swiped again, but failed. He pushed me away and stood, smiling. Blood still poured from his neck wound, only he seemed to be healing quickly. He went to grab the knife back out when a roar filled the room and a flash crossed my path, knocking Freckles at least three feet away. Blinking rapidly, I saw Isaac rise from his tackle, arms out ready for an attack.

I heard a sickening snap behind me and knew Lenny's life had just ended.

A whimper fell from my mouth. My stomach was ready to revolt.

Isaac's gaze glanced off me before he ordered in a growl, "Jeremiah, Caelen, deal with him and any others they brought."

"Already taken down the ones outside," Caelen said.

Shit, how did I not see them or even sense there were more of them? I wanted to make a telepathic connection with Isaac, but there was no chance of it. My powers were diminishing.

Caelen, is Jezanna okay?

He paused and knelt beside me. I hadn't realised I was lying down.

"She's fine, love." He ran his hand over my head.

There was a noise beside me. With my mind fuzzy, I found it hard to stay awake. *Hey, Caelen, Isaac saved me by jumping Freckles, didn't he?*

"Yes, love." He smiled down at me as the others talked around us, only I couldn't comprehend what was being said.

Hey, Caelen. Isaac's my hero and he's hot.

He let out a bark of laughter.

Darkness swirled before me. *Caelen, I don't feel too good.*

"Isaac, she's about to pass out," Caelen informed.

As I was being lifted from the ground, blackness swept over me.

Sometime later, I woke, still in my cat form. I only noticed when I went to wipe at my face and I got a full view of my paw. It took me a second to remember where I was and what had happened. I tried to move, to get up and find Isaac. All I managed was to lift my head. Weakness consumed me, nausea a close second. Placing my head back down, it landed on something firm, but soft.

"Shh, it's all right. You're all right. I won't hurt you," the person comforted me, patting my fur on the top of my head. She smelled of female. Her voice was a soft melodic tone, and slightly similar to Isaac's. My cushion was Jezanna's legs.

I wanted to ask questions and study the dark room I was in, but I felt too faint.

My black eyes would have helped me see in the dark if I weren't dizzy. Even in my human form, I could see better than most. What made it possible was because of the one eye that stayed black, which was the only visible part of my cat form showing while I was human. When I was a feline, both of my irises turned black, the green bleeding into the white area leaving no white behind.

"Isaac will be in soon. He's just finishing the clean-up with Jeremiah and Caelen." I heard the admirable tone she used when she said Caelen's name. Someone had a crush. "Your knife wound has already closed, but I'm sure you'll still feel a twinge from it. Thank you for coming to us. If... if you hadn't, we would be dead." Her voice broke at the end. I rubbed my head against her legs, reassuring her she was okay. I started to purr and eventually her sobs subsided.

She rubbed her head against mine. "Hush now, we have to be quiet if we want to listen in." I broke off midpurr and listened carefully to the voices that were coming our way.

"Caelen, tell me how Leila managed to be here?" Isaac asked. His voice was loud enough to have been in the next room. They probably thought I was still unconscious. Even if my body wanted to do just that, I refused it.

"As I said before, lad, she came into Boozers to find Hardy. She wanted to ask him for your address. Knew your papa and he are friends, but he wasn't there. So I was kind enough to give her a ride. Not realising just what predicament I was driving her into. Then you sensed I was here and told me to leave. I went to, but the woman kicked me in the gonads and ran off."

"And then what did you do?" Jeremiah barked.

"Ah, come on, mate, you already know. I took off, but my silly conscience made me come back. I hated the thought of leaving her to walk in and be slaughtered. Besides, I knew Isaac would have killed me if I didn't come back."

"Yes, I would have," Isaac said simply, which made me think he was actually stating a fact. "Especially if Leila had been killed. It was bad enough she had a reaction to Mervin's blood."

"He must be one of those few who can turn his blood to poison if attacked," Caelen said.

"Yes, must be," Isaac replied, though he seemed distracted

with other thoughts. "The real question is, why would Leila come here today of all days?"

"I can find out," Jeremiah offered. Somehow, I knew he was smiling with glee when he said that.

A growl sounded, before Isaac ordered, "You'll do nothing of the sort. I know your type of questioning, brother. What I don't understand, when we already know none of us can read her, was how you, Caelen, were able to speak with her while she was in her feline form?"

"It was all her, mate. Even with all my walls, she was still able to penetrate through them and get across what she wanted to say."

"And what was that?" Isaac asked with suspicion in his tone.

Caelen laughed. "Come on, Isaac, don't get jealous on me. I already told you she asked how Jezanna was doing."

Isaac jealous?

No way in hell.

Protective, yes, jealous, no.

"I still don't believe that's all, Caelen."

"Look, it wasn't anything important. Besides, if I told you, she'd kill me herself. She's awake by the way."

"How do you know *that*?" Isaac bit out.

"Wouldn't have the foggiest. My guess would be because of the connection *she* made."

I heard the door to the room open. I pried my tired eyes apart. The glare from the light in the other room made my stomach roll and sent a stabbing pain to my temples. I shielded my eyes with my paw.

"Jeremiah, turn off the light," Isaac ordered sharply.

How wrong did I have it? I thought Jeremiah was the one in charge when it was obvious it was Isaac.

"Jezanna, I didn't realise you were in here," Isaac said with his soft tone.

"I didn't want Leila to be alone when she woke."

"That's very nice of you." He smiled and knelt in front of us.

His eyes moved to me. I stared back. "Leila, how are you feeling?"

My mind reached out to his, only I didn't get far. A sharp pain shot throughout me, causing my body to quiver. It was too much, too soon. My mind wasn't up for anything.

Instead, I extended out to the one connection I already had. That way I wouldn't cause any more harm to myself. *Caelen, tell him I'm okay.*

"You don't seem to be okay, love."

Isaac spun his head to face Caelen, who was standing just inside the doorway beside Jeremiah.

"See there, love. You're gonna get me in trouble here."

I let my laugh echo through his mind. *I doubt that. Tell him I'm not able to make contact with anyone else at the moment. I still feel—*

"She's told me the reason she ain't in your head at the moment is because she still feels like crap. So she can't connect with you when she isn't at her fullest."

Thank you, for that, and for coming back.

"Don't fret, pet, I couldn't leave a honey like you behind," he teased. Isaac hissed.

Why does he do that?

Caelen laughed. "Lad, she wants to know why you do that."

Isaac turned back to face me. He rested his head on his crossed arms, which lay flat on the bed. Then he reached a hand out to run one finger down my nose to the side of my mouth.

"I don't like him speaking to you as he did, that's all."

Both Caelen and Jezanna scoffed, which caused them to smile at one another.

"Leila, can you answer a question for me?"

I gave a small nod, only it left me regretting doing it because the movement sent more dizziness my way.

"Why did you come here today?"

Caelen relayed everything I wanted to say. *You didn't come to get me on the weekend. I thought... When you didn't show up at school, I knew something was wrong. So I found Caelen, and he brought me here.*

"But Caelen warned you there was danger. Why would you still come inside? Why risk your life for us?" Jeremiah demanded.

Nothing changes the fact you all needed help. I knew I was the only one around who could.

Caelen quickly translated.

"You're a very foolish girl. I was unable to catch Mervin. More will come for us, and now he knows about you. You're at risk," Jeremiah snapped.

I may be foolish, but at least I saved your arse.

Caelen chuckled and repeated what I had said. Jeremiah let out a growl and left the room.

Isaac seemed amused, a smile curving his lips, but it faded before he said, "At least I know you're not scared of us... I think."

I would never be scared of you, Isaac. I wanted to say more, but not while I was in my other form. I wanted to talk to him. *Caelen, I'm sorry, but can you carry me to a bathroom? I need to shift back, and it's not something to do in front of people.*

The pain I went through with every change was excruciating, and I didn't want them to witness it. At least I was used to it, but it was hard for someone else to watch. Also, there was the fact I'd be naked. As well as the way I felt, there was a chance I could pass out or vomit. Really, none of it was a pretty sight.

"Of course, love." He glided over to the bed and leaned down to pick me up, until Isaac's hand clamped down on his arm.

"What are you doing?" Isaac growled.

"She wants to go to the bathroom to shift back."

"*I* will carry her." Isaac swiftly stood with me in his arms and took me to the door on the right. He opened it to reveal a huge bathroom. Big enough to have a party in. There was a twin shower, a double spa bath and a twin vanity sink. All of them were sparkling white.

He lay me gently on the tiled floor and sat beside me.

Is he expecting me to change back in front of him? No way is there a chance of that!

Isaac Grey was not seeing me naked.

Well, not under those circumstances.

Shut it, hussy brain.

"Ah, mate. I think she wants to do it alone."

"I won't leave your side, Leila. I saw the pain you went through to change so quickly before, and I know this will hurt you just as much. So I'll be here for you."

"Brother, you can't stay," Jezanna said from the door. "I doubt Leila is worried about the pain. I think she's more worried about you seeing her after she changes."

"Why? Doesn't she want to speak with me?" Isaac looked to Caelen for an answer. But it was Jeremiah who came back and supplied what everyone else knew.

"Isaac, she'll be naked in her human form." Once he stated the fact, he left again.

Isaac faced away, but I could still see the blush running down his neck. "Oh," he whispered.

"Isaac," Jezanna started. "We'll wait in the other room. I'll go and get Leila something to wear, and you can ring Dad to tell him we're all fine."

"Yes. Yes, good idea." He quickly stood and left without looking back. Jezanna closed the door after him, leaving me to shift back on my own. When I welcomed the pain, my body started to alter.

CHAPTER
SEVEN

The transformation left me utterly exhausted. I wasn't used to changing so fast in the first place and then altering back in such a short amount of time.

Curled up in a ball on the tiled floor, I shivered. I wanted to move, to go to the toilet and throw up, hoping it would help me feel better. Then it hit me, the other reason I wasn't coping. The vampire blood. It was still working its way out of my system.

The thought of it, of the foul taste it had left, made me move. I crawled my way to the toilet just in time for it to come up.

There was a knock at the door and Isaac's concerned voice called out, "Leila, are you okay? Sorry, silly of me to ask. I know you're not, but do you need help?"

As nice as it was for him to ask, I couldn't answer. Still, I managed a moan between heaves and prayed he didn't take it as an affirmative for him come in. If he did, it'd embarrass the hell out of me because I was naked *and* bent over a toilet in his house, puking my guts up.

"Move aside, brother," I heard Jezanna say.

The door opened and Jezanna squeezed her way in through a small gap. I didn't mind her coming in; at least she was a girl and thoughtful enough to have brought a large black blanket, which she wrapped around my shaking body.

She knelt beside me and gently rubbed my back as I waited for the dry-heaving to subside. I swore to myself I would never take vampire blood into my mouth again, and I would never shift so quickly. Well, until the next situation arose, and I had a feeling being around Isaac and his family, one could come up at any time.

Finally, the heaving stopped. I flushed the toilet and crouched over it, trying to gain control of my heavy breathing.

"Thank you," Jezanna said.

My laugh was unexpected. "For what?" I asked. "Throwing up in your toilet?"

She giggled. "No, besides, it's not my bathroom. It's Isaac's. That was his bedroom and bed you were on."

I groaned. *Great, just what I needed to think about.*

"I wanted to say thank you for not turning your back on us and running a mile when you found out what we are."

Grabbing some toilet paper, I wiped my face and then sat back, securing the blanket around my still quivering, weak body.

"I knew Isaac was different when he first came to the school. I just didn't know how." I shrugged. "Now I do know, I honestly don't care. I mean look at me, and still, *he* chose me to be his friend. I won't turn my back on him and his family."

She smiled widely. "You like him, don't you?"

"Of course, it's why we're friends."

"No, you know…" Her voice trailed off because of the glare I gave her. I shook my head and inclined it towards the door.

"Oh. Isaac," she called.

We both heard a deep sigh, and two others laughed.

"Yes?" he answered.

"Busted." Caelen chuckled.

Jezanna rolled her eyes and then leaned in to whisper, "We will discuss these things later."

Truthfully, I would've preferred not to speak of it at all. I wasn't used to feeling the way I was about Isaac, or anyone for that matter. It still scared me.

He could leave like the others had.

"I've placed some clothes for you on the basket beside the door for after your shower. I have to apologize though, because I don't think they'll fit you right." She paused to study me. "Do you think you'll be okay on your own, or would you like some help?"

Climbing slowly to my feet, to prove I could manage on my own, I smiled. I felt terrible. My legs shook, my stomach churned, my skin pulled around the healed wound and my head thumped at my temples. I'd never received someone's help in the shower before, and I wasn't about to start.

"All right, if you're not out in half an hour, I'll be coming back in to check on you."

"You might want to give me an hour. I'm going to be taking my time in here, ease some of these pains and aches."

She nodded once, gave me a quick hug and whispered, "You would be good for my brother." Before I could say anything, she left.

Stunned, I just stood there for a while. It was nice of her to say so, but I highly doubted Isaac would ever consider me that way. He saw me as a friend, someone he would protect, nothing else. And I couldn't let myself think any different.

The first thing I did was to check my side for the knife injury. *What the hell?* There wasn't any sign of it. How was that possible? Even after the time my mom hit me in the head, I woke up with a bruise. There should have been a small healing cut at least. But nothing?

Unless, the vampire blood combined with my own could have had some play in my quicker than usual healing? It was definitely a fact to consider.

After some time in the shower, I got out and dried myself, thanking the almighty above the shower had helped relieve some tension. Now, all I had to do was eat something and hope it would help settle my stomach after vomiting the contents of it. I needed to eat regularly; my metabolism burned a lot quicker than any normal human's, mainly because of being part cat. Apparently, they liked to graze all day, something I had inherited.

I looked down at the clothes Jezanna brought in and knew, just with a look, they were going to be a tight fit. Once I dressed, I surveyed myself in the mirror. Snorting out a laugh, I gazed at the words on the closely fit pink tee, 'I love vamps.' Was she trying to be funny? To go with the tee, I had on a tight pair of black pants. Neither of them I would have bought myself. I liked things baggy. Though, there was nothing I could do about it right then, no matter how self-conscious I felt.

Drying my hair one more time, I chucked the towel in the basket beside the door.

Opening the door, I looked out into Isaac's bedroom. The light was on in the empty room. I took some time looking around. Isaac's bed sat under a huge window. And that was really about it for his bedroom. He didn't even have a desk, so there was nothing for me to snoop in, damn it.

I peeked out his bedroom door and heard voices coming from the room across the hallway and down a little. Taking those few steps, I walked into a kitchen and realised, straight away, it was a different kitchen. How many rooms did the place have?

Of course, the conversation stopped once I entered, so I said, "Don't stop on my account." I smiled, tugging at the tee and looking at each of them sitting at the table. Isaac sat at the end of a twelve-seated, wooden table, his own gaze moved over me, smiling slightly at the words written over my boobs. *Shit, can they hear my heart rate pick up from that one small smile?* Wasn't that what the books said about vampires, super hearing, like myself?

Somehow, I'd have to try to control my reactions to Isaac.

To his right was a grumpy-looking Jeremiah. Jezanna was next to him, and Caelen sat opposite them. Another person, who I hadn't met, sat at the other end of the table. He was an older man, possibly in his late fifties, with thick, short grey hair, warm light brown eyes, slim and tall from what I could tell from his sitting form. He came across as a nice, friendly man, from the smile he directed at me. He also didn't flinch when he looked into my eyes for the first time, and for that reason alone, I knew we would get along.

"Hi, I'm Leila." I held out my hand for him to shake. He looked down the table to Isaac and back to me with humour in his eyes.

He took my hand, shook it, then said, "So nice to meet you, Leila. I'm Gregory, Isaac's father." He grinned. "I have a lot to thank you for," he added.

Snorting, I said, "Don't mention it. All in a day's work." I cringed inwardly. Okay, that was lame. Caelen and Jezanna covered their mouths to hide their soft laughter. I quickly took a seat next to Caelen and glanced around the kitchen for any signs of food. It was in that moment my stomach spoke up and Jezanna jumped up from the table, walked over to the fridge and came back with a plate full of sandwiches. I couldn't help but lick my lips, which caused another round of laughter.

"I thought you might be hungry." Jezanna smiled.

"Starving. Gimme, gimme." I dragged the plate to right in front of me. "Sorry, guys, but I have to eat before I start dry-heaving again. And believe me, it's not a pretty sight." I moaned on the first bite. "It's all got to do with the cat side…" I glanced at Gregory. What did he know? "Ah… cat side of the hill. I get delirious when I'm hungry. Don't mind me." I waved my hand in the air for them to continue talking and quickly shoved more sandwiches in my blabbering mouth.

"It's all right, Leila. Our father knows everything." Isaac smiled.

Looking to Isaac, who had also showered, I couldn't help but admire him. His black hair was still wet and shining. His white shirt opened at the top, so I could see his throat and part of his chest. It was enough to get my heart to take off once again. Dear God, a pulse *below* had me clenching my thighs together.

Where were these hussy hormones coming from?

Quickly looking away with a blush heating my cheeks, I noticed Isaac wasn't the only one to shower and change clothes, understandably so. Jezanna now wore jeans and a T-shirt that read, 'No. U. Suck.' Jeremiah was in dark jeans and a tight black T-shirt, showing his bulging muscles. Caelen, though, was the only one still in the clothes he had on originally. Somehow he'd managed to not get a spot of blood on him anywhere.

Taking a gulp of the water Jezanna had just sat on the table, I dragged my reluctant gaze from Isaac—stupid eyes kept on seeking him out, no matter what my mind said—to turn back to Gregory.

"Does that mean you're a vamp too?" I asked.

"No, I'm human."

"Huh? How? That can't be, right?"

They all laughed again.

"It's true," Isaac confirmed and then frowned. "Our real parents were murdered. Gregory and Kimberly took us in. They already knew our parents and knew what we were. It's easier for us within the human race to have parent figures. If we lived on our own, we would have caused too much attention. We've been with them for two decades now."

Clearing my throat, I licked my lips and asked, "If you don't mind my asking, um, what happened, to Kimberly?"

"We didn't suck her dry, if that's what you think." Jeremiah glared.

Isaac's fist pounded down onto the table. His eyes shot daggers to his brother.

Rolling my eyes, I shrugged. "It could have been possible from you, J Man, but not Isaac or Jezanna." I scowled back. He stood abruptly, causing his chair to crash to the floor. I rose quickly to be ready for anything.

He leaned over the table towards me. "Watch what you say, girl."

"Jeremiah," Isaac snarled in warning.

"Calm the frig down and I won't be forced to pull your

chain. What is your problem, dude? I haven't come here to piss on your territory. Why so grouchy towards me?"

"Jeremiah, sit down," Gregory demanded. It took him a few beats before he obliged his father.

Gregory sighed. "I'm sorry, Leila. Jeremiah is still a little upset the other men were able to trick them and hold them captive. As well as you coming along to save them."

"Yeah?" I scoffed. "How can a mere girl be able to do that? Don't fret, macho man. From this day forward, I'll leave all the saving to you."

"Anyway," Gregory intervened, "Jeremiah will calm down, because it will never happen again. We've sent for more of our people."

Gregory looked away from his son and down at the table blankly. It was obvious that memories of his past had taken over.

He shook his head slightly and looked back up to me. "Kimberly, my dear wife, passed away only a few years ago of cancer. We tried to adapt after losing her, but some other matters were occurring, so we found it better if we just moved on."

"Gregory, I think we should tell Leila the truth from the start," Isaac calmly said. He turned his gaze to me. "Our mother did indeed have cancer, although that wasn't how she passed. She was murdered, and before one of us became the next victim, we left the city. We travelled a while before coming here."

My eyes widened. That was only two years ago. Why would anyone want to murder their adoptive mum who was also a human?

"Why are they after you?" I stopped eating and pushed the plate away. The nausea rose again and I was afraid if I took another bite, I'd spew all over the table.

I thought Isaac would have been the one to answer, but it was Jezanna. "We were born in Russia a very long time ago. However, our parents were from the United States. Everything was wonderful in our home in Russia, until we were told of a seer who foretold a prophecy to the vampire King, Gerald

Holms. He was the one we all looked up to, who ruled our kind, and he's also the oldest master vampire known.

"He was such a nice man." She huffed and rolled her eyes. "Until, twenty-one years ago, when he was told by the seer there will come one who will be chosen to lead all vampires. One who will have our people's love and devotion, and who will be followed by other species as well." She sighed. "That person would be the one born with the birthmark of a dagger." She scoffed. "It sounds very corny, I know. As if it comes from an old movie." Shaking her head, she continued with, "God, I wish it had been the case. Once finding this out, Gerald changed. He showed his true self, what he was like behind closed doors. We'd heard stories, but no one believed them. We did, after we witnessed it ourselves."

The memory brought tears to her eyes. I was about to tell her we could talk about it another time, or not at all, when she took a deep breath and went on, "We were invited to come to his palace for a celebration. At the time, we were unaware of what he'd been told, so we went. We were very excited. Once arriving, a guard told our parents Gerald wished to speak with them privately. They went while we walked into the grand ball-room, and talked and laughed with others. We didn't know Gerald was questioning our parents about their child who has the same birthmark as the one foretold.

"We've heard our parents didn't believe Gerald's tale. They warned him not to believe it either, saying their child would never want to rule his people. He didn't believe them. Instead… he slayed them on the spot. A woman who overheard everything told Gregory, knowing he would help us escape. Gregory kept us hidden in the woods for over sixteen years, but they found us, and killed our other mother. That was when we fled and have been travelling since."

Waving my hands in front of me, I said, "Whoa. I… I'm so sorry for everything you've all been through." Hell, it was so much, too much even. Running my hands down my thighs, I asked, "Who, um, who's the one with the birthmark?"

Jeremiah banged his fist on the table. "Is that all you can ask? Don't you get it? You should be scared. You should be running away from us. More will come. I'd be surprised if Gerald doesn't come himself, since he'll soon find out where we are and *who* we are with."

I knew he meant me.

Closing my eyes, I breathed deeply. I didn't want to yell and scream at him because it would get me nowhere, and I needed him to understand.

Upon opening my eyes, I looked to Isaac's grumpy brother and said, "Jeremiah, maybe I should be scared and run, but I won't because this *is* my home, my town, even though I have no one here. Starting over somewhere new isn't an option for me." I shrugged. "I guess, when Isaac and I became friends, it was the worst day of *your* life because now you guys are stuck with me. I don't care what happens. I don't care who comes. I will be here for you all, whether you like it or not."

Sitting back, I waited for Jeremiah to curse at me, to yell. What I didn't expect was Jezanna to start sobbing and Jeremiah to lean over the table, grab me from my seat and pull me into a fierce hug.

He whispered, "You are one crazy girl. You're made perfectly for Isaac. I just hope it doesn't get you killed."

Blowing my mind and confusing me with his cryptic shit, Jeremiah then stood with concern showing in his eyes before he turned and left the room.

I swung my stunned gaze to Isaac, who was also just as surprised. "Please don't tell me he's the one to rule. Because I don't think the world could take it."

Gregory and Caelen laughed. Isaac offered me a small, sad smile, shook his head and started to unbutton his shirt. I *was* hoping it was because he was about to give me a striptease.

However, I knew better. Especially when I spotted a birthmark on his left rib, in the shape of a dagger. One I hadn't noticed earlier when he was on the table being gutted, or even the first time in my bedroom. Then again, maybe I had, but didn't think anything of it.

"That's a lot to deal with," I muttered.

He scoffed. "Tell me about it."

"If it's all true, then why don't you just go and kick this Gerald's arse to get him off your back?"

Sighing, Isaac said, "For one, I do not wish to be the new King, and second, it's near impossible to get close to him. I've had people try, and they've lost their lives for it. I don't want to risk more of my people."

"Well… crap."

"Love, you have the most wonderful vocabulary."

Glaring at Caelen, I snapped, "Get used to it, buddy." Only to then grin and add, "Gregory, I'm sorry if I offend you with my language."

He smiled warmly at me. "Don't apologize, Leila. You're a touch of fresh air in such a stale house."

A blush rose to my cheeks, and suddenly I found myself feeling uncomfortable, unused to compliments.

Hell, I wasn't used to being around people.

"Thanks," I mumbled. "Anyway, I had better head off."

"Leila," Isaac started before I had the chance to move. "If you don't mind, I'd like to ask you some quick questions?"

"Sure." I yawned, my hand covering my mouth.

"Does your uncle know what you are?"

Biting my bottom lip, I confessed, "No. I've never told him."

Isaac seemed surprised by my answer; actually, all of them did.

"What type of feline are you, love, and are you a shifter?" Caelen asked and then sank lower in his seat when Isaac glared at him. "What? It ain't like you aren't curious."

Laughing, I said, "To be honest, I'm not sure. I've never met anyone to clarify it for me or met another supernatural." I shrugged. "I guess you could say I'm as big as a cougar, yet my fur is dark brown to black. Your guess is as good as mine." I had wondered about those questions since the day I could shift. My eyes caught Isaac's. He looked away quickly, which normally would mean someone knew something about the situation. Did that mean he knew what I was? I wasn't sure if I was reading him wrong.

"I didn't even know you were different. You all smell like humans to me."

"Most, if not all, supernaturals have the power to block their paranormal aura. It is hard to tell who is what because of it. Do your parents know?" Isaac asked.

I flinched. "I—ah, I need to get home. I'm too tired to answer more questions. However, be ready tomorrow. I'll be at my fullest and ready for more." I smiled and rose from the table.

Questions about my parents were never easy for me. Just the thought of them sent my mind and body into turmoil.

Not only from the fact they left, but also because I hadn't had a message from my dad in over a month, and I couldn't help but worry. In the very last message Dad had sounded fearful. From what or who, neither my uncle nor I knew.

"You can't leave," Isaac said with a hard tone as he stood.

"What do you mean I can't leave?"

"You live in a house alone, Leila, *besides* an absent uncle. It's too dangerous, especially after what happened tonight."

Damn it, he was annoyed enough to do the buttons up on his shirt. I was hoping to ogle a little longer. Who wouldn't want to admire perfection?

"I can handle whatever comes my way. It's not like anything would happen tonight. We've got a couple of days at least, right?"

"She's right, Isaac. Furthermore, you've sent Hamish and Seraphine after him. They might catch him before he contacts

Gerald," Gregory said. I could tell he was always a man of reason.

"Who's Hamish and Seraphine? And when did you get time to tell them to run after Freckles?" I asked.

"They're members of my personal guard. I had given them the weekend off. They'd left town, only came back once they sensed my distress. They would have been here sooner if they hadn't travelled so far." *Say what now? They could feel Isaac? Sense him?* "I found over the passing years I haven't needed their protection as much. Now, I'm mistaken. Another reason I have sent word out for my remaining loyal friends and guards to join us here."

Holy hell, Isaac has guards. He's like a royal.

"What do you mean they could sense your distress?"

He cleared his throat and said, "Those who wish to join my guard rankings have…" he trailed off, lost for words.

"It's kinda like you did with me, love. They share a mind link. If it's too far for thoughts to carry through, they can still sense what each other is feeling."

I was going to have an information overload soon.

"There you go." I yawned, only that time was fake because a sudden stab of jealousy penetrated my gut. I didn't like Isaac having any type of *close* connection like that to his people, which I found weird for even feeling and thinking it. "So, I'll be going now. Nice to meet you, Gregory. I'm sure you'll be seeing a lot of me from this day forward."

Gregory didn't get a chance to reply because Isaac piped in with, "I don't like this, Leila—"

"Noted, Isaac." I smiled at him and blew a kiss. He raised his eyebrows at me. "Caelen, be a pal and give me a lift."

"*I* will take you," Isaac growled.

"Thanks, but it'll be fine. Caelen was about to leave anyway."

"Righto, love. 'Nite all." Caelen waved.

Before anyone said anything else, I quickly made my exit.

Isaac called Caelen back for something, but I didn't wait around for him as I walked outside to his car. After a minute, Caelen strolled out smiling. He unlocked his car and climbed in as I did. We drove home in silence. I didn't know what he was thinking, and I doubted it was the same as me because all I could think of was Isaac.

I didn't realise I'd drifted off until the engine being turned off woke me. I looked out to see my unlit house waiting for me in the dark.

"Thanks, uh, for the lift and everything. I guess I'll see you around."

"Hmmm."

I got out and walked to the front door. Only to turn when I felt a presence at my back and found Caelen standing there grinning. "What do you think you're doing?"

He coughed to clear his throat. "Quote: *'Caelen, you are to stay at Leila's tonight. I have other matters to attend to, and if you lay one finger on her, expect to die painfully slow.'* Unquote. Looks like you're stuck with me, love, unless you want me to die of course."

There was no use yelling at him. It wasn't his fault Isaac had taken it upon himself to protect me like some sibling.

Even though I thought I proved I could handle drastic matters. *Damn him.* Who did he think he was ordering people around? And he said he didn't want to rule. I scoffed internally. If he thought he had some ruling over me, then he could think again.

"Speak up, love. I can't understand your grumbling."

God, I didn't realise I was muttering aloud. "Nothing, it's nothing. You can sleep here," I said and opened the other spare bedroom door, only to then laugh when a thought hit me. "You don't sleep, do you?" I asked.

"No. Not at night anyway, and only a few hours during the day. It's all right. There are a few shows on that'll keep me occupied. You get some rest, love. You look beat."

He turned and walked back toward the lounge room.

"Caelen," I called. He stopped and faced me again. "Do you mind Isaac telling you what to do?"

He studied me for a while and then shrugged. "No. There's a lot out there who've been treated badly by Gerald. Then again, not only him. Unfortunately, there's a great amount of evil among our kind. So a lot of us are hoping Isaac will be *our* saving grace. We believe in him, even if he doesn't believe in himself."

"How old are you?" I whispered.

"I'm only 160. Still young and handsome."

Forcing myself to laugh, I walked off to hide in my room. My mind felt full, stuffed to the brim with information, yet I found myself wanting to know more.

Was Isaac older than Caelen? I had a feeling he was.

So how old was he?

If he was older, then what sort of a past had he had?

An experienced one at that.

Oh, God. I'd fallen for an old man.

CHAPTER EIGHT

Voices woke me from my sleep instead of my usual dream. I assumed it was the television again coming from the lounge room. Rolling over, I looked at the clock. Six in the Goddamn morning. I groaned. No wonder I felt cranky. It had taken me forever to get to sleep the night before. As well as the fact I'd yelled at Caelen twice to turn down the TV.

Reluctantly, I climbed out of bed. I still had at least another hour and a half left of sleep before I decided if I was going to class. The way things were going, I was prepared to chuck a sick day and stay in bed, then later, meet Isaac for some questioning.

I stomped down the hallway, knowing Caelen heard me coming, because the TV quickly turned down.

"Caelen, what the...?" I rounded the corner to the living room before stopping dead.

Shit a brick. It was full of people.

Isaac—looking scrumptious, in black jeans and a tight black long-sleeved top—Jeremiah, Jezanna and two other guys I didn't know, who seemed to be getting over the shock of seeing my eyes.

"Told you that would get her up, mate," Caelen said cheerfully. I scolded him, and then looked down at myself. Death would soon be on my hands. How dare he make me come out here in what I wore to bed, a slinky cami top and boxer shorts. By the look of it, I wasn't the only one ready to commit murder. Isaac practically ran over to me, while pulling the blanket off the back of the couch along the way, to wrap it around me.

He would do the same for Jezanna. Right? Yeah, he would.

Glancing around at the others, Isaac tried to shuffle me out of the room. They all seemed very amused by his actions.

"Whoa, hold up. What in the hell is going on here?" I grouched, stopping Isaac in the process of nearly dragging me down the hall to my room.

"I like her already," one of the new men said, the one who was the tallest and built like a body builder. He had a shaved head, green eyes and was dressed like an assassin, all in leather. The other was also tall, but slim, with long blond hair and pale blue eyes. I spotted his sword strapped to his back. He also had on a long leather jacket, but opted for dark blue jeans and a red Mambo T-shirt. Both of them were very good-looking men seeming to be around the age of twenty. And both were vampires.

"I agree. This is going to be fun." The long-haired one chuckled and then smiled at me. I couldn't help but smile back.

"Enough," Isaac bit out. "Leila, if you would go and get changed, then I will formally introduce you to these two." He winced upon seeing the look on my face.

"Are you seriously telling me what to do? If I wanted to parade around my house naked, you'd have no say in it."

"Please do." Caelen laughed, receiving a glare from Jezanna, Isaac and myself.

I sighed. "All I'm saying is that just because we're friends doesn't mean you have the right to boss me around." Looking around the room, I added, "And that goes for the rest of you."

"Oh, I do like this one, Master," Baldy said.

Master?

Seriously?

Were we on some type of sitcom for old vampire shows?

"Leila, please."

"Isaac, I'm sorry, okay. I'm just overtired and overreacting. I was unprepared for a houseful this early. It's all Caelen's fault. He kept me up all night."

Caelen gasped. "Are you trying to get me killed, love? I had the telly on too loud and that's all, lad."

"Look, I'll go and get changed. Then I hope we can start over. Let's pretend you haven't met me yet. Jeremiah, do not say anything to that." I glared, turned and walked down the hall into my room, closing the door behind me. Only to open it back up when an attentive knock came. Thankfully, it was only Jezanna.

"He doesn't mean to be like that, Leila. He can't help it sometimes. Not only because he's possessive of you, but even though he wants nothing to do with ruling, it's still in him. He has all the potential to do it. We all know this, even Isaac. Our people would be better off if he were on the throne." She grimaced. "He can't handle others wanting to swear their allegiance to him. It scares him that they see more in him than what he does himself. What also scares him more than anything else is losing more loved ones."

Sitting down on my bed, I said, "I understand that, I really do." Especially after losing so many from my own life. "But Isaac is the bigger picture for his people. He can't keep worrying about me when he has so much to deal with himself. What he really needs is to make a choice on what he's going to do, because by the looks of it, everyone else sees him as their king. All but him."

"One day, he will, and all we can do is help him through it. So, for now, please just put up with what he wants."

Rolling my eyes, I snorted before saying, "I'll try, but it's not in my nature to be bossed around. He wants those new guys to guard me, doesn't he?" Jezanna nodded. "But can't he understand I can take care of myself?"

"I'm sure he does, but since the day you two met, things changed. Not only for him, but for you as well. You now have to deal with his overbearing ways. Let's say, it's one of his quirks." She smiled.

"I'll bite my tongue for now. That's all I can promise. I've been alone for so long, Jezanna. So sometimes I don't know how to act around people and I can become a little tense."

"Really? I would never have guessed." She smirked. "Now hurry up and get dressed before he sends someone down here to make sure all is right."

I threw my pillow at her as she left. Why, oh why, was it that once I did find a friend, I had to find the one who wanted to run my life?

As I said, I would play along with it for now. However, some fun along the way was called for. I couldn't help but grin as a thought popped into my head. I walked over to my closet and moved aside all the dark, baggy clothes I had in the front to find the ones I thought I would never wear at the back. I picked out the shortest shorts I'd ever purchased. A tight, black leather pair. God only knew what was going through my mind when I bought them. To go along with them, I grabbed a red, form-fitting, low V-neck T-shirt.

Was I mean by doing what I was about to do? Yes, maybe, then again, it could help Isaac to see me as the girl I was, instead of the sisterly figure he had in his mind. With that thought, it made it all so much easier to do.

Leaving my hair down, I even applied a little eyeliner and red lipstick. To top it all off, I slipped on my knee-high, black, leather boots.

Making sure I had the smile wiped off my face, I stepped out into the living room and received the effect I thought I would. The conversation stopped. Jezanna hid her gasp with her hand. She shook her head at me. Still, I caught the lift of her lips as she tried not to smile.

Unfortunately, Isaac wasn't in the room. I could hear a conversation coming from the kitchen and guessed he was in there with Jeremiah.

Baldy cleared his throat. "Uh, Master," he called.

Moving over to the couch, I leaned my hip against it and

waited. Jeremiah walked in first and paused, his eyes nearly bulging out of his head.

"What the hell are you playing at?" he snarled.

His harsh words had me rethinking.

What was I playing at? Nothing really, I was being immature. All I really wanted out of it was for Isaac to find me attractive, and not treat me like a sister. However, I knew I shouldn't want that. I should be happy with what we had now. I was being selfish with wanting more. Regardless, I did want more. Why else would the stupid plan form in my head in the first place?

Jezanna must have seen the change in me. She took matters into her own hands and whispered something to the long-haired vampire. He nodded and walked over to Jeremiah. Jeremiah followed him back into the kitchen just as Isaac was about to walk out.

"Master, I have a question."

"In a moment, Xavier. Adan called for me."

Adan, aka Baldy, quickly moved over to the doorway, blocking the view. I took my chance and ran for my bedroom.

"It was nothing, Master. Sorry for calling to you."

Slamming my door, I quickly locked it. I didn't want anyone coming in here to see the stupid, foolish tears that broke through my willpower. I didn't have time to waste on crying. In a rush, I got out of the outfit and threw it against my wall. It slid down, disappearing somewhere on the other side of my bed. I grabbed out the first thing I touched and, with frustrated moves, I was dressed in black tracksuit pants and a dark green hooded jumper. Rushing over to my desk, I sat down and looked into the mirror. A sad, pathetic girl stared back. I splashed some liquid from a bottle I had sitting there onto some tissues and wiped all traces of makeup away.

On finishing and before I could steep lower into a pity party, I got up and unlocked my door, opening it. I was all prepared to stomp down into the living room. Instead, I found Jeremiah leaning on the wall opposite my door.

Guilt had me looking to the ground as I said, "I'm not in the mood, Jeremiah. I already know I am a complete idiot. I don't need anyone reminding me. Can we just leave it? Later, you can grill me all you want." I went to walk off, but he reached out and grabbed my arm, turning me back towards him. I sighed loudly and looked up to his solemn face.

"I don't know what's going on in that thick head of yours, but right now, before you do anything else stupid,"—I flinched at his words—"you have to know Isaac wouldn't do any of this for Jezanna. The main thing being that Jezza already lives with us. If he saw you as a sister, you would already be living with us without any argument. He understands and respects that you want your independence. He likes that in you, and he likes you just the way you are. Please, for the sake of others, do not push him to murder. If he saw you dressed the way you were, and if the guys were looking at you the way they were,"—he shook his head—"I'd be dealing with three dead bodies out there. Now me, *I* see you as a sister, and God help me, but I think it would be best if you moved in with us."

Glancing away, I quickly wiped the tears that had fallen. Jeremiah was the last person I would've expected to be sincere and caring. I looked back up at him and smiled. "Not a chance, J Man."

He smirked. "That's what I thought you would say. It's going to be hell having you around, but right now, I wouldn't have it any other way."

"Why, J,"—I clutched my chest—"I didn't know you had a heart. Did the Wizard of Oz come and see you last night?"

He let out a bark of laughter and ruffled my hair. "There's the smart-arse girl I know. Come on, before he thinks I'm killing you." He gently pushed me forward.

With blossoming emotions, I walked down the hall, flying high.

Never had I felt so happy, and it all happened in such a short amount of time. One minute, I was on my own, and the next, I had a friend that led me to more friends, and a true family that I wanted to be a part of.

It didn't surprise me that Isaac had turned my heart into something warm and fuzzy. No longer was it the cold stone that had been living inside of my chest.

Isaac really cared about me. He liked me for who I was already. As strange as that was, I loved it… him.

When you sink, you sink hard. And I had. Even if it scared the life out of me, I wasn't going to give any of it up for anything.

My smile broadened when I thought of what Uncle Jack would think if he came home. He would never believe I had a house full of vampires. Even if I didn't tell him what they were, he would still freak, because he'd warned me away from them. However, I could only hope if he saw how happy I was, then he'd be happy for me. Moreover, I hoped he'd want to be a part of this new family also.

CHAPTER NINE

As soon as I entered, I sat on the couch beside Isaac. His gaze roamed over me before he gave me a smile, which told me he approved of my attire. *Huh, go figure.* I turned my attention to the two newbies standing in front of the television. Jeremiah joined them. Jezanna and Caelen sat on the floor by the wall. I hoped the look on my face expressed what I wanted it to—an apology for my crazy behaviour.

"So," I drew out. "What's up? And why here so early?"

"Yes, sorry for the intrusion," Isaac offered. "I wanted you to meet some of my people before we went to school."

"Not sure I'm going today, but I'd be happy to meet your guys."

He looked at me cautiously. "All right." He waved his hand in the bald guy's direction. "This is Adan Kenna, and that is Xavier Trengrove. They have come here today to help, ah, me, what I'm saying is I would like for them to be your..."

Placing my hand on his arm, I smiled at him reassuringly. Him being tongue-tied told me he was worried about how I would react with the information of having guards.

Throwing Isaac a bone, I answered for him, "They're here to help keep me safe. It's all right, Isaac, I get it."

He looked at me as if I'd grown an extra boob.

He raised a brow. "Aren't you going to rant and rave at me?"

"Not today." I smiled.

He sighed and said, "Thank the gods for small favours." His smile went wide after I pushed him.

Waving to Adan and Xavier, I said, "So nice to meet you both and I apologize in advance for all I do. What can I say? Some people get me and some don't. We'll just have to see what category you guys fall under."

"We look forward to getting to know you." Xavier grinned.

Catching Isaac's gaze, I asked, "How did you guys meet?"

Only he didn't answer, Jezanna did with, "They're some of Isaac's people. They came, like many who follow my brother, to us under different circumstances. All would be willing to sacrifice themselves to keep him safe."

My eyes flicked to Isaac to see he wasn't too happy about it. I couldn't say I blamed him. It was strange how people were willing to throw their lives down for Isaac.

However, having not lived as they had, I was sure there were still things I didn't understand.

Then again, Isaac would be easy to follow. He had no intention of killing in cold blood to get what he wanted, like Gerald did. People saw Isaac for who he was. Caring, honourable and courageous.

"Right now, we seem to have a fairly easy job." Adan smiled.

Laughter fell from my lips. Jeremiah mimicked my laughter and then stated, "I give you three days tops. By then, you will want to shoot yourselves to get away from her."

"Hey," I snapped, pretending to be offended. "Anyway, now that I have you all here. I have some questions if you don't mind."

Isaac nodded. "Ask away."

"I'm assuming not all myths about vampires are true. Like not being able to eat real food, being affected by sunlight, sleeping through the whole day and being dead, because I've heard some heartbeats."

He gave me that half smile, sending my heart on high alert.

Calm thoughts, Leila. Super-hearing vampires are about.

"That's correct. We can eat, but it's not necessary. It's more of a show we put on in front of humans. We can sleep and do.

Though, we only need a few hours at the most. We're able to go out in the sun. However, in doing so, we need to consume more blood, and yes, we have a heartbeat *and* a soul. We're very much alive."

"What about, um, feeding?"

"We feed off humans, love. There're places to go where humans are willing to feed us. They even enjoy the act. But if it were in an emergency situation, we'd have to feed from who was around. In the end though, they won't remember what happened. All vampires are able to wipe the minds of humans."

Nothing else crossed my mind, except who Isaac fed from. Just thinking of it sent my stomach in a downward spiral. Whoever it was, I wanted to find them and claw their eyes out. I wanted to… Wait.

"Those girls." I gasped. "The ones I saw at Boozers…"

Caelen started laughing.

Turning to Isaac, I glared. "You feed off them?" I was a little appalled and a bit disgusted.

And *very* jealous.

"What girls?" Isaac asked.

Caelen coughed into his fist. "Heather, Chloe."

"Oh," Isaac replied.

Oh. OH. That's all he can say?

He rubbed the back of his neck. "They're happy to keep us nourished. It's hard to find trustworthy suppliers."

"Yeah, I just bet they're happy to give you something."

He raised an eyebrow. "How else am I to feed, Leila?"

"I-um. You…" I stammered and blushed. I was at a loss. I couldn't come up with anyone, other than me.

Jesus. It was time to change the subject. "How old are you all?"

Isaac's lips twitched. He knew what I was doing. Thankfully, he played along and asked, "Are you sure you wish to know?"

Not really. Nevertheless, it was better than the conversation before. "Yes." I nodded.

"Jeremiah is the oldest. He's 405. I'm 398, and Jezanna is only 101. Adan and Xavier are around that same age as Jezza and Caelen—"

"She already knows, lad."

"Very well." Isaac glared at Caelen before turning back to me. "Does it change what you think of us, Leila?"

Studying him, I pondered how someone so old could be so good-looking. It was scary really, but then it had me thinking. How long would I live for with the feline blood running through my veins? Would I have enough time to have lived a happy, loving life with Is— someone?

It was something no one knew.

Each day as you go. Dad used to say that.

"What's the matter, Leila? Something has you worried."

"Other than your feeding." Caelen laughed. We both shot him daggers.

"Nothing. It's nothing. And no, it doesn't change what I think about you all. I doubt anything could scare me away from you. I, ah, all of you."

Quick, I need to change the subject again. Hide the blush.

"So, do Adan and Xavier know everything about me?"

"I hope you don't mind, but I've informed them, because they need to be prepared for everything." He smiled.

"As long as they keep it to themselves." Tilting my head to the side, I asked them, "Can you do that, guys?" They both nodded. It wasn't that I trusted them, because I didn't. However, I trusted Isaac and his choices. He wouldn't bring people into my home if he wasn't sure of them in the first place.

Shrugging, I said, "I guess I have no more questions for now. And since I'm not going to school today, who's up for a run?" I gave them all a sly look. Then without waiting for an answer and before Isaac could question why I didn't want to go to school, I bolted for my bedroom, stripped and changed forms.

Really, the main reason school didn't appeal to me that day was because I wasn't willing for another day of questioning from our peers. What I needed was a nice, peaceful day, and school was not peaceful.

Stalking back out into the living room in my feline form, I swished my tail from side to side. I couldn't have been prouder to finally share my secret with people I cared about. People who wouldn't judge, and accepted me as I was.

Pouncing onto the couch, I watched as Caelen and Jezanna stood smiling at me.

"Leila." I looked to Isaac standing next to me. He reached out and placed his hand under my chin to bring my face up to meet his. "Even though you will be slacking today, I have to go to classes. I'll let them know you're sick, but will be back tomorrow. I'm also going to meet with another friend of mine, who will be starting at our school today. So, for now, I'll say goodbye." He bumped his forehead against mine and smiled. He waved a goodbye to everyone else and left with Adan following.

It was good to see Isaac wasn't being silly and was taking a guard with him. He also needed someone to protect him. If anyone were to attack him, it would hurt many.

"Well, love, are we running or what? I'm feeling a little peckish. I could show you how to truly hunt your prey."

My walls crashed down and I reached out with my powers. From the slight body shudder from everyone in the room, I could tell they felt the presence of my mind's strength in the room—connecting to the link I had with Caelen. *You had better watch yourself, pretty boy, or* you *will be my prey.*

He laughed and bolted for the back door. I leapt off the couch after him. He had the back door opened and ran with full vampire speed straight out into the woods, which adjoined onto my back yard. He was fast; I would give him that, and so were Jeremiah, Jezanna and Xavier. All of them only inches off my tail.

Couldn't let them have that though. I smiled to myself. Turning my head, I gave them a full-teeth grin and jumped into the air, my body ready for the impact of the tree I was heading for. I didn't stop once I touched it. I pushed from one tree to another, gaining speed and momentum.

I watched the others reach Caelen before I bounded out of the tree from above them. They all, even Jezanna, which I was proud of, readied themselves in a fighting stance, until they realised it was me.

Wanting more because I was ready to play—I always was in this form—I raced around them. Without their knowledge, I easily managed herding them into a circle.

Stopping, I sat back and watched them watch me.

"Whatever it is you're thinking, Leila. Do not do it," Jeremiah warned.

Yeah, right. I jumped anyway, landing on him, which sent him and the others falling to the ground.

"Ooph, get off, you fat cat." Jeremiah pushed at me. I placed all my weight to hold him down. As the others climbed to their feet, I stayed firmly on Jeremiah. Finally, he stopped squirming and looked up at me, smiling.

"You do know I can get you off, but I'm not willing to hurt you in the process."

Digging deep within myself, I found that part which made me able to reach out to another's mind. I absorbed it in and pushed it out to Jeremiah. His mind had a strong barrier. However, I didn't know how or why, but I was able to get through anyone's shields and, from the shocked look within his eyes, he'd just found it out.

Just try it, He-Man. I sent my laughter into his mind. I knew what was coming, but before he could retaliate, I opened my mouth and touched my big, wet, rough tongue to the side of his face, licking from his jaw to his forehead. Everyone started laughing.

"You disgusting little runt. I will get you for that."

Bouncing off him, I made a dash for the thicker woods.

The rest of the afternoon was spent with all three of them trying to catch me. I had to admit, sometimes they would outsmart me and were able to tackle me to the ground. However, I wriggled my way out and the chase began again. At least I was able to say I got the best of the three vampires by managing to pounce on them all and giving them the biggest, wettest willies they had ever had.

By the time we made it home, it was already six and the sun was setting in the horizon. We arrived at the house sated and satisfied. While we were out, we were able to hunt our own breakfast and lunch. It was strange to watch the others drink the blood from the animals, yet it was still intriguing. I'm sure they were just as interested in seeing me hunt, kill and eat my prey.

What amazed me was how well they hunted. It was as though they were animals. They hid, stalked and pounced on the incognisant deer, rabbit or elk. And even though they were still zoned in on what they were doing, I could tell a part of them never stopped searching the surrounding area for danger or uninvited guests.

We were so much alike and yet so different. Their bodies didn't change like mine, but it was almost like they had feline tendencies in them.

Jeremiah opened the back door and a new scent hit me. The hairs on the back of my neck raised and I crouched down on my front paws, releasing a warning hiss.

Beside me, Jezanna patted my head, bringing my attention up to her. "It's all right. It's only our father cooking."

Walking in slowly, still on the defensive, I looked around. How could they have known it was him straight away? The only smell, which was overpowering everything else, was garlic. Nevertheless, there he stood at a stove that hadn't been used for at least two years. He turned as Xavier shut the door.

"Good evening, all. I hope you're hungry. I've made lasagne, salad and garlic bread," he explained to everyone, only his eyes stayed on me. I understood the curiosity. Not many people had the chance to see a cat the size of a cougar walking around the house.

To let Gregory know I appreciated the effort he'd made, I walked over and rubbed my head, and therefore my scent, against his leg. His instinct, which was the same as everyone's would be, was to pat me on the head.

"You're welcome, Leila. You had better go and change, slowly this time. I'm sure we can wait for you. Besides, Isaac is not here yet with his friend."

Butterflies took flight in the bottom of my stomach from hearing Isaac's name, and the fact he would be there soon.

Bobbing my head, I moved off to my room to transform back and shower. Hopefully, I'd be ready for more food by then.

CHAPTER TEN

Tying my hair back with an elastic band, I walked down the hall then out into the kitchen, feeling refreshed and relaxed. I'd dressed in a pair of black leggings and a long black T-shirt. With the house already warm from the heater being on and the oven being used, there was no need for something warmer. It was strange to have my house cosy and smelling, well, lived in.

Upon entering, I found my usual empty kitchen table filled with people. Seeing it brought tears to my eyes. I quickly turned back around and stepped into the living room to wipe away the few drops I allowed to fall.

Stupid, uncontrollable, silly emotions. I stomped back into the kitchen.

"About damn time," a deep voice muttered. It belonged to the guy who sat next to Isaac. My obsession sat at the end of the table. The only seat left was on the other side of him, so I sat there. I returned my gaze onto the person who was rude enough to say something, and I was pleased to see a shudder run over him upon meeting my unique eyes.

Gone were the days I felt ashamed to have caused such a reaction from a person. Instead, I met his stare with confidence.

"Darik, manners," Isaac scolded. Darik rolled his eyes and shrugged.

I didn't know the connection or relationship he had with Isaac, apart from the obvious; Darik was also a vampire. His suffocating power showed me that. *Stupid dickhead wants to intimidate me by thrusting his power out, instead of hiding it like the others have.* On the other hand, was he unable to keep it under control like Isaac and the others did? Premature vamp power, no control on what he thrust out?

Snorting to myself, I shook my head so I wouldn't burst out laughing.

"Evening, Leila. I've heard you had an eventful day. I'm sorry I missed it."

As I looked to Isaac, my breath caught from the way he was dressed. He'd changed since that morning into a pair of tight, black leather pants and a black silk shirt.

"Yeah, wish you had stayed. We had a blast—" I would have continued if Darik didn't scoff at me. I turned to glare at him and felt the others around the table stiffen. Jezanna, who was on my other side, made a small sound of annoyance in the back of her throat.

"Listen here, buddy. I don't know who you are, and really, I don't give a flying shit, but you really need to quit the effing attitude, right now. I've just gotten past the problem with moody Jeremiah. I *do not* need another person here thinking time with me is not worth it." I shook my head and smirked. "No, scratch that, I couldn't care less if you like me or not. Whatever problem you have, take it somewhere else. I don't want to see it under my roof. Got it?"

"He gets it, don't you, Darik," Jeremiah stated.

"Yeah, whatever." He rolled his eyes.

Isaac slid his hand toward me on the table, stopping a few inches away. "I'm sorry for his rudeness, Leila. He's not usually like this. I've known Darik for some time now, and I trust him to guard me with his life while Adan and Xavier tend to Jezanna, our father and yourself."

"Then why is he being like that with me?"

"I'm right here, ask me." Darik glared.

Sighing loudly, I rested my chin in my hand and tapped my cheek. "Darik darling, why do you hate me so?"

"I don't think our kind should waste our time and associate

with scum like you. You're nothing but a stupid shifter." With that, he spat in my face.

The table erupted in noise. Believe me, I was impressed he managed to get his spit across the table, but I wouldn't stand for that type of treatment.

I felt, more than saw, Isaac move. He raised his hand with lightning speed ready to strike Darik. To my surprise and his, I was quick enough to stand and grab his hand before it reached his friend. Slipping my two fingers between my lips, I let out a loud whistle to gain everyone's attention.

"Stop," I said calmly and took the napkin laying on the table to use it to wipe my face.

"Isaac, I know you and Darik go back a long way, but I don't believe he should stay," said Gregory, who sat peacefully at the other end of the table.

"No, no." I chuckled without humour. "It's all right." I smiled down at Darik. He still sat across from me with a smirk on his lips. "*Everything* is fine." I nodded. "Because I'm going to kill him."

Before anyone could do anything, I jumped the table and forced Darik to the floor. Straddling his waist, I pulled back and pounded into him with my fists. Someone grabbed me around the waist and lifted me off the dick, who had his arms over his face, blocking the rest of my attempts at hurting him. I got a few good hits in.

Idiot arse-muncher. An urge to shift and rip his head off crossed my mind.

"Leila, please calm down." I didn't think I could've if it was anyone but Isaac holding me back. However, his nearness distracted me, especially when his breath fanned down along my neck as if it were caressing me. Isaac cleared his throat. "I'm sorry, Leila. He will be punished for it."

From out the corner of my eye, the look on Isaac's face had me turning my gaze down to Darik. He lay on the floor smiling up at the both of us. Darik then burst out laughing.

"You told me she was easy to get going." He took a deep breath. "I didn't think it would be that easy."

No way. No effing way. It was a test?

"You… you, dick. You little effing bitch, you were playing me?" My eyes sprung open in shock and yet my hands clenched tight, because I was still pissed.

Darik got to his feet, dusting off his clothes. "I had to test you in some way, see if you're good enough for my sire. He doesn't take on many friends, so when he does, they're forever. I had to see if you were strong enough to have his back, which you are," he said, rubbing at his jaw.

"But you spat in my face." I gagged.

"So? I heard you've been licking everyone today. What, you can't handle a little payback?"

"Seriously?" I turned to Isaac who'd only just let go of me and stepped back, *unfortunately*. "You." I pointed at him and glared. "Dear God, you brought someone here worse than Jeremiah."

"No fair." Darik laughed. "I'm way better than him. But you have to admit, it was pretty funny."

I looked back to Darik. "Just you wait, when you least expect it, I'll bring hell upon you. You won't know when, but be scared, be *very* scared. Now enough of this stuff, let's eat and be nice to one another."

Darik let out another laugh, and so did everyone else, except Isaac, who shook his head at Darik. Walking back around the table, I picked up my chair and sat down.

Darik, maybe not knowing I had good hearing, whispered to Isaac, "You have a good one there, Sire."

Only I didn't get to hear Isaac's response, because Caelen bellowed out a loud burp. "You see, love, we vampires can belch as well. We're the bomb." Rolling my eyes, I shook my head and smiled. He always seemed to be the one who acted so young, like a fifteen-year-old.

While we ate dinner, conversation flew around the table.

However, all I could think about was what Isaac's reply would have been to Darik.

I knew I probably should have been annoyed by what Darik had done. In a way, I understood his revolting test. I would have done the same, yet perhaps without the spit, if I were in his position.

In the end, did it really matter what Isaac's answer would have been? It shouldn't, but I couldn't help hoping he wanted more from me.

While Jeremiah had said Isaac didn't see me as a sister, that could just mean that he saw me as his friend, and that alone.

Goddamn, all this crap is confusing, and I swear my brain just farted from all the thoughts.

What I needed to do was be happy with what I had. I'd had no one for so long, and since had a heap of wonderful people who sat with me at my table, sharing a meal, joking and laughing together.

It was something I'd always wished for with my uncle and me.

Yes. What I had should've been enough. I needed to stop my emotions from getting in the way.

Though—*sigh*—I was worried what I felt for Isaac was because he was the first person, in so long, to pay attention to me. Who wanted to be around me just the way I was. Perhaps I felt strongly for him, because he came to me when my life had been dark and he'd shown me my life could be filled with light.

I'd been without anyone's attention for so long, which could have caused my emotions to jump to the wrong conclusions. What would happen if something did occur between Isaac and myself?

Will anyone care if I just start banging my head against the wall? It was what I felt like doing to stop my mind from over-thinking bloody everything.

"I'll help you clean the table, Father," Jezanna offered, standing. I glanced around at everyone's cleared plates and down at mine. I'd hardly touched it. Getting up, I took it to the sink, got out the cling wrap, covered my plate with it and stored it in the fridge. I was sure I'd be hungry later; if not, I'd have it at breakfast tomorrow.

"Are you all right, Leila?" Gregory asked. He'd come to stand beside me as I watched the others move from the table into the living room.

"Yeah, all good. Thank you for cooking tonight."

He smirked. "Isaac suggested it. He said you hadn't eaten properly for a long time."

God, why did he have to tell me that? My heart just melted at the thought of Isaac even thinking of doing something like that. *No, stop those mushy thoughts.*

"Yeah? Well, I've taken care of myself for a long time and I haven't starved."

Gregory looked at me, puzzled. He glanced to Jezanna who started the dishes. Only she stopped and left the room after Gregory gave her a slight nod.

"What has caused this sadness in your eyes? Is it because Isaac cares?" He shook his head. "I'm sorry, I don't understand."

Sighing, my gaze went to the floor. "No, ah, maybe. Only trouble comes when people care. I'm not used to any of this, and I'm feeling a little overwhelmed to have my house full of people. Tell me, Mr Grey—"

"Call me, Greg," he said.

"Greg." I smiled. "What happens when Hamish and Seraphine come back saying they couldn't catch Freckles?"

"Isaac will probably want to leave."

"That's what I thought. So how can I become too attached when there could be the possibility you'll all leave? I know what you're going to say, I can come with you, but I won't. Like I've said, it's not in my nature to run from trouble. I've never ran. People run from me."

"Ahh, now we're getting somewhere. I think the true problem is that you're worried about the more time you spend with us, the more you will care. Then you think we eventually won't like what we see in you and *we'll* leave *you*." He paused. "Like your parents." Tears ran down my cheeks as Greg placed his arm gently around my shoulders and continued, "Leila, I could never come up with a reason why your parents did that to you, but you have to know we're not like them. Isaac saw something in you right from the start. He knew you were to be a part of this family. He saw it. Jezanna saw it. I have seen it, and Jeremiah *eventually* saw it. As you've said to us before, you're now stuck with us."

No words came to mind, so I nodded. Scared I'd break down and show how true I thought his words were.

"Leila, what's wrong?"

Great, just what I needed.

Wiping at my face, I looked up to meet Isaac's concerned expression. I gave him a half smile; it was all I could manage.

"Nothing, all peachy-keen in here."

"But you…" he started until Gregory shook his head at him. "All right. I was wondering if you would like to go for a run with me?"

I could have, and maybe I should have, used the excuse of being tired from running all day. However, the night air, open woods and sounds of nature were calling to me and maybe it would help me clear my mind.

"Sure, sounds great. Are the others coming?" I pushed away from the bench and Gregory, but not before I gave his hand a squeeze in thanks.

"No. It will only be the two of us."

My stomach dipped and my heart perked up in attention.

"Don't forget me," Darik said, coming to stand beside Isaac. "Only, I'll be busy watching out for your arses." Isaac spun his head to his friend. "Not literally, of course. Sorry, Sire, but you don't do it for me."

Shaking his head, Isaac smiled. "I'm pleased. Gregory,

Jezanna and Jeremiah have been given a lift home by Caelen. They asked me to tell you both goodnight."

"Ah, yes. Well, I'll just clean up here and head off myself." Greg nodded.

"Adan will be driving you home." Isaac informed him.

"Thanks, son. Have fun running."

"I'll just go and change." I went to step away until Isaac spoke.

"Leila, I was thinking for tonight you should stay in your human form. I would like to see how fast you are."

Thinking nothing of his request, I teased, "Faster than you, vamp boy." My mood was already stepping up as the adrenalin and anticipation kicked in. I took off out the back door.

I heard Darik's laughter behind me before he said, "She cheats. I like her."

Chapter Eleven

I knew I was fast as a human, maybe not as quick as when I was in feline form, but nearly. Though, it didn't take long for Isaac to catch up. Within seconds, he was beside me and I could tell he was holding back. Instead of pushing, he kept pace with me.

What surrounded me was another reason I couldn't leave my house, the woods. I'd miss it all too much. They were the only stable things in my life.

Arh, there I go again with more deep thoughts. All thoughts that played with my emotions. Usually, I never overthought things. The only time I did was… Oh, of course, it was nearly that time of the month.

Great, just what I needed.

Oh, God. Could vampires tell when *it* came? Could they smell it? How freaking embarrassing and gross. What about Jezanna? Did she have to deal with the same thing every month? I needed to know, because if she did, at least then she could suggest how I was going to be around vampires for a week while my twat bled.

With my brain on other matters, I wasn't concentrating on where I was going. Next, I was flying through the air, because I was stupid enough to trip on a fallen tree branch laying on the ground. My face would have kissed the dirt floor if it wasn't for two strong arms circling my waist. Isaac turned me in midair to take that fall for me. His back hit the rough ground and I ended up landing on top of him, my hands against his chest, my whole body flush against his. I looked down into his eyes and couldn't stop the gasp escaping. His eyes had bled to all black.

"Sorry," I muttered. I went to get up, only his grip tightened around my waist, pulling me closer.

"Wait, please," he begged. Maybe I scraped myself and he could smell my blood and was finding trouble gaining control.

No. I was wrong.

Isaac's hands let go of my waist. Instead, he placed them upon the sides of my face, drawing my head down to his. A part of my mind was screaming, *Yes. Yes. Yes.* Then another was yelling, *Crap. Crap. Crap.* Because it wouldn't be good. I knew after one more taste of Isaac, I'd be addicted for life.

However, I didn't have the willpower to move away.

Before our lips touched, Darik jumped out of the darkness, landing beside us. Isaac let out a low growl. I sighed and placed my forehead against Isaac's chest, frustrated.

Damn, he smells so good.

"Sire, we have company. In the woods a few metres over are men with guns."

Isaac had us both standing within seconds. It was as if he just floated up.

"What are they?" Isaac demanded.

"I scented humans with a tinge of vampire, so they could be minions. I didn't want to get close to them just yet. Not until I informed the both of you. I would like to go back and assess the situation. I thought the two of you should leave, go home and I'll take care of them."

Isaac ground his teeth together. He didn't like the idea, I could tell, but he nodded. "Yes, all right. Leila, let's head back."

"Wait, it's probably just the Davidsons. They like to hunt in this area."

"Let Darik find out. If it is them, we have nothing to worry about."

Without another word, he scooped me up into his arms and started running. I'd been right before; he had been holding back.

After a minute of leaving Darik to fend for himself, which I didn't like, we stood at my back door.

Glowering up at Isaac, I noticed his eyes had changed back to his usual deep green. "We should have stayed with Darik. What happens if he gets hurt?"

"He won't."

"Maybe you don't care enough and want to run, but I'm not like that. I stand my ground and fight." Annoyed, I turned away and looked out into the woods. Only, I was pissed and ready for a fight, so I looked back to Isaac. Everything deflated once I saw the look of pain in Isaac's features. His jaw clenched. He breathed deeply through his nose and his eyes held a hardness in them.

"I'm sorry," I whispered. "I didn't mean it. I know you have to protect yourself by not getting into mindless trouble."

He spoke with venom in his voice, "I don't care for myself, Leila. *You* are nearly the last of your kind. I can presume this true from what Mervin said. He thought your kind had all been killed. So I will not have you playing around with your life and stand to fight beside Darik when I know he is more than capable of taking care of the matter on his own."

My hands went to my hips. I was back to glaring at him. "*You* will not have? Really, Isaac Grey?" Flopping my arms up and down in frustration, I said, "Just go. You make me so mad sometimes."

"Likewise," he snapped, and with that, he grabbed me and kissed me.

My brain shut down, my body taking over. All the blood rushed to my head, making me dizzy in ecstasy. My stomach was bursting with excitement. I couldn't get enough, so when Isaac pulled me closer, placing his hands securely around my waist, I reached up with one hand and ran my fingers through his soft, silky hair, deepening the kiss. *How can a guy have such wonderful hair? So unfair. Focus, Leila, at least you're kissing this god.*

A moan escaped both of us, all of my worries evaporating. It was more than I could have dreamed of. It was definitely *not* a sisterly kiss; it wasn't even a friendship kiss. It was more and I liked it. A lot.

Everything around us disappeared. Time insignificant as we stood there kissing, tasting and teasing each other.

I wanted to stay there forever, with Isaac completely surrounding me.

Still, he may not have to breathe, but I did, and regrettably, I had to pull back from his luscious lips. Resting my forehead against his shoulder, I breathed deeply. I was happy to hear he was having the same trouble. I couldn't help but laugh.

Isaac groaned. "That is not the response I was hoping for."

"No," I started and looked up at him, heat suffusing my cheeks. "It was really mind-blowing," I confessed and wished I could take it back. *Mind-blowing, that's the best you can do? How dicky.*

Isaac smirked, only it fell away as he ran the back of his fingers down the side of my face. "I should have never started that game with you, Leila. Because right from the start, I never wished to pretend with you."

I was sure he heard my heart skip a beat.

Licking my suddenly dry lips, I gulped and asked, "Really?"

"Is it so hard to believe I find you attractive and want to be with you?"

Oh, God, if he keeps talking like this, I'm going to start hyperventilating.

"Yes, it kinda is."

"Do you not want this?"

"Heck yes, I want this," I burst out. However, I couldn't help saying, "But you could have any girl, why me?"

"No other has shown me so much, in such little time as you have. I find you fascinating, strong, smart, sarcastic, sweet, caring." He grinned. "And I'm sure I've only seen a little part of yourself."

"You forgot pig-headed, stubborn, distrustful, and that's only to name a few."

He laughed as he cupped the back of my neck. His eyes searched my face before his smile grew. "I was being kind. I know you're all of those as well, but they're what makes you *you*." He paused. "Who I care for completely."

Lost for words, because I couldn't believe what I was hearing. The wonderful man in front of me wanted me. Cared for me. Therefore, instead of saying anything, I practically jumped him. I wrapped my arms around his neck and threw myself at him, his lips. He stumbled back a few steps, but managed to right us both, and with the same passion and desire I was feeling, he kissed me back.

Until the back door opened.

Breaking from the kiss, I glared at the person who interrupted us. Xavier. "If this keeps happening, no one can stop me from killing," I grumbled.

Isaac smiled down at me, gave me one last peck on the lips and turned to Xavier while I stood at his side.

"What's wrong?"

"Master, Darik called. He tried reaching you telepathically, but you're shut tight. There were more than he thought. He needs some help."

Isaac stiffened and asked, "Is Adan not back yet?"

"He not long left, but I called. He's coming back."

"You must help Darik then," Isaac ordered.

Xavier looked torn. "Master, I can't leave the two of you unguarded."

"He's right," I said. "I'll go." Before Isaac could refuse, I grabbed him, kissed him quickly and took off.

"Leila!" Isaac bellowed in rage behind me. "Go after her, Xavier."

"I can't. I must stay with you— No, Master, you must stay here."

"I'll be okay," I yelled. "Stay with Xavier. Besides, this is just another reason you care for me." I smiled when I heard his growl of fury.

While running, I shed my clothes and started the change. I was going to be exhausted later. Two shifts in one day would wreck me.

Still, worry drove me forward, my concern for Darik real. I couldn't deny the excitement, though, which coursed through my veins, pushing my blood hard through my system in eagerness. I was ready to play. I pumped my legs faster.

No one would die that night, not if I had anything to do with it, especially after receiving a kiss that rocked my world.

I heard the clashing of swords before reaching the area. Jumping into the trees, I silently edged my way towards the fighting bodies. Looking down, I took in what was occurring. Darik was outnumbered. There were six big, strong forms and all were having a turn at attacking Darik. He was exceptional at protecting himself from their attempts at eliminating him. However, he didn't have the chance to attack.

Opening my shields, I searched and discovered four were vampires and two were humans. The humans must have been the ones Darik had seen earlier.

One managed to get through Darik's defences and slashed him across the chest. It was time for me to join in the fun.

Leaping from the tree, I landed straight onto a vampire's back and tore his throat out.

Do not swallow, Leila. Do not let one drop in your stomach or it will be the end of you. I didn't want to risk it in case another vampire had the ability for their blood to be poisonous to me, like Freckles had.

Having bitten so deeply, my opponent's head fell to the ground and the rest of him turned to ash before me. I didn't have time to contemplate it. I bounded to the ground through the remains of the vampire. Surprise flicked through my mind when no one noticed my appearance. Though, I took it as an advantage and jumped onto the one who was making leeway with Darik, who had scored another gash across his chest. The vampire jolted with shock when he felt weight upon his shoulders. I didn't give him any time to act. I unsheathed my long, sharp claws and slashed though his neck with ease. Another one down, four more to go.

"What the hell are *you* doing here?" Darik fumed.

I hoped from his tone he wasn't another one who hated being helped by a 'mere' female.

Ignoring him, I turned my attention back to what was happening around us. One of the humans had decided to run; that only left three. There was no way I was killing a human, so I ran toward a vampire. Fear flashed through his eyes. He took a couple of steps back before he prepared himself in a fighting stance. As I lunged into the air for his face, he pulled his sword out from behind him with lightning speed. In midair, I turned my body to the left and landed on the ground, barely missing his attack. He fell upon my back before I could adjust my footing. I arched, kicking my hind legs up. His arms tightened.

Twisting and turning, so he wasn't able to get his sword under me to stab it in, I prayed all his attention was on trying to stay alive.

The next second, I felt the weight lift from me. I turned in time to witness Adan cut off the vampire's head, turning the rest of him to dust. Which, might I add, fell over me. I sneezed and glared up at Adan.

"You're welcome." He smiled.

I felt Darik's anger before he stalked over to us, noticing he'd taken care of his two other opponents. "Shit, Leila. What in the hell do you think you're doing? Huh? You aren't supposed to be here. You could have gotten yourself killed!" he screamed.

I snorted. He was overreacting.

"Why did she come? Where were you?" Darik turned his anger to Adan realising he wasn't going to get an answer out of me. There was no way I was going to connect to his mind when he was gunning for a fight.

"Doing what I was asked. I was told to drive my master's father home. I only just got back and came out here." Adan sighed. "Come on, we'd better head back."

"How's he doing?"

"Just thank the Lord we're bringing her back in one piece."

We walked back in silence. Along the way, Darik picked up the clothes I'd thrown off in my hurry. I was happy I was still in my cat form, because when he picked up my underwear and smiled brashly down at me, I knew my face would've been glowing red.

Adan opened the back door for me. I walked through and found Isaac pacing the floor, while Xavier and Gregory waited patiently, sitting at the kitchen table.

Isaac stopped, turned to face me and zoomed over. Yes, zoomed, because I didn't actually see him move. One minute, he was near the table, and the next, he was kneeling down in front of me. He rubbed his hands all over me, searching for any kind of injury. After finding none, he grabbed my head in his hands and forced my eyes to his.

"Leila Morgin, do not make me feel this way again—"

"Truly, sweetheart." Gregory sighed. "He was on the verge of killing Xavier for keeping him here when we came in."

"She fought gracefully, Sire. It was an honour to see it," Darik solemnly said.

Isaac glared at his friend, who took a step back. "I don't care if she was wonderful at it," Isaac snarled. "It's the risk she takes in doing so."

Oh, shucks. He made me want to hug and kiss him for being so concerned. Then again, he also made me want to punch him in the face for thinking that I couldn't handle it. It was *my* life I was playing with, and if I risked it to save someone else, then that was what I'd do.

Reaching out with my mind to Isaac's, after a few tries first, I told him exactly what I thought.

"Leila." He shook his head at me. "I understand. I only hope you will one day." He sighed, seeming frustrated.

What did he mean by that?

Whatever it was, it had to wait. I rubbed my head against the side of his cheek and brushed my nose down his neck, making sure my scent rubbed onto him. Did he understand my cat had just claimed him? With one last bump of my nose under his chin, I walked off to my room.

Of course I glanced back. I needed to see if he was watching, and he was. He also had a small smile upon his face. Therefore, he couldn't be that mad.

Right?

I paused in the hallway when I heard Isaac ask Darik about the ones who attacked him.

"Loner vampires and their minions. They belong to no one. I told them to leave this town. That you had ownership here. They'd grinned as if they had won the lottery and said since they were here, they might as well collect on the bounty. Gerald has set a reward for your capture or death. Whomever collects will receive $150 million. I told them they would have to go through me first. That was when the fighting started."

A whimper escaped me as soon as I was behind my bedroom door. If I hadn't turned up to help Darik, I dare say he would have lost, and then they would have come after Isaac. For that reason alone, the guilt I had for leaving Isaac disappeared.

Chapter Twelve

"What the fuck is going on in here?"

Shit, shit, shit. My uncle was home. What was he doing home?

Already altered back, I quickly threw on some clothes and ran down the hall, straight into the kitchen, and sidled up to Uncle Jack. Unfortunately, a nice warm shower was going to have to wait until later.

Gregory stood and held out his hand to Jack. "We just finished up dinner. My name's Gregory. I'm Isaac's father."

I nudged Jack in the ribs when he didn't take Greg's hand. Thankfully, he snapped to it and gruffly said, "Jack Helavay, Leila's uncle." Jack looked at Gregory with dubious eyes. "Do you condone men in *my* house with my eighteen-year-old niece? Men who have swords strapped to their backs?" he asked, eyeing Xavier, Adan and Darik. They stood in front of Isaac near the back door.

It was on the tip of my tongue to tell him to mind his own business, but I didn't get the chance.

Greg chuckled. "Surely you can understand the importance of a self-defence lesson. When my son informed me Leila was staying in a house on her own, I insisted she become knowledge-able of being her own protector. Hence, the swords."

Whoa. I was impressed.

"She doesn't live here on her own. *She* knows I'm never far and if she called me, I would be here for her anytime. I don't like this situation at all. Still,"—he looked down at me and I saw he wasn't impressed at all—"I appreciate the thought."

He knew something else was going on. He wasn't dumb. Anyone could see both Darik and Adan looked like they'd been in a fight and the ruffled look wasn't by some self-defence lessons.

I was grateful he didn't point that out though.

"So, Jack. What are you doing home?" I asked.

"I came to see you. It was lucky I did." He waved to Isaac's guards. "Hey, I'm Jack, and if any of you mess with her, I'll kill you."

"Jack!" I snapped.

"What?"

"Don't be an arse. Sorry, guys."

"It's fine, Leila." Isaac smiled. He moved forward. Darik and Xavier stepped aside. "Nice to see you again, Jack. But we'll be going now." Isaac nodded at me. "I'll see you tomorrow for school."

"Yes." I blushed for some reason. "Uh, thanks for dinner, Greg. And for the lesson, guys." They nodded and followed Isaac and his father out.

I had hoped for a goodnight kiss. I guessed that was out of the question since my uncle was currently staring daggers down at me.

The front door closed and Jack started. "So, kiddo, you have a dinner party and don't invite me?" He stomped to the fridge to see what was left.

Hell, he actually sounded hurt, causing guilt to form inside of me. Didn't he understand why I wouldn't even think of asking him home? Not that I knew we were having dinner in the first place. The fact was Jack never appeared to be interested in my life. Sure, he helped me out.

But he didn't know *me*.

He didn't know what music I liked. The anguish I'd been through with my parents leaving and what went on at school with the other students. Did he even know what made me happy or sad?

Or that I was a shifter?

Rubbing my forehead, I sighed. Maybe if he stuck around, if he showed the smallest amount of interest, then I could trust him with everything.

Still, the one thought that plagued my mind was what would happen if I did open up to him, if I told him everything. Would he run? Would he try to hurt me? Would I lose him?

I've never been happy we weren't close, but I'd be destroyed if I lost him from my life forever.

However, Isaac had taught me trust was important and I didn't have to go all the way. Baby steps would have to be enough.

Shrugging, I said, "That's because I knew you would've eaten everything and left none for the rest of us. Maybe, um, maybe next time." He spun around from the fridge with the plate of my leftovers in his hand.

I'd shocked him.

He composed himself, closed his mouth, lowered his brows and asked, "Are you okay, squirt?"

So much for trying a little.

Rolling my eyes, I said, "Fine, don't be an idiot."

"Yep, there she is. You had me worried there for a second." He sat down at the table and dug into the food. I went to sit opposite him and waited. He had to be home for a reason, right?

Jack looked up from the plate. "What?"

"Aren't you going to give me grief about having them here? Last time you asked me to stay away from Isaac, and now he's here with his mates."

Scoffing, he said, "His dad was here too, so I know you wouldn't have been having wild monkey sex."

Laughing, I caught his smile before he quickly sobered and commented, "They… they seem different."

My heart jumped. "Well, yeah. They're into combat, army stuff. That's all."

"You know, if you wanted to learn self-defence, I could have taught you a few things."

Raising my brows, I asked, "What do you know about self-defence?"

"I'm in law enforcement."

I laughed and slapped the table. "Yeah, right."

His face was serious. "Like your dad used to be."

No way. "A bounty hunter?"

"Yep." He nodded.

"Why are you *just* telling me? Is this why you're never around?"

He shrugged. "Not like you tell me anything either. Just didn't think you were interested."

That was true. My uncle and I never really talked. Regret formed in my stomach and heart. "Maybe we should change that?" I suggested lightly.

"Sound's good, kid. Anything you wanna tell me?"

There was my chance. Tell him everything. Still, too much worry was burning in my mind. "Not that I can think of."

He shook his head, a sad smile played on his lips. "Anyway, I want you to know I still don't know if I can trust those guys around you." He held his hand up. "But before you start screaming at me, I won't say or do anything until I have more of a background on them."

"Can't you just trust my judgment?"

What could he dig up on them if he started? I was worried.

"We'll see." Which meant no. I had to warn Isaac.

He sighed and sat back in his chair. "There's something else we need to talk about." I nodded and he went on, "We haven't heard from your dad in a while. I'm concerned."

"Please." I snorted. "They're just off having some fun somewhere and forgot to call."

Jack sighed. "I don't think so, kiddo. He would always call

every second Friday. I'm leaving tomorrow to see if I can find them."

My eyes went to the table. If he was going to look for them, then it had to be serious. Nerves rolled in my stomach.

Shaking my head, I couldn't think about it. Not yet. There was enough going on. They'd be fine, probably on some island having the time of their lives.

Yes. That had to be it.

"I'll leave in the morning."

Looking up and around, I nodded. "Okay."

"You 'right?" He went to reach his hand to mine, only second-guessing at the last second and picked up his fork instead.

"Fine," I said, jutting my chin out and meeting his eyes.

He smiled. "There's one good thing about those people you have around here."

"What?"

"You no longer hide. I hated it when you looked away all the time. Afraid you'd hurt someone with your gaze. But now you meet my eyes with confidence. It's good to see. You're not beneath anyone, Leila, and never let anyone tell you any different."

Thinning my lips into a line, because I knew they would have trembled, I then blinked rapidly. I had an urge to cry, to hug him. I did neither.

Sniffing up my snot, I stood and asked, "Do you want a drink?"

"That'd be nice. Thanks."

"Whatever," I said and smiled to myself as he chuckled.

After I poured us both a drink, I sat back across from him. Maybe it was because I was feeling mushy and happy, but I sat with my uncle and we talked.

It was strange.

But good.

Chapter Thirteen

A Hummer sat at the end of the driveway. As an added bonus, there was the sexiest man I knew in it waiting for me. It was only when I got in the car, my nerves took flight. Should I kiss him hello? Give him a handshake and thank him for my first and best kisses of my life?

Thankfully, he made up my mind for me. Straight away, he leaned over, his heated eyes meeting mine as his fingers slid into my hair at the back before he gave me a long, deep kiss.

After he moved away, I smiled at him and said, "So, the kiss last night, I didn't dream it."

He barked out a laugh. "No, Leila. That was no dream."

Just to make sure, I reached out to him, pulled him close, and kissed him again. My tarty hands roamed over his hard chest, stopping at his waist, but wanting to go farther.

"We're going to be late," he murmured against my lips.

"So?" I felt him smile. Then, unfortunately, he untangled my arms from around his neck—how they got up there, I had no clue—and placed them in my lap.

"As much as I would love to keep doing this, I don't wish to get you in trouble. One of us has only had one education. I'll not be the cause of you failing."

Isaac was old; of course he'd already been through school. Why he wanted to do it again was strange. Still, I found it sweet he was looking out for my education. However, I harrumphed like a spoilt child who had someone take away her new toy, and sat back in the seat and glared. He laughed, started the car and headed toward school.

Maybe Isaac didn't know he was my first boyfriend. I was eighteen, nearly nineteen, a virgin and ready to try everything. I'd been sexually frustrated for a while, and now that I had Isaac, I was ready.

God, that made me sound like I was easy. At least I wasn't until a certain vampire cemented himself into my life and sent my feelings wild.

Distracting myself, I asked, "Why do you go to school? It's not like you need it. You're smart enough."

"Thank you, I think. Both my sister and brother don't understand the whys of it either. I go because it keeps me occupied. I love watching people, even if I don't want to be a part of their pack. I also like to seem normal to the humans, so attending school helps, and then at least we're able to stay around longer if I act younger than what I am. Besides, there was also something telling me I needed to go to *this* school." He shrugged. "I guess our paths were meant to cross."

"Fate works in wonderful ways sometimes," I whispered.

He looked at me intently before turning his eyes back to the road and saying, "I couldn't agree more." His grip on the steering wheel tightened. "How is your uncle?"

Leaning my head back, I said, "Still a butt-head. Sorry about last night."

"Do you know that's the first time you've ever smiled when I've asked about him?"

"Really?"

"Yes. I like it."

My smile widened.

"Last night didn't bother me, Leila. If anything, your uncle showed he cares for you and wants to protect you."

Shaking my head, I confessed, "Sometimes I just don't see it. Maybe if he did care, he'd stick around longer."

"So, he's gone again?"

"Yes. Probably gone for a few days. He's worried, because we haven't heard from my dad in a while. He's gone to investigate it or something."

"Are you worried?"

"No. Yes. I think so. But I'm more worried about something else. My uncle wants to do a background check on you and the others." I looked at him, his smile instantly reassuring me.

"You don't need to worry. We have everything in place. Jack will find nothing out of the ordinary. I live a rather boring existence of an eighteen-year-old boy. The same for every one of my people. It's something we always have to do."

"Good. I'm glad."

We pulled into the parking lot. Isaac got out before I did and came around to open my door.

"I can do that," I snapped.

"Sorry, I have a hard time ridding myself of some old-fashioned customs."

"No, I'm sorry. I didn't mean to sound grouchy. It's just weird."

He gently shifted me away from the door and shut it. I went to step forward, but he held me against the car. I already felt the stares directed our way, but when I looked up into his serious eyes, I didn't care what was going on around us.

"It may seem weird, but you deserve to be treated the right way. I care for you deeply and I wish to do well by you." He bent his head and kissed me hard.

My breath hitched as our lips touched. My mouth opened under the slightest touch of his tongue against my bottom lip. My knees felt weak and I gripped his shirt tightly while he deepened the kiss, causing havoc to splutter to life in my belly.

Never had I been kissed like that; it was even different from the night before and I knew I'd never feel it again from anyone else. Only Isaac.

He astounded me, made my heart speed, put those funny butterfly feelings in my stomach. All of that and so much more, and it was every time he touched me, even if it was only one finger tracing along my jaw.

Christ, I'd never be able to walk away from this. Him.

I sighed when he pulled away again. It was time for class. He took my hand in his and led me to history. Only that time, Isaac took me to sit with him at his table, which made me feel like a giddy twelve-year-old. Dr Keffen stood up the front, droning on about something, but my mind was elsewhere.

I sat back in my seat to admire what was now mine. Isaac eased forward with his elbows on the table to support his head and stared up the front of the class. He knew I was watching him.

Movement caught my attention. I glanced over and saw Jenna, Monica and Bertina glaring at me. I had no idea why they even took damn history. I was convinced they were some of the ones doing 'favours' for Dr Keffen. Funny thing was though, seeing them in that moment, made me feel even better. No one understood why Isaac chose me. Hell, I still didn't, and to rub it in their faces a little, I ran my hand down Isaac's back, down to his bottom and gave it a pinch. The girls gaped. Isaac turned to look at me, heat showing in his eyes. I raised my eyebrows at him and shrugged. He scoffed, gave me a quick peck and turned back to the teacher.

The class door opened and in walked Darik. I'd forgotten he was now attending school with us, and I wondered why he was late. Dr Keffen barked at him for being tardy. Girls watched Darik, mainly his arse, closely, while he ignored everything and sat in the vacant seat beside us, glaring at Isaac.

"What's up with him?" I whispered to Isaac once Dr Keffen began to speak again.

"He's upset with me for not waiting for him while he showered," Isaac replied.

Oh, that wasn't good, especially when Darik was only trying to keep his sire from any trouble that could arise. Still, if Darik had been in the car with Isaac that morning, I wouldn't have been able to kiss him. It would have made me feel awkward having someone in the back seat watching us.

Finally, after a double class and then my computer science lecture, which we all took together, it was break time. Darik turned sideways in his seat. "Please don't do that to me again. I'm here to protect you and Leila. How can I do it if you leave me behind? I need an ample amount of time to check the perimeter before class begins. Which is the reason why I was late getting to class."

"I'm sorry, Darik. I won't do it again. I understand the position I've put you in. Let's get going. Leila must be hungry by now." Just as he said it, my stomach growled and they laughed.

We walked to the cafeteria. I hadn't been in there for a while, since it reminded me far too much of high school, but I had no choice today. I hadn't packed my lunch. Just as Darik was about to open the doors, someone called out my name. I turned and was surprised to see Raven, Sofia's younger sister. Sofia was one of Jenna's evil cronies. She stood a few feet behind us, dressed in her usual Gothic gear, with her raven-coloured hair hanging loosely around her shoulders. I only knew she was Sofia's sister because I'd overheard a conversation at the start of the year between Jenna and Sofia. Sofia was trying to get Raven into the popular click, but Jenna refused and told her that Raven was too much of a loser to be allowed to hang with them. Jenna warned Sofia if she kept bringing it up, she'd soon forget they were even friends.

Raven was already in her second year, and crazy bright. I wondered why she hadn't gone off to uni rather than sticking around at our local college.

What was weird though was that Raven had never spoken to me before.

"Ah, hi, Raven. What's up?"

She looked scared, as her eyes glanced off Isaac to Darik. I saw Darik smile at her, giving her a nod to continue, but she didn't. With one final look at me, she shook her head, blushed and walked away.

"That's strange. She's never approached me before, like everyone else here."

"Which is their loss," Isaac said, pulling me against him and then wrapping his arms around me. I tilted my head up so I could kiss him, until a throat cleared beside us. I groaned in frustration and looked to Darik, who was bloody smirking.

"Don't mind me." He gestured with his hand for us to continue. "Watching is the only way I'm ever going to get any." He grinned.

I snorted. "Ah, okay. I don't know what to say to that, only perv." He laughed and continued into the cafeteria.

Unease swirled in my stomach. I wanted to take our lunch someplace else. At least then Isaac and Darik didn't have to pretend to eat and we wouldn't have all eyes on us. But Isaac refused, saying to let them stare.

"They're only looking because the girls are jealous and the guys are pissed because the girls are staring," Darik said as we sat down at a corner table with some food.

"Th-th-that's t-t-true," someone said behind us.

Looking over my shoulder, my eyes went straight to Ty's sunglasses-covered eyes. He sat at a large table on his own. I glanced him over. He wasn't a bad-looking guy, slim, tall with short dark-blond hair and that day he was wearing light blue jeans and a dark blue shirt.

Ty was another loner. He'd started at our high school just before exams and had since attended the college the same time as me. No one wanted him to hang with them, because he was blind and stuttered. I'd heard the whispers and snide remarks, pissed off that despite being surrounded by supposed adults, few had seemed to grow up. His stuttering became worse when he was in front of someone. Once, I'd heard him on his phone to his mum where he'd had a normal conversation with her without any stuttering. He got hassled a lot for it and no one wanted to sit with the guy who'd attracted the jocks unwanted attention.

I knew they tormented him because they didn't get him.

Like they didn't get me.

Unfortunately, the teasing followed him to college, again, also like it had me.

"Ty, correct?" Isaac asked.

"Y-y-yeah. And you're I-I-Isaac," he said as he pushed his dark glasses up his nose.

"That's right. Leila is also here, as well as my friend, Darik."

"Hey, Ty," I mumbled around a mouthful of pasta.

"Hi."

"Do you want to join us?" Darik asked.

"I-I… ah—"

"Come on, Ty." I went over and grabbed his tray, moving it to our table. He made his way over by using his sensor stick and sat down opposite Isaac and myself, but next to Darik.

Sounds of snickering reached my ears. Jason, Jenna's boyfriend, yelled, "Huh, there he goes. Adopting another freak, Isaac?"

Slouching in my seat, I sighed at the immaturity of the whole damn thing. I was convinced half of the cohort only got into their courses because the college had chairs to fill. Grades be damned. Dammit, I wanted to yell something back, but nothing came to mind, nor was I willing to bite. I knew that was what they wanted. I wondered if they'd be quite so keen if they knew how sharp my teeth were. I could definitely give them a bite to remember. I snorted internally just as Isaac tilted my head towards his with one finger and kissed me gently on the lips.

"Ignore them," he ordered.

"Christ, man, how can you kiss that?" Jason yelled. His mates chuckled, high-fived him and the girls giggled.

Isaac stood abruptly, knocking over Ty's drink, which spilt all over him. I grabbed Isaac's hand before he did something silly.

"Sire, let me." Darik growled, standing. "Can I kill him?"

"No, no one does anything," I ordered. "It's not worth it. Ty, are you okay?" I grabbed some napkins and went around the table to help him clean up, most of it landed on his legs, so I didn't have to get personal with him.

Ty laughed. "I-I'm all right. Y-y-you almost s-s-sounded s-serious, Darik."

I glared at Darik, because the problem was, he *was* serious. I only hoped Ty didn't catch the 'sire' part.

Ty reached down and took my hand. He tilted his face up to where mine would be. "I-I-I'm s-sorry," he whispered, before he growled something so low even my super hearing couldn't pick it up. "I-I would have s-spoken to y-you s-sooner, b-but I thought you had enough t-trouble, w-without me adding t-to it."

"Shit, Ty. You don't need to worry about that. Besides, I'm just as bad. I thought the same thing with you. Then again, I also thought *you* thought it'd be better to stay away from the *freak*."

Isaac growled. I mouthed *sorry*.

"Th-they are j-just s-scared when people are different th-than them." He patted my hand and then let it go. So I placed it on his shoulder and gave it a squeeze.

"Yes they are. Ty, you can hang with us anytime." I looked at Isaac. He smiled at me with such adoration, causing my breath to catch. I only wished jumping him to have my wicked way was an option.

"Are you s-sure? I-I will get on y-y-your nerves."

Darik laughed. "Don't worry, Leila does that a lot as well."

"Dude, whatever." I rolled my eyes. "Actually. Ty, why don't you come to my place after school, to study or something?"

Isaac cleared his throat. "Sorry, Ty, but tonight isn't good for us."

Raising my brows, I asked, "It's not?"

"No, I have something planned." He grinned and my heart jumped.

"I'm not invited either, Ty. Isaac wants to do some romantic gesture," Darik complained.

"Th-that's all right, another t-t-time." He smiled.

"For sure," I said and sat down at the table again next to Isaac.

Pestering him about what he had planned was my first thought; however, I knew I wouldn't get anywhere. Instead, I sat there and enjoyed the company I had around me. Ty joined in the conversation every now and then, while getting frustrated with himself for stuttering. By the time lunch had ended, he felt more comfortable with us and his stuttering slowed.

I walked with Ty to software analysis, impressed with his ability to navigate the halls and people. We had the class together and, for the first time, we sat next to each other. Though, I couldn't help feeling a little lost without Isaac at my side. It was like a part of me was missing. That thought scared me, because it sounded so mushy.

I was not a mushy person.

Our lecturer, Dana, wasn't around, which was the norm. As usual, we followed the textbooks that directed us through our tasks. It was always a breeze of a lesson, learning codes and dissecting data.

We worked the first half hour in silence. Ty was using his screen reading software, so focused on listening through his headphones. I shot him cursory glances, fascinated as his fingers moved over his textbook, while he listened and pressed his keys in complete control. I'd never noticed before, in all of this time, that his textbook was in braille. I was impressed. College and being a teenager was hard enough, without the added need to learn a whole new language.

We both completed the tasks at pretty much the same time. Ty and I took the chance to get to know one another better. I found out he had a sister, who was twenty. Her name was Penny, short for Penelope. She had intended to head off to university a couple of years back, but decided to stay home and help out their mum. His dad passed away two years ago and his mum was finding it hard coping on her own. She worked at the local factory, doing nightshift, while Penny worked school hours as a receptionist.

Ty mentioned he couldn't wait to graduate, but like me, three years seemed far away. His intention was to work in program development, earning enough, and then Penny could move on and his mum could work less.

He seemed sweet, shy and considerate with other people's feelings, and I could tell we were going to get along fine.

Ty asked me about my family. I surprised myself by telling him the almost truth: My parents were travelling, because they couldn't handle what other people thought about me.

He was shocked.

Then, I moved on to my uncle, and really, there wasn't much to say about him. So I steered the conversation towards music. I couldn't believe my ears when he told me he liked the same music as Isaac. He laughed when I told him I heard The Smashing Pumpkins the other day and felt like smashing my head against the car dashboard just to make it stop.

At least he redeemed himself when he mentioned he also loved *Glee,* winning him big brownie points. He loved listening to the music.

At the end of the session, we said our goodbyes. Ty moved onto science and I headed to the library, since I had study time, with a smile upon my face.

When the day ended, I walked out the front double doors, humming some show tune. It was the first time I'd actually enjoyed my day. I found Isaac and Darik already waiting for me.

Arriving at my place, I got out of the car before Isaac made it around to open my door. I grinned at him and laughed when he rolled his eyes. Turning to Darik, who had cleared his throat and stood behind me shuffling his feet, I noticed the other car parked next to us.

My eyes went to Darik when he said, "I'll be leaving to do a perimeter check. I won't be far. If you need me, just holler."

Nerves suddenly bombarded me. My stomach took a nose-drive and my hands started to sweat. I wiped them on my jeans while my mind kept running over the fact Isaac and I would soon be alone.

Well, except for whoever owned the car in my drive.

"Thanks, Darik." I nodded.

Darik gave me a chin lift, a small bow to Isaac and then sped off.

"So...?" I said, turning back to Isaac's smiling face.

"You seem nervous, Leila. Do I make you nervous?" His smile turned into a smart-arse smirk.

Kicking at the dirt, I looked everywhere but at him. "No, why would you? I've faced many things in my life and none of them have made me nervous, so why would having time alone with you do that to me?" I shrugged. "Yeah, whatever."

He laughed, no doubt picking up on my heartbeat doing the tango. I gave him a shove, but he caught my hand and pulled me against him for a kiss. My body relaxed into his. I reached my arms up around his neck and brought him closer.

I barely registered the sound of the front door to my house opening. It was only when someone coughed that I quickly pulled away, but I didn't get far. Isaac secured his arm around my waist, bringing me back in close to him. I couldn't hide the rising blush as I looked up to Gregory standing on my front porch.

"Evening, Father." Isaac smiled. He took my hand and led me up the front steps. "Is everything prepared?"

"Yes, son." He grinned. "Have a nice night." He bounded down the stairs after giving me a quick wave and got in his car with Adan, who turned up out of nowhere. I watched them leave and then turned to Isaac to ask what was going on, but he wasn't there. The front door was still open, so he must have gone in. I walked through the front door and gasped. On the floor leading a trail to the kitchen were red rose petals. I never would have thought I'd be choked up about something so romantic, so... disgustingly mushy, but I was.

God help me, I'd fallen for my vamp, bad.

Isaac had thought of all this. Even asked his father to help him set it up, and Isaac got rid of everyone so we could be alone.

Hell, if I didn't get my heart and mind under control, I was going to be a blubbering mess.

"Are you just going to stand there and stare, Leila?" I looked up from the floor to Isaac, who was leaning against the kitchen doorframe, giving me the small half smile I loved.

"Damn it, Isaac. I,"—shaking my head, I offered a shy grin —"no one has ever done anything like this for me. You're going to turn me into a big softy. I don't want to be a softy, Isaac. I'm not used to it. I—"

With a blink, he was in front of me, pulling me against him.

"I can never see you yielding, and I'd never want that from you. I'm sorry if this makes you unhappy. I was hoping for the exact opposite and knew food usually did that."

Moving back enough so I could look him in the eyes, I saw his wince when he noticed tears showing in mine.

"Seriously, this is the best thing anyone has ever done. I'll never forget it. But if you tell anyone I was a mess over it, I'll... well, I'll think of something really bad when my mind starts working again," I scolded. He chuckled and kissed my nose.

"Now, let me feed you. By then, you may forget about harming me."

Gregory had cooked a feast. By the end of the meal, I felt stuffed and was sure I was going to burst. Yet still, there were enough leftovers for another three meals—well, maybe my breakfast and lunch the next day.

Isaac leaned back in his chair. He stared at his drink, a deep red wine, and swirled it in his cup with a thoughtful look upon his face.

I placed my hand on his to stop the motion, before he spilt it. He looked at me. I smiled and he gave me a half one back.

"Isaac, what's on your mind?"

He cleared his throat. "I was wondering how you came to live with your uncle. Why did your parents leave?"

Rolling my eyes, I smiled. "Is that all? It looked like you were going to say something I really wouldn't like."

"I know you don't like speaking of them. Why is that, Leila?" he probed, not in a naughty way either, which I wouldn't have minded. *God, woman, he's trying to have a heartfelt conversation. Control yourself.*

Audibly, I sighed. "It's true I don't like talking about them, but with you, I can handle it. Really, it's not as if I don't like talking about them; it's more that when I do or when I think of them, it makes me remember how much of a disappointment I am to them. They wanted a normal, perfect life and instead they got me, 'The freak.'" I held up my hand before he could comment. "I now know that some people *can* handle what happens in their life, the struggles some have to face." I shrugged. "My mum wasn't one of them. Don't get me wrong, they took great care of me. Showed me a lot in the time we had together, gave me a, somewhat, loving home. I guess there was too much to put up with from people around town.

"Still, in the end, she... my mum always had a need to get out of the town, out of the life she was leading, and when I turned thirteen, I gave her just that. The morning of my thirteenth birthday, I walked out into the kitchen. My mum was standing at the stove. I told her something was wrong. I was in agony. At first, I saw concern flash through her eyes."

I ran a hand through my hair. My emotions were catching up with me. Talking about it made me want to curl up in a ball and cry, but I didn't. "It soon vanished and was replaced with disgust, fright. I transformed right in front of her for the first time. She… I guess she didn't like what she saw." I snorted and then sobered. Leaning my forearms on the table, I looked down at my clasped hands. "She tried to kill me, Isaac. Before I passed out, I heard my father come running in. He managed to stop her from doing too much damage. When I woke, bruised, I found my dad was sitting next to me, petting me while I was still in my cat form."

I laughed humourlessly. "Ironic, right? He told me he was sorry, but he had to leave. Take Mum away. That… that he loved me no matter *how* I was. Still, he left with her."

Isaac reached for me. Before I knew it, I was sitting in his lap. He stroked my back up and down while he whispered, "I'm so sorry you had to go through anything like that."

"Don't, Isaac. I stopped feeling sorry for myself a long time ago. I stopped crying about a lot of things a *very* long time ago. What helps me the most, now especially, is that I have you, your family and even my uncle."

"Oh, so not *just* me," he teased, lightening the mood and it was exactly what I needed.

"Sorry, you can't take all the credit." I waited for his smart reply, but it didn't come. Instead, he gently turned my head and kissed me. I curled into him and let myself go, allowed myself to only feel and happily forgot the sadness from talking about my parents.

Much later, Isaac suggested we go for a run to clear our minds. A thrill burst through me and I told him I wanted to be in my feline form so I could whip his behind. He chuckled and then proceeded to inform me—the bastard—that I needed to be faster if I wanted to burn off the food I'd ingested, because he couldn't have *his* woman getting fat. With that, he bolted for the back door and fled into the night. I quickly stripped, transformed, and chased after him.

I wasn't sure if he was letting me, but I soon caught up to him and tackled him to the ground. I head-butted him before I licked his cheek with my rough tongue and then flew up the nearest tree. As I walked up and down the biggest branch, I watched Isaac as he laughed. He rose from lying on the ground to stand in one second, and in the next, he was up in the tree next to me. Without thinking, I leaped to the next tree and so on with Isaac following me. Eventually, he'd had enough of the chase. Grabbing me under my ribs, he flew us to the ground. With no effort at all, he held me up like a little baby with his hands under my arms and looked me in the eyes. His were twinkling beneath the moonlight, and were the darkest of blacks I'd ever seen.

"The only problem with you being in this form is that I don't get to have my way with you at the end of the chase. Next time, you stay in human form," he growled.

Oh, my God. I cursed myself black and blue for being in cat form because I wanted to know what Isaac would have done with me.

He rubbed his cheek against mine. "Now I must hunt. Dare to accompany me?" He smiled.

Purring, I rubbed my face against his again, while reaching my mind out. *Would be my pleasure,* I said through our new connection. He set me down and sped off toward the area where we both already scented some prey.

Chapter
Fourteen

The following three weeks were the happiest of my life so far. Isaac and I attended classes every day with Darik, and every lunch, we sat in the cafeteria with Ty. I really enjoyed getting to know him. And the more comfortable he got with us, the less stuttering there was in his sentences. I also discovered Ty was strong when, a few days over the weeks, he'd come to my place and there he met Xavier, Adan, Jezanna and Caelen. Even though we had a guest present, Adan and Darik wouldn't let up on my training of swordplay and martial arts.

It served as a constant reminder that there could come a day that would doom my good mood.

It was in those times I witnessed Ty at his strongest. He joined in with the martial arts, and once he started sparing with Adan, he won. It made it hard to believe he was blind. Ty explained his mum made him study the techniques so he wouldn't be picked on so much, not that he ever used it against the dickheads we knew, because honestly, it wouldn't be a fair fight. Ty could kick arse.

Other days, when we weren't training, I got to play the Xbox against Jeremiah and Xavier. Of course, I kept beating their butts every time. The steam coming from Jeremiah's ears was always a pleasure.

Gregory had a go at teaching me to cook, but after so many attempts and failing them miserably, he gave up and became everyone's personal chef. Okay, well, mainly mine, since no one else really needed to eat normal food except Gregory and me.

Each night, I got to run with them while they hunted for food. Most nights, it was animals. Still, I wasn't so stupid to believe they'd left humans off the menu, and one night, I was witness to their drinking. A hunter stumbled in our area as we were out playing. Isaac, who thought I wasn't admiring him, crept up on his prey and sank his teeth in for a feed. As I stood there watching him, his eyes met mine. It caused primal emotions from me. I wanted to be the one Isaac fed from. I wanted his teeth in me while he was inside of me.

Lust caused me to flush. Isaac removed his fangs and was in front of me in seconds. His mouth met my urgent one. At the time, there was no thought to our audience. I moaned when his tongue demanded entrance. Jumping up, I wrapped my legs around his waist. Isaac's hand went to my butt, where he ground my heated core against his firm dick.

A need pulled at me. I wanted Isaac right there and then. That was until he had to go and be the sensible one and break our connection. I swayed when I lost his support and found him metres away from me. Both of us panted hard.

Jeremiah, Darik and Xavier burst out laughing. Kicking at the ground, I swore at them under my breath and walked back to the house solemnly.

I didn't understand his restraint. His not wanting to go further with me was like a hit to the stomach. However, I understood we couldn't do it in front of people. *Though… No, Leila, just no.*

Also over the three weeks, Jezanna had become like a sister to me. We shared everything with each other. I'd never had that before, a girlfriend to talk to about anything. I ended up asking her if she had the same problem I did every month. She laughed and said, "Of course I do. Just because I'm a vampire, it doesn't mean my body isn't the same as a human's. I still have my monthlies. I can still fall pregnant. My insides are still very much alive. The only differences we have with humans are we're strong, faster and also need blood to survive."

Apparently, most of the vampire stories were filled with lies.

She told me that when it was that time for her, she wore a charm her mother had given to her to help with anyone else scenting *it*. Turned out she had two charms and gave one to me. *Thank God!*

It was towards the end of the few weeks, I could tell Isaac grew more worried about the fact Hamish and Seraphine hadn't returned. I tried to reassure him everything was okay, though I still had doubt myself. When I was over at his house one night, having dinner, I went to the toilet and overheard Isaac telling everyone he would give it until Saturday the following week for his guards to return. If they didn't return, they'd be leaving. He tried to bring it up with me a couple of times, but every time he did, I either changed the subject or distracted him in other ways.

I couldn't handle telling him I wouldn't go with them when they left. And I refused to think about it, because it hurt too much. Knowing I could possibly be losing my world soon was too much to bear. Every time the thought filtered into my mind, it left behind a residual thread of agony, one that burned its way into my soul, leaving me breathless and near tears. It was much easier to ignore the possibility and pretend everything would be fine.

It was Saturday, just a week before Isaac would be leaving with his family, when I asked, "So, what are you doing tonight?"

As we sat on my bed together, the rest of the house was quiet. Ty had just left with Adan, who'd offered to give him a lift home and then he would continue on to Isaac's house and keep an eye out there. I had the music going from the stereo on my desk, which once lived in the lounge room, but I transferred it there so our guards for the night, Darik and Xavier, couldn't overhear our conversation.

"I was thinking of joining the others at Boozers. More of my people have come to see me." He shuddered.

A couple of nights earlier, Caelen had come over from being at Boozers and told us there'd been an increase of vampires in town, ones who travelled to swear their allegiance to Isaac. Isaac hated the thought of any of it. However, I hoped one day he'd accept his responsibilities, because I did believe he was the right vampire to run things.

"Would you want to come with me?" he asked. "Although, I've been a bad influence on you. I can see you've had too many late nights." He ran a finger gently under my eye, before he placed a kiss there.

"Are you saying I look like crap?"

He laughed and pulled back so I could see him shake his head. "Always so blunt. But no, I'm not. You're *always* beautiful to me."

I blushed, which I seemed to do a lot when Isaac used sweet words. "Thanks," I mumbled and quickly continued, "Anyway, I was thinking of having an early night." I raised my brows up and down quickly.

Only he didn't get it.

"If that's what you wish, I'll get going then..."

For a 398-year-old guy, he sure could be so dense sometimes. Still, it made me smile and think he was the cutest thing out there.

"Isaac." I groaned in embarrassment for having to spell it out for him. My cheeks heated once again. "What I meant was I wanted an early *night*." I sent him a wink. My gorgeous man looked puzzled still. Looking away, I blurted out quickly, "Isaac, will you spend the night here with me?" I felt him freeze.

Great. I'd stunned the guy into shock. He should have known it was coming. Sure we did other things, but I'd been hinting at taking our relationship further. I was just about ready to jump his bones. I swore, I was so worked up to take the next step with Isaac my panties were constantly wet anytime I was around him.

Doubt grew in my bones, because he'd still said nothing or even moved. "I mean you don't have to. Gregory probably won't like it, and think of all the hell we'd get when the guys found out. Look, I get it. It's okay. It's... all right." I went to move off the bed, my heart sinking, pain travelling into my chest at his rejection, but he grabbed my arm.

"Leila, it's not that. I would love to stay here with you, to hold you all night—"

"I'm sure we can come up with better things than that." I gave him a sly look. He smiled, but it didn't shine in his eyes like it had ever since he kissed me that first time. He seemed distracted.

"Another night perhaps, when I can pay all my attention to just you. However, then I'm afraid I'll never let you go again."

I gulped loudly and stuttered, "O-okay."

He stood quickly. "I must go."

"Wait, what, why? Isaac, is something wrong? Have I—"

He silenced me with a kiss and left in a flash so I couldn't ask any more questions, leaving me frustrated and confused. Again. My gut twisted. You'd think he'd know me better. No one left me curious, and I knew something was going on. Now I had to find out what.

Darik would have gone with Isaac, so that left me to contend with Xavier. My best option was to sneak out my window. I was already in the right clothes for a late night run, black leggings, running shoes and a hooded black jumper. The nights had turned cold in the last week.

With a jump, I was out the window, only to stumble back against the house when a face appeared in front of me.

"Curiosity killed the cat." Xavier smiled.

"Don't worry about curiosity. You'll do a damn fine job of it. You scared the bejesus out of me, Xavier."

"I won't apologise for it. However, you should to me, for

trying to sneak away while under my care, which could lead to having me killed by my master. I knew the moment Isaac left it wouldn't take you long to want to find out why he disappeared so suddenly."

Placing my hands on my hips, I glared at him. "Do you know why, Xavier?"

He looked everywhere but at me. "No," he lied.

"Well, that's all right." I shrugged. "I'll find out for the both of us." I started to walk off, until he grabbed my arm.

"Please, don't go."

Sighing, I said, "I can't do that, Xavier."

"If I have to tie you down, I will, to prevent what will happen."

Spinning quickly, so my face was inches from his, I snapped, "You can try, but it won't happen. Xavier, you can either come with me or stay. But no matter what, I'm going." I knew what I was about to say was pretty low, but the way Xavier wanted me to stay here told me—and had me more worried—that I needed to find out what was going on. "Or I'll tell Isaac you hit on me."

"I would never hit a woman. My master knows this." He looked perplexed.

God, were all vampire so dense? "No, Xavier, it means you tried to kiss me, bed me." I totally regretted it as soon as it was out of my mouth, because Xavier looked flabbergasted and hurt. "I'm sorry, Xavier, but I have to do this."

"You're a cunning piece of work." He sighed. "Just don't curse me when I've warned you to not go."

"I won't. Promise." I crossed my finger over my heart. "Thanks. You ready?" He gave me a grim nod and we left.

It took us longer than usual, because I stayed in human form, but eventually we got to Isaac's just as he climbed out of the car with Darik. They both looked sick with concern. Had they taken the longest route home for us to arrive at the same time? Why *did* they take so long? I also noticed two new cars in the driveway. Great, they had company and I looked like crap after sweating to get there. Didn't matter. I could still manage a short stop over, and if no one saw me or heard me or even scented me, then it wasn't my fault, was it?

I waited a moment after Isaac and Darik went inside. Then I turned to Xavier's still grim expression.

"Wait here for me," I said. He nodded. My head jutted back as I studied him. He'd agreed too quickly for my liking.

Ignoring the foreboding lurking in the air, I crept over to the door. With senses attuned to my surroundings and my power hiding my own presence from those within the house, I stopped just outside. When I felt no one on the other side of the door, I quietly opened it and sneaked down the hallway towards the kitchen, where I heard the voices coming from.

"I told her to leave, but she won't," Jeremiah growled.

"What could she want?" Isaac asked.

"She won't say. She's waiting in the parlour for you."

Stuff it, the parlour was at the front of the house. The part I'd just sneaked by, but I hadn't sensed anything. Before I was caught, I quickly bolted silently down to the front of the house and hid in Gregory's bedroom, which was opposite the parlour. I waited and heard three sets of heavy footsteps coming my way, and then the parlour door was opened.

"Isaac, darling. It's been too long." As soon as I heard the high-pitched voice, I wanted to rip the head off whoever it belonged to.

"MaryJane, how did you find me?"

"Aren't you happy to see me?" Her voice was closer to the door now, which meant she was walking towards Isaac.

"Of course, I just didn't expect you."

"Yes, well, you should have known I would have been able to follow you anywhere. As I am sure you had sensed I was here. These things happen after sharing blood with one another."

Isaac, Isaac, Isaac, does your taste in blood donors come from your arse? First, the two bimbos at Boozers, and now, this piece of...

It took all my strength not to run into that room and beat her to a pulp. I clenched my fists and bit my tongue in case my body decided to listen to my brain.

"Still, that doesn't answer why you've come."

"I wish to speak with you alone."

Don't you dare leave him, boys. If you do, there's no telling how long she'll keep her dirty claws off him, and then if that happens, there's no telling what I may do.

"We'll not leave if you have your people still in the room," Darik barked at her. I smiled.

"Very well. Leave us." I heard shuffling. It sounded as if at least five others had been in there with them, not including Darik and Jeremiah.

"Isaac?" Jeremiah asked.

"It's fine." He sighed.

"Let's go to the kitchen," Darik ordered, more footfalls moving towards the back of the house. Still, I could feel two more presences other than Isaac's and crap-head's just on the other side of the door.

"Leave," Jeremiah said.

"Not unless you do as well. I'm paid to guard her," a new voice said.

"Fine." They stayed in the hallway.

Leaning against the bedroom door, I was able to hear what was being said with my heightened sense. "Isaac, why are you standing so far away? Come sit by me." *Don't you dare, punk.* "That's better." *I am going to stake you myself, Isaac.*

"I've missed you, Isaac. That's why I'm here."

"I'd asked you to accompany me, but you refused."

What? He'd asked her to move with him?

"I was silly to think I could live without you. It near killed me to do so."

"And now?"

"Now, I'm hoping you will welcome me back into your arms… and bed."

What the hell? Who does she think she is? That stupid, naïve slut!

"Isaac, why are you delaying to answer me? Is there someone else?" She sounded crazed. I could hear her sniffing at Isaac.

Yeah, sniff that, witch. I'm all over him.

"Why can I smell another, a human girl? Why, Isaac?" She screamed. "Who is she to you? Tell me now," she ordered.

Yeah, tell her, Isaac. Don't take her crap. Set her straight, or I will run in there and do it for you. Does it matter if I use my fists? Or murder her in the process? No, I don't think it would.

The silence was crushing me.

"It's nothing. She means nothing to me. She's someone who has a crush and refuses to leave me alone. A plaything, really. But now you're here, I have no need of her."

Every word tore me deep inside.

A plaything? Was he that bored with life he thought he'd play with mine?

Did I mean nothing to him?

I mustn't if it was that easy to brush me aside for that bitch.

Oh, God.

No!

Clenching my teeth, I threw the door wide, ready to stride into that room and tell him where he could stick his thoughts.

Jeremiah and his friend's eyes widened. "Oh, shit." Jeremiah gasped.

"Jeremiah?" Isaac called from the parlour. Jeremiah quickly pushed me back into Greg's room, shutting the door in my face, and held the handle so I couldn't get back out.

"Don't do this," he whispered through the door. "Now is not the time."

Fuck it! It was the perfect time… before my emotions and mind caught up with what my heart was already feeling.

Dammit… too late. I tumbled to the floor on my hands and knees. I couldn't seem to get in enough breath. My forehead touched the carpet. Why couldn't I breathe?

"Is everything all right, Jensen?" MaryJane called.

"Yes, mistress, everything's fine."

No. Everything wasn't fine. He couldn't have meant those words. He wouldn't, would he? I didn't know. I didn't know… how could I not know? I thought I knew him, but maybe I didn't. Maybe it'd just been a front all along.

"Who is she? I didn't feel or smell her? How is that possible?" Jensen asked.

"None of your business," Jeremiah quietly scolded.

The door opened. I looked up from the floor to his eyes as tears slid down my cheeks.

Another crack fractured my heart when I saw pity in Jeremiah's eyes.

No.

It hurts, it hurts too much.

"What are you doing here? He doesn't mean anything he says. He doesn't," he whispered in my ear.

Scoffing, I scrubbed at my eyes, but they wouldn't stop leaking. "Really, Jeremiah? Can you be 100 percent sure? Because right now, all I have is doubt, like you do. I can see it. I can *taste* it on you. Oh, God, J, why? Why has he done this to me?" I couldn't stop my voice rising at the end. Only Jeremiah didn't want me to be overheard. He picked me up in his arms and carried me outside through his patio door.

Did he also know I didn't think my legs would work? He placed me down gently and I managed to stand. *Well, good on me.* Even though I wanted to crumble to the ground, I stood tall. The rage and anger had arrived.

"Do you feel the same?" I snarled at Jeremiah. "Is your whole family in on it?" I yelled, knowing we were far enough away from the house without anyone inside hearing. Not that I cared. Hell, I didn't even care we had an audience with Jensen, who stood near.

I snorted and shook my head, glaring at Jeremiah. "Yeah, I

can picture it now. Isaac saying, 'Let's have some fun with this girl. She has no one. She'll enjoy it while it lasts.'"

"Leila, stop," Jeremiah growled low. "We've never been like that. We care for you; you should know that."

"Should I? Right now I don't." I pointed toward the house. "You tell the idiot in there that unless he comes and tells me any different, it's over."

He nodded. I felt movement behind me and knew from the familiar scent it was Xavier.

"You'll see, Leila. He will come," Jeremiah uttered.

"We'll see. I'll be at Boozers."

"Don't go there, please."

"Don't, just... don't." I looked over Jeremiah's shoulder to Jensen. "And what the hell are you looking at, hey? Havin' fun watching me lose it? If you say anything, I'll beat the living crap out of you." I turned and stomped away.

"Watch her, take care of her," Jeremiah said to Xavier.

"I will and I'm sorry, sir."

"It's all right. I know how it happened. She's a stubborn twit."

Chapter Fifteen

"That stupid, cold-hearted leech. How dare he make me feel this way. Why would he do this? Crap on toast, this sucks, like he does." A laugh escaped me. "No, I can't break. I have to wait, and by God, he'd better show up and tell me he was just conning her. Yeah, and then… then I'll rip him a new arsehole. After that, I'll enjoy shredding her to pieces with my claws for ever thinking she could have him and for being a part of his past. Why in the hell did he ever get with her in the first place? She's nothing but a ho-bag hooker. Ordering him around, she's crazy." I shrugged. "I could offer to beat the craziness out of her. Yeah, that would be nice of me, and I'd get to enjoy it at the same time."

"Leila, you need to calm down. Beating MaryJane will get you nowhere. She's strong, very strong."

Hell, had I said all of that aloud? Oh, well.

"Thanks for the advice, Xavier, but I can handle myself. Wait." I stopped and turned to face him. "You know her?"

"I've been with Isaac for a very long time."

"How long were they together? What does he see in her? Why the fuck is she here?"

"I don't think I should speak of it behind my master's back."

"Xavier, please. Please try and help me understand it."

He shook his head, his eyes to the ground. "I'm sorry, but I can't."

I harrumphed, stomped my foot, threw my hands up in the air, before turning back around and continuing. I wanted to push him, to threaten him, but really, I didn't want to get him in trouble. Besides, if I hadn't threatened him in the first place, I wouldn't have heard what I did and I wouldn't have been feeling like I was slowly dying on the inside.

Once we made it to Boozers, I went straight in, ignoring the strong, disgusting smells wafting up my nose. I strode straight up to the bar and sat down. The place was quiet, roughly around a dozen vampires. They looked at me hungrily, until Xavier stood in front of my view.

Banging my head on the bar sounded appealing. I wanted to stop my mind from overreacting, stop the spinning of my stomach as I fought to keep dinner down.

Most of all, I wanted to stop the darkness from seeping its way into my soul once again.

Just when Isaac had lit it.

He'd shattered it even more than it had been.

"Want anything there, miss?" I turned from Xavier's back to see a vampire bartender. His deep, dark blue eyes twinkled while he gazed at me. Then I felt like laughing when he tossed his silky, long red hair over his shoulder.

Shaking my head, I said, "Yeah, give me some shots and keep them coming."

Xavier spoke over his shoulder, his body and eyes still on everyone. "I don't think—"

"That's right, Xavier. I don't want to think," I said and looked to the vamp behind the bar. He hadn't moved. "Come on, I don't have all night."

"Feisty one, aren't you? I like that. First one's on the house."

Tapping my foot against the stool, I waited for my first shot. He brought it, sat it down in front of me and it looked a lot like a small cup of blood. Shrugging, I picked it up and went to drink it down, until Xavier's hand came down on mine.

"No blood, Irele." Xavier snarled. "You know better than that. You can smell she's not one of us."

Irele laughed and took the shot back from my grip. "Worth a try. She might've enjoyed the buzz from my blood."

"Yeah, and make her yours for the night. It's not going to happen," Xavier said.

My guess, Irele's blood wasn't toxic, but did something else to you entirely.

"All right, boys, settle down," I cut in. "Listen here, Irele, if you try that crap on me again, I'll go outside, carve myself a nice, long, pointy stake, bring it back in here and shove it in up your arse, then heart. You understand?"

"And she means it, mate." I turned my deathly glare to find Caelen making his way up to the bar. "Up a little late, aren't you, love?"

Scoffing, I muttered, "Yeah."

Irele came back and put the shot of some concoction in front of me. It had a light creamy brown colour on the top and a darker clear brown underneath. As Caelen sat next to me, I gulped it down and then coughed my lungs up.

"I'm guessing it's your first time drinking." Caelen smiled.

"No." I heaved. He knew I was lying.

"Rough night, love?" He turned a worried gaze to Xavier, who nodded, and then his gaze came back to me.

I took another shot and drank it down, that time without the coughing. *Yeah, look at me, I'm a pro already.*

"You could say that," I said and then added, "MaryJane's in town."

"That bitch, you don't need to worry about her. Our young master only has eyes for you."

I snorted and the next shot went down the wrong way, which brought on another round of coughing. After my lungs kicked back into gear, I turned in my seat to look at Caelen.

"I overheard him telling said bitch that I meant nothing to him because now she's back, so he can move on with her."

It was his turn to choke on a sip of his drink. "No way. He wouldn't say that."

"Then why did I hear it with my own ears?"

"Bloody hell," he uttered. "I don't know. But he couldn't have meant it though."

"He has one chance to tell me he didn't. I'm waiting for him here."

"Irele mate, keep them coming and put them on my tab."

"No, I can pay for them," I said, reaching behind to my back pocket and found nothing. Crap. "Okay, but I'll pay you back." I had some money at home.

Some time passed and I was feeling light-headed, warm and goddamn good. Caelen was the funniest guy, as well as some of his other mates I met. There was Josh, a tall dude with tattoos all over his arms, and to show them off, he was wearing a see-through tank top, with leather pants. I asked him about the tats. I didn't think vamps could get them because of their healing ability. He laughed at me, patted my head and said he got them before he was turned. Didn't I feel silly for not thinking of it. With Josh was his girlfriend Trixie. She was also tall, slim and beautiful, wearing a short vinyl skirt and a boob tube. Her hair was dyed fire-engine red, which she pulled up into a high ponytail. Another one who sat with us was Blake. He looked too young to be in the bar; he seemed only fourteen. However, Trixie told me later that he was changed by a paedophile vampire. I gasped as the shock hit me. She quickly reassured me Blake had ended up killing his sire and by doing so, not only saved himself, but others like him.

Last in our group was Toby, and his twin sister, Daphne, who, like Isaac, Jeremiah and Jezanna, were born vampires. They both had sky-blue eyes and light blonde, almost white hair. They'd also lost their parents, only it wasn't by Gerald's hands; instead, they were hunted and murdered by vampire hunters. I hated to think there were people out there who thought it right to hunt down all kinds of vampires. Even before knowing there were good ones among them, who only wished to live a somewhat normal life.

All had come to town in search of Isaac's leadership.

As I sat there and watched them, it was easy to enjoy their company. We laughed, talked and none of them were afraid of my eyes. I nearly forgot the reason I was there. Until the door to the bar opened and Isaac's scent drifted down the hall and straight to me.

It was like all the sounds around me stopped and I found my breath stopping with them. Then I saw him dressed in black jeans and a long-sleeved red silk top.

He'd come alone.

My heart skipped a beat. I started to run towards him, smiling, thinking I was out of my mind to have thought Isaac meant those things.

But I should have looked into his eyes. I should have taken notice of his stiffness, because then I would have seen my answer before I saw what came through the hall a few steps behind him.

Mary-stupid-Jane.

Hell, no wonder they were an item. She was stunning, real model material, with long legs covered in tight, black, low riding pants. She also wore a tight, low-cut, long-sleeved white shirt showing off her large breasts.

All the more to hate you for, my dear.

She had her long, dark brown, wavy hair out and it flowed down around her shoulders.

My steps skidded to a stop. My smile vanished and the alcohol I consumed threatened to make an appearance. I looked to Isaac and… oh, God, his eyes were cold, but they also held pity—or was it concern?

He came right up to me, only a step away. I could have reached out and touched him. I wanted to so bad. But more than anything, I wanted him to reach out to me, to have his body invade my personal space like his intoxicating scent was.

However, I knew I would never have any of those things again.

"I am so sorry, Leila," he uttered.

My eyes were wide and filling with tears. I couldn't hide the shock or hurt.

He'd taken the last ounce of hope from within me, breaking me and dimming all the light he'd lit.

"I let you in." *To my heart, to my home and my life.*

I felt Xavier and Caelen come to stand at my sides, just as *she* stood next to Isaac's. Her hand went to his arm and she smiled a very satisfied, cunning smile. I couldn't take my gaze away from her hand. I wanted, no, I needed to break her perfect small hand off. That would have made me feel so much better.

"So this is the little girl craving for your attention," Mary-Jane said.

I brought my gaze up to hers.

"Oh, look at her. She's going to cry. How pathetic. You pay a little attention to something and it attaches itself to you."

My head cleared and I blinked to rid my tears.

Instead, I pasted the look of hate on my face. "I'm pathetic? And how old are you, deary? As old as my grandmother—no, my great, great grandmother, and I bet you're just as loose as she would have been if she lived as long as you have."

I could hear so many sharp intakes of breath. Others laughed, like Jeremiah, Caelen and Darik. I even noticed Jensen hide his behind his hand.

"You little snake," she hissed. Her hand raised to hit me and I would have welcomed it, knowing I could hit her back, but Isaac took hold of her arm.

"She's not worth it," he said.

Looking to Isaac, I could see he meant it. He glared at me with open hostility in his eyes.

"Harsh, lad," Caelen uttered.

"So true, Isaac," MaryJane purred. "I don't wish to get myself dirty. Thank you, darling." She turned into him and wrapped her arms around his waist as he wrapped an arm around her.

I felt it then.

My heart breaking.

It hurt so much more than it did before. He smashed it and threw it away, threw everything I had into a pit of hell.

Clenching my fists, my nails biting into my palms, I refused to lose it in front of them.

"Leila, let's get out of here," Caelen said.

"No!" I barked then taking a deep breath, I continued, "I mean, I'm leaving. But I don't want you to come with me. I don't need any of you. You're all Isaac's, and everything stops here, now. No more guarding, no more friendship. I don't need anything. Anyone." Without looking at any of them, I left.

Nearing the hall, I heard MaryJane ask, "Guarding? Why were they guarding her?"

Only no one answered.

~

I managed to make it home and inside before sliding to the floor and letting it all out. The tears and pain came with force.

The agony was a reminder to let no one in.

If only I'd asked more questions. I shouldn't have let my hormones take over, but I did, and I only had myself to blame. All the hurt, sorrow, betrayal, I only had myself to blame for that too. The bitch MaryJane was right about one thing. Isaac paid attention to me and I did attach myself to him. I thought I knew him. I didn't. He had a long past, which I really knew nothing about.

He wasn't mine.

My arms circled my waist as another hysterical outburst came when the realisation hit me. I wouldn't hear his voice, his laugh. I wouldn't see his smile. I wouldn't have his touch—nothing—any longer.

Everything inside of me wanted to go back there and beat him senseless, but maybe I deserved it all. Maybe it was a life lesson. One I would remember for the rest of my years. One that would make me stronger, make me realise I didn't need anyone. I had to safeguard myself from everyone who showed me anything.

Stupid, stupid me. Stupid, stupid feelings.

CHAPTER
SIXTEEN

Darkness surrounds me. Every way I turn, I see nothing but black. My heart beats hard in my chest. My hands tremble along with my legs. I want to run, to scream, but I don't.

Because I know I'm waiting.

It isn't until I see two small red dots in the distance that I relax somewhat.

"Yes," I whisper. "That's what I'm waiting for."

The dots drift closer and closer.

And in a blink of an eye, which always makes me jump, they're right in front of me, so close I can reach out and touch them... No, touch the face that belongs to those red eyes.

I want to.

I need to.

Even though a small amount of fright fills me, I still know I'm safe.

The red eyes study me.

"You're mine," the voice growls...

I woke with a fright from someone banging on the front door, right behind me. I'd fallen asleep where I'd landed last night. I'd ran out of energy and couldn't be bothered moving, so I'd curled up in a ball and cried myself to sleep.

Crap, it was Monday. Meaning, I had lectures if I decided to go. I wondered if he'd be there. Could I stand seeing him? Could I stand all the taunting once word got out Isaac had turned to someone else? Then again, if I didn't go, they'd think the worst, that I'd either killed myself over him or I was at home brooding in self-pity.

Which really didn't sound too bad to me.

Still, I was stronger than that. I'd put up with so much before, so what was a little more? Even when I still felt dead inside.

I jumped when there was another knock at the door. I'd forgotten someone was standing out there. And no, I wouldn't let myself, my stupid brain, jump to the wrong conclusions. It wasn't him.

"Who..." I cleared my dry throat and started again, "Who is it?"

"It's Jezanna."

Closing my eyes, I begged, "Please, just go away."

"I can't, Leila. I have nowhere else to go."

What? How? Quickly standing, I opened the door to find Jezanna there, holding two suitcases in her hands. "Oh, Leila." She sighed, taking in my pathetic form.

"Don't." I shook my head. "What's happened?"

"I told Isaac what he's doing is ridiculous. It was then Mary-Jane said if I didn't like what my brother is doing I should leave. Therefore, I did. I don't like what he's done to you when it's unnecessary. Leila, he's only taken up with that witch to—"

I held up my hand to stop her from saying any more.

"I really don't want to hear anything about him. Sorry."

She nodded, her eyes sad. "I understand." She shifted from one foot to another. "So will you have me here?"

What would my uncle think? "I-uh. I really... I can't have your brother coming here because you are. It's going to be hard enough to see him at school."

"I understand." She looked upset and turned to leave.

Shit. She'd left her own house because she didn't agree with what *he* had done. She was here, because she'd stood up for me.

"Jezanna, wait." She looked over her shoulder, giving me a pouty look that would have guys eating out of her hands. "Don't look at me like that, girl. I ain't no guy to fall at your feet. Still, you can stay, but *only* you. I don't want any others coming here. And we'll figure out something to tell my uncle."

She ran up to me and gave me a big hug. "Thank you, thank you. Except we have just one problem. Jeremiah wouldn't let me leave without someone guarding me."

"Oh, Jezza. Who?" I mumbled. Xavier appeared in front of me, smiling shyly.

I sighed loudly and moved aside, waving my arm inside the front door. "All right, whatever. Come on in. I have to get ready for classes, so make yourselves at home. There's a spare room you'll have to share. But under no circumstances are we to speak of Is—" My stupid voice cracked. "Him, not one word. You're here, because Jezanna guilted me into it, and because no matter what I think of *him*, I still like you guys." I followed them through and shut the door, only to pause, turn and ask, "Wait, you're not going to double-cross me or something, right? Because if that's all you're here for, then leave right now. I-I couldn't handle it. Sticking a dagger in me would be less painful right now."

Jezanna walked over to stand in front of me. Taking my hands in hers, tears shone in her own eyes, like mine.

"I will only bring him up this once and then never again. None of us, even his people, are happy with what he's done to you. He'll not listen to our reasoning. He thinks he knows best. We want you to know that what he's done has no involvement to what we think of you. We all care for you, Leila. You have become a part of our clan. Nothing will change that." She wrapped her arms around me.

"Here, here," Xavier whispered. I couldn't hold it back any longer. I broke down once again, this time in Jezanna's arms.

I still had people who cared. I wasn't alone. I didn't have to be alone. My world had not ended.

Only a part of my soul had left me when he'd crushed me the way he did.

Eventually, I pulled away, wiped my face and said, "Enough of this emotional crap. Life goes on, right, and that begins with college. Sorry, for being a blubbering idiot."

"You don't need to apologize. Go and get ready. We'll drive you. Otherwise, you'll be late. We already understand why you'd want to go, and we think you're a strong woman, Leila Morgin." Jezanna smiled.

Snorting away the compliment, I said, "Hey, I didn't see a car out there."

Both of them had a cunning grin upon their faces, but it was Xavier who answered, "Jezanna had me park at the end of your drive, behind some trees."

"Smart girl. If you had of shown up in a car, I wouldn't have answered the door in the first place. You're nearly as tricky as me. Though, now you're living with me, I'm sure I could teach you a few extra things."

We pulled into the car park with all of us in the front. Xavier was driving, Jezanna in the middle and then me. She grabbed my hand as my heart rate accelerated when I saw a certain Hummer parked near us.

Can I do this? I knew I was brave. I knew I could be strong, but would all of it fall away once seeing him? Would he try to talk to me? Would he want to explain? Question was, did I want to hear anything that came from his mouth? There was only one way to find out. I opened the door. The cool air from the overcast day rushed into the car, bringing on a shudder. Funnily, usually the wind didn't affect me.

"We'll be here to collect you after schooling has ended," Xavier offered.

"Thanks, guys. I, uh, I really appreciate everything." I nodded. Not wanting to hear a response, I quickly closed the door. Pulling my hood up over my head, I turned and made my way into the building. I had history, with him.

Time to put on my big-girl knickers.

I walked in with my heart near jumping from my body. I didn't look around and kept my hood up. My heart slowed a little once I saw our—my—desk was empty. I slid my backpack off and sat down. I could feel all eyes were on me. Taking no notice of them, I grabbed out my history textbook and pencil case. *I can do this. He isn't here and that makes it better. I have this under control.*

"Can you move so I can sit next to my boyfriend?"

Fuck me drunk.

Of course I knew straight away who that annoying voice belonged to. How could *he* bring her here? Why would she want to bother with school? Why did he even bother himself? I kept my gaze down on the desk, my hood hiding most of my face. Breathing deeply through my nose to calm my heart was a big mistake. His scent filled me up and I felt he was standing to the side of the desk, while she-devil was in front.

The room filled with whispers and giggles.

Jenna was kind enough to say something aloud, "Oh, my God, he dumped her already. Come on, who's paying up? I won the bet."

Then a guy laughed and said, "Any wonder she got dumped. I would have done the same if that hottie came my way. Then again, I wouldn't have touched her in the first place."

"Hello, anyone in there at all? I said move." MaryJane tapped the desk with her knuckles and then sighed. "Isaac, does she have brain damage as well as her deformity?" The whole class erupted in laughter.

My fist clenched in my lap. Couldn't I just kill the bitch? I grabbed my stuff and moved to the opposite desk in the other back corner. No one usually sat there. No sooner had I flopped down when the chair next to me was pulled out and Darik sat in it.

"Le—"

"Don't." I spat. "I don't want to hear it." Pulling the hood down farther over my eyes, I pleaded, "Please, if you were ever really a friend of mine, please don't talk to me. For my sake, leave me alone. I only ask you take care of Ty. Protect him from her cruel words."

"He won't want to be around us with her there. He won't agree with what my sire is doing, like others don't—"

"Darik, please, just—"

"If he chooses to be around us, then you have my word she will not harm him in any way."

I nodded and said no more. The door opened and Dr Geffen came in and began talking. I was grateful he didn't say anything to me about having my hood up through class. I needed it to hide the view to my left.

The one positive thing I achieved was writing down different ways I could murder she-devil. I didn't even care if Darik looked at what I was doing. He gave no indication he was, so I continued.

By the end of the session, I felt remotely cheerful. I'd come up with 100 gruesome ways to kill her. My favourite was a little boring to some maybe, but the best for me was looking into her eyes as I pushed the stake through her chest. Only I wouldn't pull it out and end her life quickly. I'd have to have a little fun first.

Okay, I was sounding like a lunatic. I would harm a person who was endangering someone I cared for, but *he* meant nothing to me anymore. Besides, at least I hoped he suffered enough by just being around her.

Darik rose from his seat straight away and quickly placed his hand on my shoulder before he left. I waited for everyone else to exit the classroom and destroyed the evidence of my craziness, ripping it into tiny pieces and throwing it in the bin. At least it had made me happy for a little while.

By lunch, I made my way to the library, in need of some

quiet time. The whole way there, I heard a range of jibes at my expense from those still immature enough to revel in gossip and low digs. It was getting to me. For once, I'd hoped maybe at least a few would be able to put aside their torment and consider I may be hurting enough since I'd been dumped, thrown away and made a fool of.

In the library, I found Jim at his desk. He looked up smiling as I approached, but his worry was transparent in his eyes. No doubt he'd already heard what happened. It was *that* small of a campus that even the staff was brought up to speed on the student gossip. I wished I'd never brought *him* here to meet the librarian. But I'd wanted Jim to meet the man who'd made me happy, content. I regretted it. I regretted so much.

Placing on my pretend smile, I said, "Hey, Jim, how you doing today?"

"Miss Morgin, so good to see you. My day's been fine, and yours?" He gave me that look, which said, 'Don't lie to me, young lady.'

"Not too good."

He sighed. "I know. However, you're strong enough to get through this, but, if you need anything, you know to just ask. And you know, he didn't deserve you anyway. Took you away from me and your corner. So get back to it. It's missed you."

My bottom lip trembled. "Thanks," I uttered and walked off before I started to bawl like a baby.

I hated crying. I'd get snotty, my eyes would go all red and puffy and then sometimes I'd get that mouth bubble thing going on from all the slobbering. It wasn't something for me, and I tried not to do it too much, especially in front of people.

I had already cried enough.

Without realising, I found myself rubbing my chest. My heart felt raw.

Would that feeling ever go away?

Shaking my head, I opened my lunch bag. Jezanna had organised my food for me while I'd been showering. It was one of her special sandwiches, a bit of everything included in it. She knew it was my favourite. It was so big I had trouble getting my mouth around it. Still, it was way worth the struggle. She had also packed some biscuits, an apple and a pear. If she kept living with me, I would definitely appoint her my lunch wench every day. She could take over from Gregory doing it.

I knew that she-devil wouldn't allow Gregory to cook for me again. And even though I'd also pushed them all away, I'd miss them.

Shuffling footsteps came from the right side of me. I looked around to see Sofia hiding behind a bookcase. What was she doing up here? Had she come to make fun of me to then run back to Jenna so they could have a big laugh?

"What do *you* want?" I asked.

She came out from her hidden spot and took a few hesitant steps over to me then stopped.

Looking up, I held back my gasp. Besides the fact she was blushing, her perfect pale face had a big black bruise covering her right cheek and eye. And even though she tried to hide it under a heap of makeup, it was too obvious to go unnoticed.

"What happened to you?"

She shifted uncomfortably. "Nothing. I, well… Sorry, I don't know what I'm doing here." She shrugged. "I heard you came here, so I thought I'd come and have a look, and yep, here you are. But now… now I don't think… No, it's useless. No one can help. God," she groaned. "I've gone and said too much and you probably think I'm a freak. Oh, sorry."

"Don't fret. But why all the gibbering and why would *you* come and seek me out? Are you after an exclusive about the breakup so you can run and tell the rest about the find you made? Well, sorry, it's not happening. You can run along now." I flicked my hand at her in a shooing motion.

Closing my eyes in exhaustion, I placed my head in my hands. Hadn't I already been through enough?

Shaking my head to rid the confusion, I glared up at her. She couldn't hide the quiver that passed over her body when she met my mismatched gaze. It happened to many people. Except Isa—ah, Jezanna.

Sofia quickly looked away and down to her hands, which were clasped together in front of her, and then she glanced behind her. Did she expect to find someone? Obviously it wasn't only being in my presence that had her so jittery. Scared even. Still, why would she come to me? All she had to do was talk to one of her many friends.

The silence was killing me. I watched her flick her long, dark red hair over her shoulder and blow at her fringe to get it out of her eyes. Dear God, then she went back to having her hands together in front of her.

Am I going to have to do all the work? Seems like it.

"So, what do you want?" I asked again before taking a bite of my apple.

"I don't know," she whispered. "I'm sorry. Maybe I shouldn't have come to find you, b-but I need help. I have no one else to go to. No one who would believe me. I thought you may, but then again, maybe not. It's strange. It's all too much, no one will understand. Except, maybe, you. Then again, why would you help me?" She shrugged. "I've done nothing for you except be mean and I'm really sorry for it. I am."

Tears welled in her eyes and then overflowed down her cheeks. Still, she continued, "I can't comprehend how much you have gone through and all on your own. Maybe you're stronger than anyone else here. I really think you are, because if it had been me, I would've killed myself by now. But this, what's happening to me, I can't do it on my own. I'm not strong like you."

Everything she'd said held truth. I was positive of it.

She stood there wiping away her tears while keeping her gaze on me. What was I supposed to say? How could she expect me to help her with whatever was going on when she was one of the many who'd given me hell for so long. Then again, she was right. I was a stronger person than most—in some parts—and I could see she definitely needed help, but I wasn't sure I was the right person to do it. Didn't I have enough going on in my own life to deal with without adding more to it?

I wanted to be selfish and say eff off, but that wasn't me. It would have taken her a lot of strength to come and talk to me, so I couldn't turn my back on her. Even though I knew she would on me.

"Afternoon sessions are going to start soon. How about we ditch and you can tell me what's going on?"

Her eyes widened. "Really?" she squeaked with surprise. "You're willing to help me?"

"Yeah." I sighed. "Only if I can."

She sat down next to me. My own eyes widened when she started to reach her hand out to touch mine, only uncertainty quickly washed over her features. Instead, she blushed and looked down. "Thank you so much. I really don't deserve it."

Ignoring the deserving part, I said, "Don't thank me just yet. Start explaining." Opening my lunch bag again, I pulled out my cookies and offered one to Sofia. She took it, but didn't eat it. Instead, she held onto it as if it were a lifeline. I glanced at the clock. It was time for phys ed.

Snorting wasn't an option, but I wanted to. Because I felt it funny that I was ditching class with someone from Jenna's group.

Sofia looked terrified sitting next to me and I couldn't figure out why.

She took a deep breath. "Last month, I was out with some people. I was supposed to get a lift home with Bertina, but she went off with Malcolm in her car, so Jason offered to give me a lift home with him and Jenna. He dropped Jenna off first. Maybe I should have gotten out then, but I was excited to be alone with him." She stopped, a blush rising to her cheeks.

She groaned and admitted, "I'd been crushing on him for some time. We were nearly at my house when he pulled over and turned in his seat to look at me. Smiling, he reached out to run his hand down my cheek." I wasn't sure if she knew she was following the action with her own hand on her cheek only to fall away when she grimaced. "He went lower. His hand reached under my top. I tried to get his hand off me, but he's so strong. By this time, I was crying and he was laughing, saying he knew how much I wanted this, how much I liked him. I kept telling him to stop, but he didn't. He ripped my top off." She sniffed and wiped her eyes. "I somehow got up enough courage to punch him in the balls. When he was doubled over, I got out and ran."

Reaching out, I placed my hand on her arm. She looked down at it. I waited for her to pull away from my touch, but she didn't. If anything, she found courage from it and continued. "He caught up to me. I'd made it to my neighbour's backyard, but before I could call out for help, his hand was over my mouth. He told me not to worry, because soon I'd know more about him than anyone else did." She laughed humourlessly. "He wanted us to be together. However, the only problem was he'd have to share me with five others like him. He didn't think that mattered though. He said I'd love the attention. Then he bit me. Right here." She pulled her shirt away from her shoulder. I could see the scar of teeth marks embedded into her. Shit, I wasn't sure they were human teeth marks. He acted and sounded like something different.

"What is he, Sofia?" I asked through clenched teeth.

She gasped and dropped her hand away from her shoulder to her mouth. More tears flowed.

Behind her hand, she uttered, "You do believe me. You know there are other things."

"Yes. What is he?" I repeated.

"I'm, I mean, he's... we can change into large dogs," she cried before covering her face with her hands.

I wasn't sure if she was crying for what had happened to her or for the fact she was hiding something from me. I could taste deception on the tip of my tongue.

Which meant I had to find out more. "Sofia, calm down. I need to know everything." She sniffed, pulled up her shirt and wiped at her face. She took a couple of deep breaths to compose herself and looked at me.

"I knew, I knew you would understand. I don't mean because of your eyes, but, because you're a witch, right? You'll put a spell on him or something, from far away, right?" She nodded at me, hope shining in her eyes.

A burst of laughter fell from my lips, but I quickly shut it down. "Sorry, Sofia, I'm far from a witch. Maybe there are some out there, but I'm not one—"

"But then how? How can you help me? You can't, can you?" She whimpered. "I'm going to be their sex slave for the rest of my life."

"Wait, what? Sofia, what do you mean sex slave? Are they raping you?"

She nodded, a sob caught in her throat. I placed my arms around her and held her tightly.

Disgust crawled up my throat. They had no right to touch her, to hurt her. Payback was a given, and I thrived on the fact they were shifters, which meant the human authorities were too fragile to deal with it, so it would come down to me. My teeth throbbed at the thought of ripping out their throats for what they had done.

Sorrow brought tears to my eyes. "It'll be okay, Sofia. Even though I'm not a witch, I can help you. No one should be put through what you have. You have my word, Sofia. I will stop them."

"You will? How? When?"

"Where and when do you usually meet? I can't do anything here at college. No one can know about any of this. They have to continue living their ignorant lives."

"I know, I get that. Um, the next time is Friday night. Jason wants me and his friends out in the woods, behind his place. But, you don't have to come. I'll think of something else. I'll—" Something tugged at the back of my mind and I knew doubt was the cause of it. I didn't trust Sofia.

"It's all right. I'll be there," I interrupted.

"Thank you," she sniffed.

"Like I said, don't thank me yet."

"L-Leila?" Ty called from a few rows down. Sofia's whole body stiffened.

"Hey, Ty. Down the end," I called.

I could hear his approaching steps, as well as his cane hitting the floor. I smiled up at him once he came into sight. Not that he would notice my smile, but ever since he started hanging with us, it always made me happy to see him.

"You have c-company. I'll come b-back."

How does he know? Lately, he's been surprising me with that sort of thing. It was little comments here and there that told me he was unique in his own way. For example, when he was over at my house one day studying, he told me someone was at the door before there was a knock. More importantly, even before I was able to scent it was Jeremiah. I'd asked him how he knew, though he didn't say, only offering me a small, cheeky grin. After Jezanna's brother told Jeremiah about it, it made him suspicious of Ty and said he would look into his background. I hadn't heard any more of it.

"No. You can stay," Sofia said, getting up off the ground.

"I-it's all right, S-sofia, I d-didn't mean t-to interrupt. You can s-stay."

Okay, how does he know it's Sofia? Does he know her?

"I-ah, no. I have to go anyway. Thank you though. Bye." She blushed and left.

"S-sorry to drive her off," he said as he sat where she'd been next to me. "S-she must have wanted s-something important to have been here..." He winced. "S-sorry."

Nodding, I finished what he was about to say, "To have been seen with me. It's all right, Ty. I know that, and yeah, it was."

"C-care to tell?"

Always inquisitive, but recently about too many things. Once was why Darik kept slipping and calling, you know who, Sire. I told him it was a dare Darik lost. Another question he'd asked was how at times one minute either Darik, Xavier, or Jeremiah were there, and then the next, they'd gone. I didn't have an answer, so I'd steered him towards another subject.

He had many questions, and sometimes it was hard to have him around, because I couldn't be truthful with him. I hated I couldn't tell him everything. I wished I could, but there were too many risks in doing so. If it were only about myself, then I wouldn't hesitate. I trusted him. He'd become a real, loyal friend. However, there were other lives that could be endangered than just mine and I wouldn't put them in the line of fire.

Although, trust was a funny thing. I thought I could trust *him*, and look where that got me.

"I'm sorry, Ty, but I can't. I promised her I wouldn't."

He shook his head. "Leila, y-you're the most unselfish p-person I know. Even though S-Sofia has been terrible to you, you're still w-willing to help her, with whatever it is. I'm glad t-to know you and am very s-sorry for what that shmuck has done to you."

His words brought tears to my eyes. For the first time, I was glad he couldn't see, only because I was acting like a softy.

Wrapping my arms around his shoulders, I gave him a squeeze and whispered, "Thank you."

At the end of the day, and after asking Ty to come to my place to help me with my computer science assignment, I walked out to the car park. I found Jezanna and Xavier parked in the same spot where they'd dropped me off. The only problem was—a problem that made my steps falter and my heart stop—that *he* stood next to the car. Jezanna had her window down while she spoke. She didn't look too happy about what he was saying. I glanced over to his car and saw fathead MaryJane sitting in it with a grumpy-looking Darik. I pulled my hood up over my head and walked to Jezza's car. I knew they could feel me coming, like I could smell their scent. However, he didn't turn and no one said anything. Therefore, I opened the back door to the car and got in, slouching down in the seat.

"Goodbye, Isaac." Jezanna sighed.

Still, no one moved and the car didn't start.

"Leila." His voice held sadness. I flinched. "Please, Leila. I don't mean to hurt you, but—"

"Xavier, if you don't move this car, I will shove a stake in your eye."

The car started, only the noise of it didn't hide the frustrated sigh from Isaac. As we pulled away, a part of me wanted to tell Xavier to stop, but I didn't.

I wanted to look at Isaac. I wanted to hear his voice again. Feel his arms around me.

I still wanted so much of him.

My heart and soul seemed to pine for him in a ridiculous way.

Groaning, I banged my head against the window and closed my eyes.

Stuff it. No more thinking of him.

Instead, I thought of what I had to do Friday night and how I was going to get away without anyone seeing.

We drove along in silence, while I formed a plan. The only way I was going to be able to get out of the house undetected was to install the help of someone, and that someone was going to have to be Jezanna.

Once we pulled up to my house, I got out and walked straight inside. I went to go straight to my room, but stopped after hearing Xavier speak.

"I'm going to make a sweep of the property. Please don't answer the door to anyone."

"Thank you, Xavier," Jezanna said.

"Okay." I sighed.

The front door closed. I waited a few minutes to make sure he was out of hearing range and turned to Jezanna who stood in the living room looking back at me.

"He asked me to speak with you."

My head went back, eyes to the ceiling. "Jezanna, I don't want to hear it."

"But maybe if you do you could understand and not hate him so much."

Scrubbing a hand over my face, I then looked at her and told her the truth, "I-I don't hate him. I could never. It hurts. It hurts so much inside and I feel foolish for it. It's still so raw, so please just leave it."

"Okay." She nodded and then added, "For now." She smiled.

Shaking my head, I asked, "I need to ask you to do something for me."

"Anything." She didn't hesitate.

"I have to go out Friday night, alone. I need you to distract Xavier for me so he doesn't follow."

She stiffened. "Why? Where do you have to go?"

"I have to do something for someone, but I can't tell you what or why."

"You can't ask this of me and not tell me why. What happens if something goes wrong? I need to know where to find you. Or a timeline at least, so if you're not back by then, I'll come for you. You mean too much to me, Leila. If you can't give me those answers, then I can't help you. I'm sorry."

"All right, okay. I'll tell you what I can. I'll be in the woods off Drummond Street. Do you know where that is?" She nodded. I added, "And I should only be an hour."

By the way, I'm going to see a pack of dogs, so if I'm not back within that hour, then I've failed and I'm probably dead.

Guilt gnawed at me. I pushed it aside.

"Thank you. And just how am I supposed to keep Xavier occupied?"

"I don't know, flash him your boobs or something." I laughed when her hand went over her mouth and her cheeks pinked. "You're going to have to figure it out on your own." I smiled and she rolled her eyes.

We fell into silence as the front door opened and Xavier came in with Caelen following.

"What are you doing here? Does no one understand I don't want you around?" I asked with amusement in my voice.

"Sorry, love, but I ain't that easy to get rid of. Besides, you just don't scare me."

"I can change that." I glared, placing my hands on my hips.

He scoffed, winked and said, "Sure you can. But then you'll not have two strapping men taking you out tonight."

"Find me two strapping men and I might rethink it."

"Ha ha, you kill me. Come on, ladies, go and change. We're off to Boozers to have a good time."

"Sorry, can't. I have assignments, and Ty's coming by to help me." I grabbed my bag I'd dropped on the floor earlier and walked off to my room. It didn't take Jezanna long to follow me.

"Please, please, Leila, come with me. Jeremiah and—yes well, you know who, don't usually like me going there, but now that they're not around to tell me what to do, can't I indulge in a little fun?" She gave me her puppy-dog eyes.

"You only want to go, because a certain English guy asked you."

"Can you blame me? He never pays me attention. I'm hoping to change his mind on the subject if we can only spend some time together. Maybe with a little liquor to help my nerves."

Snorting, I told her, "You don't need the liquor. He fancies you anyway."

She gasped. "You really think so?" She bounced around my room like a little schoolgirl. It was adorable and weird at the same time. She was, after all, an old vampire. However, the way she acted made me wonder if she'd had any lovers. Then I remembered she did have two very protective brothers.

"Jez, have you ever..." I raised my brows up and down.

She stopped bouncing and asked, "What?"

"Been with anyone?"

She blushed. Holy shit, how was that really possible?

"But you're old," I blurted.

She shrugged. "Schooling had always been important to me. Then, when I started taking notice of men more, things seemed to happen to capture my attention. Then there was always the bad luck I had with finding the wrong men, who only wanted one thing from me. To build their status with my family."

"You've kissed right?"

She grinned. "Oh, yes."

Sighing, because I was about to take one for the girl team, I said, "Okay, I'll go, but what about Ty? I won't blow him off."

She beamed. "He can come with us. Ring him and tell him we'll pick him up on the way. It's not as if he'll be able to see the bar is for supernaturals."

I really didn't want to go to Boozers. It was only the previous night I was there and too many things had happened. But as I looked up into Jezanna's eyes, I knew I couldn't let her down. She was like my sister and she'd already done so much for me.

Sighing loudly, I said, "I'll ring him and then get changed. You can be the one to tell Caelen and Xavier a human will be coming with us tonight."

"Thank you so much, Leila. You're wonderful." She gave me a quick kiss on the cheek and ran towards the lounge.

CHAPTER SEVENTEEN

I opted for a pair of jeans and a black tank top under one of my many hooded jumpers.

I took my hair out of its ponytail and brushed it, leaving it straight. I walked out to find Jezanna looking wonderful in a long leather skirt and short-sleeved, dark grey silk top. She had her dark curls pulled up onto the top of her head and wore no makeup, like myself. Where I couldn't be bothered wearing the stuff and may have needed it, Jezanna didn't need to wear it at all. Her skin was flawless. I could tell by the look in Caelen's hungry eyes he very much approved of the way she looked.

Xavier stood by the door, grumbling about how it was a bad idea. Not only about going in the first place, but having Ty come along as well. For some reason, I thought so too. However, I was doing it for Jezanna, so I wouldn't complain. Yet.

As we piled into the four-wheel drive, I noticed Xavier had also changed. Instead of his usual leather pants and tight T-shirt, he wore something similar to Caelen. Dark slacks and a light coloured shirt. They both looked like sex on a stick. Not that I'd tell them it; it'd just go straight to their heads. We pulled up to Ty's small, brick home in the middle of town and found him standing out the front, looking just as good as the other two, in black jeans and a white, long-sleeve dress shirt.

"Taxi for a Mr Ty Rivers," I said as I opened the door for him.

He pushed away from the wire fence, smiling. "I h-hope this isn't going to c-cost me anything though."

"Not tonight at least."

He chuckled. "Well, th-thank you. You're too kind, *sometimes*. Hello, Xavier, Caelen, and the lovely Jezanna," he greeted as Xavier pulled the car away from the curb. Jezanna and Xavier said a friendly hi back and Caelen mumbled something rude. He didn't like that Ty was obviously attracted to Jezanna and was so open about it.

"So, what kind of bar is this?"

"It's a friend of the family's bar," Jezanna said.

The parking lot was full. Boozers was going to be packed. I couldn't resist glancing around to see if I could spot a familiar Hummer. I breathed a sigh of relief when I didn't see it.

"Why so busy tonight?" I asked Caelen while walking toward the door.

"Karaoke night, love."

A smile settled on my lips from the thought of vampires getting excited about singing. Tonight may just be fun after all.

At least I hoped. I quickly swept away the deep sadness to the back of my mind.

As I held Ty's hand, Caelen led us to a reserved booth in the corner while he continued on to the bar for drinks. I looked around the place. The dance floor was already busy with bodies bumping and grinding, while a male vampire was belting out an Evanescence song. He wasn't doing too bad a job either.

Caelen came back with a tray of five shot glasses filled with the same concoction I'd had the previous night. He also had five other glasses of what smelled like cola and whiskey.

Wincing from the memories of the night before, I downed my first shot.

"I won't be drinking," Xavier said. "Someone has to be the adult here."

"I'll have his," I said, dragging his over to me. Gulping it down, I slammed the shot on the table and took a sip of the cola and whiskey.

"Easy, tiger, we've got all night," Ty said.

"That is true, but you only live once." *And have too many regrets to count along the way.*

We sat around and talked, laughed and teased one another. I relaxed enough to enjoy myself and felt a little merry. I wasn't the only one. I looked over to Jezanna to see she was smiling and had gotten up enough courage to place her hand on Caelen's thigh, which he didn't seem to mind at all. He grinned away while leaning back in the booth. Every now and then, he'd glance to Jezanna with something akin to adoration in his eyes.

"Come on, X and T. Let's go dance." I took off my jumper, grabbed both of their hands and pulled them out of the booth. Xavier came reluctantly, Ty more willingly. I wondered what kind of dancer a blind guy could be? I guessed I'd soon find out. Turning back to the table, I gave a sly wink to Jezza and then went off to the dance floor.

We danced through three songs. All self-consciousness washed away, even when I got up close and personal with either of them. Mainly because I knew they didn't think of me in any other way than a friend, like I did with them.

It turned out, Ty could really get his groove on. A couple of times he bumped into people, but once he apologized and explained he was blind, they didn't care. By the time the third song finished, I was thirsty. I sent Xavier back to the booth to find out if the other two wanted a drink as Ty and I made our way to the bar.

Climbing up on a stool, I waited my turn, which gave me a chance to look around, while Ty stood silently beside me listening to the music.

"Miss Leila Morgin and Ty Rivers, what are you two doing here?" I turned my attention to the bar and was very surprised to see Coach Bacon, the phys ed teacher, standing on the other side of the bar, as though she was there to work. "Close your mouth, girl. You never know what may fly in."

Snapping it shut, I gawked and finally asked, "What are *you* doing here?"

She laughed and smiled at me. "My father owns the place." She grinned.

"What? Then he… No, that means, ah… You know?" I signalled with my fingers and eyes that Ty didn't know anything about supernaturals. I could only hope she understood what I was saying and didn't think I was having some kind of attack.

Again, she laughed just as Xavier came to stand beside me.

"Yes, I know, not that Isaac"—a flinch went through my body—"knows I'm related to Big Hardy. I don't come here unless Dad needs help and tonight he did. It's good to see you enjoy yourself, Leila." She leaned in. "Of course, neither of you can tell the other students of my involvement here. They'd want free drinks, and really it's not their sort of place. Anyway, what can I get you?"

"Um-ah." I turned my shocked face to Xavier. "Did they want anything?"

He bent down to my ear and whispered, "I think they are a little busy."

Looking over his shoulder to the table, I found Jezanna kissing Caelen, or was it the other way around? Didn't matter what it was, because it was great to see it finally happen.

"Ty, would you like anything?"

"No, thanks. I'm fine." He smiled.

"Just a whiskey and Coke," I said sweetly.

Coach Bacon raised her brows. "My instincts tell me not to serve you, but I know you'll only drink in moderation, as well as the fact you have very nice people taking care of you." I could feel Xavier nod at my side.

When she left, Ty leaned into me and whispered, "I think I may be missing something important here about this place, but I doubt you'll tell me."

Wish I could, Ty. I really do.

"No, sorry."

Coach Bacon came back with my drink. Thanking her, I paid and promised not to say anything. I wasn't really sure it had sunk in yet. It was laughable really. My phys ed coach just served me alcohol and knew about the creatures of the night.

The three of us sat at the bar while I drank. I'd just sat my glass down after finishing it when Xavier stiffened beside me. He turned his attention to the crowd around us. My heart started racing, thinking it was because he saw *him* here, but as I followed Xavier's stare, I spotted Jensen standing in the corner on his own, leaning against the wall looking like a Greek god. Once he noticed us staring, he made a move our way.

He stopped just in front of me. "Leila, isn't it?" He made it sound like a question, but he already knew my name and it wasn't like he really cared. His eyes stayed on Xavier.

"Jackal, isn't it." I smiled.

He laughed. "Xavier, good to see you."

Xavier did his usual nod and… wait, was that—holy shit, it was—a blush on his cheeks.

"And who do we have here?" He turned his gaze quickly to Ty, but then back to Xavier.

"No one you need to know about." I smiled. "What are you doing here?" *Please don't say she's here.*

"It is my night off. I came to see what the talk is all about," he said, looking at X.

Thank eff she wasn't there. *Oh, crap.* Now I wished she were, because that meant she was back at the house with *him.* Maybe in a position I didn't even want to think about.

Jensen finally graced me with his gaze. *Damn it, why is there pity in his eyes?* "They're coming tonight. I thought you would like to know."

That's why. Crap a duck.

My stomach pivoted. "Yeah. Thanks," I uttered. Only Jensen's eyes were back on Xavier; however, X was looking down to the floor, his eyes flicking to Jensen every few seconds. What was the go with all the heat between those two?

Unless. No way, I would have noticed. X would have told

me, right? Then again, probably not. He really hated talking about himself.

Wow. Xavier wanted him, likewise for Jensen. Still, I knew neither of them would make the first move.

The distraction eased my stomach and calmed my heart a little. "Let's just have some fun until they turn up to ruin it. Care to dance, Jensen?"

His shocked gaze fell on me. "I… sure, thank you."

"Come on, Xavier, Ty." Grabbing their hands, I led them to the dance floor with Jensen following behind. I wove my way through the crowd until we were fully in the middle. Turning, I faced Ty and placed my hands on his waist as he did on mine. Pulling him in close, I swayed with him. It didn't take long for Xavier to join us. He came up nice and close behind me. It was as if the three of us were joined at the hips. Xavier placed his own hands at my sides. Jensen stood back watching the three of us move.

"You should go and dance with him, Xavier," Ty whispered. Xavier growled. Was the tension that obvious even a blind guy felt the heat from the two of them?

"I can't," Xavier muttered. Despite his reluctance, it didn't change Jensen's train of thought. He came over to us and moved in closely behind Xavier. Xavier jumped from the contact, but he didn't move away. I rested my head down on Ty's shoulder, trying to give the two at my back as much privacy as I could. We stayed that way for two songs until Jensen swore and I knew it was time to leave.

Eyes were on us. I knew it was *him*.

Pulling away from the group, I said, "We have to go."

I turned away as Jensen gave Xavier a quick kiss on the cheek and whispered something in his ear. Xavier's whole body sagged. He looked up to Jensen and I saw the loss, the pain. Both of them mirrored each other's feelings.

"Jensen, maybe on your next day off you can come to my house for a while?"

He smiled. "I would love it." He turned to Xavier. "If that's okay with you?" Xavier nodded.

Jensen stepped closer to me and whispered out of Ty's hearing range. "Thank you, Leila. If my mistress had seen or heard about this, about the way I am, then she would kill me."

My eyes widened, appalled by the thought and with how blunt he was about it. How could she take away the chance for Jensen to be who he was meant to be? To love who he wanted. We were in the twenty-first century, for God's sake. It was time someone told her that.

I wished I could be the one to do it, but it was impossible. I knew once I started, I wouldn't be able to hold back.

Jensen disappeared. I went to ask Xavier something, but he shook his head. "Not here."

"All right," I said and cleared my throat. "Thank you, guys. You two are the best dance partners so far."

"You won't find anyone better." Ty smiled.

"I guess only time will tell. Now, let's try and get those other two lovebirds away from here. It's time to go."

And hopefully we'll escape without seeing them.

We moved through the crowded floor back to our booth where Jezanna and Caelen were still seated.

Shit a stick.

The booth was also occupied with *him* and her.

My head fell back, my eyes to the ceiling. *Couldn't I get a break, just once, please?*

Not wanting to make a scene, I stopped where I was with Xavier behind me and Ty at my side, my hand in his. As we stood on the edge of the dance floor, I opened my shields and reached my mind out to Caelen's.

What I wasn't prepared for was Isaac's face to snap straight to me. He must have felt my power. Mary-fungus-Jane kept talking to Jezanna and Caelen, unaware her man's attention had wavered to someone else.

I couldn't keep standing there looking at him, seeing the

pain in his eyes, as I was sure my own reflected a different pain. Only what did he have to be hurt about? Nothing. It was his choice to rip my heart from my chest, throw it to the ground and stomp on it.

Damn him. Why did he have to look so bloody wonderful in black slacks and a long-sleeved white shirt? His hair was loose and it flowed down around his shoulders. My eyes drifted to his shoulder and then followed his arm down. That was when I saw he had his hand placed gently on her fucking fat thigh. Cringing at the sight, he pulled his hand away quickly. Only that made her look to find out why. She saw me straight away. Her stare turned into a fierce glare.

Ignoring her, I turned to Jezanna and nodded to the side; she knew what I was saying. She rose from the table, as did Caelen, and followed me, all while I dragged the unaware Ty out of Boozers, with Xavier following quietly behind us.

Walking straight to the car, I bent over trying to catch my breath. It seemed I couldn't get enough air in and it was hurting.

"Leila, what's wrong? I-is Isaac here? Did you s-see something? Fuck him, Leila. He's an arse anyway."

Jezanna came rushing up to my side, rubbing her hand up and down my back. Goddamn, I wanted to cry again.

They look like the perfect couple, nothing like what we were.

Clenching my fists, I gave myself a good shake and stood tall. Jezanna held out my jumper and I threw it on.

"Ty, would—"

He held up his hand. "I'm going to c-catch the taxi home that Xavier has flagged down. I-I know you just want to get home. Don't worry about it, o-okay? I understand. But, listen, you c-can trust me, you know. About anything at all."

My arms went around him. I hugged him hard and nodded into his shoulder.

The car was quiet on the drive back home, everyone in their own thoughts. I spent the time trying not to think about someone. I was sure the other three were thinking of the ones who took their breaths away, and I was happy for them.

Even if my own life was so fucking messed up, at least they could bring some normalcy to it. Well, sort of.

I left Jezanna to say goodnight to Caelen alone and went off to my room. Xavier followed behind me. I closed the door and flopped down on my bed, hiding my face with my arm. I felt the bed sink next to me and peeked out to see Xavier watching me.

"Are you all right?" he asked.

"Yeah, I will be. Though, I'd be better if you took my mind off things and answered some questions."

"I'd be glad to."

Sitting up, I scooted back to lean against the headboard, patting the spot next to me. Xavier took off his shoes and jacket, unarmed himself and sat next to me. I needed some type of comfort, so I put my arm through his and laid my head on his shoulder.

"Is it easier to touch me now you know I'm gay?"

I thought about it. "Yeah, in a way, I guess it is. At least I know you won't get the wrong idea from it."

He smirked down at me. "That's true. It also gives me the chance to have someone touch me and not be repulsed. I have gone without having someone show me they care for so long. All we need is a little comfort every now and then. No matter who we like."

Yawning, I said lightly, "I don't think Jensen was repulsed at all."

His rumble of laughter ran through the ear I had rested on him.

"Yes, well, I have you to thank for that."

"No way, it was all your godly doing." I laughed. "Does, you know, does I-Isaac know?"

"Yes, he does. He was the one who saved me from my previous sire. Someone I long to forget, but have the scars that won't let me. You see, being gay is very much looked down upon with a lot of the older vampires. Though, it's not only from the vampire society, but also still with the humans. Only, it's worse with vampires, because"—he shuddered—"we're beaten, usually to death. I'm guessing something similar has happened to Jensen and that's why his new mistress knows nothing about him. I was lucky enough Isaac stumbled upon me one night after being beaten. He gave me his blood, which broke the bond of the person who made me a vampire and Isaac became my master. He chose to save me knowing who I was and then faced the wrath of my previous sire." He stopped and took my hand in his. "I don't like what he's doing in your situation. However, he has his reasons and he's hoping one day, as well as I and many more, you will understand and forgive him. He's a noble, strong man, but we all have our faults."

Wiping my tears away after hearing about the hell Xavier had been through, I sighed. "Deep down, I know he's being noble and all, which is why I still care for him so deeply. However, my anger wouldn't let me admit it aloud until now. Hell, I couldn't even admit it in my head. Nothing can erase the hurt swirling inside of me or the slap of betrayal across my face and anguish that still burns me." I shrugged. "Maybe one day, we can be… friends again. But not if she's in the picture." I scoffed. "Something tells me I could never get along with her. Then again, friendship with Isaac would probably only upset me so much more, because I will never get to feel what I had with him again. And having him around, seeing him only makes me remember what I lost." I sighed again.

"At least you were able to say his name this time."

A snort. "Yeah, big improvement." We were silent for a few moments, then I broke it, saying, "Can I ask you something else?" He nodded, so I asked, "Why do you call Isaac master like off those old vampire movies?"

"Like I said, Isaac was the one who broke the bond from my sire—the vampire who turned me. Therefore, I use it for him as a term of respect. When a vampire makes you like them, you call them sire. Then, if for some reason your sire is no longer around or you have won the rights to leave the clan you were reborn as a vampire into, to join another, then the one who rules the new clan, you call them master. Again, it's out of respect, because they do so much for you."

I gulped. I knew he had heard it. "Has, ah, Isaac made anyone?"

Darik.

Of course, Darik was the only one around who called Isaac sire instead of master. I wondered how it happened and why Isaac chose Darik. Had they been friends before it happened?

"My master has made only a few. Although, he has saved many, like myself, by giving them his blood. Which in turn, wipes out the connection from their other sire or master's bond."

I wanted to ask who the others were that Isaac made, but somehow I knew Xavier wouldn't tell me.

CHAPTER EIGHTEEN

The week passed quickly. Each day, I woke with the dream fresh in my mind. I attended school, kept my distance from Isaac and whore-face, all while managing to dodge Darik's attempts at talking to me. However, he caught me one night while I was out on my nightly run in my other form.

Xavier had magically disappeared when Darik popped up out of nowhere. "Leila, how have you been? Of course I don't expect an answer." He chuckled.

I hissed at him and kept my pace.

"Now, now, kitty cat. No need to be testy. Seems you've been avoiding my attempts to try to speak with you. So I thought this would be a better idea. The best, in fact, because you can't talk back." He laughed again.

A growl escaped as I stopped running and turned to Darik. He grinned down at me. Was he waiting for me to meld my mind to his? It was not going to happen.

"All right, I can see you want me to get this over with. All I want to get across, for now, is that Isaac only wants to protect and take care of everyone in his circle. Including you."

Snapping my jaw in frustration, I pounced at him, landing at his feet. He didn't move. I turned and took off, hoping he wouldn't follow.

They needed to get through their thick heads, I may still be friends with *his* people, but I wasn't one of his to protect and take care of. Not any longer.

～

Later that week, I turned my thoughts to another matter, one that had me worried. I hadn't seen Sofia around or even Raven, her sister. I asked a few people where she was. They, of course, told me to get out of their faces. I was tempted to go to her house to see if she was okay, but then I'd have to explain to Xavier the whys of it. Xavier had also taken it upon himself to be my shadow. He'd dropped and picked me up from school, took me to the supermarket and then ran with me every night.

Caelen had been around a lot, and by a lot, I meant he was there every afternoon when I got home and didn't leave until early hours of the morning. It was great to see Jezza and Caelen so happy. Too happy sometimes, to the point I felt like puking from the little lovesick gazes, touches and whispers of sweet nothings in each other's ear. Still, they deserved to be content, and the thought of that made me stop throwing things at them.

For some reason, I didn't get a chance to spend much time with Ty through the week, other than in class. I asked him around a couple of times, but he said he was busy at home helping his mum.

By Thursday night, I'd had enough of the sweetness between the happy couple, who were sitting on the couch together, and went to bed early.

I'd just gotten to sleep when I woke with a start from my bedroom door being thrown open. I was on my feet on the bed in seconds, ready for whoever entered.

Jezanna turned on the light. She looked terrible. Tears stained her cheeks and her body shook violently. Something was wrong, very wrong. I jumped off my bed and ran to her side.

"What is it, Jezz?"

Oh, God, please don't let it be Isaac, please.

"I have to get to the hospital. It's Father. He's... Something attacked him. Oh, Leila, it doesn't look good. Please, will you come with me? I can't get a hold of Caelen. He left two hours ago. Otherwise, I wouldn't ask this of you, because my brothers will be there."

"Of course I'll come. Let me just get dressed."

"Xavier's preparing the car. I'll meet you in it." She gave me a quick hug and flew out the door. I grabbed the clothes I'd discarded on the floor and threw them on. It ended up being my running clothes, my black leggings and T-shirt. I shook my head knowing they stunk, but there was no time to change.

Rain poured heavily from the dark sky. I quickly took the long black duffel coat hanging beside the door and hurried out to the car.

The three of us sat in the front, my arm around Jezanna, trying to console her as she cried. Meanwhile, I tried my best to hold my own emotions and thoughts at bay.

My heart constricted. I hadn't managed to spend enough time with Greg. He'd better be okay. He couldn't leave us, not now, not ever.

"Why doesn't someone just change him?" I thought, but I must have said it aloud, because Jezanna sobbed harder.

"He won't let anyone," Xavier said.

Oh, shit, really? Although, I understood why, at least he'd get to be with his loving wife, who he missed every day since her passing. But couldn't he see he was needed here? It may have been selfish of me to think it, but… Crap, no, I couldn't let my emotions control me. I needed to be strong for Jezanna's sake. I had to stop thinking.

We pulled into the hospital's emergency car park. I jumped out, as did Jezanna. Xavier mumbled something about parking the car and he'd be along in a moment. Only Jezanna had already started running for the door, so I followed her.

She reached the information desk, screaming where to find Gregory Grey, before I had the chance to catch her.

"Jezanna," I whispered into her ear. "There're humans around. You can't run off like that." She nodded.

We waited for the administrator to pull up the information

on her computer. Before I had left the house, I grabbed some tissues off the kitchen bench, and now handed some to Jezanna. She took them and wiped her tears from her face.

She hiccupped. "I can't help it, Leila."

"I know." I turned to the lady behind the desk. "Geez, woman, how long does it take?"

"Don't take that tone with me, young lady. You will find him on floor two, south. Room thirty-five. If you go straight around the corner, you'll find the lifts."

"Thank you," Jezanna said.

We sprinted around the corner. The pain-in-the-arse part was waiting for the lift to come back down. We jumped inside and I pushed the button. I then proceeded to tap my foot impatiently while holding Jezanna's hand.

We didn't have to walk far to find the room. As soon as the doors opened, we spotted Isaac leaning against the opposite wall to his father's room. I glanced behind me as I stepped off the lift and saw Adan guarding the area. Darik was pacing the floor in front of his sire. Isaac looked up to see who was coming out of the lift. His eyes were tired and sad. He straightened from the wall as Jezanna ran to him and threw herself into his waiting arms. I didn't want to seem like I was intruding, so I walked slowly down the hall, Darik meeting me halfway.

"Is Gregory okay?" I asked.

"It doesn't look good, Leila. They've given him until morning."

"What? How? What happened? Who did this?" I gripped his tee. "It's too sudden."

"We don't know anything yet, but we have people searching for answers. He's taken a lot of internal damage and lost so much blood. We know it's one of our kind. He... he had a stroke right after the attack."

My hand went to my mouth. Tears filled my eyes, but I blinked them away and wiped my face. I had to be strong for

Jezanna. She'd need me. Remaining strong was something I was used to. I'd cry later, alone.

"You'll get answers? You'll make who did this pay?" I asked.

His nod was stiff, but the hardness in his eyes told me vengeance was just around the corner.

I watched Jezanna walk into the room where Jeremiah's voice came from within. She closed the door behind her. I looked to Isaac to see how he was holding up. He was turned away from me. My heart clenched when I saw his shoulders shaking; he was crying.

Oh, God. I ached to reach out to him. Squeezing my fists into tight balls, I walked over to him. Darik stayed where he was.

"Isaac," I muttered. He didn't turn and I didn't expect him to. I knew he'd hate anyone to see him as he was, so vulnerable. So I did the only thing I could. I wrapped my arms around him from behind, hugging him tightly. He stiffened on first touch then crumbled. He turned, his own arms coming around my waist, and buried his head into my shoulder. I held him close, my own eyes filling with tears once again, only that time I let them out. I was honoured he'd let me console him, hold him. And hurt that it would take such a tragedy to have him in my arms again.

We stayed that way for a while, even after I felt his crying subside. He didn't move away from me and I didn't pull away from him. Only one thing ruined it. We both heard the lift doors open. I knew it was her by the way Isaac quickly dropped his arms from me and moved away, not meeting my gaze. I stepped back and shifted so I didn't have to witness him take her in his arms. I shrugged out of my jacket and placed it on the ground.

"Darling," MaryJane cooed. "I'm so sorry. If only I was with you at the time it happened instead of out hunting."

"It's all right. It can't be helped," Isaac replied softly.

"Well, don't worry now. I'm here for you."

The door to Gregory's room opened. I turned to see Jeremiah filling the doorway. He looked around at everyone. Darik, Isaac, snot-head and her three guards, including Jensen.

But when Jeremiah saw me in the back, he grimly said, "He wants to see you."

My body went rigid. *Why me? God, no, I can't. I won't be able to hold back if I see him, talk to him.*

Jeremiah moved out of the way for me to enter. He quickly gave my hand a tight squeeze as I walked past him. The first thing I saw was a pale Gregory. He lay on the bed in one of those hospital gowns, his lower half covered by a blanket. He whispered something to Jezanna. She nodded, got up and left the room, shutting the door behind her.

I closed my eyes. I couldn't do this, be in here on my own with him. I wasn't strong enough for this.

"You can come closer. I don't bite like the others," he said, humour evident in his weak voice.

Snorting, I opened my eyes and went over to sit in the chair beside the bed.

He held out his hand to me and I took it. It was cold. "Do you..." I cleared my throat and began again. "Do you need another blanket?"

He smiled but shook his head. In an exhausted whisper, he said, "I've asked you to come in here, because I wanted to say a few things to you in private." He pulled my hand to his mouth and kissed it then placed it back on the bed within his own. "I'm so glad you came into our lives, Leila. You've made my household alive again. I only regret we haven't got to spend much time together." He paused to take a few deep breaths. I hiccupped back a sob and rubbed at my eyes with my free hand.

He smiled. "At least I know when I leave this world, I leave my family in safe hands—yours." I went to argue, but he squeezed my hand to silence me. "No, don't say anything. Not yet at least, please." He gave me a chance to grab some tissues. I blew my nose and rubbed at my face. Curling into a ball and hiding from what was happening to such a wonderful man wasn't an option. No matter how much I wanted it.

"You're a level-headed, strong, caring woman, and I love you like another daughter. However, you're stupidly stubborn as well." I raised my brows at him and he smiled.

He licked his dry lips. I offered him a drink, but he declined. "You won't listen to people. Leila, you need to fight for what you want. For *your* family, for us, them. You know that's what we are to you, your family. I understand you're hurting and Isaac has his own foolish reasons for doing what he has, just... I only ask you don't give up on him. I don't trust MaryJane one bit." Another deep breath. "For me, will you keep a close eye on her and be prepared for whatever she may throw your way? She can do things others can't of their kind. Ask Jeremiah to explain about her."

He sighed. "Our people, family, will be better off without her around. I'm afraid it will come down to you to do something about it. Because I fear that Isaac will have his own battle on his hands very soon. Be careful, sweet Leila. I don't want to see you up there too soon." He smiled at me. Hearing those words brought me back to what was really going on in the room.

He would be gone soon. It wasn't fair.

"No. Don't cry or be upset for me. At least we got to meet. As I said before, I go happy knowing you're here with the ones I love. Take care of them, like I know you can." Another squeeze to my palm. "I need you to get them back in here. Stay with us?"

"I, ah, I have to go." He nodded, understanding shone in his eyes. "Oh, God, Gregory. I love you. You've shown me so much, you... Thank you." I kissed him on the cheek and ran to the door.

Not caring I probably looked an emotional mess, I opened the door and told his family, "He wants you back in there." Taking a deep breath, I moved aside as they walked in and closed the door behind them.

I went over to the wall, away from everyone, and sank to the ground, my head in my hands, but not crying as I wanted to. Instead, I thought of all the good times I'd had with Gregory in the short period we knew each other.

He'd asked me to help them through their loss, to be there for them. Of course I would, but would all of them let me? I had to agree with Gregory. We would be better off without MaryJane around. Hell, if she hadn't shown up in the first place, things would be different.

Would I still be with Isaac though? I didn't know.

All I knew was if it came down to it, I would protect them with my life. They were my family and I could no longer turn my back on them just because Isaac hurt my feelings.

Putting everything aside was what I had to do. No matter how much I ached for him inside.

I lifted my head to see Xavier sit beside me. His arm came around my shoulders. I gave him a half smile and leaned against his weight, while filling my mind with wonderful thoughts of Gregory—him trying to teach me to cook; the talks we had; the funny stories of the past, when he would start laughing at the main part and then it was hard to get the rest out of him, so in the end I'd just be laughing at him. So many good, happy memories and in such a short amount of time.

Gregory Grey would always be remembered by me.

I drew in a sharp breath.

"What is it, Leila?" Xavier asked.

"Someone needs to tell Caelen. Jezza will need him."

"I'll go get him," Xavier said and then quickly left.

Silence filled the hall. Unfortunately, it didn't last long. "Come on, how long does it take to die already," Mary-effing-Jane said.

Before I even thought of it, I stood and strolled towards her, ignoring her three guards at her side with their guns pointed at me. Just as I was about to reach her, Darik flashed in front of me, stopping me in my tracks. He grabbed me by the arms. I looked up to his face and he shook his head at me.

"Oh, let her go." MaryJane laughed. "It's not like she'd get to lay one finger on me anyway." She crossed her arms over her chest. "Look at you. You're only here so you can have a chance to comfort what's not yours. Tell me something, *Leila*. Who warms your bed at night? Oh, that's right, no one. You're alone. No one would love something like you. So while you have no one, I have Isaac. It's not like you could keep up with him, sweetheart. We're at it. All. Night. Long." She laughed at me.

My body shook with rage. For the first time in my life, I didn't have control over the change. I was fuming, pissed off with how uncaring she could be in a time like that. I wanted to rip her head off, claw out her eyes. Kill her.

"No," Darik growled, bringing my attention back to him. He lifted me off the ground while I shook from the change and dragged me to the wall. He held me against it, hiding me from everyone. "You will not do this, Leila. Take control of yourself. Now is not the time. Do not let her baiting win." He was right. I closed my eyes and clenched my fists. Calming my breaths, the shaking eventually stopped.

The lift doors opened and out walked Caelen and Xavier. Caelen looked defeated. They walked down the hall, taking in the tension that was obviously in the air, coming to a stop in front of myself and Darik.

"I was on my way here. I felt something was wrong. Foolishly, I left my phone at home. I went to your house. When you weren't there, I tried Isaac's. Some of the other lads told me what happened. I can't believe it. This is going to wreck her. She still lives with the pain of the loss of her parents, and now Gregory?"

"I know. She's going to really need you," I said. He nodded.

The door to the room opened. Jeremiah came out. His cheeks were wet but his eyes dry. Through clenched teeth, he told us, "He's gone."

Oh, God, my chest tightened as Isaac and Jezanna followed him out. Seeing the pain in their eyes was so hard. But I knew it matched my own expression, not only for the loss of Gregory, but also for what they'd gone through in the past. Jezanna spotted Caelen. He held his arms out to her and she ran into them, burying her face in his chest. I watched Isaac step into she-devil's embrace. Jeremiah stepped away from them all. I went to him, pulling him into my own arms. His body stiffened. I knew he wouldn't cry, like me, not in front of others. But I was rewarded with him giving into the hug and placing his arms around me. I glanced over his shoulder, looking straight into Isaac's eyes as he stared back over her shoulder.

I wanted that to be me. Still, I was glad I could be here for any part of my family. I mouthed, '*I'm sorry*,' as one tear escaped and ran down my cheek. We were near enough he was able to reach out his hand and, with one finger, he wiped that tear away.

"Master, we have incoming," Adan called from down the hall, just as the elevator doors opened and a doctor, with a nurse, walked out.

CHAPTER NINETEEN

Class wasn't in my cards Friday. We'd spent half the night up at the hospital, then the other half making arrangements. During the early hours, we were at my house talking. Not all of us though. Isaac went back to his own place with shithead, Darik and Adan. Jeremiah said he couldn't stand to be around all the falseness and came with us. I was pleased he was comfortable enough around me to let everything go once we got through the front door. I made everyone come down to my room where we all huddled around on my bed. Jeremiah, Jezanna, Caelen, Xavier and I talked, cried and laughed, and remembered everything that made Gregory the amazing man he'd been. Later, we curled up and slept.

I wished Isaac had been there for it. I felt terrible he'd gone back to a house with someone as cold as her. I could only hope Darik and Adan were taking care of him.

~

Darkness surrounds me. Every way I turn, I see nothing but black. My heart beats hard in my chest. My hands tremble along with my legs. I want to run, to scream, but I don't.

Because I know I'm waiting.

It isn't until I see two small red dots in the distance that I relax somewhat.

"Yes," I whisper. "That's what I'm waiting for."

The dots drift closer and closer.

And in a blink of an eye, which always makes me jump, they're right in front of me, so close I can reach out and touch them… No, touch the face that belongs to those red eyes.

I want to.

I need to.

Even though a small amount of fright fills me, I still know I'm safe.

The red eyes study me.

"You're mine," the voice growls…

When I jolted awake, I found an elbow in my left eye and one in my right rib. I pushed Jeremiah's arm from my face and Xavier's elbow from my rib and sat up. I looked around and smiled. They were all still sound asleep with emotional exhaustion. Jeremiah took up most of the space. Caelen was on the far end with Jezanna in his arms and while she had one hand on him, the other was holding Jeremiah's hand. I turned to Xavier next to me. He lay as stiff and straight as a board. Probably worried he'd fall off the bed, because he didn't have much room.

Slowly and quietly, I crept down the end of the bed, managing not to wake anyone. I grabbed some clothes and went for a shower. I looked out the window in the bathroom and saw it was already late in the day. The sun was nearly set over the horizon. I really wanted to go back to bed and then spend the rest of the night with my family. It hurt to leave them. But I'd made a promise to someone who needed help. I could only hope they'd stay asleep long enough and wouldn't even notice I'd disappeared.

My mind drifted back to Isaac, wondering how he was and what he was doing. He should have been at the house with his brother and sister.

Sighing, I got dressed, and on the way out of the house, I grabbed an energy bar to eat, as well as Jezanna's mobile. I quickly placed it in the front pocket of my hoodie. I had a feeling I was going to need it.

Guilt ate at me for leaving the house when I knew they

could need me. However, I was also worried about Sofia's safety, especially when I hadn't seen her in so long.

Jason's parents' house wasn't far from my own. In human form, I made my way over. Something told me I didn't want to show my feline part just yet. As I reached closer to his property, I slowed. Doubt ran through my mind, causing the hairs on the back on my neck to rise.

Taking a deep breath through my nose, I absorbed the many scents in the air. Bark, leaves, grass, dirt, humans. The only one that shocked me was the familiar woodsy scent of Ty. Was he here? Was he a part of this? I really hoped not.

Tension boiled, causing my stomach to flip. It was funny how calm I was until I scented someone I knew.

I had to relax myself, go in with a clear mind. Closing my eyes, I took another deep breath, shook out my limbs, and then crept closer.

Voices came from the right. It was close to his house, which was strange, unless he was having a party. A clearing came into sight and in it stood Jason, Mathew, Ronan and Steven, who were all from the football team.

Who I couldn't see was Sofia. Suspicion took over all other feelings. I stepped into the clearing and the conversation halted. They all turned to me smiling.

"Well, well. She did pull it off." Jason laughed.

Alarm bells rang through my mind. *Shit, it was a trap. RUN, RUN, RUN.*

The back door to his two-storey house opened and about ten more people came out. All students from college, including Jenna and her cronies. Within them was a concerned Sofia; she was being held by two guys.

"I'm so sorry, Leila. They made me. I had to get you here or they said they'd kill me and my family. Leila, please, please forgive me."

Crap.

She'd believed them when they said they'd kill her family. A snort left me. I highly doubted they would. But killing me. Yes, I could see that happening. No one in the town would care if I disappeared.

Was everything Sofia told me a lie? How stupid did I feel, falling for her story hook, line and sinker.

Though, how did Sofia get that black eye? Or those marks on her collarbone?

The group surrounded me, forming a circle. I let them. I wasn't going anywhere. I wanted and needed answers, plus I was in the mood to teach them a lesson.

Looking at my fingernails, I asked, "So who wants to be beaten first?" I smiled and placed my hands in my pockets, rocking back and forth on my feet. Trying to come across less afraid than I truly was.

Fuck, I'd better not die tonight. Any other night would be all right. Just not there, not by those people. I looked out at their scowling faces and thought it could be a possibility.

"Thank you, dear Jason, for bringing her here. I will reward you all later."

Double crap.

I knew that voice. Anyone would after hearing it only once —the irritating sound, which made you want to clench your teeth together.

Turning, I watched as Mary-fucking-Jane walked out of the woods.

"Really? You need all this help to take me down."

She laughed. "No, silly. I don't need their help. I want it. You see, I was so excited to find out you're so loathed. These sweet people want nothing more than to get rid of you. All this hate gives me chills and the chance to use them to do what I want. Then I don't have to get my hands dirty." She giggled. "At least then Isaac won't blame me for your death. I know, *Leila*, I know he still cares for you and it makes me so sick." She screamed. "So now, if I have you out of the way, we can go back to how things were, until Gerald gets here, of course."

Scoffing, I shook my head. Why was I not surprised she was in cahoots with Gerald? My hand went into my pockets. I rocked back on my feet while my fingers pressed the buttons on Jezanna's phone, praying I pushed the right ones to receive some help.

Something MaryJane said triggered me to look out around the crowd. What I hadn't noticed before was most of them had vague looks in their eyes. *They're being controlled.* She was using her vampire power to make them hers. So they'd do her bidding, to kill me. The only ones who didn't have the glazed look was Jason and Sofia.

"So you can control minds. What other tricks can you do?"

"You will just have to wait and see."

I should have—no wait, I'm not going to start on the I should haves or wishes. This just plain sucks and I can't do anything about it.

Shifting forms was one solution, but I wouldn't until it was the last resort. There were too many of them around to know my secret.

"Where are all your guards?"

"Around. Come, people." She clapped. "Hurry up with the task."

Jason, Jenna, and their so-called friends started descending upon me. They moved closer, but slowly. Were they waiting for me to do something?

"Bring the girl to me first. I could use a little snack." Mary-stupid-Jane motioned towards Monica and Bertina, who were now holding Sofia. They dragged her struggling body over. "I want you to watch what you helped organise," she said and held Sofia's face with one hand so she looked at me. Sofia whimpered. I knew a vampire's hand could crush a skull.

I was hit from behind first and fell to my knees. I looked over my shoulder to see Steven holding a baseball bat. *No wonder it hurt like a motherfucker.* I took a kick to the head and a punch to the back. They all joined in at the same time, kicking, punching, pulling and screaming at me.

"Freak, Witch, Weirdo, Bitch, Satan, Loser," were just some of the taunts thrown my way as they beat me.

Everything in me wanted to fight back. To change into my feline form and attack them all. Hurt them, because the agony they put me through was viciously raw. I whimpered. I yelled and I cried out in pain.

But I didn't shift. Because if I turned, if I started, I wouldn't be able to stop, and then I'd have death upon my hands. Death of humans. If they had been anything else, they would have more strength than they were using, which was lucky for me in one way. No matter how much they hated me, wanted *me* dead, I couldn't bring myself to retaliate.

Therefore, I took it all and prayed once they finished, I'd still be alive enough to kill the one who deserved to be dead.

Even with all the sounds around me, nothing blocked out Sofia's gasp as MaryJane bit into her.

What I was surprised to hear was the spitting and cursing. "What in the hell are you? You taste disgusting."

Turning my head, I was able to see, through my swelling eyes, MaryJane take a step away from Sofia.

"It's called dog." Sofia took the distraction to her advantage. She punched MaryJane in the face and ran towards me. "Get the fuck off her." She pushed and punched her way through the people to fall to her knees beside me. "Leila, oh God, Leila, can you hear me?" She pulled me against her. My left eye, the black one, was still somehow able to stay open and searched her worried face. I managed a small nod. There was no chance I was going to be able to speak for a while. I already felt the skin around my face, back, stomach, legs, arms—okay, practically everywhere—swelling and bruising.

The agony in my body was unlike anything I had ever felt. The fear from it beat my heart hard in my chest, had my body shaking like a leaf. I didn't want to move, didn't want to breathe; even that hurt.

The people around us shuffled from foot to foot. I could sense their unease. They wanted to continue, but whatever they saw with Sofia made them pause. Laughter started to the left. MaryJane came forward, giggling away.

"You silly girl, do you honestly think you can stop this? It's too late." Her laughter abruptly stopped. Sofia stiffened as MaryJane's gaze took hold of her. "Grab her. She will no longer give you trouble while I have control," she ordered the others. They moved closer, grabbing the stiff Sofia by the arms and dragging her a few feet away.

MaryJane sighed. "I can see I'll have to finish this myself." She bent quickly and in one swoop had me by the neck, dangling in front of her. "I would love to taste you, drink you dry, but I have a feeling Isaac would sense your blood flowing through mine. So I won't. Such a pity. Still, now at least I can witness your life end, as I squeeze it out of you."

Her grip tightened. My hands came up trying to loosen them around my neck. Kicking out, scratching her arms and ignoring the stabbing, aching pain wanting me to stop, I fought.

I wasn't going to let her do this to me and leave her with my family. I dug deep within myself for the strength I needed. Pushing the pain down, I dropped my shields. Her look of surprise actually brought a smile to my aching face, and no matter how much it was going to be excruciating, I was prepared to do it before my last breath ran out, and before my lungs burst in my chest.

I shifted into my feline form.

A scream ripped from my throat then turned into a growl. MaryJane hadn't moved her stunned body. At least her shock gave me the chance to move. Her grip had eased a little after my neck grew in size and, because of that, I was able to breathe again. I swiped my left paw with my long, sharp claws at her face, opening up a huge gash down her right cheek.

Unfortunately, it brought her out of her stunned silence. She dropped me and bounded back, levitating up into the sky. I landed on my feet, like all cats did, and glared up at her. Screaming started behind me; a couple of the others ran for the house, leaving Sofia on the ground.

"Leila?" Sofia whispered.

From MaryJane's lack of concentration, Sofia was no longer held under her spell. Violent screams ripped through the night as the rest of the others came out of their trance. They quickly fled into the house. I watched as Jason followed them with a frown.

"What a nice little trick you have, *Leila*. I wonder, does Isaac know? Oh, well, doesn't matter. You'll still end up the same way. Dead." She circled me in the sky.

Even I had to admit it was cool she could fly like that. Was Isaac able to do it too? I shook my head. I didn't have time to admire it. *Focus, damn it.* The air around me thickened. I felt her power building. She was preparing herself for something and I had no doubt that *something* was going to be aimed at me.

Her movement stopped. She hovered above me, her hands out at her sides, her fingers twitching. What was she going to do? Next thing I knew, I dodged to the left as a bright blue glow came from her hand, shooting down towards me. I only barely got out of the way.

Growling started behind me. I jumped around in time to see a large dog running toward MaryJane. It leaped into the air, bouncing off a tree, which shook from the force behind the bound. The dog had its mouth open heading straight for Mary-Jane's foot. The same blue light hit, and the shifter fell to the ground in an unconscious form, but its body shook from whatever the bitch had done to it.

I ran to its side. My own body wanted to break down and stop working with every step I took. I breathed deeply at the dog's side. Its scent filled my nose and I knew then it was Sofia lying there as a large, Samoyed canine.

She had been telling the truth.

A sizzle sounded behind me as MaryJane fired off another shot. I moved just in time to see it land where I'd been next to Sofia.

I've had enough of this bitch. I have to take her down.

Running off into the woods, I leaped into the trees and circled around on her. Hoping to take her by surprise. I jumped into the next tree to my right, knowing from the scent it would bring me out near her.

"Leila, you can't win this," she yelled.

Silently, I crept forward from one tree branch to another, and just as I came out behind her, ready to attack, she turned. Still, I jumped, landing right on top of her. The force from my weight brought her to the ground quickly. We landed with a thump. Immediately, she wrapped her arms around my waist. Tighter and tighter they squeezed.

A rib or two cracked and I howled in pain.

The only thing I could do was bite through her neck. She must have sensed it, because a second later, I was thrown off her, landing several feet away.

I got to my feet quickly, my body screaming at me to stop, to just lie down and rest. I had no time for that. MaryJane slowly rose to her feet, never taking her eyes from me.

"I didn't want to do it this way. It's a quick way to die and I wanted you to suffer. But I see I have no choice now." Her power stretched out and surrounded me. I could feel it wanting to crawl inside of me. Thankfully, I had my mind shield raised.

"Let me in," MaryJane screamed, her insanity riding her hard. She really was one crazy bitch.

Before I could even blink, she picked up a rock and threw it at me. It slammed into my face. It didn't matter. She could bring on all the hurt she wanted, but nothing would be able to break through my shield, even distraction.

Using speed unknown to humans, she disappeared into the woods. Backing away from the tree, I took myself into the centre of the opened area, while making sure all the advantage points were visible from her coming attack. Only in the last second, I remembered to look up, and there she was, descending fast. I jumped up to meet her, my jaw sinking into her arm. She screamed in pain, but managed to wrap her other arm around my neck.

"Let go, you beast."

As I tightened my jaw, she let out a fierce hiss. Her own grip increased around my neck.

I scissored my jaw back and forth, remembering not to swallow the blood pouring out. I had only a few inches to go before her whole arm would fall from her body below the elbow.

No. Not now. My vision blurred; I was on the verge of passing out, and if I did that, I'd be as good as dead.

"Stop!" a voice bellowed into the night.

Once MaryJane's body stiffened, her grip loosened. At the same time, bodies fell from the sky. Okay, so maybe they jumped from the trees, but it was a bit hard to see when I was busy chewing down on the arm of my enemy.

"I said stop."

And that was when all my focus went down the drain.

Ty moved forward into my view. He was dressed entirely in black. Earlier, I'd come to the conclusion, once I didn't see him there at the start, I'd imagined his scent.

However, there he was.

With five others standing behind him, also all dressed in black. With the new distraction, MaryJane was able to pull her arm free, throw me to the ground and pin me with her foot on my throat.

My strength evaporated from within me. I had nothing left to fight. My body was tired, my mind consumed with all the suffering my body had been through.

I was empty.

In the background, I heard weapons drawn and then guns being cocked and... growling?

"You will s-stop or you die," Ty ordered.

MaryJane released the hard pressure on my throat, though I remained pinned to the ground. She looked up to Ty and laughed.

"You can't stop me, fool." She raised her leg and I knew it would be my end as soon as she brought it down upon me.

"Maybe he can't, but I will."

Oh, sweet Lord, I know that voice. I loved that voice.

CHAPTER TWENTY

"Isaac," MaryJane squealed, her eyes wide and set in panic. She backed away from me quickly. I felt his power surrounding me. It was almost choking. I turned my head in time to see Isaac walk calmly from the woods. Following him were Jeremiah, Jezanna, Caelen and two of Caelen's friends from Boozers.

All of them, except Jezanna and Isaac, were tightly holding another person. MaryJane's guards? Also approaching from within the woods with their own prisoners were Adan, Xavier and Darik.

"What do you think you're doing, MaryJane? I told you no harm was to come to her, and yet here you are. Explain now." Isaac stopped a few feet away.

She dipped her head as if in shame. "I would, but you'll not like it."

"Try me."

Her head raised. She turned her angry glare to me. Not daring to move, I stayed on the ground, on my side. My eyes healing enough for me to see.

"She will always be between us if she's here." She looked from me to Isaac. "I wanted to remove the pest, so we can go on to how it was before. I want to help you lead. *I* deserve to be the one beside you."

"No, you don't. You deserve nothing when you're in allegiance with the one who wishes me dead," Isaac snarled. MaryJane's breath hitched.

"You, you know?"

"Yes."

"Then there's no longer any reason for me to be here." With that, she disappeared from sight.

"Peter, Henry, Kalvin, s-spread out and look for her. Sh-she has to be taken into custody," Ty ordered... his people?

"Darik, Adan, go with them. Find her, kill her."

"You have n-no right here, Isaac." Ty glared.

"I have *all* the right. She's one of my people, and by the laws, I have every right to do to her as I wish," he barked.

Isaac didn't wait for a reply, but turned his attention to me. Who, I might add, was not stupid, so I was still lying very still, trying not to be noticed. He glided over to me and knelt, reaching out a hand to run through my fur at the side of my face. I couldn't stop the flinch, even if I wanted to, because the power he had pouring out of him made me wary, besides the fact he'd just ordered a death sentence on his girlfriend. Wouldn't it be better to capture her, find out all the information she had? Maybe beat her along the way. That could be fun.

He removed his hand quickly and sighed loudly. "Please, Leila, don't be too angry with me. I've had my reasons for the occurring activity over the last week. I can only hope you will understand them."

"You need to back away from her, Isaac," Ty warned. Isaac didn't move. He looked over his shoulder at Ty, who trained a gun at him.

"You dare threaten my master," Xavier yelled. He threw MaryJane's vampire he held to the ground and unsheathed his sword, pointing it toward Ty's neck.

Ty didn't even acknowledge him and continued, "You may have a lot of explaining to do, but right now isn't the time. Sh-she's hurt badly and bleeding, so back the hell off."

"Do you think I would chomp down on her when she's like this? All I've wanted is to protect her," Isaac growled. He gave a signal only some would notice to stop Xavier. Instead, Xavier grumbled about something and went back to the other vampire, roughly securing his arms once again. At least MaryJane's vampire didn't attempt to fight or leave.

"Funny way of showing it. Now move," Ty demanded.

"Come, brother," Jezanna called. "Let's all take a step back and think clearly."

Isaac stood and took one small step away. "You have some explaining to do yourself, Ty. Leila will have her questions, as do I. Will you be ready to answer them?"

"Of course," he said.

Hell yes, I had many questions. Was he another one who'd played me all along? Who could I really trust?

It was Ty's turn to look over his shoulder to one of his men. "Penny, you ready to do your thing inside? We have too many w-witnesses."

Okay, I was wrong. There were men and women; there could even be a super-agent goldfish for all I knew. People did like to lie to me. Wait, didn't Ty have a sister named Penny? Was that her, or was it another lie?

Penny moved off towards the house.

"Jezanna, Caelen. Go with her and help, please."

Before Caelen left, I reached out to his mind. *Caelen, you need to contain Jason in there. He helped set all of this up. He needs to pay.*

He will, love. Do you give me permission to deal with it?

Even though I wanted my own revenge, I wasn't up for it and I wanted Jason dealt with as soon as possible. I knew Caelen was gleefully ready for the job. *Yes.*

"She doesn't need it." Ty glared.

"Just in case."

"Yes, master." Caelen bowed and then nodded to me.

"Brother." Jezanna tilted her head down in respect.

They were acting so formal and I knew why. Anyone would if they could feel the power rolling off Isaac. It didn't help that Isaac still felt there was danger around with Ty and his merry men and women being there.

Jezanna and Caelen walked off, following Penny into the house. Commotion erupted, people screamed and stuff was thrown around, until quickly, it quieted. After a second, the back door banged open and I saw Caelen dragging a struggling Jason out. I wondered why he wasn't screaming, until I saw something shoved in his mouth. Before Caelen dragged him off into the woods, Jason's eyes caught mine. In them, I saw fear. He deserved everything he got and I felt no remorse. In fact, if I were in my human form, everyone would have seen a wicked smile on my lips.

I looked to my side as footsteps approached. Ty headed my way. Isaac watched him with deadly eyes.

"Leila, I'm going to pick you up now."

Shit, it would hurt. I even cringed at the thought. I ached all over. My whole body throbbed to its own tune of pain. My stomach churned and I wanted to crawl into a tight ball and just sleep. If I didn't wake, it wouldn't bother me, because then at least the pain would stop.

Ty scooped me up into his strong arms and held me gently against him. I whimpered into his neck. Internally, I screamed.

He turned back to his last man, or woman. "Steph, I'm taking her home. Meet me there when things are cleaned up here and the others have returned."

"Yes, boss," a quiet voice replied.

"You're not leaving without me," Isaac said.

"Master, what about these?" Xavier asked, gesturing towards MaryJane's other guards.

He exhaled loudly. "I don't wish to kill any of you. Will you swear your allegiance to me and my people?"

All of them looked startled by his question. All but one agreed.

"No," the only idiot yelled. It was one of the guards from the hospital, the taller, largely built one, with brown hair and dark grey eyes. He was also the idiot who'd held the gun on me. "Our mistress is right. You deserve to be destroyed by Gerald's hand."

"I see. I'm sorry you see it that way. Nevertheless, I cannot let you go and harm one of my own. Xavier." Xavier moved quickly. Within seconds, he was positioned behind the guy, twisting his neck until his head popped off his body. Xavier stood tall, threw the head away and dusted himself off from the particles the body left behind after disintegrating into nothing.

"Xavier, please take the rest to my home and have the others there watch them. I'm sorry, but until we can adjoin in the blood ceremony, so you're all under my protection, I can't trust you. Xavier, after that's done, come back to Leila's house. I've already informed the others of my plans. They'll be returning here soon to help with the clean-up and then will continue on to Leila's."

"Yes, Master." Xavier gave a small bow, collected up the rest of MaryJane's men and left with Caelen's friends helping him.

"It would be better and faster if I carried her," Isaac said. My heart soared from the thought of having his arms around me once again. I couldn't let it happen. I stiffened.

Ty felt it, because he said, "No. I will carry her."

Isaac uttered some swear words I'd never heard come out of his mouth before and disappeared into the night.

What about Sofia? She needed help more than me.

Thankfully, Ty answered my unasked question. "Don't worry, Leila. I won't drop you, and I will have someone bring Sofia along. Steph, have Peter do it." Ty smiled down at me, and I suddenly saw a flash of silver through his eyes before it disappeared.

What was that?

He took in a deep breath and started running. He was just as fast as I was in my human form.

Who was this guy?

Did I really know anything about him?

Was he actually blind? Because honestly, no blind guy could run through the woods like he was and not hit a tree.

Lies. There were too many lies.

CHAPTER TWENTY ONE

Ty walked in through the already opened back door to my house. I looked at the door as we passed through and saw it was nearly pulled off its hinges. *What happened to it?*

Other than the door, the rest of the house seemed unharmed. Ty bypassed the living room, where Isaac sat stiffly on the couch, and went straight to my bedroom. He laid me down on my unmade bed.

"I will l-leave you to…" he cleared his throat, "change. Just call if you need me. I'll wait outside your door."

Once the door closed, I wanted to lay there and succumb to sleep. However, I had no chance of it. Grunting and groaning, I moved into a sitting position. Blood had started to dry into my fur. I was in pain with every move I made, and now I was about to make it worse. But I had to shift back. I needed answers.

Still feeling nauseated by the small amount of blood I had managed to ingest, I started the shift.

My bones cracked, shrank, and moved around inside my body. Most had healed from my beating when I'd laid watching on in the woods. Still, every bit of me was tender.

I whimpered, growled and hissed through the agony, and once I was in my human form, the sounds changed to screaming, panting and cursing.

"Leila, what can I do?" Ty asked. I couldn't answer him; it would take too much out of me. "That's it, I-I'm coming in."

A crash echoed in the hallway.

"You will not dare enter Leila's room," Isaac yelled.

"She's in pain."

"I know and neither of us can help her." Isaac's voice cracked, his sorrow showing. "Take your hand away from the door," Isaac hissed. Something crashed to the floor.

"S-stop ordering me around, Isaac. I'm not one of your groupies and throw something at me again, I'll fucking hurt you."

Isaac scoffed. At least their bickering helped distract me for a little while. I fell back on the sweat, dirt and blood-soaked bed, breathing hard.

I wanted to take time to think, to lay there and rest, but I didn't. Weakly, I stood from the bed on shaky legs, grabbed some clothes and swayed to the door, leaning my head against it.

"Ty." I cleared my dry, raw throat. "Ty, move away. I want to go to the bathroom."

"Do you need help?" Ty asked.

"Help will not come from you. Jezanna, please attend to Leila."

Jezanna's here? Please, Jezza come help me.

"Ty, move away please so I can get through. I think it best if you watched your own people in the living room. They seem tense enough to shoot one of us."

You go, girl. I smiled at her teacher tone.

Ty's footsteps retreated. A knock on my door jerked me away from it.

"Leila, I'm coming in." I backed up and the door opened. Jezanna gasped at the sight of my bruised, beaten body. "Oh, darling. Oh, dear God." Her hand went to her throat. "Look at what she's done to you."

My control cracked and I broke down. Jezanna was at my side in the next second, wrapping me in a blanket and taking me into her arms. "She will pay for this. Mark my words, she *will* pay." She gently pulled me over to the bed and sat me next to her, holding me in her arms until the tears dried up. I wanted to cry more, guilt clawing away at me as it felt like I was cheating Gregory from the time I'd taken away for grieving him.

Jezanna stiffened beside me. "Someone's coming."

A soft knock at the door soon followed.

"Leila, can I come in?" Sofia asked with a shaky voice. Instead of having to answer, Jezanna went over to the door, opened it and walked back to sit next to me, placing her arm around my shoulders. I knew it was to show she would protect me if she had to.

Sofia looked as bad as I felt. Her hair was a mess. She had dirt, scrapes and bruises all over her and her clothes. Warily, she entered and closed the door behind her. Instead of sitting on the bed, she sat on the floor near the door.

"You should not be here. You caused this to happen. You tricked Leila. For that, you had better watch your back. I don't take kindly to people who hurt my family members." It was the first time I'd heard Jezanna speak so threateningly.

"Jezza."

"No. It's all right. She's right, Leila, you and I both know it. I was glad when that Peter guy brought me here. I needed to talk to you, to check you're okay and to apologize a thousand times over."

Licking my dry lips, I asked, "Just tell me why, Sofia."

"Let me start at the beginning, please. Then I hope you can… I don't know, understand. Maybe, forgive me?"

"That will never happen," Jezanna snapped.

Sofia nodded. "I get that. I do," she said then sighed. "My parents were both attacked by different people who carried the canine disease. It wasn't until many years later they met and married. Then Raven and I came along. They thought we'd be born like them, but we weren't. We were human. So they gave us a choice. They offered to turn us when we turned sixteen, to make us like them. We both saw the advantages of having canine blood. So we said yes." She looked down to the floor, absent-mindedly rubbing at her collarbone.

"Everything was going along fine. We were all happy. I really loved the days we'd be out running together as a pack. Until one night Jason had caught Raven and I shifting."

Tears fell freely from her eyes.

"The night I told you about, Leila. It did happen. Only it was different. Jenna had left the car and Jason kept driving. Then he pulled over and turned to me. Before he, he r-raped me. He said if I wanted to keep my secret, I had to do whatever he wanted. To start off with, I refused. Which was when he hit me and, and… I was too shocked to run. I just started crying. He said if I didn't do as I was told, my family's secret would get out and we'd be driven out of the town. I was sure my parents wouldn't care. They'd be proud of me for fighting back. But then, he said if I didn't follow the rules, he and his friends would have some fun with Raven, before… before they killed us all. Do you see? I couldn't let that happen, so I played along." She wiped at her eyes. "I'm so sorry for the pain I've caused you. I know I should've told you right from the start it would be a set-up because he wanted to impress MaryJane. But I thought… You see, I didn't believe those things about you. I still thought you were an average teenage girl. I had hoped a witch, but now that I know you can change as well, we could have helped each other and we wouldn't be like this now." She sobbed into her hands. I wanted to console her. It wasn't her fault I had someone gunning for me.

"Sofia. Sofia, listen. I don't blame you for anything. There's nothing to forgive." I shrugged. "You were tricked as much as I was."

Jezanna cleared her throat and we both looked at her. "I still think none of this should have happened, but I can understand your reasons for protecting your family."

"Thank you," Sofia whispered.

"I would get up and hug you, but I'm naked under here and that would just feel weird." I smiled, making her laugh.

"Don't your clothes change with you?"

"No. When I shift, my clothes fall away. Why, do yours?"

"Yes." Sofia nodded.

"I believe the difference is that Sofia is a shape-shifter, where Leila is a were. Your cat form is at one with you; they're both the same person. Leila was born this way." Looking to Jezanna, she saw my questionable look. "I've been Googling."

Sofia and I burst out laughing at the random answer from a vampire.

But if what Jezanna said was true, then *Holy crap*. There were many different species out there.

"Jezza, since you have all the answers, what in the hell happened to my back door?"

Jezanna laughed. "Uh, yes. That would be because Isaac received a mysterious call from someone using my phone."

That was right; when I put my hands in my pocket at Jason's, I found the phone and dialled the first number on it, hoping it would be someone who could help. Turned out it worked.

"He came straight here looking for you and in the process of entering the house quickly, the door just seemed to come right off. He found us all in your room, demanding to know where you were. I knew something happened, so I told him what you'd planned."

Now I was grateful I'd mentioned to Jezanna where Jason lived or else they could've turned up too late.

"Leila, I'm going to have to go," Sofia said sadly.

"That's okay. I'm sure you feel as I do, ready to crash. Look, I hope you'll come by more often."

Fresh tears filled her eyes. "I would love that. Thank you, Leila, and I'll bring Raven with me. She's always wanted to get to know you." She stood, came over and gave me a quick hug. I tried not to grimace in pain at the contact. "Bye, Jezanna," she said as she opened the door.

"Yes, goodbye. And don't fear. Jason has been dealt with,"— she glanced to me quickly, I nodded—"for what he did to Leila.

He was not allowed to live, and now that I know what he did to you, I wished we had prolonged his death a little longer. Still, know this. He did suffer." Sofia nodded, taking it all in before Jezanna added, "The others will no longer remember what happened this night or even if Jason had said anything to them regarding you and your family."

Sofia sniffed, gratitude shining in her eyes. "Thank you, thank you so much."

Once she left, Jezanna turned to me. "Come on. Let's get you cleaned up."

Chapter Twenty Two

Jezanna helped me to the bathroom. She stayed that time because from my swaying, I couldn't convince her I'd be safe enough in a shower on my own. Not that she got in with me; she stood silently by the door. I turned off the water and Jezanna handed me a towel. I tried to be quick drying myself, but there was no hope in that. My body still ached too much with every move. I got out with the towel wrapped around my body, and the first thing I saw was my reflection in the mirror. MaryJane *had* done a wonderful job on me. I was covered in bruises and scratches.

At least you're not dead.

Well, there was that to be grateful for.

Jezanna helped me dress in a warm hooded jumper and tracksuit pants. I tied my wet hair up in a ponytail and looked to Jezanna's concerned face.

"I'm all right." I gave her a small smile.

"I know you're not, Leila. We can do this another night. I can tell them all to leave."

Scoffing, I said, "Yeah, right. No, it's better to get it over with. But thanks."

She gave me a nod, opened the door and walked out first to the quiet living room. As I came out behind her, the first movement I saw was Isaac rising from the couch coming towards me at the same time Ty was.

They pulled up in front of me, standing next to one another. Isaac went to reach out to me, but I stepped back.

"Don't," I whispered. I couldn't look him in the eyes, knowing he'd be hurt by my word.

Instead, I walked around him and Ty to stand near the front window, next to Jeremiah and Jezanna. Isaac's sigh was loud enough for everyone to hear. I heard him move to sit back down on the couch as Ty took back his position on a kitchen chair in front of the television.

My stomach growled. I was starving, but I knew if I ate something, I'd be bringing it back up in the next second. My stomach was unsettled. I was unsure if it was my nerves or fear from what they had to say or just plain exhaustion.

I opened my mouth to get the show on the road, only to clamp it shut again when some commotion started outside in the back yard. I turned to face the back door as others moved quickly to stand in front of me, ready to take on whatever was coming in. My heart thumped hard to see Isaac was one of them.

He wasn't alone. Before me was also Ty, Jeremiah, Caelen, Jezanna and another of Ty's people. All I knew was it was a guy, from the build—tall, broad, strong. The scent wafting off him filled in the rest. Yes, definitely male. The testosterone was too strong to think otherwise. It was too bad a black balaclava hid his face, like all of Ty's people, except Ty. For some reason, I wanted to see what he looked like.

The back door opened and in walked Darik, Xavier, Adan, Jensen and two others Ty had sent off to track MaryJane. Jensen didn't pause at the doorway of the living room, like the rest. He kept coming and then fell to the ground on his knees in front of Isaac.

Bending low, his face touched the ground. "My apology. I didn't know what she had planned. I would have stopped it if I had. Please, if you will have me, I wish to swear my allegiance to you and your people."

"Rise, Jensen Neon," Isaac ordered. Jensen was on his feet within a second. "I will accept your oath. Tomorrow night, the ceremony will be held for those who want to be a part of my family."

A small smile lit my face. At least Xavier would be happy.

"Thank you, Master." Jensen bowed and stepped into the background.

People started to relax around me. I sank to the floor, crossed my legs and looked out to them all.

"Someone had better start," I said.

"I would like to explain my part, but I'm not permitted to speak in front of the vampires," Ty said as he walked back to his seat, with the other fella, who kept my attention, following. The sway of his body, the liquid movements did something to me deep within my stomach. I let the blush come, because it was obvious to anyone who was watching me I'd just checked out the guy's butt. And, bloody hell, even that said guy knew and started laughing. His laugh was deep and rich, and I wanted to drink it down. I turned away and shook my head. Unfortunately, I'd turned toward Isaac on the couch. He openly gave the guy a death glare. When he looked to me, his expression softened.

"Sire," Darik called. "We need to update you."

"Very well," Isaac said.

Darik dipped his head. "We couldn't catch her, Sire. She's still out there. I'm sorry."

My stomach dropped.

God, she was still out there, still after me. What would she do next? Murder me in my sleep?

"Leila," Isaac said.

But I didn't—couldn't stop all the thoughts of how Mary-Jane would plan to kill me next. Panic rose in my chest, but I didn't want to break in front of everyone. Even though most of them already knew or had heard I had a near breakdown in my bedroom before. So why not let the terror take over? Why not let myself drown in it?

It was bound to happen, because I was destined to be dead.

"Leila. Look at me." Someone shook me. My gaze focused on Isaac crouched in front of me. "She will not harm you again. I will not allow it."

Could he stop it? He couldn't before. Would he want to? I didn't know. I knew nothing, and it was mixing all my thoughts up. What was right? What was wrong? Who could I believe?

Hissing and growling started around me. I shook off my stupid paranoia. Damn it, she would not beat me down. I was stronger than that.

I can do this. I have to do this. I want to live. I want to love and protect my family freely.

Clenching my fists, I took a deep breath and looked up to see Jeremiah holding back Isaac, while Ty was... holding back the masked guy with the cute butt.

What's that about?

Standing, I yelled, "Stop." Everything quieted. "I don't care what's going on. I need answers and I want them now. Ty, if you want to speak with me, you have to do it in front of my people. They're my family. Everything you say, I'll just tell them anyway."

Isaac shrugged off his brother and gave Ty a smug look. Ty shook his head and let go of who he held.

Rolling my eyes, I added, "And, Isaac, the same goes for you. Everyone speaks freely in front of everyone or I'm going to scream."

"I agree, Leila," Isaac said.

"Yeah. I guess. They'll just kick my arse later for it," Ty replied mildly.

Who was going to kick his arse?

"Good, great." I nodded. "Now who's starting?" No one said anything. "Okay then, I will. Seems you two are being stubborn jerks." A few laughed. Only I wasn't trying to be funny. I looked to Isaac, who stood by the wall near the front door. "How did you know she worked with Gerald?"

He came back to sit on the couch, glancing up at me as he

said, "I found out the day she arrived. After leaving *your* room that night." I didn't miss the emphasis, but I had no idea why or to whom he was trying show off to. It seemed all men, regardless of species, could be confusing idiots. "Darik and I were driving home when Seraphine and Hamish came out of nowhere. They explained they followed Mervin,"— known as Freckles to me —"to MaryJane's residence. There, they overheard Mervin informing her of where I was. The strange part was, he never mentioned who and what you were, Leila. She ordered him to stay at her house, because she would be the one to take care of everything by controlling and delivering me to Gerald, along with my people. Seraphine and Hamish quickly left to inform me of her plan. I asked them to return to her house to… end Mervin and stay there in case they could learn more."

My breath hitched. "So you played along with her, why?"

How could you do that? I wanted to scream.

"I wanted information. She knows where Gerald is. She has inside information. I did it to protect everyone I care for." He glared and then sighed. "Now, it's all for nothing. She'll be heading straight to him and then he will come."

That just pissed me off. I needed to kick him so hard it would hurt for a week.

"You prick. You overprotective little shit," I snapped, my hands going to my hips as I glared down at him. "You stayed with her, you slept with her, you let her touch you, kiss you, all for what? What information did you get? You told me once you could never hurt me. Well, you have. Question is, was it all worth it? Please tell me it was worth it!" My chest heaved with my angry breath. I shouldn't have lost it in front of everyone there, but the fire that burned within me wouldn't let up until I'd had my say.

He looked absolutely wrecked from every word I'd delivered. My heart hurt, because I was the cause of it. Yet, I wanted to throw my hands up in the air and stomp my foot because I was annoyed also.

"I have nothing. I thought I was doing the right thing, Leila. I never wanted to hurt you. Please know that—"

"Just shut up. Don't you get it? You did hurt me. Every touch, every caress you shared with her, cut me deeper and deeper each time. And now I *know* you did it to protect me, us." I shook my head. "I—we can take care of ourselves. We fight our own battles. You need to get some things straight and start asking for some help or you will never be the right ruler for your people." I stopped once I saw Darik draw his dagger. "Darik, if you want to use that on me, then do it right now. I don't give a shit. But if you're not, then back the fuck off." He shrugged and used it to pick out dirt from under his nails. I sighed, dropped my arms and calmed my voice before I continued, "Gerald will come and eat you up if you don't get off your high horse and believe in everyone here. All of your people are willing to help, to fight alongside you. None of us want to see you injured. It would kill us all. But I'm afraid you will, if you continue like you are, workin' alone, taking on *everything* alone." I rubbed at my eyes to erase the few stray tears wanting to fall.

Looking to the floor, I composed myself. "Your turn, Ty. Start explaining." I glanced up to give Ty my full attention. I knew Isaac was still looking at me. His gaze burned. All of the other vampires stared openly at me too. I'd shocked them all with my outburst.

Ty cleared his throat. "I'm not sure if I want to now. Will you chew my head off as well?"

Snorting, I hid the smile wanting to come out. Instead, I turned my whole body to face him. "Depends on what you have to say."

He grinned and began. "Two years ago, I was approached by... some people. They asked me if I wanted to work for them. I s-said yes. They also approached my sister and the others here. An assignment came up, where I was told to keep an eye on you, Leila, so I did. I often wondered why they asked this of me, until tonight that was." He removed his glasses and rubbed at his hazy eyes. He left the glasses off and continued, "This—us here, we're a team who have special abilities. As you can see, I am blind, but I can also see, only shadowing outlines. I can run fast and I have excellent hearing. My sister can control minds and erase thoughts." He gestured to Penny, who sat on the floor beside him. She pulled off her black balaclava and wow, she was beautiful with her long blonde hair, which was tied back. Her shining blue eyes were mesmerising.

"Is your name really Penny?" I asked.

"Yes." She smiled.

"Does your mother work two jobs?"

"No. Not since we started these jobs. She no longer needs to work."

At least Ty hadn't been lying about everything. Maybe stretching the truth, but not a lie; it counted in my books.

Ty gestured to another, who stood behind him. "This here is Peter." Peter pulled off his balaclava. He was short, with red hair and light green eyes. "He can talk to animals and is very strong." *Okay, impressive.* "Over by the kitchen is Henry. His sister Steph is outside, no doubt. Henry is a pyrotechnic and Steph can read emotions and control metal."

I could understand why Steph would be outside with so many emotions flying around in the house. It would be hard for her. I wondered if she looked anything like her brother who had dark brown, shoulder-length hair and light brown eyes.

Eagerness filled me as I turned my gaze to the last person to be introduced. The one I wanted to know. Ty smirked at my impatience. Isaac growled at it.

"Last, we have Kalvin." Ty chuckled.

Kalvin took off his cover, and damn it, the sight of him made me gasp, sending a nice shiver down my spine. He was stunning. Absolutely eye boggling with short and messy, light brown hair and deep honey-coloured eyes. If I had to guess, he'd have to be a vampire to be that good-looking. "Kalvin here can—"

"Boss, let me do it," his deep throaty voice said, making me squirm a little. Ty nodded.

Then Kalvin dropped his shields.

We all felt what he was. My body stiffened. I had to gain control over myself, because right then, I wanted to run over to him purring and rub my whole body against his.

"You're… you're a…"

"Yeah." He grinned. "I'm a werecat. Like you."

A sharp snapping noise broke what felt like the intimate gaze Kalvin and I had going on. I glanced over to see that Isaac had broken off the armrest on my couch.

However, I didn't care. I looked back to Kalvin and he smiled.

Amazing. I'm not the only one. There are others.

How could it be?

How was he working for Ty?

And just who was Ty working for?

Reluctantly, I dragged my gaze from Kalvin to Ty. I asked, "What does this mean? Who do you work for and what do you want from me?"

"We all work for a s-secret special force within the government."

Whoa, what the hell?

"No!" Isaac bellowed. "She will not. Never," he ordered, standing. All the vampires took fighting stances.

"What?" I asked, obviously not understanding what Isaac already had.

Ty smiled and said the words I wasn't ready for. "We want you to come work with us."

CHAPTER TWENTY THREE

No one laughed or smiled, so I knew Ty's request was a real one. They wanted me to work for a special branch in the government.

Me.

God, I wanted to laugh at the thought of it.

"What does it entail?" I asked. Curiosity pushed the question forward.

Isaac spun to me. "You can't do this," he growled. His hands fisted at his sides. His jaw clenched and his eyes showed determination. He wouldn't *allow* me to join them. Little did he know he had no say over the matter, or over me at all.

Ignoring him, I looked to Ty again, even though my eyes and body pleaded with me to take in Kalvin again.

"I need more answers before I even contemplate it," I said.

"Of course. Our boss should be here any moment. He can tell you everything you need to know."

Nodding, I sighed, not sure I'd be able to honestly think of important questions. I was too exhausted.

"Leila, please. You don't even know anything about them, you can't possibly."

"Isaac," I said wearily. "You're right. I don't know anything about them, which is why I'll find out everything I need to from their boss before I even consider it."

"They're hunters, Leila. *Hunters.*"

My eyes widened. Hunters hunted supernaturals to kill them. They saw us as pests.

"Ty?"

"It's true. We are. Then again, we're not. We don't hunt anyone who doesn't deserve it. Otherwise, Isaac and his family would be dead already."

The vampires hissed their complaint.

Holding up a hand to silence them, I asked, "Was I supposed to be hunted?"

"No. Never. Like I said, my team and I were here to watch you. Protect you."

"Who ordered you to do it?" I asked.

"I did," came from the kitchen.

People parted and my eyes landed on… What the fuck?

Uncle Jack.

He gave me a smirk as he stalked forward. In my shocked state, he was able to take me into his arms and hug me before he whispered into my ear, "Glad you're okay, kid."

Frozen in place, I struggled to comprehend everything I discovered. Uncle Jack was there. In a room full of paranormals, and *he* was the one who ordered Ty and his team to protect me.

What the actual fuck?

Pulling back, I looked up into his tired face. My heart beat irregularly, thumping hard and fast in my chest.

"What, you're, so you, you're not an actual bounty hunter?" I shook my head.

"Just a hunter. Like your dad used to be."

My dad had been one also. It explained so much, how he didn't freak out when I shifted my first time. Why he would send my uncle to look out for me.

My mind was about to overload with all the shock.

"Leila," was whispered behind my uncle. Glancing over his shoulder, I gasped.

Stepping back, my hand went to my mouth. My eyes teared and my stomach twisted in nerves.

Reaching out with my other hand, I cried out behind my fingers, "Dad?" Right before blackness swirled in my vision.

"Catch her," Jezanna yelled as everything blinked out.

~

Darkness surrounds me. Every way I turn, I see nothing but black. My heart beats hard in my chest. My hands tremble along with my legs. I want to run, to scream, but I don't.

Because I know I'm waiting.

It isn't until I see two small red dots in the distance that I relax somewhat.

"Yes," I whisper. "That's what I'm waiting for."

The dots drift closer and closer.

And in a blink of an eye, which always makes me jump, they're right in front of me, so close I can reach out and touch them... No, touch the face that belongs to those red eyes.

I want to.

I need to.

Even though a small amount of fright fills me, I still know I'm safe.

The red eyes study me.

"You're mine," the voice growls...

Sun shining in through the window warmed me. I stretched lazily, my body twinging, my muscles sore. Voices woke me more, my mind already knowing I'd want to listen in.

"She's been sleeping for the last twelve hours. Let me in to check on her," Isaac demanded.

"She's fine. Exhausted from the fight and shocked from seeing her father," Uncle Jack said.

Dad. Springing from the bed, I tangled myself in the sheets, tripped and fell flat on my face. My dad *was* back. He was there in the living room. I hadn't dreamed him up.

My bedroom door came flying off its hinges and Isaac appeared, fangs out, hands up as if he were ready to kill someone.

Fighting myself, I stayed where I was instead of reaching out to him.

Looking up through my hair, I puffed out, "You really have to stop breaking my doors."

"Leila," he whispered, a small smile ghosting his lips.

"Get out!" Jack yelled. Glancing through Isaac's legs, I watched my uncle slowly climbing to his feet. "If you throw me like that again, I'll damage you."

Isaac threw my uncle to get to me. My body drummed with a tingling feeling. Why did he drive my senses wild still when he'd hurt me so much?

It was like my body acknowledged something in Isaac I didn't understand.

If I did, it would be easier to detest him for what he'd done.

Isaac slowly approached me, ignoring Jack who was still threatening him. He bent to help me up, but before he could touch me, I moved backwards and was on my feet.

He let out a pained groan. Which was when I looked down at myself dressed in only panties and a camisole.

"Jesus, kid," Jack grumbled, covering his eyes and reaching out blindly to grab Isaac. Only he moved out of my uncle's reach.

"Leila, please let me talk to you," Isaac asked.

"Now's not the bloody time," Jack yelled.

Isaac's hand cupped my cheek as he stepped forward. I felt like backing up, but the grief in his eyes had me halting my movements.

Behind him, Jack curled blindly with his hand, still trying to find Isaac, while cursing him as well.

"Isaac—"

"You're right," he started, stepping closer still, until his front pressed to mine. I raised a brow at him. My hands itched to touch him, but I left them hanging uselessly at my sides. "I do need to take charge, to work with the help around me so I can be a better person to lead my people how I should. I was blinded with worry to protect, when I should have asked for help from the ones I trust the most. All I wanted was your safety. If I lost you…" He shook his head. "She was never anything to me. You have to believe me. I may have touched her hand or even kissed her, but I never slept with her."

"Isaac, I don't want to hear—"

"Me either. Just get the hell out." Jack lunged, but Isaac stepped us aside before Jack reached him.

"You must know, Leila, I *will* fight for you. I will do everything in my power to gain your trust back. I will do anything to make you mine again."

Shaking my head, I groaned. "I can't—"

"That's it." Uncle Jack removed his hand covering his eyes. I quickly moved to pick up the sheet and wrapped it around me before Isaac sped to the door.

He looked back to me. "I *will* prove myself to you, Leila," he said and then disappeared from my view.

"Fucking vampire," Jack barked, his eyes also on the door as my dad stepped in.

"Not sure I like him for you, sweetheart." Dad smiled. My eyes stung as I held back my tears. My dad looked the same, except for a few grey hairs at the sides of his dark hair. His eyes were still the same, only sadder. He gave me a chin lift before adding, "Get dressed, honey, and then we'll talk. Yeah?"

Nodding, I waited for Jack and Dad to leave before moving to my drawers. I took a quick shower to wake me up more and to think over what Isaac had said.

However, before anything could run through my head, a certain name popped into it.

Kalvin.

He was a werecat. He was like me and he was… mouth-watering. I wanted to talk to him, get to know him. To see if he knew his family, if they were still around. A blush rose to my cheeks at the thought of us in our cat form rolling, playing and enjoying each other. Only to slip back into our human form to finish the fun in a different way.

No.

The image fled my mind and another appeared. Of Isaac naked on top of me in bed. This picture was powerful. A fierce bolt of desire shot through me. Always for Isaac. I moaned, my hand running lower on my stomach as I pictured him entering me slowly.

"Leila," Jezanna called with an urgent tone. I shut off the shower, wrapped a towel around me and went over to open the bathroom door.

"Is everything okay?"

She blushed. "I'm not sure, um, what it is you're doing, but you need to stop. Both Isaac and the werecat can..." She coughed. "Can feel your arousal and they're ready to kill each other because they sense it's over both of them."

Now it was my face to flush beet-red. Pinching the bridge of my nose, I slowly died of embarrassment.

"Are you serious?"

She giggled. "Quite."

"Oh, my God, Jezza. Get them out of the house. How in the hell did they know I was thinking of them both?" I whispered.

She bit her bottom lip before answering, "It seems you somehow projected some thoughts into their minds."

"No," I gasped, shaking my head. Slamming an extra shield into place in my mind, I prayed everything in there was locked tight. The only answer I had was because I'd passed out my shields weren't working and I'd let them slip after I'd woke. "Won't happen again," I said. I couldn't be thinking of them that way anyway. I had enough to sort out with my uncle and dad.

Stupid sexy men and crazy hormones.

"Can you get rid of everyone? I want to talk to my uncle and dad alone." She nodded. I reached out to grab her wrist. "I don't want you to go though. Please, don't ever think that."

"I'm always here for you." She smiled.

After she walked down the hall, I ran across it to my bedroom. My door wasn't fixed, so I dressed quickly, pulling on my jeans and a tee. My temperature seemed to be running hotter than normal.

By the time I walked down the hall and into the living room, there was no one there. Voices came from the kitchen, so I headed there and found my uncle, Dad, Jezanna and Jeremiah sitting around the table.

Glancing to the back door, I saw it was fixed. I went to take a seat next to Jack when Dad suddenly stood.

"Don't I get a hug?" His arms went wide. For a second, I paused. I didn't really know the man any longer. He didn't know me. He'd left me.

His smile faltered. He nodded to himself. "I understand," he whispered. "I'll regret the day for the rest of my life for leaving you, Leila," he said to the floor.

I hated he was hurting. I had to understand, like another man in my life, he'd left me to protect me in some way.

No matter how much it had hurt.

Taking the distance, I stepped in front of him and buried my face into his shoulder, my arms looping around his waist. He uttered a noise in the back of his throat as his arm wound around my shoulders. "You've grown so much and into such a beautiful woman," he whispered.

"Dad," I choked.

"I'm sorry, sweetheart. So very sorry for leaving you."

Pulling back, I offered him a small smile. "I wasn't alone, not really. I had my boof-head, annoying uncle with me."

He chuckled.

"Hey," Jack snapped and then gave me a wink. "Come on, kid. Sit, we have so much to talk about."

Giving Dad one last squeeze, I went and sat next to Jeremiah. He bumped my shoulder with his, offering his support in his own way.

"You smell different," he whispered. My head jerked back at his statement. I hadn't done anything different. Therefore, I sniffed my underarm. Nope, I wasn't stinky. I shrugged it off and focused on Jack who'd just cleared his throat.

"I should be angry with you," I said before he had the chance to talk.

"What? Why?"

"For hiding things from me."

He snorted. "I could say the same thing to you. Your dad didn't even tell me you're a werecat. I found out the hard way when you were sixteen and I caught you leaving the house with a blanket wrapped around you. I nearly freaked when I saw you on your hands and knees and then from under the blanket crawled a bloody large cat." He whistled low. "That was when I called your dad to confirm it. Always knew you were different, didn't know how though." He reached over and shoved my shoulder. "Shoulda told me, kid."

Biting my quivering bottom lip, I nodded, shrugged and then admitted, "I was worried you'd leave if you knew."

He nodded solemnly. "I guessed that, which was why I didn't confront you about it. Wished I had though, 'cause then I could have shown you I,"—he cleared his throat—"I care for ya no matter. Work got in the way for you to really see it though."

"Things will be different now."

"They will, kid, for the better too."

The emotional words shared were getting to me, so I sniffed and then asked, "Did you know who Isaac was before you saw him here?"

"It's my job to know what shows up in these parts of town."

"Why didn't you tell me you were a hunter?" I knew it was selfish in asking it, because I hadn't also shared. Regret singed my mind.

"I hinted in a roundabout way I was a hunter." He shrugged.

Rolling my eyes, I said, "A bounty hunter."

"What was I thinking leaving you two together?" Dad sighed. "You're both as bad as each other with all the bickering."

He was right and I realised I liked arguing with my uncle; it was our way of showing we cared.

"What was the real reason you left?" I asked my father, deferring my questions to him instead of Jack.

He rubbed the back of his neck. "I wanted to protect you."

Groaning loudly, I stood, anger boiled once again. "Protect me?" I threw my hands up in the air. "Jesus Christ."

"Kid," Jack scolded.

"No. That's all everyone wants to do is protect me, but none of you get it. All it's ever done is hurt me in the end. For God's sake, I'm more than capable of protecting myself. If I wasn't, I wouldn't have been able to save Isaac's family by tearing out a throat and getting the jump on Mervin. I wouldn't have been able to kill those rogue vampires if I can't fucking protect myself," I yelled. "You all need to learn to work with me, instead of trying to stuff me in cotton wool. Does anyone consider I want to help to protect you *all*?" I ran a frustrated hand through my hair.

Every single one of them had hurt me. Dad leaving. Jack never being around, and Isaac… All of it, because they thought they were protecting me.

I'd had enough.

"You all need to decide now to either stand at my side while we fight what's coming or leave me to it. I'm not running and I'm not standing back while everyone else joins the battle. I'm sick and tired of people trying to protect me," I snapped. My chest heaved, my hands screwing up into fists. I wanted to punch someone.

Jack stood with his hands on his hips. "What do you mean you goddamn tore out a throat and killed rogue vampires? Why haven't I been told this? What in the hell were you thinking?"

Scoffing, I glared and then screamed, "I was trying to protect those I love." Hands to the table, I leaned over it. "What goes around comes around. At least *I* didn't hurt anyone, besides the damned bad guys, while *I* was protecting."

"I think everyone needs to calm down," Jezanna said.

Jack threw his arms up and demanded, "What are they even here for? This is a family meeting."

"Don't," I barked. "They"—I pointed to Jeremiah and Jezanna—"are my family also. They've been there for me through so much. They didn't turn their back on me. Hell, even Jezza trusted me to take on the situation with Jason and his friends."

"Now hang on—"

"What?" a new voice growled. We all turned to the living room entryway to see Isaac there with Darik. "You let her go into a situation on her own? What were you thinking?"

"Don't you dare talk to her like that," I spat. "She's been the only one who's had my back when you've been too busy boinking—"

"I told you that never happened." Isaac's growl was low and dangerous. He stepped closer and got his face into my space. His upper lip raised when he said, "I would never touch her like that, not when I had perfection already in my arms. One day, Leila, you *will* forgive me and you'll regret even thinking I would do something like that behind your back. Still, I will forgive *you*. Yes, I hurt you, but I was stupid to think I was doing it for your own good."

Heaving out my breath, I noticed our noses touched right before I snarled, "How dare you again. You do not get to—"

"Stop!" Dad yelled.

Everyone did and turned to him. Thank God, I was seconds away from jumping Isaac. Then I remembered all the heartache he'd caused me. My insides fluttered.

Isaac must have seen it, because he whispered, "Leila."

One day, I could get over what he'd done, even if he thought he was doing best by me. However, it was still too fresh.

So when he reached for my hand, I stepped away.

"You're not very good at listening, vampire," Jack sneered. "We told you to stay away."

Isaac stood tall. "My family is here. Therefore, I am."

"We're getting nowhere with all this bickering." Dad sighed. "Everyone, take a breather and sit down." Everyone sat. Isaac and Darik moved to the other end of the table while I sat between Jeremiah and Jezanna. Dad said, "Leila, I need to tell you something."

"Justin," Jack warned.

"She needs to know."

"What?" I asked.

"Your mum, she's not your real mother."

Well screw me sideways. Of course, I'd already guessed it, but it was still a shock to actually hear the words.

Mentally tired once again, I rubbed my eyes and said, "That explains why she tried to kill me when she saw me shift for the first time."

Jezanna gasped. Isaac and his brother hissed.

"I'm sorry I haven't told you before, but I couldn't. If others found out what you were, they would have taken you from me and locked you up. So I pretended I found you one night and brought you home. Stacey and I were new in a relationship, but she was willing to pretend to be your mum. For me."

"Wait, are you even my dad?"

"Yes." He smiled. I breathed a sigh of relief. "Your real mum, Izzy, had disappeared two years before I met Stacey. I didn't know she was pregnant at the time she left. When she found me, she told me people were after her and her kind. She begged me to take care of you. Little did she know she didn't need to beg. I would have done anything for you, for her, but before I could ask her to come with us, she ran and I haven't seen or heard from her since."

"Why would Stacey try to harm Leila if she was willing to take care of her?" Jeremiah asked.

"She thought she could handle it. But, she wasn't strong mentally. When the town kept saying things about her, about Leila, it was hard."

"Hard? Hard for her? What about me? I had to live being different. Being teased every damn day."

"I know, sweetheart. But *you* are strong. Look at you now."

Shaking my head, I said, "You took her away and stayed away for so long, why?"

He looked pained. "Because she threatened to tell everyone about you and I knew if she did, the people who were after Izzy would want to come after you."

"Where is Mum?" Shaking my head, I corrected, "Stacey now?"

A grimace from Dad made my heart ache. "I don't know. All of a sudden, she left. I was searching for her when Jack found me and told me what's been happening around here. All the leads I had on Stacey were amounting to nothing. So I came home."

"What exactly did Jack say?" I asked.

Dad smirked. "Just that you had new friends."

So Dad rushed home to protect me from the big bad vampires. Except Isaac and his family weren't bad.

"I won't let you harm any of them."

Jack sighed. "We're hunters, not executioners, kid. We only hunt those who don't abide by the laws." He shrugged. "So far, they've been behaving."

"And we'll continue to as well." Jezanna glared.

"Then why has there been an increase of supernaturals in our area? Planning a war?" Jack asked.

Jeremiah scoffed. "If we were, you'd be the first on the list to kill."

My fist banged on the table. "No one talks about killing one another."

"It's because I've taken to live here," Isaac offered.

"Sire," Darik warned.

"No, they're a part of Leila's family. They need to know what's going on."

"They're hunters," Jeremiah snarled.

Isaac's hard eyes snapped to his brother. "Who can help us. We all want the same in the end, to live free and safe. A person once told me I should reach out for help to obtain a goal we all want." Isaac looked to me. I rolled my eyes. He laughed, before turning back to Jack and Dad. "There has been an intake of more supernaturals, because they are my people."

"What do you mean by *your* people? As far as we know, there's only one governing vamp and he's in Russia, goes by the name of Gerald."

Isaac went to answer. I waved my hand at him and told them, "Long story short, Isaac was prophesised to become… I guess you could say King, with not only the vampires, but all supernaturals. Gerald didn't like what he heard from his fortune cookie, so he wants him dead."

"Why here?" Dad asked.

Why Isaac's eyes came to me, I was unsure. However, they did, and in them held something I didn't understand either. He quickly looked back to my father.

"I was informed this was a safe place and I can understand why, knowing there are many hunters who live here."

"Right," Dad said, as if he didn't really believe him. I wasn't sure I did either.

Rubbing my hand over my face, I thought I would have gotten enough rest when I'd passed out, but I yawned and then said, "Honestly, I don't think my brain can take any more. I need some sleep. We have a sad day tomorrow, so I'd like everyone not at each other's throats before it."

"Agreed." Isaac said.

"Of course. I heard about your loss. I'm sorry," Dad offered.

Kicking Jack under the table, he jumped and said, "Yeah, sorry." He then added to me, "Kid, you need to eat some food first." I nodded as my stomach growled.

"Leila." I looked up to Jezanna. I hadn't heard her move. In fact, all of them were standing. "Since your father and uncle are home, I'll be going back with Jeremiah and Isaac."

Of course, it made sense. Still, I didn't like her leaving. I was used to seeing her all the time.

Her hand took mine. "I'll see you tomorrow and every day. No one could keep us away from you."

Smiling, I said, "Same."

"Good." With a final goodbye, she left with her brothers and Darik. Not before I felt both brothers take it in turn to reach out and touch me in some way for comfort. Jeremiah touched my shoulder, while Isaac... he ran his fingers through my hair, causing me to shudder, and then ended with his hand at the back of my neck. He gave it a gentle squeeze.

"Don't like that guy," Jack mumbled after we heard the front door close.

"Hmm," was Dad's reply, which didn't tell me anything.

CHAPTER TWENTY FOUR

Standing back as I surveyed the funeral about to take place, I realised life was too short. Even if you were immortal, there weren't enough days to be with the ones you loved. Isaac and his family knew the day would come when they lost their second father to them. They just didn't know how soon it would happen. The way Gregory had been taken away from them was brutal, unfair. So really, we had to appreciate each day. I knew I should, even when it was hard, live and love the best I could, because there were dangers in the world no one could stop, no matter how much people tried. There were moments where accidents happened or even illnesses took away a life. Any day. Any moment.

Regardless of it all, the pain and hurt, what Gregory taught me the most was that through those times, it was good to have your family close.

I had mine.

And there was nothing that would separate us again.

Isaac and I had our issues, but one day, those painful memories would pass. It didn't mean I didn't stop having feelings for him, stop caring about him. He was important to me.

So many people were important to me, and I would do anything for them.

Especially for Gregory. He'd asked me to help take care of his family and I would.

Gazing at the people around me, at those who were ready to help Isaac and his family through this pain, who were there to show their support for their leader, I couldn't help but think, even though it was a sad day, I was lucky.

Lucky to have found them. Lucky to have been included in their world. They were like me and I like them. Nothing normal, above average in fact.

So the day would be a day that left a hole in our hearts for losing such an amazing man, but it would also be a day to remember what he taught us.

Family meant so much.

Taking the few steps I needed, I stopped between Isaac and Jezanna as they stared down at the grave dug out for their father, his coffin supported above it. The hole didn't seem to be right for Greg. No man as good as Gregory should be put to rest into a hole in the ground where dirt would be thrown over him.

Still, it was how he wanted to go. He wanted to be buried as his wife had. If anything, I knew Greg. He would be looking down upon us all, with his wife standing in his arms, thinking we all looked like a sad bunch of idiots. Well, he'd just have to get over it because feeling the loss of him left us hollow.

The reverend stepped forward, but his words blurred into one another. My hands reached out blindly to take Isaac's. Jezanna was already curled into Caelen. Jeremiah stood on the other side of Isaac. Both brothers looked the same, their eyes hard, jaws clenched and body tense. I wondered if they were listening to the words of the reverend or if they were remembering their father in their own way. My eyes widened as Sofia stepped up beside Jeremiah and took his hand. He glared down at her and tried to shake her off, but she wasn't having it. She held strong and I was grateful for it. Because his body seemed to sag, give in and in his eyes, I saw appreciation.

My eyes turned back to the man next to me to find his eyes on mine. Oh, God, the pain I saw in them nearly took me to the ground. If Isaac hadn't whipped his arm out and around my waist, I would have fallen to the ground. He brought me close to his side. All I could think was that it was all wrong. *I* should be the one to console him, hold him, not the other way around. But then, as my arms wound around his middle, I realised we were helping each other. We were supporting one another through the loss.

We held each other right until the end. Even as Gregory was slowly lowered into the ground, we watched on together.

Tears fell down my cheeks as the dirt was placed in over his coffin. I gripped Isaac's black shirt tighter. His hand threaded into my hair, bringing my cheek against his chest and held me there. His heart beat solidly in his chest. I wondered if mine was in tune with his.

We stayed there until the last person left. The only ones still solemnly standing around were close family and friends. The sun peeked out behind the dark clouds. The day was cool; however, it didn't faze any of us except maybe my uncle and dad. Though, they were dressed for it. Again, I found myself burning warmer than usual, so I'd picked to wear a black sundress. Everyone seemed shocked by it.

Raising my chin, I looked up to Isaac while Jeremiah was thanking the reverend and I whispered, "He'll always be missed, but he'll always be in here." I placed my hand over his heart.

His nod was minute, but I saw it. His hand threaded into my hair where he gave it a tug. "I wouldn't have been...," his voice wavered, "strong through this without you by my side."

My heart ached.

Shaking my head, I said, "Yes, you would have."

"No, Leila. You make me strong. You make me want to be so much."

"You need to be who you want without thinking about me."

"You're right. I have been hidden for so long, leaving my people to fend for themselves. It's time I stood up, be the one my people need." He paused, sadness flashed through his eyes. "I just worry I will lose myself during it."

"You won't. I— no one will let you."

"You will help me then?"

"I won't be the only one."

"You're the only one I need at my side."

"Isaac," I groaned. My head fell forward, hitting his chest with my forehead. I needed to step back, put some distance between us. It wasn't what I wanted though. Staying in his arms, his warmth drummed inside of me. Isaac Grey owned me, but I wasn't sure I'd be strong enough if he decided to hurt me again.

"I realise I'm putting you on the spot, so I will stop. However, I need you to understand, Leila, *you* as well as ruling are my destiny. I see it no other way. One day, you will forgive me—"

Quickly looking up, I told him, "I already do, but—"

"Then one day you will learn to love me as I do you."

What?

It was then I took a step back. Eyes wide, I searched his face for the truth and I saw it; his eyes shone with it.

Isaac loved me.

"I-I…"

Screaming I loved him was impossible when the anguish he'd caused still flowed through my veins.

Smiling sadly, he shook his head. "You don't have to say anything." He shrugged, such a human thing to do. "I needed you to know it has always been you. I've been foolish, so very foolish, but never have you been from my thoughts, my dreams."

"Isaac, I really—"

"Kid," Jack called. I turned to him and he gestured to the car. I was caught up on deciding to go with my uncle, to get away from the awkward situation, or staying, talking it out and being with Isaac and his family.

"Go," Isaac said. Facing him, I was surprised when I felt his kiss on my cheek. *Stay with him, help him, hug him, kiss him.* My soul seemed to yell.

Shaking my head, my eyes sought out his. He grinned. "You still have so much to talk to your uncle and father about. Spend some time with them. We're going to Boozers. If you have time, come there later."

Nodding, because my mind was busy with so much racing through it, I watched him silently turn and walk off to meet his brother and sister. They gave me a wave, which I returned, before they disappeared in swift movements into the thick woods behind the graveyard.

Isaac Grey loves me.

I was giddy with happiness.

My hand covered my mouth to hide my smile. *He loves me. Holy shit, Isaac Grey loves me.*

But he also hurt me.

Shut the eff up.

He did it because he thought he was protecting me.

Was the excuse enough?

Maybe. Just maybe.

If felt surreal sitting in the living room with my father. However, there he was. We'd come back from the funeral, had some lunch and we were since sitting quietly while Jack was out doing something with his team.

"Feels strange, doesn't it?" Dad's question startled me, causing me to jump.

"If you mean having you here in the living room after five years, then yes."

He sat forward on the chair, his hands clasped in front of him. "Do you understand why I left, Leila?"

I offered a shrug, because really I wanted to hear it again. Hear how he chose Stacey over me.

"It wasn't because I picked Stacey over you." Great, he could read me well. "I would have stayed if I could. I wanted to stay so much. I never wanted to leave my daughter after what you'd been through." He sighed at my raised brow. "You mean more to me than what she ever did. I kept her around to play a part and that was all. I left with her to keep you safe. If she had gone to someone and told them about you—"

"We could have fought that battle together," I snapped.

"I'm your father. I wanted to protect you."

"By taking away the only person who showed me I wasn't a monster?" I whispered with such raw emotion my tears threatened to fall.

His head fell back to look to the ceiling and when he looked back to me, his own eyes were filled with tears. "I'm sorry you think I picked wrong. I'm still not sure I did wrong if it kept you safe all these years. But I will forever be sorry I lost five years of my daughter growing up." He stood, stepping over to the couch where I was sitting and sat next to me. I stiffened when his arm came around my shoulders. Anger burned too close to the surface for me to let down my guard. Still, he didn't remove it. He took a breath and when he spoke, his voice was soft. "There's something you have to understand. Do you know why we chose to protect you?"

"Because you all want me safe."

"There is that, but most of all, we do it because we love you. We love you more than anything, even above our own lives. Even though I don't like what I see when Isaac looks at you, that boy was doing what I did. We left, we hurt you because we loved you enough to want so much more for you."

"But what you all don't understand is I can help. I can fight." *If I'm not outnumbered.* Still, I'd give it my best shot to come out on top.

"We know this, sweetheart, we do. No matter how much we hate it, we understand it because you care for us as much as we do you and you want to protect us as we have done for you. I know I do, and I'm sure Isaac does as well, but we will forever regret our choice."

"It made me think I wasn't worthy," I whispered.

"God, no. Never think that. Never, Leila. I love you." He

kissed my temple. "I don't believe in your choice to want to fight, but I'll stand by you as I'm sure they all will."

"Seriously, you men give me a headache."

He chuckled. "And I'm sure it will happen many times more."

Nodding, I said, "That's true, especially with Isaac in the picture."

"Ah, is he, are you two…?"

"Dad, right now we're friends."

"I've noticed some tension between the two of you. Do I need to kick his arse for you?"

Laughing, I shook my head. "No, thanks though. I'm pretty good at arse kicking."

"I believe that." He smiled and then gave my shoulder a squeeze. I looked up to him. "Are we going to be okay?"

"Yeah." I grinned. "I think we will be."

"Good." He kissed my temple.

The back door suddenly opened. I stood immediately, with Dad beside me. We looked toward the kitchen as Jack walked around the entryway.

"Kid, there's someone here who wants to see you."

"Who?" I asked. Kalvin appeared beside Jack and my heart stuttered at the sight of him. "Um, hi." I waved lamely.

His smile was big. "Hi," he practically purred. A blush lit my cheeks. "Do you mind if we talk?"

Not at all, I had questions for him.

"I'll meet you outside."

"Thank you." He grinned and left the room.

Turning, I gave Dad a hug. His arms wound around my shoulders and he held me close. As I went to pass my uncle in the doorway, my wrist was caught.

"We good, kid?" he asked.

We were. We always had been. Even though he wasn't around much, I knew my uncle didn't have a clue with how to deal with a thirteen-year-old in his life.

He still annoyed the hell out of me. However, Dad was right. We were very much alike.

"You're still a boof-head, but..." *Shit.* Tears filled my eyes. Jack's eyes widened. I waved a hand around and mumbled, "Don't worry, I'm just due for my period."

"Crap, kid. Do not talk to me about that shit."

Giggling, because I couldn't help but remember the time my tough uncle told me I was going to be menstruating. His exact words were, 'Kid, as you get older things change. Worse for women because to have babies you need to bleed outta your privates for a week every month. Life's tough. We just have to deal with it.' And then he'd left.

Suddenly, I had an urge to hug him. So I did. My arms went around his waist. Hesitantly, his wound around my shoulders.

"Thank you. You drive me nuts, but I have appreciated everything."

"Same, kid, same."

With a nod into his chest, I spun and walked out the back door.

A smile settled on my lips as I stepped down the back steps off the deck. Kalvin stood near the woods. He looked up and spotted me, grinning.

When I was close, he said, "How have you been?" He'd asked me as if we hadn't seen each other in a long time. Weird.

"Okay and you?"

"Better now." He winked. My body tingled in awareness. He was so damn handsome.

Purring and rubbing was out of the question. I hardly knew the guy, so I wouldn't let myself do what it wanted to.

Turning to me, he leaned against a tree. I found myself wishing I was that tree, yet I also knew the pull I had to him wasn't as strong as it was to Isaac.

Did I wish it were?

Maybe.

At least then, I wouldn't give Isaac the chance to hurt me again.

But you love him.

Oh, God, did I?

"Leila," Kalvin called my name longingly. Glancing up at him, I waited for something else. "You're very beautiful."

You're very forward.

Shrugging off the comment, I asked, "Why don't you have an eye like mine? I thought all werecats would."

He smirked. "I'm not sure. My only guess would be your feline is stronger, so it shows while you're in your human form."

Nodding, I looked back to the house and then Kalvin. "Do you know of any more werecats?"

"No, not until I met you."

"Why aren't there any?" I asked more to myself than Kalvin.

Still, he answered, "I've heard that Gerald hunted them and killed them."

Shock had my heart beating hard in my chest. "Why?" I whispered.

"A prophecy of some sort."

"Do you know what it says?"

He glanced behind him into the woods. "Not all of it."

My brows drew together in confusion. "Are you going to tell me?"

His eyes met mine with heat. He took a step toward me, reaching out a hand and trailing his fingers down my cheek. "I'd rather talk about something else."

A thrill shivered through my body at his touch. His eyes told me he wanted me. "I can't stop thinking about you, Leila," he whispered, his lips closer to mine.

"K-Kalvin…"

"We're meant to be together." His hand threaded into my hair, pulling my head back so I would meet his gaze. His other hand went to my waist while I stood there like a limp biscuit.

Then his lips touched mine. It wasn't gentle. It was rough,

wet and hard, but good. His tongue forced its way in. My hand went to his shoulders. Half of me wanted to push him away, yet the other half liked what was going on, causing me to kiss him back.

His lips left mine and trailed down to my neck where he nipped. "Say you're mine. Be with me. Come with me now and we can escape all of this and live peacefully."

Yes.

Wait, no.

What?

Stop, I needed to stop it.

I shoved at him. He faltered back a step and looked at me with surprise.

"You want me." He grinned. "I can feel it, taste it even. All you need to do is trust that I can take care of you." His eyes widened a fraction. "We need to leave. Come with me, be with me and live happily with the one person who knows all of you." He swiftly kissed me again. My body caved for a moment, until I turned my head away from him. "We need to go. We have to hurry before evil gets here."

Huh?

My mind was a fog. An urgency thrummed through me to listen to Kalvin. He could protect me. He wanted me. He was like me.

Shaking my head, I tried to clear it. Nothing was making sense.

Why would I think those things when I fought so hard to be my own person? I didn't need anyone to care for me, to protect me like I was weak, because I wasn't.

A feeling of pure contentment washed over me.

"Kalvin?" I uttered.

"Yes, baby. Yes, come on, we can leave and love each other forever. We will be happy. We'll have a family. A perfect future."

It all sounded nice. Sweet. Perfect.

Smiling up at him, I nodded. His grin was gorgeous. His

hand reached out for mine and we started walking into the woods.

"Leila!" was roared in the distance, and a shudder ran over my body. I knew that voice... Didn't I?

Kalvin, with swift speed, picked me up and threw me over his shoulder. From my position, I watched the backs of his legs as they blurred together with how fast he ran into the woods.

Why was he running? To keep me safe. Something bad was after us. Kalvin wanted to take care of me. He was my love, my life, and I would do anything for him.

A deep, painful throb in my head had me gasping for breath and cradling my head between my hands.

Leila, do not let him take you from me.

Who are you?

No! Snarled through my mind. *Leila, remember. Remember me, who you are, where you belong. Why you want to fight.*

Flashes of images ran through my mind.

The sexiest man I had ever seen standing in my bedroom only wearing jeans.

His smile.

His kind eyes.

A kiss that seared my soul.

A touch that caressed more than the spot he touched.

People surrounding me.

Family.

Isaac.

Gregory.

My dad, uncle, all the reasons why I wanted to fight.

To help protect the ones I loved, instead of them going head-to-head on their own.

With a severe intake of breath, I flung myself off Kalvin's shoulder. He stumbled, righted himself and faced me.

"What did you do?" I snarled.

He smirked. "How did you break it?"

CHAPTER TWENTY FIVE

Standing, I glared at him. "None of it matters, but if you want to live, you'll tell me why."

He stalked towards me, his movement angry. His hands clenched at his sides as his face pulled into a sneer. "Why, you ask? Because *you* have killed all of my family," he yelled in my face.

"What are you talking about?" I asked, not backing up. I would not show fear.

"MaryJane told me."

"MaryJane. You're doing this for her? But she works for Gerald. He probably killed your family."

"He did, but he did it because of you." He shoved me back. "I should take care of you myself, but my mate wants to do it, and her, I would do anything for, even lay my hands on such filth." He spat to the ground before my feet.

"Mate?"

Had he been smoking pot before trying to kidnap me? Because he certainly wasn't making sense.

Leila?

Isaac?

Yes, we're coming. Keep him distracted. Relief washed over me. Isaac was on his way. He saved me, broke the spell Kalvin had on me.

"What did you do to my mind?" I asked.

He laughed. "As you know, we can make connections with

our minds. You're probably too stupid to work out we can also do other things. Take thoughts, change feelings. Even kill."

"My shields don't let anyone in. How did you do it?"

He rolled his eyes. "Being the same helps and there's only another who could force entry, your mate."

"Wait, stop. Nothing you're saying is making sense."

He snorted. "MaryJane did say you were dense."

"Whatever. Tell me why you joined Ty's team if you've sided with MaryJane and Gerald."

"I've had enough questions for now, Leila. I can feel his power coming closer. My mate didn't want me to harm you, but I see no other choice."

His hand wrapped around my neck and I watched as he shifted his other hand into a claw. "You will die tonight. Isaac will have nothing worth living for and then Gerald will succeed."

As if slow motion took over, I saw his clawed hand pull back. He intended to force the blow to my stomach, maybe even stab me with his sharp claws. I couldn't allow them to touch me or I would die. Hate burned in his eyes. I didn't understand it, but I could see it and he meant to kill me.

Raising my feet off the ground, I kicked out just before his claws would have sunk deep into my stomach. Instead, the force behind my kick loosened his hold on my neck. I jumped backward and he stumbled back and hissed.

"I won't be an easy target to kill, Kalvin."

"We'll see," he growled and pounced, shifting on movement, turning into a large cat. The only difference I noticed was his form was more solid than mine, his fur darker too. I scrambled backwards, away from him and called forth my change.

Bones crunched and popped. It was the fastest shift I had ever done, but I had to.

Silently, I screamed through it.

In the final stages, I reached my arms up and jumped high,

landing over Kalvin in my feline form. Kalvin turned. I started to run, but he caught me, his paw taking out my back one. I rolled to the ground. He was on top of me snarling and hissing in my face. Growling, I snapped my jaw at him, anywhere I could. We rolled and I dug my claws into his sides. He howled in pain and then managed to sink his fangs into my flesh at my side.

A blur of black and white passed me. Kalvin was knocked off me. Staggering to my feet, I found us surrounded. Isaac had Kalvin pinned to a tree. His arm across Kalvin's chest while Darik and Adan held his claws at bay. Kalvin snapped his teeth at Isaac, until Isaac gripped Kalvin's fur on the top of his head and forced it back so they were eye-to-eye.

"No one touches her. No one rolls her mind. You will be killed tonight, you will..." Isaac stopped snarling in Kalvin's face, and Kalvin's eyes widened and something flashed in them. Isaac smiled, his fangs showed. "Hello, MaryJane."

Startled, my gaze roamed the area. However, she wasn't around. Xavier came to my side and whispered, "Master sees her within her mate."

"You will be happy to know your mate has failed you. His game of taking Leila away from me didn't work and now we have him." Isaac's smile was vicious. "No, MaryJane. I will kill him for even thinking he could take her." He paused. "Crying and screaming will get you nowhere. Not after what you've put us through. Siding with Gerald has got you nothing, and even now it will be less. You must thank your master for it." Isaac reared back, his mouth wide and his fangs long.

Isaac, no! Knock him out, but keep him alive. We can bargain with MaryJane for him when the time is right.

If Isaac heard me, he chose to ignore it. His hand snapped out, vise-like, gripping his neck. Kalvin howled and hissed, but Isaac had other plans. Darik adjusted his stance as Isaac freed his hand from Kalvin's neck and lifted Kalvin's front leg up.

Isaac's fangs were out sharp, long and ready. He was going to drain him, take every last drop of Kalvin's blood. Isaac tore into his arm. The sound of flesh tearing apart echoed through the woods. Kalvin growled in pain, yet I didn't look away as the man I loved, drank until it was done. The three of them stepped away as one and Kalvin slumped to the ground, his form shifting back to human in death.

Isaac turned to me, wiping his mouth with the back of his arm, his eyes wild with fury. "Lessons must be taught if I am to rule, and that lesson was to everyone who thinks they can harm you. Think they can take you from me. No one will touch a person in my fold, not without a fight."

He was right, of course. I didn't like the lesson. I didn't like he'd just killed the second last of my kind, but he was right.

Life had changed.

Isaac had taken control. He was making a stand and chose to be king, and with that type of responsibility came consequences. He would have to take lives when others fucked with his people, and Kalvin was one of them. Through his blindness for Mary-Jane, Kalvin had signed his own death warrant.

Footsteps approached. My dad and uncle came into view.

"What the fuck?" Jack bellowed.

In a blink, Isaac was in front of Jack, backhanding him to the ground.

Isaac!

With swift speed, Isaac had my uncle off the ground, his hand fisted into Jack's shirt at the front. Jack was smart not to move or talk.

Never had I seen Isaac so viciously furious.

"You endangered her," he snarled in Jack's face.

"Sire," Darik said in a calming tone.

Isaac ignored him and shook Jack. "How did he become a part of your team? Do you know how to do your job? He could have taken her. He rolled her mind. Made her forget. He. Could. Have. Taken. Her." Isaac threw Jack backwards. He sailed into the air, thumping to the ground. I thought he would have been knocked out, but he wasn't. Jack slowly sat up.

Isaac, you listen to me right now! He spun to me and hissed. *Back the hell off right now, Isaac Grey. You have to remember Kalvin was a good actor. Hell, I'd seen him a couple of times and I would never have expected him to be MaryJane's mate. Do not blame Jack and take it out on him. It was my own stupid fault for letting it happen. I didn't know our kind were able to do what he did.* I sighed. *Everything's okay now. We all just need to calm down.*

"Calm down?" he bit out. "How can I calm when I nearly lost you?" He threw his hands up in the air.

Isaac, I whispered. *You can't keep acting this way. There is a battle to come and one I will be fighting in. I don't want you distracted in fear of what could happen to me. I want you to fight the best you can and defeat Gerald once and for all. I need you to fight without worry. I need you to live. The thought of losing you would be too much to bear.*

"Leila," he breathed. He shook his head. "From this day forward, you will train with our people, as well as Ty's. We will need your mind and body strong. The battle to come will be hard, but I see no other option but to survive. For you, for family and our people."

Agreed.

"Is it safe to come back now?" Jack asked from where he'd fallen.

"Yes." Isaac gave a small nod and turned to him as he walked towards us. "I will ask that your people are questioned. I need to know if Kalvin was working alone or with others."

"You can't—"

"Done," Dad blurted. "Jack, you need to give this to him. He saved my daughter, your niece, once again." He looked to Isaac and said, "Forever I will be grateful." Then he bowed, showing his support for the future king.

∼

Later that night, Isaac didn't go to Boozers. Instead, while Jack, my dad, along with Adan and a few others of Isaac's people questioned Ty's team, Isaac came with me to my room. He sat on one side of the bed and I sat on the other. I'd just told him everything Kalvin had said to me and the kiss we'd shared. His eyes flashed with fury, but it went quickly. After all, my mind hadn't really been my own. Sure, I had an attraction toward Kalvin, but everything inside of me knew Kalvin wasn't the one for me.

No one outshone Isaac.

Instead of speaking of it, I wasn't sure why, but he seemed to want to change the whole subject.

"I think your father finally approves of my being around you." He smiled.

Laughing, I said, "I think so, too."

Isaac sighed, his smile turning sad. "Will we ever get back to what we had been before?"

Gazing down at my bedspread, I shrugged.

"Do you think me a monster after what I did to Kalvin?" he whispered.

My surprised gaze met his concerned one. "No, never. You're right, people need a lesson. You are the next king and you can't let people walk all over you." I laughed humourlessly. "I could ask the same question to you, Isaac. Do you think I'm a monster after taking the lives I have?"

"No. You have done it to protect. Your compassion and heart are something I admire, Leila. Among a lot of other qualities."

"Isaac, do you know what Kalvin was talking about? Why he would accuse me of killing his family when I've never met them?" I paused, but he said nothing. "Do you know of this other prophecy?"

"I'm unsure if what I know is true."

"What do you know?"

He quickly reached out and took my hand in his, moving

closer to me on the bed. I jumped with how fast he'd moved. "I think what Kalvin accused you of and the prophecy are rolled into one."

"You mean the prophecy is about me?"

"Leila." He sighed. "I need more time." He shook his head. "No, not exactly. In order to tell you the truth, I would like to suggest you wait for the answer. Wait just a little longer, because I don't think you're ready for it."

"Of course I am. If it's about me, I need to know."

"I understand your need to know. I do. However, I'm asking you to trust me once again. I know I don't deserve it, but please give me a little time to tell you. Instead, you need to prepare for the battle, make it your number one priority."

"Isaac," I whined.

"Please, Leila. Please, I beg you to give me time." *Let me show you how to trust me and love me first.*

Watching his thumb rub over my hand, I knew I wasn't supposed to hear the last part, which whispered through my mind.

Trust, I already did. Of course I did. He stuffed up big time, causing me to hurt, but like so many, he did it because he *loved me.*

Love… I was already in love with him.

So what was a little more time?

And grovelling.

Smiling to myself, I nodded while meeting his gaze. "Okay, we prepare for Gerald and *soon* you will tell me everything you know."

His smile was gracious and mischievous at the same time. He was happy. I was giving my trust to him, yet he was playing at something and his next words told me what. "Yes, Leila, soon. For now, we must practice making your mind impenetrable from any form of attack."

Rolling my eyes, I asked what I already knew. "And how do you propose we do that?"

"Why, we must kiss."

How did I know he was going to say that? "How would that help?"

"You seem to let your guard down when intimate."

"But, it could have been because Kalvin was the same as me. Maybe our species aren't able to keep each other out."

"I had come to that conclusion." He sighed. "The real reason why I want my lips upon yours, why I *need* my touch upon you, is simple. I do not like the thought of anyone else tasting what belongs to me."

"I could say the same for you."

"Instead of fighting, I would have welcomed you into open arms to wipe away her touch. Your anger, which was justified," he quickly added, "overwhelmed you, preventing you from even thinking as us vampires do."

"Which is?" I asked, inching closer. Our noses brushed together.

His eyes flared with heat. "You belong to me and me alone, Leila. If anyone touches you, I must, after killing them, erase any scent they have placed upon you."

"Then do it," I whispered. I was on my back in a second with Isaac looming over me. His long dark hair floated down around his shoulders and face. He studied me. I smiled up at him. His eyes widened and then—*God, he was gorgeous*—he smiled back before his lips touched mine.

I've missed this. Missed you. I said through our connection.

You do not know how much I have missed you. My heart stopped beating while you were not around. My life was dull when I didn't see your smile.

Our arms and legs tangled as our mouths melted into each other. He rolled us, so I was on top. I moved against his body, my legs straddling his waist.

He growled against my mouth. I whimpered against his.

Is it always like this?

No, never. Only with you.

Isaac moved a hand from my butt up and slid it under my tee. When he brushed it over my breast, I gasped as my body shivered.

Yes!

Leila. He groaned.

A knock on the door brought us apart and panting. We should have heard whoever approached, but we'd been too caught up with each other.

"It's Ty," Isaac growled.

A giggle left me. He didn't like we were interrupted, but maybe it was for the best. We needed this, us to work, so maybe it was good to slow down.

Even though it would be one of the hardest things I did, it was probably for the best. Though admittedly, right then, I wanted to scream at Ty to rack-off and tear Isaac's clothes from his body.

A mew of complaint left me as Isaac lifted me off his body. "One second," he called to Ty in an annoyed tone, and I swore if Ty hadn't listened and walked in anyway, Isaac would have taken Ty's life.

Isaac took my hand in his and helped me stand. Without thinking, our bodies sought out one another until they aligned with our fronts touching. Our arms wound around each other. Staring up at him, my heart beat wildly with his and then he said quietly, "It has always been hard to restrain myself when I am around you. So in a way, I am grateful for the interruption because I would like to deem myself worthy of you and not take advantage of the situation by getting carried away."

Jesus. He definitely had a way with words.

Words, which tugged at my heart.

Sighing, I pushed my forehead against his chest. "I agree, but..." I gave a dramatic huff.

He chuckled. "I know. However, when the time comes, it will be worth the wait." His hand tugged on my hair until I looked up at him. "I'm very fortunate tonight to gain you back in my arms. To have the heat between us lit once again. I will never endanger what we have again, Leila. This, I promise."

Tears filled my eyes. "Can we send Ty away?"

His laugh was joyous. "I'm afraid not. And unfortunately, we will be very busy. I have people to lead and you have training. Nevertheless, every night I wish for us to connect in here,"—he touched my temple—"keep our link open, so never will I be far from you."

"I will," I whispered.

He kissed me one last time before he tore himself away from my grabby hands. He laughed to the door. There he composed himself and opened it, glaring at Ty.

Dismissing Ty altogether, he glanced back to me before saying, "I'll have guards posted. Stay safe, Leila."

Snorting, I rolled my eyes and saluted him, "Yes, Captain."

He went to pass by Ty, until Ty caught his attention. "Isaac, I have an understanding Leila will be t-training with both our sides."

"Yes."

"Thank you for trusting the rest of us after Kalvin did what he d-did."

Isaac shrugged. "If you were to harm Leila, you would have done it already."

Ty smirked. "True."

"Besides, Darik has already informed me the rest of Jack's team is legit." Ty nodded. "For Leila, we have come to a truce with Jack and his team. However, if one was to stab us in the back, there will be a swift punishment."

Ty stiffened. "It won't happen again. I trust my team with my life."

Isaac's eyes narrowed. "Would you have trusted Kalvin with your life?" he snarled.

"No," Ty snapped. "He was new, sent to us. But the rest of us *are* dependable."

"We will see." My man glared.

Clearing my throat, I said, "Okay, boys. Enough testosterone. Isaac, I'll see you soon, and Ty, come on in if you want to talk."

Isaac smirked, winked and walked down the hallway without another word. Ty watched Isaac's outline leave before he came into my room. I patted the bed and sat near the pillows. Ty sat next to me.

"What's up?"

He snorted. "I can't believe what happened. I never thought Kalvin would have turned on you. Not when he spoke of his loss."

"He seemed to blame me for it."

Ty's head jerked back. His sightless eyes met mine and they were wide. "What? Why?"

Shrugging, I said, "I'm not sure. As soon as I find out, I'll let you know." I leaned in and nudged his shoulder with mine. "Thanks for coming to check on me though."

He nudged me back and smiled. "Always. You've come to be an annoying little sister to me."

Laughing, I teased, "And you're a pain-in-the-butt brother."

"So," he started.

"So what?"

"I know you haven't had time to scratch yourself, but have you thought about joining us?"

I licked my dry lips and bit a nail before answering, "Not really." Looking to him, I asked, "Are you happy doing what you do?"

He nodded. "Yeah, I really am. We're like cops, but for the supernatural. We don't hunt anyone we don't have hard facts on, Leila. We don't just kill random supernaturals for the fun of it."

"I'm getting that. How's it been working with Jack?"

Ty laughed. "He's tough, but I know if he puts us through hell, he'll be there with us doing the same. He's a great teacher."

Who would have thought my uncle would have high praise on him?

"You seem like such a tight-knit group. I'm not sure I'd fit in." I wasn't sure I wanted to either. There were other possibilities I had to think of.

"You would. Everyone is easy to get along with."

"Can I think about it a little longer?"

"Course you can. In the meantime, you get to hang with us while we kick your arse."

Rolling my eyes, I shoved him. "Like that could happen."

He chuckled. "The good part about it, we won't get in the shit about it from Isaac." He searched my face for something.

"Just ask."

"Are you sure you'd be happy with him?"

"If you start to offer yourself up for the taking, I think I'll be sick."

His nose screwed up. "Jesus, no." He shuddered. "No offence, but that's just wrong on so many levels."

"Good." I laughed. "But yeah, I'm happy. I know Isaac would bend over backward to make sure I was."

"He would." He pretended to gag. "I guess he's an okay guy."

Shaking my head, I smiled and said, "One day, the two of you will be friends."

He laughed loud and long. "When hell freezes over."

Problem was, hell could be coming sooner than we thought.

CHAPTER TWENTY SIX

A month had passed with no sign of Gerald. College seemed nothing compared to what was really going on in the world. Therefore, two weeks earlier, I decided to leave. Instead, I was joining Isaac's team. My uncle, Dad and Ty had tried to persuade me to reconsider nearly every day, but I didn't want to be a hunter.

Now that Isaac had taken the step closer to become his people's leader, I knew the battle had just started. Gerald would be only one enemy against Isaac. I felt my help would be more beneficial with Isaac and his people than with the hunters.

However, even though all the training and meetings continued, some harder than most, everyday stuff still happened. Which was how I was in the local store food shopping.

Jezanna strolled down the aisle with me. She was telling me about how Caelen had been so great after they'd lost Gregory. It didn't seem as though it had been a month already. It still felt fresh. Sometimes I could see Isaac staring off in the distance and I knew, like I had many times, he was thinking about the man who took them in after their parents were slaughtered. It would still live with them for a long time to come.

She placed my favourite cereal into the trolley when she paused her talk and whispered out the corner of her mouth, "Why do I get the feeling people are staring at us?"

Shrugging, I leaned over to grab some Pop-Tarts off the bottom shelf. As I stood, I said, "It happens all the time when I'm around."

Her hand went to the trolley and my step forward halted. I let out an "Oof," when my stomach crashed into it. When a vampire wanted you to stop, you did.

"Leila, this is not normal. I've been here with you before and there was a mixture of males and females looking at us. Now, it's mainly men."

Glancing around, I stiffened. She was right. Down both ends of the aisle, even scattered through, there were men of different ages looking at us. Actually, their gaze would flick quickly from the shelves to us and back again. But they were definitely watching us.

"What's going on? Do I have something on my face?" I asked.

Jezanna shook her head. She was as tense as I was feeling. "Leila, what did Xavier say this morning as he drove us here?" She'd been on her phone and probably only heard a murmur of it; Xavier had been quiet saying it.

"He said I smelt different." A lot of people had been saying the same thing to me for a while now. I thought nothing of it, only them being strange because I hadn't even changed my shampoo or body wash.

"Your birthday, Leila, when is it?"

A pretend offended scoff escaped my mouth. "I'm upset you don't know already, no matter how busy we've been."

She spun to me, her eyes wide and worried. "Your birthday, Leila?"

"It's coming up in a couple of months. Why?"

Shaking her head, she mumbled to herself, "It's too soon then. It's too soon."

Grabbing her arm, I gave her a shake. "Jezza, what are you talking about?"

"Your uncle loaned me a book. A book the hunters from the beginning of time put together. In it is information about every supernatural species. Leila, it was only a few days ago I read about your kind."

I knew why my uncle hadn't given it to me to study, because I had refused to tell him about my feline side. Still, he could have given it to me recently, instead of Jezanna.

"Don't be upset with your uncle. You were out. I was supposed to pass it along to you, but I got caught up reading and couldn't stop."

I offered a stiff nod. "What are you getting at, Jezza?"

She opened her mouth to answer, but someone behind me cleared their throat. "Excuse me." It was a familiar male voice.

Turning, I came face-to-face with Rodney. He was a friend of Jason's, only he was a nicer one. At least he wasn't there the night Jason and his mates helped MaryJane.

What was even stranger than the men staring at us was Rodney had never approached me before. So of course, I wanted to know why. "What can I do for you?"

His smile was big and bright. His eyes lit with something I wasn't used to seeing, kindness, eagerness as well. "I was hoping you'd want to go out with me tonight?"

Um... Huh?

"No," was yelled. Spinning, I looked over Jezanna's shoulder to see Malcom. He worked in the Chinese takeaway place down the road. He stepped up to us. "Go out with me, please, Leila."

My shocked gaze turned to Jezanna. Her eyes were as wide as mine. Men around us started shouting out their complaints towards Rodney and Malcom, and then following through with their own invite for dinner. Some even forwent the invitation for dinner and had went straight for a party in their bedroom.

"Shit, shit, shit," rattled off Jezanna's tongue. It was the first time I'd ever heard her swear, so I knew whatever was happening was serious. She pushed the trolley towards the approaching men, then took my wrist in her hand and pulled me down the aisle to the front of the shop, shoving men out of her way as she went. They tried to grab me, grope me and begged me to stay. Jezanna picked up speed as she ran us through the front glass sliding doors.

Xavier was at our sides the next second, his face full of concern. He'd been waiting out the front after checking the grocery store was clear of anything other than humans. "What is it?"

"We must get Leila home and now. Call in Sophie, Raven. Jesus, any female fighters we have close."

"What?"

"No, Xavier, please just do it."

A nod and he propelled me into his arms where he raced us to the car. Behind us, I saw the doors to the store open again and all the men rushed out of it. Before Xavier threw me into the car, all I could hear was my name being called over and over. Their voices sounded so pained, filled with anguish and loss because I was leaving.

This shit was starting to freak me the hell out.

Xavier jumped in and started the car. Jezanna was already in the passenger seat, her phone to her ear.

"Jezanna?"

"Please wait." She hit her hand to the dash. "Come on, answer," she cried.

Looking to Xavier, he also had his phone to his ear, mumbling something I couldn't hear into it. "What's happening to them?" I mumbled to myself. "Is there a new drug going around?" Maybe some type of gas had leaked into the town.

"Jack, finally. We have a problem. Leila tells me she doesn't turn nineteen until a couple of months and you would have read what I did in the book—"

"What in the hell happened?"

"Men swarmed her at the store." Jezanna glanced behind her and out the back window of the car. "We're being followed by at least five different vehicles. We'll be taking her to our house. There's a basement we can hold her in until this passes. Make sure you warn all men to stay away. Xavier, who is not feeling the pull, is calling in the women within both our circles to help keep them out."

"Fuck," he yelled. "Fuck, we had time. We had time."

"Did Leila's mother tell Justin her birthdate?"

"Christ, hang on." We could hear Jack call out the question to my dad. "Shit. No, she didn't. He just placed it at the day he got her."

Jezanna sighed. "Meaning we have a big problem to deal with and no time to prepare."

My heart sank to the pit of my stomach. My body shook. I felt cold, but my body was extra hot still.

Answers, I needed them.

"Exactly. I'll warn the men. Call Isaac, he'd left early on a mission. Tell him what's happening and to stay away." He swore again. "You take care of her, Jezanna."

"With my life," she whispered and then slid the phone away from her ear. She looked to Xavier. "Tell me they're coming."

"They are and Seraphine arrived back last night."

"Good, we'll need her."

"Hold the fuck on. Can someone please tell me what the hell is going on with *me*?"

Ignoring me, Jezanna asked Xavier, "Since you're not affected, please call in Jensen as well."

"I will as soon as I know what's going on and before Leila bursts a blood vessel with concern."

Jezanna turned in her seat to face me. "I'm sorry, Leila, but I needed to act first before the information was passed because things are about to become difficult for us."

"How?" I snapped.

"A passage in the book caught my attention, which is another reason I hadn't passed it along. I wanted to prepare for it and help you through it in any way I could because it will be hard to... comprehend."

"Jezanna," I whined. "Get on with it."

"On your nineteenth birthday, you will go into 'heat.'"

My hand went up to silence her. I studied her face for any signs of hilarity, but couldn't find any. "You have got to be kidding me. I'm not some dog." She couldn't be serious, not really. Shaking my head at the thought, I started laughing. It was plain-old ridiculous. I was going into heat. Heat like a bloody cat. What the fuck? No way, no how.

A hand touched my knee. Seeing it was Jezanna's, I glanced up to her. "No, Leila. I'm not joking. House cats go through it as well, but again, it's different for werecats," she stated with an apologetic tone.

"That shit does not happen. This is real life, people. Why in the hell would I go into heat?" I scoffed. "No. Nope. Nuh-uh."

"How can you explain the reaction from the men down the street?" she asked.

Hell. I didn't know. Therefore, I offered a shrug.

"Leila, I am sorry this is happening, but it's uncontrollable. The desire the men feel is undeniable. They will lust after you until this passes. They will try anything to get within arm's reach of you. They want you. They need to hear your voice, touch your skin and the urge to want to be inside of you is unmanageable. Their mind only has one thought, which is to claim you."

"When will it end?"

"Either in a couple of days or..." she trailed off. Her pinched eyes told me she was worried.

"Or what, Jezza?" I growled.

"Or it will pass if your mate claims you."

Mate? I didn't understand the mate talk. But it was coming up more and more. MaryJane and Kalvin. Even Isaac mentioned something about it, but I couldn't recall what he'd said.

"I don't have a mate, so it looks like I'm going to have to put up with stalkers for a few days. Jesus."

Jezanna shook her head. "Everyone has a mate. It's lucky if we find them in this life. Some have even gone through many lives and never found theirs."

Believing it was another story. I wasn't ready to burst Jezanna's bubble because I could tell she thought she'd already found hers with Caelen.

"Why don't I feel any different *if* I'm in heat?"

She bit her bottom lip.

"Jezanna?"

"The only change you will have is the difference in your scent, which is a calling card to men, and feeling warmer than usual. That is until the night passes onto your actual birthday."

"And then?"

She cringed. *Shit, I'm not going to like this.* "Then, you will feel the change. Your body will… God, I don't know how to say it." She ran her hand over her face. "Your body will desire a release."

Slumping back in the seat, I crossed my arms over my chest and glared at Jezza. "Are you trying to tell me I'll become some horny slut?"

"Um, yes." She nodded.

I snorted. It was all unbelievable, yet the men's reaction to me at the store was proof to some of it. Still, I couldn't see myself wanting to fuck everything in sight.

"So what, I just have to twiddle my nub and I'll be okay?"

Xavier coughed out a laugh. I leaned forward and hit him in the back of the head.

"Sorry." He smirked.

"Watch it or I'll hump your leg."

He cringed. "Note to self: stay away from Leila."

"Leila," Jezanna said, catching my attention. "If you did do what you said, it will only give you release for a moment. You will not be satisfied until this passes or your mate hears your call."

"My call?"

"What the men are feeling from taking in your scent is mild compared to when midnight comes. Your body will send out a pulse until it finds your mate. It will call to him and he'll have no control over it until he seeks you out and claims you."

"And this is if I have a mate."

"Yes."

"Fuck, what about Isaac?" It would kill him if some stranger came to claim me.

"Isaac may be your mate, but…"

Nodding, I said it myself, "He's not here. How far away did he have to go?"

"A few of his people needed his help. He couldn't have left them, Leila. They were in trouble."

"Meaning, he's too far away."

Sinking into the seat, disappointment washed over me. Then again, I was being stupid thinking Isaac could be my mate. Especially when I didn't believe in them.

"I feel like I'm on some other planet. Why does this only happen to werecats?"

"Apparently, because the werecats were a dying breed, one went to seek a witch's aid for their species. A spell was placed upon all werecats so they were able to find their mates in their first lifetime, which could lead to reproducing more of their kind."

A dry laugh escaped me. "So a witch spelled us into horny wenches that put a call out to our mates so we can get knocked up?"

"Nice way to sum it up, Leila," Xavier commented.

"Shut it, you. Okay, tell me."

"No more time for stories." Did that mean Xavier didn't believe it either? "We're here."

Jezanna tensed and ordered, "As soon as the car stops, you get out and run for the door. I'll be with you."

It had been a long time since I was at Isaac's house. Since the night my heart was crushed. Luckily, he'd mended it or I would have refused to enter the house. Everything looked the same. The house was still outrageously big, the drive was still long and the gardens were gorgeous, as always.

The only difference was out the front stood Sofia, Raven, Ty's sister, Penny, Trixie and Daphne, who I'd met at Boozers, and three other vampire women I'd never met. One of them would have to have been the ever-absent Seraphine.

My gaze was torn from them when the car stopped in a jolt. No time to think, I threw my door open and I was out it, racing with Jezanna at my side for the house.

Trixie was at the opened door and I would have made it, if it wasn't for the body tackling me to the ground.

"Jeremiah!" Jezanna screamed.

I was rolled over and Jeremiah loomed over me. His nose twitched as he drew in my scent. "You smell delicious."

"No, brother," Jezanna begged from our side. She gripped his arm, but he was strong. His nose ran along my collarbone.

"Boy, are you going to hate yourself for this in two days," I said.

He pulled back to study me. "I won't."

"And I won't for doing this either." I cocked back my fist and threw it into his jaw. He tilted sideways, enough for Jezanna to drag me out from under him.

We started for the house. I glanced behind me to see Xavier, Penny and Trixie were holding back some men from the store who'd caught up with us. Sofia took Jeremiah to the ground after he tried to come at me again. Daphne ran to aid Sofia and together, they dragged Jeremiah away.

Chapter Twenty Seven

We'd just slammed the front door closed when it opened again, causing me to scream, which I was ashamed of. But hell, weird shit was happening. Of course, I was going to be scared when the strange stuff was because of me, and because men wanted to hump me.

Penny leaned her back against it, breathing hard. "I-I," she panted, her hand went to her chest. "I can't control them, can't take away their thought of Leila. Nothing I do works." Her voice was tight with agitation.

"I was afraid of this." Jezanna sighed. "Penny, thank you for coming to help. For now, stay inside and let the vampires control the situation."

She nodded. "I'll have to. I'm strong, I know how to fight, but they're crazy out there and even the vampires are having a hard time."

Jezanna left my side and walked into the sitting room. There, I saw her look out the window. "Jensen is here, which will help, and…"

"What?"

She actually giggled. "Sofia has knocked out my brother. I hope he stays that way, the stubborn git. He would have stayed, thinking he was strong enough to ignore the pull."

"It's going to be a long two nights," Penny said.

"So you know what's going on?" I asked as Jezanna came back to my side. She steered me down the hallway. Only instead of heading to the kitchen, she made a left and we went down another long hallway.

"Yes, Jack rang and filled us in."

How fucking embarrassing.

Her hand touched my back as we walked. "Don't worry about it. It's not like any of it really is your fault."

Scoffing, I said, "Feels like it."

"It is not," Jezanna bit out. "You weren't to know a spell was put upon werecats. You should have been prepared. Maybe with more time it would have helped." I snorted. "You're right. Nothing would have helped."

"This is something that will only happen this year, right?"

"Thankfully, yes. Which is also why the spell isn't 100 percent guaranteed for you to find your mate."

At least there was that. One year of total embarrassment. "Where are we going?" I asked when we turned down another hallway.

"To the dun—basement."

"You were going to say dungeons? You're taking me to the dungeons?" Pictures of dark, dreary, damp dungeons flashed in my mind. "Are you going to chain me as well?"

She laughed, stopping at the top of some stairs that wound down and around. "Don't be silly," she said before starting down the stairs. Frozen in place, I wasn't sure if I wanted to go down there. Closed-in places scared me senseless. "Leila, get down here. Maybe if we have you underground, the pull may ease enough for Penny to work her magic or for us to get them away from here without too much of a fight."

It made sense. It really did. However, it was a bloody dungeon. Underground. Small. Dark. Scary.

"You will be safe," she called back up.

"I'm a person who loves freedom, Jezanna," I called. "Not being cramped in a tiny, stinky room. Probably with dead people from ages ago." I turned to Penny with wide eyes. Her pity showed, but I also saw she thought I should do it. She nodded towards the stairs.

"Let's walk down together." She took my hand in hers and stepped down on the first step. I hesitated, until she took another step and tugged on my hand. Soon, I found myself following her.

What felt like a million steps later, we came to a door, which was propped open by Jezanna. She shifted and a light sprung to life.

Penny walked in first, then I followed with Jezanna behind me. My mouth dropped open. The room was huge. Dropping Penny's hand, I turned this way and that, looking at everything around me. A TV was mounted on the wall next to the door. A slim desk was under it holding a DVD player and Xbox. To the far side of the room was a couch and coffee table. In the middle lay a four-posted king-sized bed. Paintings were scattered on all walls. I calmed immediately. To the right of the room was another door. I walked to it and opened it.

The bathroom resembled Isaac's en suite. It was spacious with a double shower and large Jacuzzi, a toilet and washbasin. There was even another TV mounted on the wall above the bath.

Turning, I asked a smiling Jezanna, "Why do you have this down here?"

"Newly-turned vampires are sensitive to light. For their comfort during daylight hours, until they grow out of it, they stay here. As soon as we arrived to town, we changed the dungeon into a room where they would be happy in. It never takes vampires long for renovations."

"You could have said this upstairs," I said, exasperated.

"I know." She smiled.

We all jumped when something crashed upstairs.

"Incoming," was yelled.

"We must go. I'll get food down to you soon. For now, open the coffee table top and you'll find snacks and bottled water."

"Fuck!" a female screamed. "You're lucky you're human or I would have sucked your bone marrow out, you little shit."

"Who—?"

"Seraphine." Jezanna spun and walked out of the bathroom. I followed. "Come, Penny, we have to help." She looked back to me. Penny waved over Jezanna's shoulder before Jezanna said, "We will keep you safe. I promise."

"I know. I'm just sorry I can't help fight."

"There will be no blood spilt tonight. It's best you keep yourself for the real battle to come." With a nod from me, she walked out, shut the door and called back, "Lock it, Leila."

I went over and did just that. Turning back to the quiet room, I eyed my surroundings once again. Another bang sounded from above me. It was unfair to let them deal with this because of me. But I had no choice and it sucked.

Staying still wasn't an option. My body twitched in agitated movements. I needed to relieve the ache between my legs that my whole body felt. My skin was tender to the touch. I was burning up and my breasts felt tingly as much as my core did. Wetness soaked my panties. I would remove them, but if I did, I knew I'd do anything to have someone help me with the throbbing sensation. I paced around virtually naked, my clothing long gone because it hurt to have them on my sensitive skin, all except a sports bra and my panties.

An urgent need for release rushed through me. My body convulsed. My back arched and a whimper escaped me. I wanted to drown myself in someone's body. Lose control and take what my body needed because no matter how many times I touched myself, it wasn't enough. Exhaustion rolled through me, but sleep wouldn't come. Not when my body was so needy. Sweat slicked my skin as I lay on the strange bed, giving up my pacing.

It was all worse than I could have thought.

There was non-stop background noise. Even when I was deep below the house, I still heard it all. Seraphine yelled orders while men called out to me. Others screamed and things crashed. I only wished it all would take away from what I was going through. Never had I thought it would be this bad.

A scream burst free from my mouth and echoed around the concrete room.

Two days, I had to put up with this.

And I wasn't sure I could.

Already, I fought myself from running out of the room and grabbing the first man I laid eyes on. Only I knew it wouldn't help me find my release. I wouldn't be satisfied until it was my mate.

So I was stuck within this hell for two days.

"Isaac, no!" Jezanna's high-pitched yell hit my ears from above me, telling me she was on the floor higher than I was.

"Move!" Isaac's growl was animalistic.

"You will regret this, brother."

"The only thing I will regret is harming my sister for keeping me from my mate."

Jezanna gasped. "Isaac, are you sure?"

"She calls to me." His voice was soft. "I feel her pain. I feel her need. I must ease her suffering and claim her."

Yes. My Isaac. My love. My mate.

I could feel it now. The pull towards him. His heat, his scent, his soul. *Mine, all mine.*

I rolled off the bed and crashed to the floor, limbs tangled, before I even thought of it. I needed to get to Isaac.

A moment later, the bedroom door was smashed in. I cowered, whimpered, and covered my head when splinters of wood flew my way. Peeking out, I screamed when a form pounced through the doorway dressed in dark jeans and a hooded cloak.

Scrambling up and backwards as the dark figure stalked me,

I lost my balance on the floor and I tumbled. My back hit the cold floor hard as another wave of desire filled me.

My mate was close.

Opening my eyes, Isaac glided swiftly into the room and launched himself at the newcomer. He had the man twisted around and slammed into the wall in mere seconds.

"I told you to stay away," Isaac snarled.

"Her scent filled me, the act to take her, have her was far more important than listening to my sire."

"You will not have her, Darik. She is mine to claim. *My* mate."

"No," Darik's low rumble was ripped out of his mouth. He pushed backwards, forcing Isaac to back up a step. There he swirled and ran towards my prone self on the floor. My body then convulsed and heat pooled between my legs.

"Stop!" Isaac roared. Only Darik didn't listen. He spun out of Isaac's reach and came at me. It was as if he flew through the room. Only inches from me, he managed to brush his hand over mine before Isaac grabbed him.

He wrenched Darik's arms behind him, to near breaking point and knelt on his back. Leaning in, he hissed out, "No one touches her."

"Stop!" A flurry of movement and Isaac was pushed off Darik. Before I could blink, I was up and forced behind Isaac, his arms caging me in, but not touching me. He looked down upon Raven, kneeling beside Darik.

"You saved his life, girl."

Raven nodded. Tears glistened in her eyes. "I know." With her shifter strength, she rolled Darik over. Fear touched my tongue for her because Darik wasn't himself. Only, my fear wasn't just for her, but for Darik also. If he didn't gain some amount of control, Isaac would kill his best friend.

Even with everything going on, my desire didn't die. My hands trembled for my mate, I reached out and he took a step forward. Licking my dry lips, I pleaded, "Isaac."

Soon, my love.

Darik growled low. He stretched his hand out my way until Raven grabbed his face in both hands and forced him to look at her.

"Darik," she called. "Don't do this. You do this, you kill me. Is that what you want?"

What was she talking about?

"Darik," she pleaded. "Do you want to harm me?"

Slowly, he sat. "No," he choked.

Tears broke and ran down Raven's face. "Then come with me."

"Yes," he hissed. He was up with Raven in his arms and stalking quickly from the room.

"Isaac," I breathed and started to reach out to him again.

"Do not touch me *yet*, my mate." He sped over to the door and left before I could say anything.

Why would he leave me?

My knees buckled. I was about to fall, but hands caught me. Desire bubbled up throughout me again and I was lifted into strong arms.

"Isaac," I whispered.

"I have you. I'll never let go." He glided us over to the bed, and somehow, he managed to sit us in the middle of it with his back against the headboard, with me in his lap. With my legs straddling his waist, I felt his hardness beneath my hot core and I rocked against it. A moan escaped me.

Isaac's hiss was low, a sweet sound to my ears because it meant he was affected as much as I was.

"Leila, do you understand what's going on?"

"No questions," I growled and went to kiss him.

"Love." He chuckled.

"How can you… think, not act like them out there?"

"I'm a master vampire, Leila, and my love for you helps me control myself because I need to know you understand what is going on."

"I do." I sighed happily and then smiled. Leaning in, I rubbed my head against his cheek gently. A purr tumbled out of my lips. *Claim. Mate.*

Yes. Isaac's voice growled through my mind. *You are mine. My mate to claim. Do you want me?* His voice held a little uncertainty, as if he were unsure I would want him.

Yes. I purred. *Always have, always will. My love for you will never die.*

His groan filled the room. He tore my panties away as well as my sports bra. Naked in front of him, there was no room for unease or embarrassment. There was nothing but heated desire and love in his eyes. In fact, confidence bloomed and I rocked to my knees, where I placed my breast right in front of his mouth.

A moan fell from my lips as I waited with baited breath for him to make the move. And then, Isaac licked his lips, attaching his mouth, lips and teeth to my nipple. His suck sent a throbbing pulse into my core.

Want. Need. Have.

While one of my hands gripped Isaac around the neck, the other slid between us. There, I shifted my nails into claws and sliced through his pants. Surprise caused my eyes to widen. I never knew I could partially shift, until then. My shock was driven out when I looked down and moaned at what I saw.

My hand wound around his gorgeous erection, causing Isaac to jerk up and hiss.

My breast fell from his mouth as I slowly sat down onto Isaac's hardness. A gasp escaped. I didn't realise how tight I would be or how big Isaac felt.

His hands came to my hips to stop me. I met his eyes. He knew I had never had anyone inside of me before. Hell, he liked the fact I hadn't. The possessiveness in his eyes told me so. There was also a small frown upon his beautiful lips and I knew he hated the fact this would hurt me. He would hurt my body.

So I smiled, letting him know I was okay. His gaze travelled to my mouth and when he saw my curved lips, he nodded. I wasn't sure if it was more to himself or me. When his grip loosened, I took the choice out of the equation and slammed myself down upon him.

A pain-filled cry whimpered out of me. My forehead hit Isaac's shoulder.

Then suddenly, something changed within me. I moved my hips and the scent of us hit me. I groaned. Isaac tried to hold me still for a moment as he inhaled deeply.

Us. Mate. Claim. Mine, was snarled through our connection.

"Yes," I whispered, pushing back down on him. His hands gripped my butt tightly, helping me, helping us find the perfect rhythm. The sensation of Isaac moving in and out of me was something I knew I would remember forever, and already, I found myself looking forward to the next time.

A wash of warmth swept over me. Butterflies fluttered low in my belly and still I couldn't get enough. Isaac's hands slid up my back while mine went from his shoulders to wrap around his neck. We both knew what we wanted. Our kiss was demanding, hard and yet sweet.

I whimpered and purred against him as my core spasmed around Isaac. He growled deep, long and low as he pumped his seed inside of me, filling me.

It was after we caught our breath when Isaac gently lay me down onto the bed before he removed the rest of his tattered clothes and shifted in behind me, bringing my body flush against his.

Silence. Nothing but amazing silence filled my ears, which meant the fight upstairs had stopped.

I felt sated, a part of me was claimed and therefore happy. Yet, something was still missing. I curled into Isaac, wanting to talk, but sleep took me under.

Darkness surrounds me. Every way I turn, I see nothing but black.

My heart beats hard in my chest. My hands tremble along with my legs. I want to run, to scream, but I don't.

Because I know I'm waiting.

It isn't until I see two small red dots in the distance that I relax somewhat.

"Yes," I whisper. "That's what I'm waiting for."

The dots drift closer and closer.

And in a blink of an eye, which always makes me jump, they're right in front of me, so close I can reach out and touch them... No, touch the face that belongs to those red eyes.

I want to.

I need to.

Even though a small amount of fright fills me, I still know I'm safe.

The red eyes study me.

"You're mine," the voice growls...

Light suddenly shines everywhere and arms circle my waist. I look up.

"Isaac," I whisper. His red eyes fade into black before his lips meet mine. His arms draw me in tighter against his body. The kiss takes a new level and a hot heat engulfs my body. I worry I'll burn him, so I pull away and smile up at him, reassured he isn't harmed, but his eyes are red once again.

"It's been you all along," I say.

"I dreamed of you for so long, your eyes. I was meant to find you. Claim you. You are my soul, my saviour, my mate. You were made for me. To love, to cherish and to lead with me. Together we will rule the world, make our people safe and allow them to live peacefully among all species."

A dull pain drew me from my sleep to find Isaac over me. His lips against my neck. With his teeth in my flesh, my blood flowed freely from my body into his mouth. Gasping, I threaded my fingers into his hair, holding him close to me. He growled against my skin, sending a delicious shudder throughout my body, while one of his hands forced my legs apart. Honestly, my legs opened willingly. They and my hot core wanted what Isaac had to offer.

His fingers danced over my folds and I trembled in bliss.

Isaac was mine. My mate. He must have worked out what was missing, or maybe he was scared of my reaction to it, but I wanted it. I wanted him to drink from me, for us to join and claim *all* of each other.

"Yes," I breathed. He hummed against my neck and I felt him move between me. His hand disappeared from my heat. I would have complained, but then I felt his hand against my thigh as he gripped himself. The tip of him slowly entered me, so I spread my legs wider as he gently pushed himself further in. It was too slow. I gripped his back and lifted my head slightly, but not enough to dislodge his fangs as I kissed his shoulder.

Drink from me, my love. Claim me, he encouraged.

But your blood?

Is safe. Mine is not toxic, and even if it were, it would never harm my mate.

A muffled roar of pleasure left both of us as soon as I sank my teeth into his skin, causing Isaac to slam inside of me. He pumped into me over and over while we drank, touched and claimed one another. Our souls slid together, and finally, I felt as one with my mate as I climaxed around him. His teeth left my skin and he grunted through his own release.

With him still inside of me, he pulled back to smile down at me. "My queen."

A laugh fell from my lips. "My king." I gasped when he pulled out and pushed back in. Only he stopped.

Looking up, I saw his expression had turned serious. Then he said, "Are you happy?"

Reaching up, I caressed his cheek and then lifted to kiss his lips. "More than you'll ever know."

"Good," he growled. Without a stir of wind, he was standing beside the bed with me in his arms and still hard within me. I grabbed his shoulders and lifted myself up, only to slide back down on him.

Isaac closed his eyes. His head fell back, eyes to the ceiling and he groaned. When he looked back to me, his eyes were red. "Mine," he roared.

"Yours." I smiled.

He walked us to the bathroom where we made good use of the large shower.

CHAPTER TWENTY EIGHT

After our playtime in the shower, we lay in bed together naked in a freshly made bed. It must have been what Isaac was doing while I dried myself. Because when I'd come out, he was already in bed with my side of the clean sheet thrown back. I climbed in, even though all I wanted to do was rip the blankets off Isaac's sexy, sleek form and ogle it for at least a year more. What I'd seen in the shower didn't give me enough time to study him. Though what I did see, I liked, a lot. His pale skin was smooth all over his body. He didn't just have a six-pack, but eight, with tight pecs to go along with them. His body held enough muscle to tantalise me with his thinner frame.

He was perfect.

Stunning.

Goddamn hot.

"I enjoy the way my mate is looking at me. However, we must talk." Isaac smiled and half rolled over me. Placing his head in his hand, he looked down at me. His black hair fell into his eyes and I had every right to run my fingers through it, pushing it back, so I did.

Hell, I had every right to do to him what I wanted. That thought brought a smile to my face.

"Where is your mind taking you?" he asked, chuckling.

Shrugging, I said, "Just thinking, since we're a couple now—"

He growled and nipped at my bottom lip with his teeth. "We're more than just a couple."

Grinning like a fool, I slid my hand over his back and down to his bottom, where I pinched it. "Oh, I know. You claimed me good and proper."

His eyes bled to red. "You are very good at distracting me." His lower half pushed against me and my back arched. I loved the feeling of him. "Unfortunately, it will not work." A disgruntled mew slipped from my lips as he shifted us. Isaac lay on his back with my body along his and my head rested on his chest. "We must talk."

Sighing, I grumbled, "Fine." Smiling to myself, I tickled a trail with my finger down his chest, over his abs and... He grabbed my hand and held it against his heart.

"You are devious when you want something." He chuckled.

"Very true, but you'll get used to it."

"Something to look forward to. Actually, all my days will be spectacular with you at my side. Even when you are trying my patience."

Cheeky man.

"Same to you, mister."

"Do you wish for me to tell you about the prophecy now?"

A laugh erupted out of me. "Smooth move to catch my attention."

"It worked, yes?"

"Oh, yes, as long as you put out in the end."

His laughter was full and free. "Of course, I would not like to disappoint my mate."

"Good. You better remember those words, Isaac Grey."

The arm around my shoulders gave me a squeeze before he said, "Always."

"Okay, let's talk."

He kissed my forehead and started, "The same seer who foretold Gerald the prophecy regarding me, also foretold another that same night. It was said there would come a woman who holds her feline form close. One who has a green eye and a black one. This woman, who is also a werecat, would rule beside the new king. She and the king would be one together and would lead all supernaturals to live in harmony alongside one another."

God, no.

My body stiffened when realisation hit me. *I* was the cause of the extinction of my species.

"Gerald killed my kind." It wasn't a question because I already knew the answer and it fucking hurt.

"Yes," Isaac whispered and his grip upon me tightened. "None of this is your fault though. You have to remember this, Leila my love. All of this happened before you were born. You cannot help being born the one who was meant for me."

"But it killed my people."

"I know the pain you must feel burning deep inside you because I have felt it when I lost my parents because of the prophecy. We were both born into a life where we would have many hurtful times. It is not a life we would have asked for ourselves, especially when we have lost so many. However, I see the purpose now. We were meant to find each other. We were meant to lead. To be strong, not only for each other, but for our people."

Leaning into him more, I lifted my head and rested my chin on his chest, looking into his normal coloured eyes. They were remorseful. "It all makes sense. It does."

"Still, it doesn't make it any easier."

He knew me. He understood. My anguish for being the cause of my people's death gripped my heart and churned my stomach. It was something Isaac would have felt and probably still felt because I wasn't sure it would ever go away.

However, life went on and it was up to us to be who we were meant to be. To each other and to our people.

Kissing his chest, I settled back down. "We will get through this together."

He sighed, a small smile touching his lips. "Yes, we will."

"Now, do you want to tell me what was going on with Darik and Raven?"

"Before we speak of it, I must tell you where I have been and why it took me so long to get here and claim you. The thought of what you went through, what you felt, will haunt me. I am so sorry."

"Don't. It's not like you knew about what was going to happen to me." He stiffened. I sat up, bringing the sheet with me, holding it against my chest. Turning, I glared down at him. "You knew?"

He had the nuts to look sheepishly at me. "I did. Jezanna informed me. Though, we all thought we had time."

"Hang on, hang on. Did you know we were meant to be a mated couple right from the start?"

He pushed himself up, his back to the headboard. "Yes. As soon as I walked through the classroom door and saw your eyes, my breath caught and I nearly stumbled. I never stumble," he said matter-of-factly.

It came to me then. The way I'd always felt about Isaac. I knew there was something about him I needed to know. A place, a part of me, reached out to him that first day. He intrigued me. Only it wasn't just that. It seemed my body always knew he was meant for me. I'd denied it though, because the thought of a mate, a partner intended for me, was something that had never crossed my mind. I had been alone for so long and I'd always thought I would die that way.

Glancing to the bed, I whispered, "I never believed in mates. I even told Jezanna there wasn't one out there for me, no matter the connection we had. I was foolish." Looking to Isaac, I asked, "Did Jezanna know you were my mate?"

"No, I even kept that prophecy to myself. Gregory knew though. He was the one who told me and never second-guessed me, like my siblings when I wanted to move from one place to another while I searched for you."

Shifting up the bed, I snuggled into Isaac's arms. No wonder Gregory was adamant about me staying and protecting his family, our family. He knew I was meant for his adopted son.

"Speaking of Gregory, it was also why I was delayed coming to you. I had information about his attacker. As we suspected, it was one of MaryJane's men. Though, after he had brutally attacked my father, he fled. We managed to find him, Leila. I went after him."

"Tell me you made him suffer."

He kissed my temple. "Another reason I love you. You are bloodthirsty when it comes to people you care for."

"True." I nodded without an ounce of remorse for it.

"Yes. At my hands, he suffered for a long time and still it wasn't enough."

"Because he took away a good man."

"He did."

"You know, Gregory would be a happy man where he is now, with his wife."

"I do know it."

"But the loss of him is still hard."

"Exactly."

"Life is truly mean sometimes." I sighed.

His fingers touched my chin and he tilted my head around to his. Placing a soft kiss upon my lips, he then whispered against them, "Which is why we must live like it is our last. We must smile, laugh and love with all we have, and make each day special in some way."

Pulling back, I smiled. Isaac opened his eyes and they were red. Turning my head, I asked, "Why do they go red?"

"It's a sign I have claimed my mate."

"So not just because you want to do the wicked with me?" I grinned.

He threw his head back and laughed. When he calmed, he kissed me again and then said, "It is that as well; however, the claiming is what brought them out."

I ran a finger over his brows and down the side of his face. "I think they're freaking amazing."

He chuckled. "I'm glad, because you will see them a lot."

"Will others?"

"No, it's mostly when we're intimate. My eyes only bleed red for you and you alone."

"I wonder if Caelen's go like that for Jezanna."

"Leila, I refuse to talk about Caelen," he bit out Caelen's name with a growl, "while in bed with you."

"Wait." I sat straight. "Does mating have anything to do with Darik and Raven?"

He sighed. "I believe so. As well as with Jeremiah and Sofia. Also, yes, I do believe Jezanna and Caelen are destined mates for one another. Though, I'm unsure if they have claimed each other as yet."

"What's holding them back?"

"They're both scared. I think, once this trouble with Gerald passes, things will change."

"Is Darik going to claim Raven? And Jeremiah, Sofia?"

"I cannot answer for them."

Shrugging, I said, "I'll ask them."

"Leila," he groaned. "I think it best if we stay out of their business."

"Maybe," I teased.

He grinned wickedly at me. "What would make you promise to stay out of their love life?" Slowly, he touched my neck and then slid his hand down over my arm, only to come back up on the inside. My eyes closed and I moaned when he ran his fingers down my side.

However, they sprung wide and I let out a squeal when I found myself on my knees facing the headboard with Isaac's powerful body behind me.

His hands inched slowly from my sides to cover my breasts. "I'm sure I could make you promise." His voice was husky and low. I pushed my arse back against him to find he was already hard and resting against my lower back.

I grumbled when he moved away slightly, so our lower halves weren't touching.

"Isaac," I snapped.

His chuckle blew his warm breath over my shoulder and neck. "Leila my love, do you promise not to get involved?"

"I…"

Isaac's right hand glided down my stomach and paused just above my pelvic bone.

"Promise and you can have what you want."

Breathlessly, I panted, "What do you think I want?"

"Me," he growled and nipped my earlobe. "You want your mate *deep* inside you." With his fingers, he ran them whisper-softly through my coarse hair below. He slid a finger up and down my opening. Teasing me, taunting me, but it was in the best way possible.

"Please," I begged.

"Promise me?"

"N-not fair, Isaac," I bit out when he parted my lips and placed a finger over my clit. Only he didn't move it.

He chuckled. "I know, my love. However, this I need you to yield over because they need to figure things out on their own."

Yield? Me?

The best option I had was to tell a little white lie to get want I wanted. "Okay," I whispered.

Isaac bit my neck and then earlobe. "You lie to me, my love."

He flicked my nub. A shudder shivered over my body and a moan dropped from my lips. "Please."

Isaac cupped my mound and forced me back, so my arse jutted out. He ran his spare hand over the globes of my arse cheeks and then slapped one. "It is difficult to say no to my mate," he growled. I felt his hand then and I knew he was holding himself and lining it up to my entrance. The tip had just touched my opening when he added, "I will have to find another way to make you promise." And then he pushed all the way in, the tip hitting something amazing inside of me, ripping a half scream from my mouth.

Looking over my shoulder with hooded eyes, I saw my mate's eyes glowing red. He was enjoying this as much as I was.

"Fuck me," I panted.

"Yes," he snarled. He took hold of my hips and thrust in and out of me hard. My hands gripped the headboard in a tight hold. I threw my head back and purred through my fast release.

Fangs sank into my shoulder, pulling another climax out of me. I yelled out my pleasure. Still, Isaac didn't relent. He pounded me over and over while he drank my blood deep from my shoulder.

Suddenly, his mouth released and with another snarl, he emptied inside me with thrust after thrust.

We both panted to catch our breath. Would it always be like that? I hoped so.

The love I felt for Isaac was so hard to explain, to put in order, but I knew I would fight for him. I would bleed for him and I would love him until I passed into the next life, where I would find him all over again.

Love you.

He kissed my back and slowly slid out of me. *And I you, my love.*

Forever.

Chapter Twenty Nine

When I woke, my stomach growled in complaint. Stretching, I reached out for Isaac, only his side was cold. Sitting, I looked around the room just as the bathroom door opened.

"You took a shower without me," I complained.

He smiled. "I knew I had to or else I would have been distracted once again with your delicious body. Besides, I need to feed my mate and before that, I have to clear the way to get out." He looked at me with a sheepish grin.

"Isaac, what did you do?" I asked, standing and pulling the sheet from the bed to wrap around my body.

Stepping up to me, his hands went straight to my waist and then he leaned in and ran his tongue over my lips. Pulling back, I said, "Now you're distracting me." I smiled. "What did you do?"

He rolled his eyes. "I only pulled some things down the stairs so no one else could enter."

"What type of things?"

He cleared his throat and my big, strong, ever-courteous vampire mate muttered, "A couch, piano and table. They were the items close to the stairs and then Jezanna would have filled in the gap with more items. Like I had asked."

After a big gulp of air, I burst out laughing. My hand went to his chest to hold myself up.

That explained why he'd left the room for those few moments. He was making sure no one could enter and interrupt us. It was hilarious and gorgeous at the same time.

Isaac's hand at my waist tightened. He pulled me into him so our fronts collided. He smiled down at me, but his eyes were heavy and hot red. "I love seeing you laugh."

"I love you." I grinned, winding my arms around his shoulders where I pulled him down and kissed him.

When my stomach growled, he mumbled against my lips, "You must shower so I can feed you."

Looking up at him, I asked with raised brows, "Sure you don't want to go back to bed?"

He sucked my bottom lip into his mouth before pulling back and saying, as he walked toward the stairs, "We will have more time for that, Leila Morgin."

"Oh, I hope so."

He winked over his shoulder and started up the stairs. I went to the bathroom with a smile upon my face. Never had I been so happy. I could only pray it would stay that way.

By the time I made it out of the shower and dressed in the clothes laying on the bed, Isaac wasn't in sight. Therefore, I made my way up the stairs and walked down the long hallway until I could hear voices.

As soon as I entered the kitchen, silence nearly burnt my ears. Rolling my eyes, I ignored everyone and walked up to the far end of the table where my mate waited with a smile upon his lips. There, he grabbed my wrist, twisted me and tugged me down into his lap. His mouth met mine in a hungry kiss. If he didn't care showing affection in front of everyone, then I wouldn't either.

I decided I liked to grope my man whenever I had the chance, so I was happy.

A giggle started and then a wolf whistle, while someone else cleared their throat.

Dazed, I shifted back where I felt Isaac was very happy to see me and looked down the table. Jezanna was the one giggling. Her smile was of pure joy. Of course, Caelen was the one who whistled. I caught him in the action doing it again. I had to guess who the person was who cleared their throat and it would be Jeremiah. He sat down at the other end of the table looking a little embarrassed.

Besides the three of them, there was also Xavier, Darik, Jensen and two other people, a guy and a girl, who I didn't know.

"So, what's going on?" I asked as I dragged a plate of cold meat towards me.

When no one spoke, I looked up to see all of them standing. I hadn't even heard them move. My fork with meat on it slipped from my hand and clattered to the table when they all went to their knees.

"What's going on?" I whispered out the corner of my mouth to Isaac. He didn't even answer me.

Watching in awe, every one of them placed their hand over their heart and spoke at the same time, all saying the same thing, "We pledge our allegiance to our queen."

Holy shit.

"Okay, um, thanks. I think." I picked up my fork again and added, "Get up off the floor. You're all starting to freak me out, and none of that queen stuff in this house."

"I like her," the new female vampire said with a smile. I'd caught a glimpse of her outside when I'd arrived in my heat frenzy, so I knew she must have been Seraphine.

"It's what we all said after she opened her mouth to talk," Xavier laughed. They all got to their feet and sat back down.

"Queen Leila—" the nameless guy with fiery red hair said.

"Nope."

"Ah,"—he looked to everyone for assistance—"Queen Leila."

"Sorry," I mumbled around my food.

Isaac chuckled behind me. "My mate means what she said, Hamish. She would like to be only called Leila within these walls."

"And if we're down the street shopping. Really, any time we're around humans. My uncle would get a kick out of you calling me Queen, but he'd also tease the hell out of me for it. Not happening. Oh, and when we're in battle, Queen Leila is too long. Just Leila is fine."

"In other words, like myself, only in formal situations will you call us by our titles."

"Yep, really like her." Seraphine laughed. I winked at her.

"Good to have you and Hamish back safe and sound." I smiled.

Her eyes widened slightly. "Thank you."

Shrugging, I turned my gaze to Jeremiah. His eyes narrowed. He knew what was coming.

"How's the jaw?"

"What's this?" Isaac asked.

"Leila," Jeremiah warned.

Laughing, I sat back in my man's arms and told him, "Darik wasn't the only one who wanted to do the hanky-panky with me."

"Brother," Isaac growled. "Explain."

Jeremiah's eyes told me he would be getting payback on me one way or another. "It was nothing. I tackled her to the ground and Sofia stopped me from doing anything."

"Why were you here?" Jezanna asked. Her brother's glare turned on her.

"Because, sister, I was stubborn and didn't listen to you."

"True."

"Don't worry, Isaac." I smiled. "I clocked him a good one in the jaw and then Sofia knocked him unconscious."

"Good," Isaac bit out.

Darik stood. "I would like to apologise for what I did in the room."

I waved it away. "No one could help it, so all is forgiven."

"With Leila maybe, but I will be teaching you and my brother a lesson later on."

Which meant swordplay, and I knew it would leave Darik and Jeremiah with a few extra holes until they healed.

Darik accepted his punishment with a nod. Jeremiah rolled his eyes.

So I could meet my mate's eyes, I placed my arm around his shoulders and said, "They really weren't themselves. You can't punish them for that."

"No, but I can for their inability to listen. Jezanna obviously warned Jeremiah and told him to leave. He didn't. And I had ordered Darik to stay where he was. He didn't. Maybe after I'm done with them, they will understand the importance of following instructions."

It was fair. Isaac had to set rules. I understood it and now I was mated to him and—*eek*—queen. I should also lead by example.

I hoped like hell I could.

With a nod to Isaac, I then turned around and asked the room at random, "Was anyone injured last night?"

"No casualties," Seraphine said. "Only a few scrapes and such. Once things stopped, the men came back to themselves, so we had Penny erase their minds."

"Good. I wanted to thank you all for taking care of an awkward situation. I'll be glad to fight at your side when the next one comes."

"We would be honoured. I've heard many great things about your fighting talent." Seraphine bowed her head.

Smiling, I offered a small nod. "I also wanted to thank the other women who helped. Where are they?"

"They had to leave after everything was back to normal," Jezanna said.

"I'll make sure to invite them around." I turned to Isaac and asked, "Um, maybe we could organise a dinner or something as a thank you?"

"That's very thoughtful of you and I'm sure they would love it."

"Only I'm not sure Dad's kitchen will be big enough for everyone."

Isaac's brows drew down. "Why would you have it there when you will be living here with me?"

My head jerked back. "I will?"

He smiled. "Of course. We are mated now. Have claimed one another. There will be no other for us, and I wish to have my mate under the same roof every night. Especially if you are having our child."

I balked. My hands slipped from Isaac and I would have fallen to the floor if he hadn't grabbed me. "I-I-I-I..." was all I could manage.

"I think it best if we leave you two to talk." Jezanna offered a small, sad smile. She knew the thought of me being knocked-up had never crossed my mind.

While I sat in my stunned state, the room cleared of people. I listened to their chairs being scraped back, their shuffling feet exiting and I wondered if I could sneak out and follow them to hide away from the thought, from even talking about it.

Really, I wanted to bury it all because the thought of a child growing inside of me when there was still danger coming for us filled my heart with fear.

"Leila." Isaac ran the back of his hand down the side of my face. "I never thought it wouldn't have crossed your mind. We didn't use protection last night. Unless, are you, as they say, on the pill?"

Shaking my head, I uttered a small, "No."

"Do you not want children?" His eyes were worried; obviously he'd already thought about them. One would after living so long.

"I do, but I never thought. I mean… Can I even fall pregnant from a vampire? And if so, how"—I gulped, hating the thought—"do you not have mini vamps running around all over the world?"

He quickly wiped the smirk off his face—luckily for him, as I may have throat punched him if he'd laughed—as he ran a hand over his mouth. "Simple, my semen only becomes fertile after I claim my mate."

"No shit." I gaped.

His eyes crinkled. I knew he wanted to laugh at me, but he held off. "No shit."

"Oh, wow, wow." Looking down, I placed my hand over my stomach. Tears filled my eyes. I blinked repeatedly and glanced up at Isaac. "What happens if—"

"Nothing will happen to you. Your life will be safe. Not only will I protect you, but our people will, too." His hand covered mine. "Children are as rare as mates. We are fiercely protective. Do you believe me, Leila? You will be safe."

A tear slid down my cheek and he kissed it away. I smiled. He was happy with the thought I was pregnant. No, his eyes shone with a new excitement. He loved the idea. My belly rolled with nerves. I wasn't sure I was ready to have a baby. If I'd be a good mother.

However, I knew the love Isaac and I had for each other could possibly be enough for most of my worries to subside. Though, the thought of popping our baby out was another worry altogether.

Taking a gulp of air, I said, "As long as you stay safe with me. I wouldn't be able to do the child thing on my own."

His grin was big. "I will do everything in my power to keep it that way, so we have a future and family together."

"Do we know for sure?" I asked.

"No, not as yet. We will find out together when we visit a human doctor."

Nodding, a thought came to me. "If I am, *you* can tell my uncle and Dad."

He cringed.

"Don't look so scared. You did throw Jack just the other day." I laughed.

His eyes searched my face. I wasn't sure what he was looking for until he asked, "Would *you* be happy if you were with child?"

He wanted a serious answer out of me, so I took the time to contemplate it. Thoughts swirled in my mind. Then pictures of Isaac holding a baby. A baby we made together with love. Of Isaac, walking along holding the small hand of our child. Of all of us together, snuggled up on the couch, watching a movie.

It *was* a future I wanted.

I could only hope it would happen.

"Yes." I nodded with certainty, hoping he read as much in my eyes. "A child with you would make me very happy."

He tucked my hair behind my ear, a smug smile playing on his lips. "I'm glad. It was always something I had wished for, a large family we could live forever with."

"What happens if they're like me, a werecat?"

He looked puzzled and then something dawned on him, his eyes widening a fraction. "You do know that you are immortal like me? We will live forever, and so will our children."

Again, I nearly fell off his lap. "Are you serious?"

He smiled kindly. "Quite."

"I-I… my mind has been blown once again." I threw my arms around my mate and hugged him close. "I look forward to our future, Isaac Grey."

"So do I, my love," he whispered against my neck before he kissed me there as well.

Footsteps fast approaching had Isaac out of his seat, placing me on my feet next to him. We both tensed when the kitchen door crashed open.

"Gerald is here and taken Boozers." Jeremiah growled the words.

My bubble of bliss washed away in an instant.

Turning to Isaac, I saw his eyes were hard, his jaw clenched, and a hiss slipped past his lips. It was time to fight for our future.

Glancing back to Jeremiah, I said in a tight voice, "Then we take it back from under him and destroy him."

CHAPTER THIRTY

We stood just on the outskirts of Boozers, waiting for the rest of our party to arrive. I'd opted to change out of my hooded jumper and leggings. Instead, I wore a tight-fitting black tee with a jacket over it, combat boots and jeans. Nearly every part of my body hid the weapon of my choice. Knives.

Isaac stood next to me, gripping my hand in a firm hold. He'd also changed and God, did I love what he had on now. Black leather pants with kick-arse boots and a long-sleeved black shirt. His skin looked paler against all the black. He had no weapons on him. He was a weapon enough himself.

Leaves rustled behind us and out stepped my uncle, Ty and their team. I walked over to them and hugged Penny, Ty and Jack.

"Thanks for coming."

"It's what we do, kid." He ruffled my hair as if I were ten. "So, you're Isaac's trouble now. Finally outta my hair."

Rolling my eyes, I smiled. "Yeah, I guess I am. Well, that is until we ask you to babysit." *Oh, Shit.* It just came out and I couldn't take it back. Though, deep down, I knew why I shared it before enjoying the show when Isaac would have told them. I wanted my uncle to have that fierce urge to live. If a great-niece or nephew didn't do it, then wanting to murder Isaac could.

Isaac wheezed out a breath behind me.

"What the fuck, kid? The bastard knocked you up already? I'm gonna skin the hell outta him."

He went to stalk toward Isaac, but I placed a hand on his

shoulder. He looked down to me and I said, "This is why you need to fight with everything you have. I need my uncle to meet our child. I need you to live through this night."

His eyes softened. He knew I'd just given him something extra to fight for. Jack nodded and again ruffled my hair. "It'll be good, kid, and your dad wants the same from you." I nodded. I'd asked my dad not to attend. He'd been out of practice being a hunter for a long time and I knew I would be too worried for him. Everyone who stood with me, I knew was ready and prepared to fight. Had been training for it.

Before I moved away, I reached out and caught Ty's hand and gave it a squeeze. He looked up and smiled before he nodded. I offered a quick hug back. My hands drifted over the guns strapped to his holster. I knew, like he did, we would do our best for victory.

I walked back to Isaac, his hand already stretched my way. I took it. He got in close and said in an amused tone, "Well played."

Looking up, I sent him a wink and glanced at the people already waiting with us. As well as our family and friends, there were a few others I hadn't even met; however, they were willing to fight at our side.

Please, Lord, let us all survive the night.

More footsteps approached. We all turned to see Sofia and Raven step into our circle. My eyes widened at their presence.

"No," Darik snarled and stepped to Raven's side. His hand wrapped around her wrist.

"I agree," Jeremiah bit out. His jaw clenched as he eyed Sofia.

"We're not going." Sofia glared.

"Both of you are," Darik grumbled low.

"We don't have time for this," Raven stated. "The more time that man has in there, the more damage he will do. Do you want that?"

She was right. We had discovered Gerald had many of our people in there and God only knew what he was doing to them.

"They stay," Isaac ordered.

"Sire," Darik snapped.

"No. They are willing to fight, then they will."

"Goddamn it." Darik threw Raven's wrist out of his grip and turned his back to her. A hand ran through his hair. Raven stepped up behind him and placed her hands on his shoulders. She leaned in and whispered, "Everything will be fine."

Darik's stiff form sagged. He nodded. "Stay close to me," he ordered.

She kissed his neck quickly. "I'll try."

He groaned and shook his head.

"This is bullshit. They're just girls," Jeremiah blurted, which was really the wrong move.

"A girl who could knock your dumb-arse to the ground," Sofia snapped, her hands going to her hips.

He snorted. "I wasn't myself then."

She cocked her head to the side and asked, "Do you want to try it again?"

Seraphine clicked her fingers together. "Can we stop with the foreplay and get this show on the road?"

My gaze spun to Isaac, his face a mask of fury. "What is it?" I asked.

"He has started the torture."

"Okay, everyone, we're going in."

With no chance of a surprise attack because Gerald would have felt us arrive, we walked calmly to the front door. Isaac and I were the first to enter. We made our way down the hallway and out into the large room.

What I saw made my stomach curl. Bile threatened to rise, but I swallowed it back down. Isaac's hand in mine was applying more pressure. He was feeling exactly what I was: disgust and a rush of vengeance.

He let out a snarled hiss. Glancing up to him, I followed his gaze.

"No," I gasped, my heart in my throat.

The scene on the floor in front of us was enough to turn my stomach. Our people were on their knees. Their wrists and arms were pinned down by silver chains and nailed into the floor. He wanted them bowing before him.

Sick fuck.

Worse was what was on the stage, where karaoke had been only months ago. Gerald sat in a throne. Where he got it, I had no clue. Beside him stood a smug MaryJane. And just behind her were Daphne and Trixie, naked and bound to the wall by their ankles with silver. Both were bloody, swollen and bruised.

Tears welled in my eyes.

Rage. Pure rage boiled inside of me. A shiver ran over my body. My heart beat so fast I could hear it in my ears.

Isaac's arm wrapped around my waist. I hadn't even realised I'd taken a step forward.

"You sick bastard," I hurled venomously towards him as our team came to stand at our backs.

Leila, no. You need to stay calm.

How can I, Isaac? Daphne, Trixie…

I know, my love, and we will kill all who did this to them. However, they will need our help to get through this. They will need their king and their queen. Stay strong and calm.

I'll try.

There was a soft caress deep in my mind. *That is all I ask.*

Gerald, a man who looked in his twenties with long blond hair, and eyes that held nothing but coldness and death, smirked down at me.

He glanced up at MaryJane, gaining her attention, and then looked back to me. "This is what the fuss has been about?" He sneered at me as if I were nothing. His eyes slid to Isaac.

"It has been a long time, Isaac."

"I am sorry to say, Gerald, but it is not long enough."

He chuckled and then shrugged, before leaning back into his throne. "I thought it time I rid myself of a problem."

"I do not understand why we cannot live alongside one another without all this hostility."

He stood swiftly and boomed, "Because I rule alone! No one will take my place. I am master. I am Lord. I am—"

"Long-winded," I offered.

Crap, I just had to open my big mouth. His eyes flashed to me. Hatred shone hot in them.

"You speak so freely when I have your people captured." His hand waved in the air toward Daphne and Trixie. "Do you want to watch while they suffer more? Or will you all be willing to bow to me? If you do, I may just let you live."

"No!" MaryJane screamed. "They must pay for killing my mate. You promised me."

Gerald looked to her and whatever she saw in his expression had her cringing and backing up a step. Panic flashed in her eyes. She was smart enough to know her life could also be on the line as well, because Gerald was one fucked-up vampire with an ego issue.

Isaac released my hand and stepped forward. "You do all of this for what, Gerald? What does it prove to *your* people? It shows nothing but proof that you are scared with what the seer foretold." Gerald snarled, flashing his fangs. "You are scared because you are weak. You have let a prophecy take hold of your life. You have ruined many lives, and I can no longer stand by to watch it happen."

"You don't get to change—"

"I do," roared Isaac. "I do have the chance to change the future because... I. Am. King." His hand reached back to me. I took it and stepped forward to his side. "With my queen at my side, we will rule with an iron fist, but we will be fair. We will listen to our people and reach for the freedom we all long for. Instead of living behind a man who lives his own life in fear."

Gerald threw his head back and laughed. Throwing both

arms wide, he said, "You think things will go your way when I have insurances that tonight you die and not I?" He shook his head and smirked. "You are naïve, Isaac. You do not stand a chance here. It is best you bow to me now or die."

Isaac's eyes met mine. I smiled in reassurance. Gerald could not live past the night.

We both looked to the people behind us. Jeremiah and Darik wore an expression of fierce determination. Actually, now that I studied them all, they all had the same look.

Gerald could no longer go on doing what he had. Already our people were suffering. It was enough.

We fight.

Stay safe, my love.

You also, Isaac, or I'll hurt you myself.

He kissed me gently. *I will look forward to it.*

Gerald must have guessed our play—we were ready to battle —because he lifted his hands and clapped them together.

Vampires appeared from all different directions. There were so many of them, worry pounded through my veins. Our people already captured were sitting ducks.

I'm going after Daphne and Trixie. And I was going to kill the bastard standing by them with a superior smile upon his face.

I have asked Darik to help you. Raven will be with him. Penny is unable to reach Gerald's mind. Like all master vampires, our shields are guarded. I will be seeing to him with Adan. The rest are spreading out to help our people and battle Gerald's.

Running my hand down his arm and folding my hand in his for one last touch, I sent into his mind, *I love you.*

And I you, always, my love.

For the life of me, I was going to try to stay in my human form in case there were others like Freckles, with toxic blood. If there was, I would be useless to everyone.

My legs kicked into gear. I bolted for the stage while battle cries broke out behind me. Two vampires tried to jump me; their teeth extended, ready to rip into my fresh. I dove and they crashed into each other. I quickly got my feet under me ready to stand, only to be dragged down again. A body climbed up me. Pushing back, I twisted and pulled a knife from my pocket. Just as he was over me, I plunged it into his heart and twisted. His remains rained down over me.

A scream hit me. Glancing through my hair, I saw Daphne tugging at her restraints while the vampire I wanted to kill bit into her.

With the knife I'd just used, I placed the sharp end in my palm, aimed and threw it. It landed straight into his back, only just below his heart.

His pain-filled cry was music to my ears, but it wasn't enough. I searched for Darik and Raven. They had their own battle going on with four vampires surrounding them. Raven had transformed into her shifter canine form.

Back on my feet, I swiftly ran towards them. Two vampires stepped in front of me and I halted. They made their move. There was no way I could let anything happen. I had too much to protect now.

I gripped their hair and smashed their skulls together. Strength I never knew I possessed caused their skulls to cave in. They screamed and I stumbled back, shocked. Darik appeared and sliced their heads off.

"Go!" he yelled.

I should not be that strong.

Leila, I didn't realise after our claiming we would share each other's powers.

Searching, my eyes landed on my mate. With his fangs extended, his eyes were black. He snarled as he danced around Gerald. He looked amazing. His hands flicked out to his sides and I watched as his nails grew as if they were mine.

We were sharing our gifts.

"You stupid bitch," was cried. My eyes found the source. MaryJane climbed to her feet while Jezanna stared at her smiling. Only Jezanna lost her smile when MaryJane moved swiftly into her space and backhanded her, sending Jezanna flying through the air and landing with a thud. Caelen roared his fury and flew through the people, knocking who got in his way, friend or foe, out of his space to get to Jezanna who was slowly sitting up.

My upper lip raised. The bitch was gonna pay.

Changing directions, I sped my way to MaryJane. Someone stepped in my way, ready to take me to the ground, until Darik was there, cutting him down.

A knife in each hand, I threw the first. Landing it in Mary-Jane's lower back. Her gasp of agony made me smile. I'd just severed her spine. Before she had the chance to reach for it and remove it in order to heal, I was in front of her.

Her eyes rounded and just as she slid the knife out of her back, I plunged one into her abdomen.

My free hand went to her shoulder where I brought her in close and whispered in her ear, "The amount of pain you put me through, taking *my mate* for those precious few days, will never be forgiven, and the pain I'm about to inflict will never be enough. Still, I'm more than happy to deliver it." Shifting back, I smiled brightly. "Goodbye, MaryJane." Then I sliced the dagger up her stomach. She struggled and cried, but I was stronger and held her at bay.

My knife glided through her intestines with ease, right up to her heart and before I eliminated it, I winked and relished in the panic and pain I saw in her features as I tore into her heart, shredding it to nothing. Her ashes floated down around me and I found myself wishing I could kill her all over again.

There was no time to enjoy her death because Darik urged me into a running speed once again with a hand on my lower back. I had to get to Daphne and Trixie. I looked down to see Raven panting beside me.

With a leap, I was on the stage and stalking towards my prey. He'd managed to get the knife out of his back and dropped it to the floor.

"Come and play, pussycat," he taunted. "I've had my fun with your friends. They've bled enough already, wouldn't you say?"

"I'd say they should never have bled at all."

Movement to the side and I glanced there to see Sinister Dude had friends. Darik stood at my back and Raven growled at my feet, low on her hunches.

"Oh no, there would be no fun in that." He licked his lips suggestively. "My, my, they tasted good."

Daphne cried out. Fuck, another was at her now. Drinking from her. Trixie, beside her, whimpered and then yelled, "They'll drain her."

No!

With a snarl, I started forward. Two vampires charged me. My claws grew where I sank them deep into their stomach. They gasped and looked down. I twisted my fist inside of them and pulled my hands back out. Their intestines dropped to the floor.

"Raven," I called. I knew she would make the kill. I just needed to make a show of my strength and it worked. The one who'd bragged about taking my girls backed up with wide eyes.

"I'm not some meek and mild queen. I will fuck you up for touching our people, and I will do it with a smile upon my face."

Kicking out, my heel connected with his jaw. With the force behind it, he flew through the air. I was about to go after him when a jolt of pain stabbed me in the shoulder. I spun, my eyes landing on my mate falling to the floor with a sword sticking out of his back.

"Stop!" Gerald roared.

We did.

He pulled the sword from Isaac's back and kicked him over to place the tip over his heart.

Isaac's eyes met mine. In them, I saw pain and regret.

"No!" I screamed. *No, Isaac, fight. You promised you would. Fight for us.*

Gerald laughed and ordered, "Then bow to me in defeat."

Isaac?

We bow to no one, Isaac growled through my mind.

I smiled and saw surprise shine in Gerald's eyes. He pulled the sword back, ready to plunge it in, when Isaac flew up from the floor. He knocked the sword out of Gerald's hold with one hand while the other, with claws extended, drilled into Gerald's chest and twisted.

His ashes floated to the floor.

Silence filled the air.

Weapons crashed to the floor as Gerald's fighters sank to their knees, heads to the floor. They were giving in.

A flurry of movement started. Isaac's people started to cart away the injured and captured.

Casualties? I asked Isaac.

Adan, as far as I know.

He will be missed.

Yes, my love.

Turning, I watched Daphne and Trixie being helped down by Ty's people. I caught Darik's eyes and pointed to the one who'd harmed them and said, "He stays alive for now. They deserve to have their own payback." I looked to the girls. "If you want it?"

"Yes," Daphne uttered. Trixie nodded. The man wasn't so tough now. He was being carted away by Xavier and Jensen, screaming, pleading with the new King.

Leila. I looked to Isaac. He stood in front of the throne and gestured to me. As soon as I was close, I threw my arms around him and held on tight.

You scared me.

I'm sorry, my love.

It's over.

It is. Now it is our *future.*

Pulling back, I smiled. *Yes.* Then kissed him.

We separated and I stood beside him, looking out at the

mess. Many lives were lost. Adan's wasn't the only one. I could see this by the forlorn looks upon faces. There were so many I didn't know, but would still mourn. Jezanna was off to the side in Caelen's arms. Jeremiah was snarling something in Sofia's face. She laid her hands upon his chest and pushed him back, only to grab him again and pull him towards her before she kissed him. I watched Jeremiah melt into it and take her into his arms. Darik was doing the same with Raven, celebrating with a kiss. I saw Seraphine and Hamish huddled in close together, and Jack smiling and talking with Ty and their people.

Whispers caught my attention, and people parted as a cloaked woman headed our way. Looking out the corner of my eyes, I saw Isaac wasn't worried, so I immediately calmed.

The person stepped onto the stage and threw her hood back. Pure white hair cascaded down around her shoulders. I gasped when she turned to us and smiled. Her eyes were also white.

Who…?

The seer, my love.

She threw her arms up in the air and cried, "To our new King, Queen and their child."

A flutter swept through my belly. My hand went to it. I beamed at my mate. His eyes shone with delight and heat.

Isaac took my other hand and brought it up to his mouth. He kissed it before raising it into the air. Eruptions of cheers and claps echoed around the room.

We were the start of a new era, a new freedom for our people. I was eager to lead it with my mate, Isaac, at my side. Hope blossomed in my chest at the possibility of our future. Together, I knew we were strong enough to face any enemies who attempted to take it from us. And we, the people, would no longer be forced to live in the dark.

ALSO BY LILA ROSE

Hawks MC: Ballarat Charter

Holding Out (FREE): Zara and Talon

Climbing Out: Griz and Deanna

Finding Out (novella): Killer and Ivy

Black Out: Blue and Clarinda

No Way Out: Stoke and Malinda

Coming Out (novella): Mattie and Julian

Hawks MC: Caroline Springs Charter

The Secret's Out: Pick, Billy, and Josie

Hiding Out: Dodge and Willow

Down and Out: Dive and Mena

Living Without: Vicious and Nary

Walkout (novella): Dallas and Melissa

Hear Me Out: Beast and Knife

Breakout (novella): Handle and Della

Fallout: Fang and Poppy

Standalones related to the Hawks MC

Out of the Blue (Lan, Easton, and Parker's story)

Trinity Love Series

Left to Chance

Love of Liberty (novella)

Young Adult

Senseless Attraction

Romantic Comedies

Making Changes

Making Sense

Fumbled Love

Paranormal

Death (with Justine Littleton)

In the Dark